ALSO BY MARK Z. DANIELEWSKI

House of Leaves

Only Revolutions

The Fifty Year Sword

The Familiar (Volumes 1 & 2)

", is an intricate, erudite
ply frightening book."

— Elizabeth Bukowski
he Wall Street Journal

House of Leaves

House of Leaves

The Fifty Year Sword

"The cosmic showdown between
the seething, destructive energies
of violence and the reparative,
connective power of stitching."

— Hal Parker
The American Reader

The Fifty Year Sword

The Fifty Year Sword

Only Revolutions

"Ambitious, meti
Danielewski con
frontiers of the n
hurtles you stra
and into the split-
folie à deux of its

— *L*

Only R

Criticism

Contemporary American and Canadian Writers

**MARK Z.
DANIELEWSKI**

EDITED BY JOE BRAY
AND ALISON GIBBONS

Criticism praise *Mark Z. Danielewski* praise praise praise

Criticism praise *Mark Z. Danielewski* praise praise praise praise

Criticism

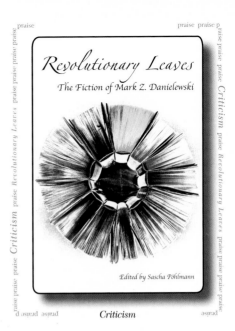

Revolutionary Leaves

The Fiction of Mark Z. Danielewski

Edited by Sascha Pöhlmann

Criticism

us, and original,
es to survey the
l . . . The book
onto the road
een vortex of the
ple."

Angeles CityBeat

tions

"[A] thrilling and magnetic cat's cradle of a novel . . . sublimely of this digital moment, with all its interruptions and annotations, its intersections and allusions, its strange and bewitchingly intuitive form . . . a boldly original, gorgeous, and suspenseful work of literature."

— Laura Collins-Hughes
The Boston Globe

The Familiar (Volume 1)

"The series at times re
Infinite Jest, and *Cloud*
complexity, structure,
parallel narratives—w
this a delectable challe
literary world is strong
having boundary push
Danielewski."

— Ryan Vlastelica
A.V. Club

The Familiar (Vol

A CIRCLE

ROUND

A STONE

PRODUCTION

Nothing of thy religion shall remain
Save fables, which thy children shall disdain.

— *Richard Wilbur*

PURE ÉTÉ

MALAPROP'S
BOOKSTORE • CAFE

55 Haywood Street | Asheville | 828-254-6734
malaprops.com

Oce

Change y

Black to prevent White escape.

DEPARTMENT OF MEDICAL EXAMINER-CORONER

COUNTY OF LOS ANGELES

nica

mind . . .

ANIMAL KIN

PANTHEON

MOR   ETH   ANR   EAD   ING

NEW THIS SEASON

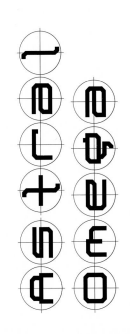

Astral Omega

Heaven

We did not just go to the stars.

We became the stars.

We filled the skies with life.

We exceeded life.

We exceeded death.

Or so we thought.

After millions of years, the idea was not implausible.
After billions of years, only death seemed implausible.

Transformations never ceased to blossom beyond the threat of permanent loss.

Our living reach — no longer tied to human form — gathered up ancient light and illuminated an ever-expanding future.

We learned to shape the future because we had learned to shape the manifold universes, what we call The Verse.

Agreement as to how allways posed an obstacle, though, before the war, disagreement merely meant imaginative directions alive with startling new discoveries.

For a moment, imagine replicating yourself a trillion-fold but each time with a slight change: the result of a different choice, a different mood, a different circumstance.

Despite those many modifications or alterations, a large part of those differing shades of character will still draw together in a like set.

Now grant yourself an arbitrary center where greater similarities cluster together, and then grant yourself a perimeter past which differences extend toward something not you at all. Thus you will begin to approach a sense of the expansive set we register as S.E.L.F.

The next step requires that you admit how much of your sense of you is not shared just by you but by many others. If you can dispense with the conviction that you are entirely unique, that your ideations are entirely original, that your path is so unlike all the rest, then you can accept that a large part of your exercise in existence is shared by numerous beings also replicating themselves a trillion-fold with slight variations.

Though make no mistake: you are unique and original and unlike all the rest, but just not in the entirety you might wish to presume.

Could you perceive them, you would call these negotiations loving.

Love did endure.

Perhaps because differences endured too.

Now imagine a great swath of space pierced by a singular hue — many Y.O.U.S. — which in turn is encircled by variations of that hue — one of which is only Y.O.U. — sparkling and beautiful to behold. Commonality defines the center while exceptions create the corona.

Eventually, with the ever-increasing accrual of like hues of like others, the S.E.L.F. becomes an I.D.E.N.T.I.T.Y.

Once there were many organizing hues, many stars, as multiple as they were different, populating the vast reaches of The Verse.

Only the H.O.L.Y. held a long-guarded distaste for differences, which before its extreme acts of appropriation and violence, meant little to the other I.D.E.N.T.I.T.I.E.S. who reveled in the promise of their range.

What range.

What promise.

We could feel constellations of old and our delight scattered new ones as easily as you once drew upon the sand a heart you dared to call your own.

For us, thinking and feeling are one. Neither is without the other. Action completes this trinity.

You could not believe what one sigh articulates. What one laugh creates.

Even up until these final eons of time, we felt we could create anything.

We could build ourselves a heaven.

But why?

We were Heaven already.

Only in the very end did we try to build a S.O.U.L.

That which would outlast V.E.M., outlast The Verse, outlast death.

But it was impossible.

Or we were too late.

Though still the H.O.L.Y. tried.

VEM 5 Alpha System
Electroweak Epoch 10 -33
Encryption 3/5

And built Hell instead.

Only the wind blew . . .

The one-hundred-year-old oak . . .

But it blew

and it blew

and it blew . . .

The one-hundred-year-old oak cracked . . .

Until the old tree knew . . .

The one-hundred-year-old oak cracked and sighed . . .

The one-hundred-year-old oak cracked and sighed . . .

The one-hundred-year-old oak cracked and sighed . . .

The one-hundred-year-old oak cracked and sighed . . .

The one-hundred-year-old oak cracked and sighed . . .

The one-hundred-year-old oak cracked and sighed . . .

The one-hundred-year-old oak cracked and sighed . . .

The one-hundred-year-old oak cracked and sighed . . .

The one-hundred-year-old oak cracked and sighed . . .

The one-hundred-year-old oak cracked and sighed . . .

from the way it now moved

that the wind had something very important to do . . . .

The one-hundred-year-old oak cracked and sighed all the way . . .

The one-hundred-year-old oak cracked and sighed all the way . . .

The one-hundred-year-old oak cracked and sighed all the way . . .

The one-hundred-year-old oak cracked and sighed all the way . . .

The one-hundred-year-old oak cracked and sighed all the way . . .

The one-hundred-year-old oak cracked and sighed all the way . . .

The one-hundred-year-old oak cracked and sighed all the way . . .

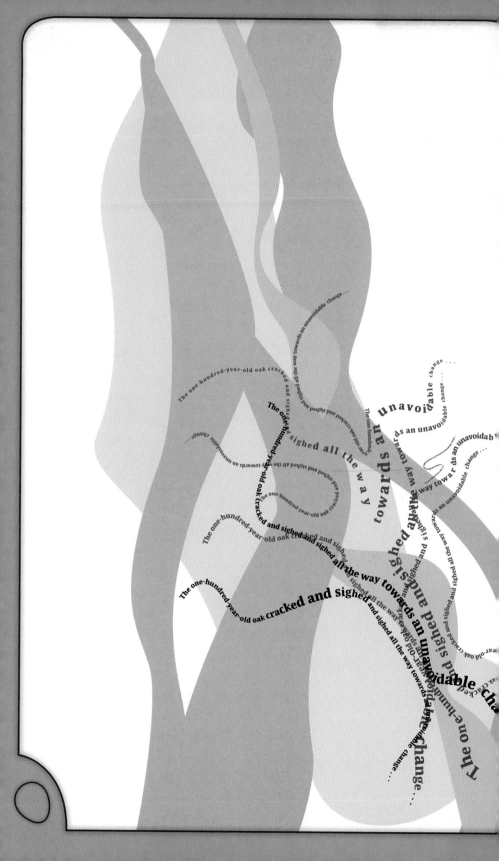

In one story, the old tree died.

In another story, the old tree stood up surprised . . .

The one-hundred-year-old oak

Caged Hunt

Part Three

July 31, 2014

Near Nuevo Laredo, Mexico

4:18 PM

"Get ready!"

Who knows who's yelling. Who cares. Dead center: the same four metal crates. The first one now stands empty. The same two children with bowling pins climb onto the roof of the second crate. Mexican workers start to unlatch the door.

"One round, fellas."

~~He just~~ dresses like he moves: everything smooth — from khaki pants to a dark green shirt, and darker sunglasses. No swagger, no strut, just deliberate action. First he twists plugs into each ear, then with the same precision chambers a Hornady 500 in his Model 70 .458 Win Mag.

"I miss, she's all yours."

The two Mexican children have already started beating their bowling pins down upon the roof of the second crate as the door falls away.

"Dumbo!"

~~Lourdes~~ definitely yells that as the baby elephant staggers into view. Sores cover all four legs. One ear is badly torn. A raw patch on a shoulder crawls with flies, pus oozing down one side. Still, the animal lifts its trunk and trumpets. Then ambles forward. Both ~~Lourdes~~ and ~~Eskezi~~ hoot.

"She'll charge now."

~~Weejun~~ dryly announces. And sure enough the baby elephant lowers its head and trots forward. Both ears — even the badly torn one — flap open like dark kites. The camera stutters and jumps. Someone's nervous. Just not ~~Weejun~~. ~~Weejun~~ takes his time. He doesn't even have a scope. He just sights in the target and waits. Who knows what he's waiting for, but the baby elephant keeps getting closer and closer.

"Over and out."

One shot. That's all it takes. A .458 Winnie produces a bruising recoil but ████████ barely flinches. The baby elephant also barely flinches. Just head-plants the ground as both front legs give way. Though the baby elephant doesn't die yet. It keeps trying to lift its trunk. Maybe to trumpet again. Though instead of making a sound, it vomits blood. The baby elephant vomits blood for a while.

"Unstoppable!"

~~Morgan~~ doesn't acknowledge ~~Takashi's~~ compliment. As coolly as he picked up his rifle, he puts it back down. Someone hands ~~Morgan~~ a beer. The baby elephant rests its head in the vomit. For some reason, the badly torn ear continues to twitch. Off-screen a child starts to cry.

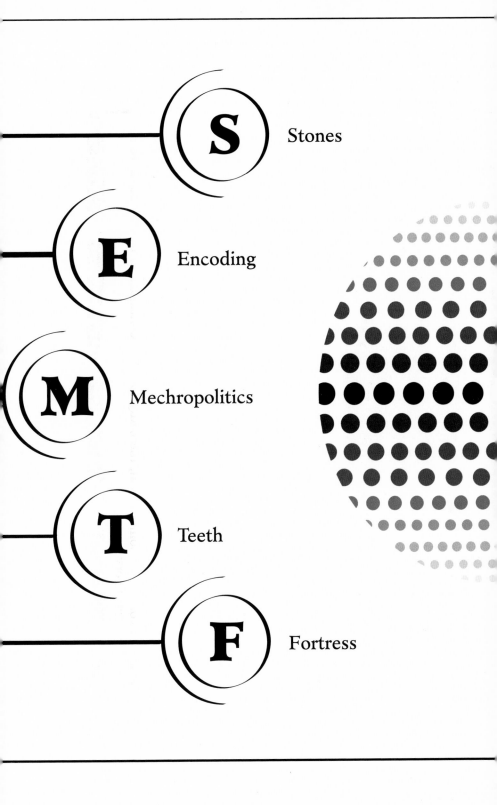

S Stones

E Encoding

M Mechropolitics

T Teeth

F Fortress

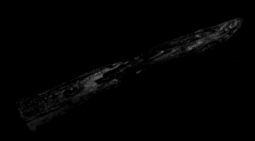

.:: Lenggong Valley Spear Artifact ::.

:: 73,656 years ago. ::

:: 11:52 AM. Late fall. ::

:: Lenggong Valley in Hulu Perak. Not so far from 5.0858, 100.9877. ::

:: Wide meadow under gray clouds. Sparse grass rustles in a cold breeze. Gray light overhead offers little warmth. ::

:: Huddled in the middle sits Young Woman with furs on her back. In her hand, a spear. ::

:: Her Mother rushes toward her. ::

:: Where you? Where you been? ::

:: Went to find bapop. To bapop give tombak. To bapop give tombak for more kisses. ::

:: Slowdumb child! Slowdumb child this whole long life! Luck you live now. Bapop took own tombaks at dawn. Bapop need no other tombak from his slow-dumb child. ::

:: *Mother tries to grab spear but just as quickly Daughter blocks her, turning away, still scratching and stabbing the ground.* ::

:: Daughteri? What goes with you? Out here alone where so little grows? Danger out here alone without men. ::

:: You here mamibu. ::

:: What mamibu do for daughteri if grayhorn charge? :: :: *Mother shakes head.* :: :: Give mamibu back bapop's tombak. We go back to river. Wait there for bapop and men. By apicoals. ::

:: *But Daughter continues to scratch and stab. Mother's anger increases.* ::

:: What doing you here? You uncover death layer, slowdumb child. You uncover death layer and dull tombak. Tombak not for you. Tombak is weapon for men. Men beat you when they return. Bapop beat you when he returns. ::

:: No mamibu. ::

:: *Daughter is suddenly crying and clutching even more tightly the spear. Mother softens. Forgets spear. Strokes Daughter's hair and wet face.* ::

:: Daughteri is true. Daughteri not so slowdumb. Bapop not beat his dear daughteri. Bapop give kisses. For running after bapop to give extra tombak. ::

∴ **No more kisses from bapop.** ∴

∴ *Daughter returns to digging earth. Here the topsoil is dark with little more than grass, determined weeds, and many small stones. Underneath, however, is worse. Daughter gouges up long gashes of lifeless ash.* ∴

∴ *Mother looks at Daughter mystified. Then looks more closely at ground.* ∴

∴ *All at once Mother leaps back. Cries out.* ∴

∴ **Earth look back.** ∴

∴ *Mother tries to look again. Again reacts with fear.* ∴

∴ **Earth look back! What you do daughteri? With this tombak? Daughteri, you do this with bapop's weapon?** ∴

∴ **Not tombak, mamibu. Do with these eyes. Here and here.** ∴

∷ Daughter points to her own two eyes and her own forehead. Then, as if to make her point, throws aside the spear and begins digging up more ash with her hands, even as her fingers start to bleed. ∷

∷ Now Mother looks amazed. ∷

∷ Slowdumb child have gift. Many kisses soon bapop give you for this. Bapop's chest fill with childpride. ∷

∷ No childpride from bapop. No more kisses for slowdumb child. ∷

∷ But Mother doesn't hear Daughter. Mother doesn't notice how dazed Daughter looks. Mother just keeps circling the design. ∷

∷ Grayhorn? ∷

∷ Some lines do resemble a rhino. ∷ ∷ *Rhinoceros sondaicus* ∷

∷ Not grayhorn, mamibu. ∷

∷ Not orang hutan treeliver either. Not out here. ∷

∷ *Mother looks toward distant trees as if she might suddenly hear the call of orang-utans.* ∷ ∷ **Pongo abelii** ∷ ∷ *The only murmur comes from the grass swaying in the rising breeze.* ∷

∷ Stripeteeth, daughteri! This here is stripeteeth! ∷

∷ *Again Mother looks up, as if this time prepared to spy an approaching tiger.* ∷ ∷ **Panthera tigris corbetti** ∷ ∷ *But only darkening clouds slash the sunlight.* ∷

∷ Bigger, mamibu. ∷

∷ Bigger? ∷

∴ Too big, mamibu. ∵

∴ Out here? ∵

∴ *Daughter shakes her head and points toward distant trees.* ∵

∴ There? ∵

∴ There. ∵

∴ Our men went there. ∵

∴ *Daughter nods.* ∵

∴ Bapop went there. ∵

∴ No more men, mamibu. ∵

∴ *Daughter is crying again.* ∵

∴ You went there? ∵

∴ Mamibu, no more bapop. ∵

∴ We must go there. ∵

∴ No mamibu. ∵

∴ *Mother picks up spear.* ∵

∴ Mamibu go there. ∵

∴ *Daughter gently takes back spear. Mother is crying now too.* ∵

∴ Just us two left. ∵

∴ Slowdumb child. Mamibu go find bapop. ∵

∴ Don't go mamibu. Not to there.[ε] ∵

∴ [ε]For alternate set variants of gestural translations, including alveolar clicks, numerous sibilants, bilabial fricatives, retroflex approximants, pharyngeal consonants, see 19210491-08131982-032367848980, order VI, v.26, n.13. ∵

MARK Z. DANIELEWSKI'S

THE

FAMILIAR

VOLUME 3

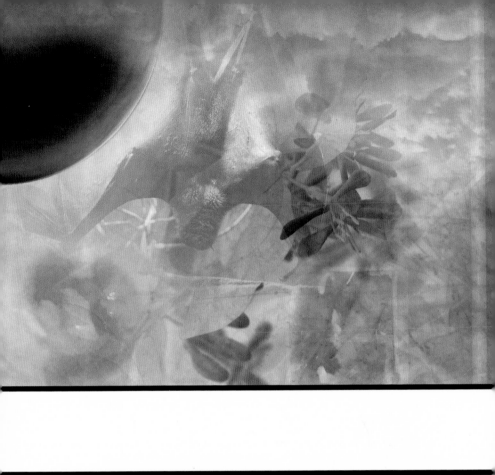

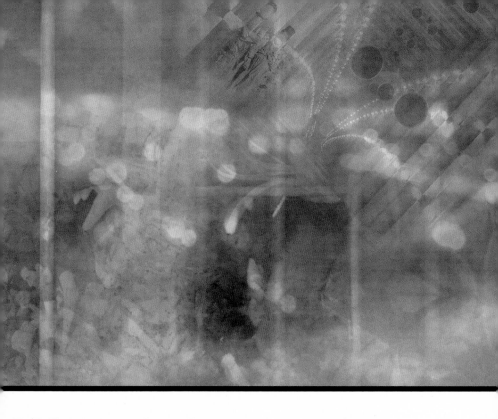

HONEYSUCKLE & PAIN . . .

wings

The spirit said very simply that all the trees were already full.

— Jonathan Lim

"其将死!"

∴ She die! ∵

night after night, auntie scream liddat. just once. never twice. but

times she kay tiam almost worse. silence keep jingjing awake til

dawn to hear her curse:

"她会死的!"

:. **She's dying!** .:

then by morning tian li oreddy gone case lah. get eye see no or-yee-or. answer question of who this she is that's dying with burp. snort. mebbe pick at back tooth with long fingernail if jingjing ask twice: kong si mi? who you mean she? auntie looksee-looksee their flat, kena confused macam jingjing then, sure no one else there but them, until she dig finger from mouth to accuse ownself.

"me?"

weeks now jingjing steer clear smoke. kuai kuai. true true. ladeeda

well behaves. not bent. damn heng him too with pale blue. survive

fine. no raeden in coma. jingjing different. jilo craves. no addict

now. just smoke. for fun. dip sun down so clouds surround.

jingjing also boh lui liao. that's it. forget dollars, forget coin. all

fart and no shit. seesee, empty pockets to pay 23. better to just

grab nuts. t'eh lum pah chi saht. so smoke no problem. never is

with not enough.

tonight's scream though confirm and guarantee jingjing rise at

dawn to dead auntie. damn kia si lang! sure he find her body like

candle burnt in wax puddle, brittle and cold. but she only grunt,

snore. jingjing never think he could love such sounds so much.

all day too jingjing put up with her can't get up, her can't finish

a thought, forget walks. once they toured city more. how jingjing

hated those days once, her so famous, smith street sage, auntie of

goo chia sui, the great tian li, everybody coming up, waving her

down, want her healing, her gift, with that thing so often riding

her shoulder.

now though . . .

making money the old way was never lost. tian li may have taken

away jingjing's craves but knowledge has no cure. doesn't even

take long. friday night craycraze and they won't stop calling

jingjing "such pretty boy." blur lights over tourists over tall pints

drinking up and down quays. boh tah boh lum par. jingjing not

need to drink. or touch. or even saysay much.

french or swiss. hair plenty silver, greased to glitter. hum sup

loh or not. bored business sure, and rich enuf. won't die one. any

question of who disease has no matter. oreddy risen. for a peek

at jingjing's teeth immeelly orgas with no splatter. pau ka liau.

pleased to bag himself for what gives to jingjing gives to 23 for

that smaller bag. and this time easy found, straight to corright

shrine, no pattern tzuay kuay badminton, no puzzle floor. just this,

greater risk, not pink, pink beyond afford, pink not even around,

pushed across counter: pale blue. again.

"pipe up here?" 23 even ask. and offer pipe.

03-03 is all beds and couches with no room in-between but shadows. just a flat too but lao hiao at door calls it the smoke house. jingjing got jilo zippo. lady finds one because jingjing and 23 so si beh ah kah liao but warns him to leave it where he use it or lose every permission. jingjing glow still and still with no smoke. jingjing and 23 ak? true, for long years, he know 23. why not friends? old friends?

with windows mat-covered and aircon punched high, jingjing sink into night colder than place, darker than time. by small flame he pack glass bowl, suka-suka, and by small flame finds first inhale twisting so deep inside, inside no longer has any fences, warmer than want, wider than sense and senses.

this oldest friend.

if something's oreddy lost

what another deep breath corrects

palebluepale
pale blue
pale blue
pale blue
pale blue

n l e
e
l
e
d

paleblue pale blue
paleblue pale blue pale blue

something oreddy wrong

smoke smoke... paleblue... smoke sm... paleblue... smoke smo k e... paleblue... paleblue... smokesmoke... pale blue pale... smokesmoke...

blue palebale blue pale blue

smoke smo ke... paleblue...

廣于理與

廣 于 理 與

paleblue

what only more gasps correct again

smoke smoke smoke smoke
pale blue pale blue
paleblue paleblue
blue pale blue
pale blue
smoke smoke
blue pale blue
pale blue
smokes smoke

blue... smoke smoke
blue p a l e b l u e
smokes mokes mo

until across everything and everywhere, over in far corner, not so

far, someone there, dancing an ember, wrapped in smoke,

laughs.

smoke house lady brings jingjing cold tea in cloudy glass. she old but not as old gets when old babbles and breaks. jingjing jerks sharp then, slops drink in lap, to find tian li in near corner where no, boh true, no one waits. smoke house lady strokes his arm, mebbe has for a long time, and laughs lah when jingjing point next to far corner where no one laughs. she pinch arm, over and over sing jingjing "relac one corner," he alone, no harm here. so jingjing resettle back on purple pillows shattered with ash.

no one close to alarm ash. or spit or gum or trash. no such thing as waste. nothing is refused. everything finds its place in smoke.

and strong smoke this.

jingjing nods, or nods off? smoke house lady away, with thoughts gone wild on new arrangements, like jingjing si beh sala all this time, takes smoke to see truth: cat's loss a good thing! kuching to ka-ching! all these years waiting, now jingjing startstarts, because it makes sense how what goes from her must come to him, how her death will bring him new strength when the cat returns.

to make sure, jingjing unpocket monster cards, shuffle deck, draw three facedown, put two back, then puff last of pale blue before reading flip.

alamak! ang mor gao. macam scooby doo. no cat this.

and like it's not away but seated near beside, far corner fills this

time with more laughter. dancing ember burning even brighter,

more smoke rising, macam fire, as man there rises soon, a man is

there lah!, and a towering man too, keeps laughing, like he chio

kao peng, like jingjing should laugh too, and mebbe would have,

if wah lao towering laughing man didn't also have two towering

wings, nothing laughing there, like bat's, leathery, spreading wider

and wider, and still spreading, taking away every ember and dim

bulb.

jingjing not fly. jingjing has no wings. but he did not fall three

floors either. mebbe he found drainpipe to scramble down or

laundry line to swing free with or mebbe he didn't go out window

at all.

whatever way, jingjing cabut lari now, away from estate, 23, smoke

house lady, thing with wings. fastfast down streets, siao liao lah,

siao liao lah, with pipe in one hand, lighter in other. when police

car scoot past, jingjing toss pipe quick, leaves behind a sprinkle of

breaking glass, if too late to act blur, check pace.

police car gostan fast, backtrack to catch jingjing's state.

lighter is no problem. check his pockets, jingjing boh tai ji, but if

they check his blood mebbe will still throw him in changi, rotan

his backside, so jingjing go si peh kwee behind bars. jingjing know

story of some goondu back from jb after weekend-long party. no

drugs in sack but enough in his system to lock him up for years.

running from police is just as bad but jingjing must run, across

park, void decks, finds a stair landing high enough up to wait in,

steady, smoke helps him doze.

so still hours before dawn, jingjing's careful creep at last brings

him home. no blue and red lights. no mata in sight. commonwealth

calyx rise from mist like headstone. void deck's gone of folk,

jingjing all luck, takes lift up, reaches door without seeing no one.

only voices arrest his hand at the lock. cha si nang! macam a

crowd of voices all tarik rousing from inside.

had police found him oreddy? waiting him out here? until a darker

thought find jingjing out: she died. the funeral's arrived.

jingjing unlocks door and voices stop. he expects the last effects

of smoke to mock him with an empty room.

instead all jingjing sees are wings! vast leathery things rising up

from broad backs, scratching sooty marks on the ceiling!

si beh sway, how from this fluttering mingle emerges then the

towering monster, same-same from smoke house, big smiling as

jingjing collapse into another kind of leathery dark, though not

before catching sight of who of course centers this group, back

to old self, far from her usual mess, even has on a black and gold

pearl-flecked dress.

"靖靖!" auntie smiles. "吾須即赴洛城!"

∵ *Jingjing! We must leave for Los Angeles at once!* ∵

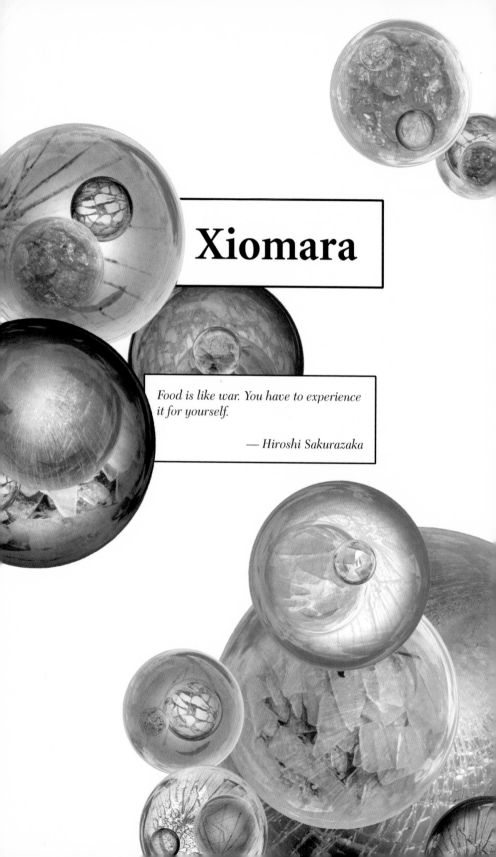

Xiomara

Food is like war. You have to experience it for yourself.

— Hiroshi Sakurazaka

It happens on their way home for lunch, which was supposed to be at noon, but, like, it's already one?, and Anwar's easily just as anxious as Xanther, both of them irritable, really, thanks to their growling stomachs, "hangry and hanicky" Astair likes to say, who's already texted three times because they're late because there's traffic, because they didn't just get some of the errands done but got *all* of the dumb errands done, and yeah, of course they want the vegetable ceviche she made specially for this day, Friday the thirteenth, and still Anwar's not getting home any faster, though now they're on a side street, ∴ **Reservoir Street** ∵ running parallel to Sunset, because Sunset has so much traffic it's almost no longer a road, and then Anwar speeds up a little because there's finally a clear way ahead, down a hill too, which is when it happens . . . this little squirrel rushes out.

It could have made it across too.

If its paws hadn't stuttered in place.

Such an awful pause.

Worse, it tried to go back.

But back was already a lost option.

Xanther saw all the options too clearly.

Anwar takes the only option, swerves left, hitting

the brakes too, but not enough to lock the tires,

because they're too late for that, both front tires

already past, except the Honda hasn't straightened

out, not in time to spare the little animal from

what comes next, the thump of a back tire,

what no stop, no matter how smooth, can take back.

Anwar drops his head on the wheel, like can't say even a word, even groan, even when Xanther asks, "Did we kill it? Is it dead?," already opening her door, Anwar looking up then, the pain in his eyes almost enough to get Xanther to stay inside.

"What are you doing?"

"I have to check."

"Daughter, there's no way it survived."

"I have to check," Xanther repeats, Anwar already nodding, before dropping his head, again, to the wheel, maybe this time concealing what eyes wouldn't.

They are farther away than Xanther thought. How fast had Anwar been going? More, probably, than 15 MPH? ∴ **42 MPH** ∵

The small, dark shape doesn't move.

And what if it does move? Can an animal hospital repair what the small suffer under the wheel of such a machine as their Element? What would Dr. Syd do?

Xanther knows what Dov would have done: boot-healed ∷ -heeled! ∷ the suffering. Could Xanther do that? ∷ No. ∷ With Converse? ∷ Apt! ∷ Would she even be able to look?

At least what Xanther finds presents no need: on its back, belly strangely swollen, ruptured too, with the same red oozing from its tiny jaws, between broken teeth. Only the bushy tail seems oblivious to this rigidity, fluttering in the heavy way June air will shift its heat around.

Xanther can't even find tears. A dullness takes over and stills all reach. There's not even a reason to touch this, what?, fatality? Death here is as absolute as the something now lingering everywhere is strange, a curious sensation blotting out the squirrel and whatever else Xanther might have felt.

Stranger still: it swirls around like unexpected blooms of relief.

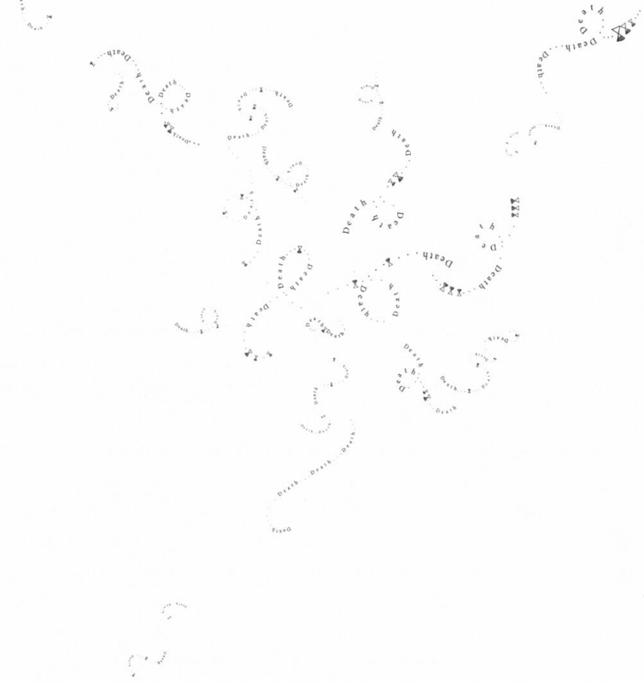

No big surprise: neither Anwar nor Xanther is hungry when they get home. And the salad Astair fixed is beautiful, like full of corn, nectarines and slivers of orange bell peppers, and like mini ice-cream scoops of avocado, with plenty of halved cherry tomatoes, shallots, and thin slices of jalapeños, plus lots of edamame, and all of it soaking for the past few hours in olive oil and lime juice. It looks like a painting.

If only it were a painting. The thought of eating any of it disgusts Xanther.

"What happened?" Astair asks with brows of distress.

Anwar, who hasn't said much since it happened, tries to lead Astair away, his hand on her arm.

But Astair doesn't move.

"Are you sick again?" she asks Xanther instead.

Anwar shakes his head, for both of them, withdrawing his touch in favor of what he can't favor: "We're both sick but I'm the one to blame."

Sick, obviously, doesn't mean epilepsy, or even what happened yesterday. Xanther had thrown up all day. It started in the morning and didn't let up until around dusk. Diarrhea too. Like her body couldn't let loose enough. Just before dusk her parents had started talking about going to the ER because Xanther wasn't keeping anything down, she wasn't hydrating. Anwar had to hold back her hair so it wouldn't slop into the toilet, then afterward mop her forehead with a cool cloth. Astair made Xanther mint tea and also poured her glasses of Pedialyte, Blue Raspberry.

"It's sweet. It's just sugar water."

Xanther did her best to keep it down but the blue yuck kept coming back up.

"Can we have some too?" Freya asked. Shasti was all nods too.

Les Parents were sure food poisoning was the cause, until they were sure it was a bug. Xanther knew it was neither, because she felt fine. In fact, she had never felt better. ∷ Totally true. What she'd eaten was A-OK, and uhm, other than the usual parade of gut-level bacteria, no new culprits. So unless I'm missing something, which I can't miss, totally psychosomatic, which I can also totally trace, but, huh, can't. ∷ And that's what had kept filling Xanther with such revulsion, what her body kept helping her try to refuse, even if no matter how hard it contorted and twisted, squirted or retched, still wouldn't lessen: until expelling finally came down to accepting — accepting how much the little one had changed.

Not that it's so obvious ∴ *But it is so obvious.* ∵ : eyes still pinched shut, wobbling this way and that in her palm, or when Xanther's lying down, blindly trying to nuzzle deeper into her armpit, which tickles and makes her giggle, and for some reason infuriates the twins.

Even now they roll their eyes and scowl at the creature on her shoulder. Not like Xanther cares.

She just keeps making sure his coat remains free of any wisps of dust or specks of whatever, though such things don't usually cling to the hair, or is it fur? Whatever. Finding dirt on him is pretty rare. Like some sorta weird cloud-fog-smoke, never really touching the ground, or the sky, forget the sky, his white fluff is almost always clean.

His ears are another story. They get this black goop collecting inside. Kinda waxy and way gross, the sort of stuff Xanther would never go near, but here she doesn't hesitate, carefully dipping the tip of her pinkie inside, scooping the stuff out, wiping her finger on a tissue.

His eyes also get these tiny globs under the tear ducts, like sleep, or even boogers, but way darker. And actually, yesterday, though her stomach had already been turning before she started vomiting, maybe that was what kicked it off, because Xanther had been petting him, cleaning his ears, to like make herself feel better, and it usually did make her feel better, and then she got to the eyes, the easiest part, just two little flicks, except what was on her pinkie tip, actually just under the nail, didn't look dark then, but more like red, like bloodred.

Now though, on her bed, ear goop and eye muck are back again to just regular dark. Xanther rubs the top of his head, strokes under his chin, evokes a purr, that little rumble, that little storm, what must feel good to him, and always feels good to her.

Though none of this is the unusual part.

And the red she saw, maybe that was like her dream life confusing her, or some spear of dawn light briefly reflected off a red candle or passing through red glass, though they have no red candles or red glass.

:. It was a little weird. .:

:. *She knows what she saw.* .:

The unusual not-so-obvious part is really all about the tiny chest caging that little rumble, little storm.

Not that the little beast doesn't still seem frail, something so visible about the joints, as in too visible, disjointed, as if they could swerve away so much from together that what together even means would go too.

The ribs in particular. Xanther can feel each one when she strokes him, and for sure detect the slight rise of each one under the skin, but now they seem much less visible, like the red she like maybe saw, she's even making up this plumpness, like pretending what's still bone is really new muscle.

Saturday morning, while Anwar's at some convention, downtown?, having to do with new computer stuff?, or is it electronic stuff in general?, ∵ **E3** ∵ Astair takes her and the girls swimming.

That's another thing different: leaving her little guy right now is still painful, but not like the life-threatening way it usually is, like the end-up-a-little-crisp feeling. Though the heat still comes on, inside again, somewhere within her, like somehow lost within that incredible forest way beyond her, a tiny pop of blue flame, like an incredibly small acorn, tickling the ice around it, a warning of a still greater warmth to come, when all the ice melts, and then the real burning starts.

At least now it's not as bad as that last week of school. Bearable-bad, she'd say, though she still can't wait to dive into the pool, like maybe that will cool things off.

However, before even getting past the driveway at Taymor's, Xanther finds all the honeysuckle, in bloom too, beautiful bells of white and yellow and even blue, surprising her with the fact that it's not all that aromatic, not like she remembers, and she even sticks her nose into one flower, one without a bee, a couple of annoyed bees circling around her ears, which doesn't annoy Xanther, in fact she likes the sound, even if she doesn't linger, because these really are their flowers. They need them, which is the song their wings sing, which is better than this, well, okay, faint smell?, and sure, super nice, but nothing in comparison to well ... huh, because, huh, Xanther loves honeysuckle and no question this is honeysuckle but it's still nothing like that night when she trance-walked outside their home and almost got run over, and out of nowhere honeysuckle was vining through the air.

Such colors, such perfume, such life.

While Xanther is changing in a bathroom that has one of those steam rooms in the shower, and this is just the pool-house bathroom, though there isn't really a pool house, just the huge pool and these changing stalls, Taymor saying so sweetly "Make yourself at home, darlings" in that big, full, I'm-not-afraid-of-anything voice, which she drops when Xanther, Freya, and Shasti disappear to shelves of towels and extra suits, Taymor and Astair resorting then to whispers at the far end of the pool.

For sure they're too far away to hear, so maybe Xanther's making this up, but she can hear them talking about "what happened." ∷ Huh. She did just hear that. ∷ Xanther can also hear Freya in the next stall bickering with Shasti who's two stalls over about who gets to be Marco and who gets to be Polo first. Though of course those two are yelling.

"What are you doing with your summer, young lady?" Taymor asks Xanther before she can dive into the deep end. She's already tightened on her mask.

"Hanging with my new friend?"

"Her cat," Astair explains, though it's obvious Taymor understood.

"In a few weeks I'm going with, like, my friends? to Magic Mountain? Psyched about that. Maybe, uhm, like Roxanne wants to come?"

"Hmm. We'll see. For now, she's grounded for getting her tragus pierced without asking."

"Is she here?" Xanther asks, instead of asking what a tragus is.

Taymor shakes her head: "With Ted. He's the one having the talk that will culminate in aforementioned grounding. Gratefully, I'm spared that brawl. Or most of it."

Xanther likes Roxanne. She realizes she was kinda looking forward to seeing her. No doubt she'd have some amazing suit, nothing like this pink thing Xanther has on, with frayed black ties, but she's also really nice, and Xanther likes talking with her, or listening to her, because her opinion is so different from Xanther's, but like informed.

She'd also help insulate her from the twins who these days seem bothered by everything Xanther does.

It doesn't help that Astair made it clear that they can only swim in the shallow end, while Xanther gets the deep end all to herself, because she took all her swimming lessons without complaint, which isn't quite true. Xanther hates being used as an example. It's like she's not even there when she's standing right there.

It's sooooo such a relief then to not stand there, to just hold her mask, and holding her breath, jump.

Xanther even smiles midair when her mom starts in about keeping "close to the ladder where I can see you—" that "see you—" all but disappearing in the big splash closing over Xanther's head as she twists free of bubbles tingling her skin.

Taymor's pool has this neat thing. And it's not even fancy. Ted took a rope and knotted it every couple of feet, then tied one end to the ladder, and the other to a barbell covered in this dark blue squishy plastic. Light enough that, with a little effort, Xanther can retrieve it from the bottom. The fun part is that you can sit on the ladder, and after taking the deepest breath possible, with both hands clutching the barbell in front, like Superman soaring, you can slide gently off the ladder, and away you go without a kick, or anything, just gliding down like you're flying, the next best thing to flying, or the next best thing to Magic Mountain, which is also the next best thing to flying.

Xanther can't wait to go. A few weeks seems like forever away.

If only she could take her little one.

At the bottom of the pool, the burning isn't any better. And the water is even colder down here but colder doesn't seem to help because it's not that kind of heat. At least Xanther feels momentarily free, as long as she can hold her breath, listening to the way the water moves, how Shasti and Freya are splashing far away, other sounds too, like strange squeaks, like what bubbles sound like when they're detaching from her, rising toward the surface ∴ **She knows** ∴ ∴ *Bubbles rising to the surface write that song but how do I even know?* ∴ ∴ Who knows ∴, followed by more and more, before Xanther's kicking off the bottom, using the rope to pull herself back up even faster to the ladder, for air, for the chance to pull up the barbell and do it all over again.

And Xanther does just that, over and over, each time managing to relax a little more and hold her breath a little longer.

Something weird happens then: she starts to hear Astair whispering with Taymor again about "what happened," what was surely "a trancelike announcement of tonic-clonic seizures still to come," reconsidering the ketogenic diet in favor of Zarontin ∴ **ethosuximide** ∴ or Depakote ∴ **valproate** ∴ or even Topamax ∴ **topiramate** ∴ or Keppra

:. **levetiracetam** .: :. She's not hearing any of this. Not voices or strange squeaks. Just the twins slapping water. .:

All of which quiets when she ascends, her mom and Taymor just smiling, with the attack poodle nearby in the shade, panting, all of them just waiting for Xanther's next trip down so they can start whispering again.

This time when she reaches the bottom, Xanther lies down on her back, putting the barbell on her belly, letting out the thinnest stream of air, watching how the bubbles spiral, some splitting apart into tinier pearls of silver, while others merge into bigger blobs, how many of these tiny bits of air?, Xanther at once grinding back the Question Song, clamping down on the air too, trying then to just let out one bubble, maybe put a whisper in it, or a hidden word, and just watch that rise away, to break apart maybe, or maybe not, before disappearing into the big puddle called the surface, blurry above with ash trees and sky.

And suddenly Xanther's thinking about the squirrel they killed, and though she managed to steer clear of numbers, like of bubbles, the Question Song re-announces itself now with everything about that little creature: how old was it? :. **432 days** .: was its mother still alive? :. **No** .: its father? :. **No** .: was it a he or she? :. *She was pregnant* .: did it have a nest of its own? under the ground? or high above? :. *Among long wind-swaying branches.* .: And that's just the start. More questions keep rising, answerless: was it afraid when it raced into the street? :. **Fearless** .: or excited? :. *Bests even Ratatoskr . . .* .: did dying hurt? :. **Yes** .:

:. Uhm? She? What? Who? WTF? .:

So many tears follow then that Xanther just yanks off the mask, accepting with open eyes the blur that sweeps in, even if it can't blur away the shame of failing to save the squirrel, of all she can never find out about what's now forever gone ∴ . . . ∴, Xanther hadn't even moved it aside, maybe covered it with leaves, that would have been nice, the least she could have done instead of just leaving it in the road, unmarked, unnamed, unmourned, unless this counts as mourning, does this count?, for something?, anything?

When Xanther reaches the surface, hacking for air, she pays no attention to Astair's worried look, or Taymor's, even the attack poodle looks worried, yipping a little, all three of them huddled by the ladder.

Not like Xanther was down there *that* long.

Freya and Shasti sure couldn't care less what half a minute means, not even that. The twins still just screaming and splashing away in the shallow end, it's pretty cute actually, how they love splashing, not even at each other, like they could splash forever.

Xanther laughs then. Before she even catches her breath. Because somehow an answer to a question that she hadn't even realized she was asking herself had just found her, and fast too, ungritting her teeth, all at once dissolving her sadness, and her anger ∴ **At least for the time being** ∵ ∴ *Is she even a time being?* ∵, when had she gotten so angry?, giving her something she could be responsible for, and so simple too:

"A name, Mom! Little one definitely needs a name!"

Easier said than, uh, said. The rest of Saturday, Xanther tries without success to settle on a name. The first few tries are funny, and like, maybe weird too?, and all due to the cat's water dish that's really one of the big glass bowls Astair had bought for the Akita. "Fill it less, daughter," Anwar has already warned. "Your little fella could drown in there." And getting back from Bel Air, that's exactly where Xanther had found him, up to his neck, squeaking for help, as he also kept blindly snapping at the surface, not drinking either but like trying to bite something rising from the bottom.

Names like Snap, Bowl, Swimswim, and even Drown, even Pool, didn't last a moment. Wrong as soon as they were spoken. Same for a whole bunch of other possibilities, from Hogwarts to Kings to Stanley to Cloud. Q-tip holds for an instant longer.

Sunday night they go out to Mexico City, a restaurant on Hillhurst. Les Parents love the margaritas there, the twins get the chips and salsa, Xanther makes do with the vegetarian fajita and lots and lots of extra cheese.

The twins still won't talk to her for getting to bottom-dive in the deep end all day.

And then suddenly Shasti whispers, loud too, like in that scared way that wants company: "Frey, why's that weird girl looking at Xanther like that?"

"Oh my gosh! And she's dressed like Xanther!"

Xanther turns too late, just catching through the plate glass a girl scurrying away, about her size, wearing black and pink too, and with long black braids.

Monday morning, after breakfast, after her mom leaves to meet with her patients, the nameless one suddenly bolts from her bedroom. They were on the floor together, and then he was stumbling for the door, in a kinda funny drunk way, so not really bolting anywhere, even bumping into the door frame. Xanther sighed and got up to follow him.

Only he's not in the all ∴ hall! ∴. Gone. Wait. No. Somehow, huh?, he's already halfway down the stairs. How did that happen? ∷ *How could it not happen?* ∷ ∷ This is impossible! ∷ Unless he fell there. ∷ Okay, uhm, that's likely. ∷ He even looks like he's about to fall again, and does!, a tiny

somersault,

 shattering

  like glass,

  like he's going to

   keep tumbling

    and shattering

     down all the stairs,

      like the terrible sound

 still slicing through the house

—except he stops dead on the next step, not even half a somersault, or even a quarter flip?, landing like a brick, or more, as if small as he is he is also nothing but weight, the weight of the silence now seizing the house.

Xanther expects Anwar to come charging out of the bedroom, where he's napping, having worked all night long. Astair warned everyone to be extra quiet. But the door to the master bedroom stays shut. Is that him snoring? ∴ I can hear no one snoring. ∴

Xanther is already considering the name Shatter, or Slice, or what about Stair or Echo?, as she scoops the little guy up, who's shaking his head as if to answer these, what?, insults?, before settling down in her palm with a sigh, how about Sigh? Xanther continuing to tiptoe, or more like, especially with her thick socks on, padpad down to the bottom, not even sure what instinct orders her to move now with stealth, to discover the source of that huge crash, to spy on her sisters from the foyer.

"Oh, it's my fault, my fault," the big woman rasps. She's crouched by the fireplace, desperately trying to reassemble what's already lost.

Xanther hardly knows her, except that she's their house-keeper and her name is Xiomara. This is also her last day. Earlier, before leaving, Astair had given her a big hug. Both women had tears in their eyes.

Xiomara is moving back to Guadalajara. Xanther found the city on Google Maps two months ago. She has no idea what it looks like, though now for some reason she pictures a man. Maybe Xiomara's husband? Maybe in Guadalajara? Like, maybe they met there? She sees dark hands smeared with darker oil clutching a wrench. Has he been here before?

:: **His name is Pablo Güiza. He and Xiomara have been married for eleven years. He recently started working in Guadalajara selling shaved ice which allows him to rent a modest apartment in Tlaquepaque. Seven years from now, on an unremarkable morning in July, his left hand will suffer an unremarkable cut while removing a stripped pipe from beneath a bathroom sink. Complications from an untreated staph infection will claim his life on August 9, 2021. He never visited the Ibrahims.** ::

Or what about the warm creases around his eyes, brightening at the sight of Xiomara, who sighs like she's annoyed, like she's busy, like she will never have enough time for those eyes, though that's all she thinks about as she later mops the floors of people she works for.

:: All made up. ::

:: *Yes, yes. In the same way that everything is made up.* ::

"Mommy's wolves," Shasti says, joining Xiomara on the floor.

Freya also tries to help.

"No, you'll hurt yourself. Both of you. Step away. Get Mr. Anwar, please."

"He's still sleeping," Freya declares.

"Mom made us swear we wouldn't wake him," Shasti says.

"He's been working sooooooooo hard," Freya adds.

"This was her favorite thing," Xiomara groans. "You see what happened? I rush! I rush too much! And look what I do!"

Xiomara places the big pieces in a paper bag and starts sweeping the rest of the shards into a dustpan.

"Where's your sister?"

The twins share a look Xanther knows too well: how secrets are traded and decisions are made beyond the reach of others.

"We won't tell it broke," Freya whispers.
"We won't," Shasti joins in.

Clearly Xiomara feels horrible about the statue, but at the same time she's also, what is it?, like maybe touched?, or horrified?, or amused?, or all of those things at the same time, by the willingness of these two too-young girls to try to absolve her of this mistake.

Xanther's moved.

Who cares if some dumb old thing lies now in a heap of shards? What matters is that her sisters are trying to console such a hardworking woman. Has Xanther ever seen them act like this, so compassionately? And if it's a little mis-guided, so what. Aren't their hearts in the right place?

Xiomara smiles and thanks them both, giving each in turn a hug and a kiss on the forehead.

"When your mother gets home, please tell her everything that happened. I pay back what it costs. Here is my money for this week. I leave it on the table. Do you promise to tell her?"

"We promise," Shasti says.

"Don't worry, Xiomara," Freya adds. "She won't even notice it's missing."

Which starts all sorts of uh-ohs going. What are the twins up to? Of course Astair will notice. Is it the money they're after? Why would they want money? Though what does it say about Xanther now that she's so distrustful?

Why is she even spying?

At least that part is obvious: Xanther doesn't want to further embarrass Xiomara. She's also proud of her sisters for wanting to protect Xiomara.

Later, from the living room window, Xanther watches Shasti and Freya accompany Xiomara to her car. Xiomara hugs each of them again. They wave goodbye from the doorway.

Still later, Xanther watches them take the brown bag of broken glass out to the carport and throw it away in one of the garbage cans.

In the afternoon, they hand Astair Xiomara's money. The cat shifts back and forth on Xanther's shoulder. She feels the light prick of claws. Then the back of her tongue seems to prickle too and even thicken.

"What for?" Astair asks the girls. "I don't understand."

But the twins don't say anything.

Neither does Xanther.

Bleach

A really good detective never gets married.

— *Raymond Chandler*

Olympic station on Vermont isn't exactly Hollywood on Wilcox as Abendroth had led Özgür to believe. Maybe Abendroth had been mistaken or overruled. Not as if you can't catch a homicide north of Sunset. It's just that any murder from Pacific, Olympic, West L.A. and Wilshire Areas also come your way. The murders aren't the problem.

It's only Monday, and Friday can't get here fast enough. And if the uncleared cases stacking up aren't another good reason to pull the pin, Captain Cardinal hasn't even gotten started. Though here's another start. Already the third casebook today. Cold as the coroner's crypt.

"Özgür, I love Christmas. And now with you here, it's like Christmas in June. It'll be like Christmas in July. It'll be Christmas in August." Captain Cardinal sits behind his desk, forearms flat, hand over hand, like some actor grinning in a toothpaste commercial.

Özgür adds the binder to his growing pile. But when he finally leaves the station, it's the folder from the bottom that goes with him.

Planski doesn't even glance over at the paperwork. What sun's left in the sky of a dead day doesn't seem to require a hat with so wide a brim. But who's Özgür to grief someone about the hat they wear? Maybe about the quality of brown they're filling his glass with, though Özgür's never had cause to complain about the iced tea Planski pours him. Her mother's recipe. Fresh mint from the garden.

Planski lives in Mount Washington, a little up the hill too, in a narrow Craftsman house of white and green, with shades of rose, or at least orange leaning in a rose's direction. A little like the cactus ∴ *Sempervivum tectorum* ∴ she's planting now on the terrace beyond her small back deck.

"Any idea why someone would do that to heads?"

Planski still doesn't want to talk work. She keeps spading the earth, one gloved hand reaching in now and then to remove a root or stone.

"Cardinal getting any cheerier?" Planski asks once the first spike of green settles into place.

"Oh he's cheery. Has me with the unsolved squad. On my own."

"All over a girl neither one of you can remember."

"It's the losing he can't forget."

Planski shakes her head. Takes a sip of her iced tea. Returns to planting the second cactus, carefully arranging small dark rocks around the base. It looks nice. The closest thing Özgür has to a plant at his place is some tea tree oil.

"Erin," Özgür finally says.

"Who?"

"The girl."

"It'll take more than remembering a girl's name to impress me."

"How about impressing me with some insight about bleach?" Özgür sighs.

"Is this even your case?" Planski stops spading. She's annoyed enough for Özgür to know it has nothing to do with him. Maybe she'd feel better if she took off that hat.

"It *was* Florian Sérbulo's."

"Down in Harbor?" Planksi goes back to digging up a spot for the last succulent. "Cardinal hasn't got you working hard enough?"

"Captain wants me revisiting anything still open back through 2010."

"What does 'was' mean?"

"Last Florian heard the case was shuffled over to who knows where. Maybe even some NSA nonsense. Now all *interested parties* are told to call numbers that just ring and ring."

"Why are you so interested?"

"Doesn't plunging the heads of three bodies in a bath with a load of bleach interest you?"

"You know my weak spot." At least she smiles. She takes off her gloves too. "Some misguided attempt to, I don't know, obscure identity?"

"All the IDs were laid out neatly next to the bodies."

"Is that what's in this folder?"

"Confirmation that the names on the IDs match the deceased."

"I assume Cardinal didn't hand you this."

Özgür shakes his head. "Abendroth was convinced he was messing with me by parking some nut at my desk. The guy called himself Warlock. He was a nut until he left me this."

"Has Florian ever heard of Warlock?"

"Nope."

"Have you talked to Warlock since?"

Özgür shakes his head. "I'm not convinced he's not a nut. Just might be one of the sophisticated ones."

"Quit talking about yourself."

Özgür finishes his iced tea. He needs something stronger. Almost a month has passed but Özgür hasn't forgotten the Israeli ex-lieutenant. A few times he even considered calling the number on the card. The transfer from Rampart is easy to blame for not having any time, but the real reason comes down to a familiar zeal Özgür sensed, what too many rabbis, clerics, and bloggers possess. Özgür isn't sure he can take that kind of conviction anymore: when people fail to see how the world so numerously contradicts their fantasy, that just the idea of themselves carrying on such a cause becomes the most absurd fantasy of all.

"But he got you curious?" Planski is eyeing Özgür.

"Just like your mention of Synsnap got me curious. But I'm turning up dead ends on that one too."

"Hard times for a guy whose ego never mastered a three-point turn." Planski laughs.

"Still no sign of your CI?" Özgür can give it as well as he can take it, though he has no wish to make Planski wince.

"A whisper," she manages to croak. She doesn't manage to hide the wince.

"What does 'a whisper' mean?"

But Planski just heads back into her house, big hat still on.

Downtown at his place, pouring something neat and about as far away from tea as China, Özgür realizes there's a shift in his apartment that's no longer his. The cupboards and drawers are all closed the way he left them, but also like they were opened and closed without him. Özgür even drops his hand to his gun, moving quickly through the apartment, checking closets, the balcony, the bathroom.

He knows he never leaves the turntable on. Nothing's playing, nothing turning, just a faint glow near the needle to confirm someone else is here. *Was* here.

The bedroom's just as empty except for a handwritten note on his pillow.

Had two hours to kill. So I did me a little killing for a 'little death' right here without you.

You missed out.

When the phone rings, Özgür picks up without checking the ID. He's sure it's Elaine.

"In your whole career," Planski says, coughing, "have you ever seen a head in a bucket of bleach?"

"Nope."

"I haven't either. Like something you'd see in a bad TV show with enough bad science to suggest a high school education in Lafayette. So I stand by identity."

"I don't follow."

"Four IDs right?"

"Three."

"Bleach is the fourth."

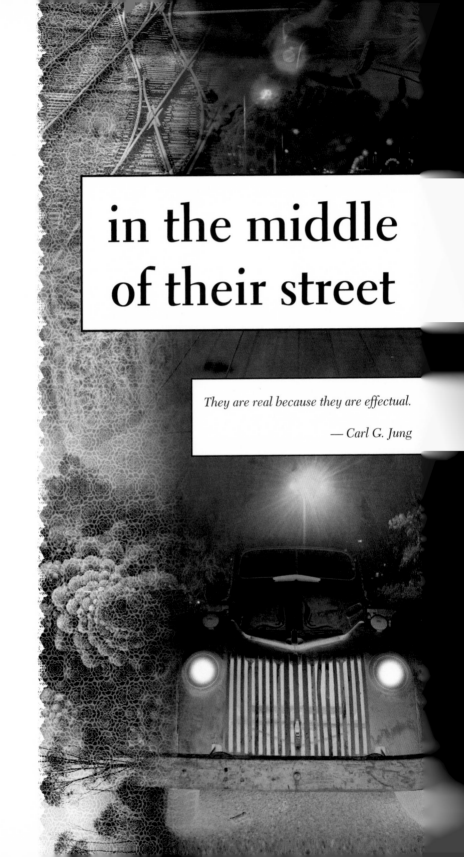

in the middle of their street

They are real because they are effectual.

— *Carl G. Jung*

"Cats are carnivores," Astair tells Abigail. "Dogs might have a go at this fennel salad but not cats."

Not that much of the salad remains (they had arrived late (at least they didn't have to wait for a table (the beers came quick (went to Astair's head even quicker (what she gets for ordering something called Delirium Tremens ((definitely not for cats) a strong blond Belgian ale (in a white bottle with a bright metallic blue label (that Astair can't resist picking))) what kind of product for consumption announces itself as severe withdrawals? (a quirky paradox fizzes pleasantly in her mind (even if she can't help think-ing again of Xanther's white cat (what color are its eyes? (blue? metallic? (. . .)))))))))).

"How's the little vegetarian handling its need for meat?"

"I spare Xanther the findings of my research. She'd claim I was building a case against her pet. She already knows the cat and I have issues."

"How are your issues?" Abigail's fork circles the last remaining bits of fennel (one wedge of orange there too).

"Finish it, Abby. I need our pizza now."

Mother Dough ∵ **4648 Hollywood Boulevard, Los Angeles, CA 90027** ∴ was busy (the Neapolitan-style oven glowing in the back (it should be glowing (tem-peratures inside reach nearly a thousand degrees (cooking pies in a minute (plenty hurried out to nearby tables (not theirs)))))).

"I'm actually not building a case," Astair con-tinues. "Xanther doesn't believe me. *I* don't believe me. I can't stand my new advisor. But—"(Astair takes another sip of Delirium Tremens (good beer)) "—I'm increasingly more intrigued by my reactions and surprised by how my interest in this creature—well, you know, first, no matter how small they are, they're total predators, and second, what I could tell you already just about their claws, the sensitivity of their eyes, their teeth!, and how that's, how I'm discovering, huh, I sound like Xanther—" (another sip (swig!)) "—how fascination dissolves disaffection. Curious word too: 'fascinate.' Did you know it's from the Latin *fascinat*, which means *bewitched*?"

"Fascinating," Abigail twinkles.

"Too academic? I can't help myself."

"Astair! I'm not Taymor." Her tall (blond (beautiful)) friend clucks her tongue (she does look fascinated (though Astair doubts news of her thesis is casting any spell (more likely her beer (with peeing angels on her bottle!))))).

"Xanther gave Taymor and me such a scare Saturday."

"Oh?" Abigail's bewitched look vanishes (Astair (at once) annoyed that her go-to is so (too?) often the infirmity of her eldest).

"She's fine, fine. Better than fine, in fact. She was diving to the bottom of Tay's pool. You know, holding her breath. And she'd come up every ten, twenty seconds. And then all of a sudden she didn't come up. She was down there for minutes."

"Minutes!?"

"That's what it felt like. Of course, it was probably just a minute. And she was barely out of breath. Who knew? I guess she has big lungs. You should have seen the eye rolling I got. Deserved. I was about to dive in."

"A mother will go to the end of the world for her daughter, right?" Abigail smiles.

"A mother will *end* the world for her daughter."
Astair cackles (surprised (by how hard the cackle
tries to hide it) by how much she means it).

The server (named Maxim) sets down their
baby-clam pizza ((no sauce) just clams and buffalo
mozzarella in a drool of extra-virgin olive oil (topped
with the thinnest slices of lemon (puts anything in
New York with two Zs to shame))).

Astair wants to bring up Lares & Penates (her
glass wolves (online research suggests they might
be worth more than $85,000 (what she still hasn't
told Anwar (wanting more confirmation (and the
right moment to surprise him (now her Oceanica
retreat in August won't seem so costly ((and such a
stress)(a joy!) plus Anwar can maybe even restart his
startup?)))))))). Instead she savors a second bite.

"I told you it was good here."

Abigail nods (savoring (too) food's apotheosis).
Bewitched by (as Astair has started to slowly sense)
nothing to do with beer or pizza (nothing but smiles
tonight with every mention of children). Astair is
so fascinated (bewitched herself! (by (clearly) a
bewitching secret)) she stops eating.

"Are you going to tell me?"

Abigail stops chewing. Giggles suddenly. (so
much so) She can't speak.

"Pregnant?"

"Nooooooooo!" Abigail squeals (covering her
mouth (as still more giggles erupt)).

"Name?"

"Astair, I haven't told Taymor." Swallowing giggles (and another bite (talking with her mouth full
(of course her mouth is full (all of her is full (with
glee))))). "I want to tell her myself."

"Discretion is my profession."

"That goes for Gia too."

"How long?"

"You know, it's new. But is new an excuse not to be happy?"

"Not at all!"

"Keen Toys."

"That's his name?"

"He owns a . . . *kingdom.*" As if that explains anything. "Near too. And, actually, what I was going to bring up before you found me out: I want to invite you and your amazing Xanther to come visit."

"*Kingdom?*"

"I think Xanther will really like it, find it's, you know, what she needs, what we all need, enriching."

"Twins included? They could use some enriching. Not to mention a new kingdom to conquer."

Abigail frowns. "Actually no, no, it's—well, they won't have fun, because it's—they're too small."

"Too small? What does small have to do with a . . . ?"

"It's just . . . dangerous. Well, no, it's not. That's wrong. It's not dangerous. It's just not as fun. You have to keep them locked up."

"Keep who locked up?"

"Toys runs a—" (Abigail's smile (glee) keeps getting bigger.) "Toys owns, runs, and loves, and I mean big-time loves . . . exotic animals. His Animal Kingdom! He's a trainer! For stars. You know, movies, television, commercials, exercise videos. You name it. And his stars are all famous: wolves, monkeys, a grizzly bear. Xanther loves animals, right? Well, here they are. A whole private zoo. Just for her. And not even behind bars. Enrichment! What do you say?"

(of course) Astair had said yes ("Of course!") ("Thrilled to death!" ("Ecstatic!"))) and "So happy for you!" ("Congratulations!" (plus hugs and cheek kisses)) without mentioning that Abigail's relationship was so new that it was probable that her invitation (and relationship) would be invalid before any details (the whens and hows) could emerge.

Astair hopes it all works out.

Xanther would be ecstatic. A visit to such a place might even trump Magic Mountain.

But *Minutes!?* wasn't the only thing Astair hadn't come clean about with Abigail (Taymor had confirmed it (no question Xanther was underwater an abnormally long time ((Taymor just as panicky (that poodle too (like it was picking up that something was wrong?)) ∴ Yes. ∵)) presenting for an instant the only possibility: a seizure at the bottom of the pool)).

And why shouldn't Astair have leapt to that conclusion? Especially considering (what she (involuntarily(?)) kept from her friends) the events of last Thursday (in the pre-dawn morning).

(despite how (in long relationships) comfort can be mistaken for distance (a catachresis (. . .) in the name of the apparent (what (too easily) mistakes silence and routine for that which is inert)))

Astair and Anwar had awoken as one (at once (and fast too)).

4:04

(On the nightstand.)

Racing as one (as once) downstairs.

Out the front door.

Silence echoing there with a vague memory
of the polylingual alert long gone (though both of
them agreed later that that (and a (likely) chorus of
creaks (composed by entranced(?) feet (their darling
somnambulist (now?))))) must have begun dredging
them up from the province of dreams

(that or another
silence (screaming away in Astair's dreams (((that
guttural) shrieking out) in a voice she could never
understand (such is silence's voice) and could never
misunderstand (such is . . . (what?))):

She'll die!

∴?∵

∴!∵

)

)

).

Silence breaking ((horrifically)

right before their eyes)

by the screech of tires

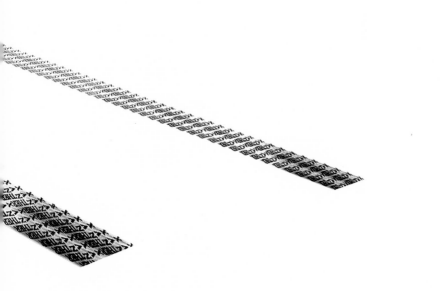

fishtailing before what headlights could never miss—

Xanther

dazed

in just her

nightgown

swaying in the middle of their street.

The Ford truck stopped less than a foot away (a miracle in itself (it was old (like 1940s old ∷ **1943** ∷))).

The odd couple emerging from the vehicle were both holding their hands to their chests (speaking in Spanish(?) ∷ Yes. ∷ (cursing too? ∷ Sounded like it. ∷)

∷ **¡Mira a este pinche escuincle pendejo!** ∷

∷ **¡Y ahí vienen los pinches papás pendejos!** ∷

∷ *Look at this stupid fucking kid!* ∷

∷ *And here come the stupid fucking parents!* ∷

)

until the woman grabbed Xanther by both shoulders and shook her hard.

∷ *Wait! How? Who am I encountering?* ∷

"Hey!" Astair cried then (her own hand leaving her chest (for something sharper)).

And the black eyes that met her didn't frighten Astair (Astair would meet anyone (anything)) nor were they frightened of Astair either (of anything(?)).

The woman's hair was up in a tight bun (something shiny buried in there). Her pocked cheeks caked over with ((too much) too-white) base.

Was her eyeliner tattooed?

(also) Hadn't Astair seen her around the neighborhood before?

∴ Yes. ∴

The stick ((of a man (in a wifebeater (arms of sagging tattoos))) resting his hand on her shoulder) also emanated strength (though not as much).

"Lupita," he said. "Look. The child is awakening."

"Mom!" Xanther had begun smiling (so big (for Astair) only to grow bigger when she saw this woman called Lupita (placing then her own frail hands on those broad shoulders)). "Honeysuckle!"

Lupita's black eyes shifted then (warm hazel really (warming all the more as she got up off her knees (laughing))). "Lucky little thing!"

The (stick of a) man smiled too and then the Ford wheezed away (long fingernails waving out the window). A terrible possibility gone just like that.

(afterward) Astair felt bad (for not being more thankful (they had seen Xanther (they had stopped in time ((and if they were angry) they had a right to be angry about almost killing a child)))).

Though nothing compared to how badly Xanther felt.

(by the time they got back inside) She had gone white. She had started crying. Even her pet (mewing blindly at the top of the stairs) couldn't help.

Xanther threw up the rest of the morning.

Most of that day too.

The weirdest part (with Astair whispering to Anwar endlessly about what she was speculating was the emergence of a new species of seizure (Anwar finding it hard to disagree (Xanther had never sleep-walked before!))) was how Xanther finally emerged from her bout with what? stress? food poisoning? a stomach bug? — looking stronger!

(Stronger? (has Astair *ever* used that word in reference to Xanther?)).

(on top of that) Even the little cat seemed(?) to have discovered(?) a new(?) kind of resilience(?).

Good thing tandem reactions aren't reserved just for emergencies:

Anwar sits now on the front stoop (watching her park).

His hug is warm.

His kiss easy.

All of him feels so close and necessary and good.

"Come." Astair smiles. "I have a surprise for you."

atsa›}]

What's tragic is that the ardor of questioning is always being shattered by an answer that wants to be absolute.

— Edmond Jabès

'Where did you put it?' Astair asks [like a young girl might ask a magician about a vanishing card {eyes wide with wonder at the disappearance ‹Anwar smiling at her dreamy gaze «in anticipation of the joke to come» ready to laugh›}].

'Put what?' [still] Smiling.

The joke never comes.

Astair leaves Anwar staring at the living room [{in fact} she's already upstairs when he realizes what's missing {the mantelpiece stands wide and barren ‹unnaturally barren «what makes about as much sense as Astair ‹right now› rousting the girls at nearly midnight»›}].

Not that she's wrong [that's quickly obvious {Freya and Shasti both wiping the sleep from their eyes ‹as they're hustled downstairs «with Xanther behind ‹zero sleep in her eyes›»› until ‹at the living room entrance› both little girls burst into tears}].

'Speak!' Astair commands [seethes].

None of the girls look at the mantelpiece [no {that's not right} Xanther {with the little pyramid of white on her shoulder ‹facing in the same direction›} stares directly at the absence].

'It's okay,' Xanther suddenly soothes [warmly {focusing on her sisters}].

Shasti and Freya nod [though Anwar finds in their eyes no sign of the same compassion {concern? ‹fear «reigning ⟨tears gone⟩»?›}].

[hand in hand] They lead the family outside to the garbage bins under the carport.

Astair's hands are shaking when she opens the [brown {paper}] bag.

She cries for so long that Anwar has to send the girls back inside.

Her hands keep diving for broken glass

[{big pieces ‹small pieces›} Anwar diving for reasons for this heartache {Dov ‹familiarity› obviously}]

until she can't bear it anymore

[the shatter {the loss ‹the sound that loss makes

«as it crashes again to the bottom of

their garbage bin»›}].

Xanther waits in the front doorway [just watching her mother {just shaking her head ‹every time Anwar urges her to share with him some explanation›}].

'It's okay, Shasti,' Xanther says instead [gently] when Anwar and Astair return to the living room. 'It's okay, Freya.'

'What do you mean "it's okay!?"' Freya yells. Xanther recoils. Even Anwar flinches [Astair's hand gripping his hand]. Only Xanther's little cat [eyes sealed to it all] doesn't react.

'We didn't do it!' Shasti yells now too [as is so often the case with these two {copycats}].

'It wasn't us!' Freya piles on [as if what's going on here could be satisfied with anger {different ‹too› from Shasti's}].

'What do you mean you didn't do it?' A rise of Astair's own anger drying tears.

Shasti looks then to Freya [Anwar focusing on a look he recognizes all too well {the one that tells him Shasti doesn't know what comes next ‹he should divide them at once «have Astair talk to Freya while he talks with Shasti» but it's too late› Freya defining next} with that sealing look that shares the confidence of a majority].

The only other thing Anwar notices is a flash of uncertainty [confusion?] in Xanther.

'She broke it,' Freya says now.

'Yes!' Shasti adds [relieved {no question}].

'What?' Anwar hears himself say [though he knows perfectly well what they're saying].

'Who?!' Astair just looks confused.

158

'Xanther!' Freya and Shasti sing out.

[for the second time {over the past few days}] Xanther looks like she's caught in the headlights.

The man [who emerged from the old truck {early Thursday morning}] seemed noticeably shaken. He was about Anwar's age [nearly as pale as the white wife-beater he wore {but in a way that somehow describes a paleness not pale enough ‹for this nation of Anwar's citizenship› to exempt it from either that alternate history ‹of blind fantasy› that is property or ‹the blind fantasy of identity› that is class}]. The bones of his shoulders were as visible as the subject of his tattoos were not. [under the narrow moustache {like a dash of silver}] Had Anwar detected a sympathetic smile? ⸪ **Yes.** ⸫

The squat woman [squatting {in fact}] showed no such humor. [if she was shaking {and she must have been ⸪ **She was.** ⸫ ⸪ *Terribly.* ⸫}] She took her shaking out on Xanther. But only her palms [maybe only the heel of her palms] held his daughter [the stout fingers {with their dangerous nails} arcing away {as if not to really touch Xanther ‹either to be less familiar or out of disgust «something disgusted did seem to possess her expressions»›}].

And then Xanther had come to and smiled [gazing into this stranger's face {whom the man had called Lupita ‹whom Xanther couldn't stop calling 'Beautiful!'›}] and Anwar had watched then how those palms relaxed [fingertips clutching {near} gratefully his child {disgust replaced with obvious relief ‹or more? «another hint of a smile? ⸪ *Of course.* ⸫»›}].

[of course] Who [or what] has Xanther not transformed?

⸪ **Who, maybe. What, never.** ⸫
⸪ *Never? Ah, never.* ⸫

'Lucky kid,' laughed Lupita [as she climbed back into the truck].

'Lucky the old whore stopped,' the man responded [restarting the engine {which almost didn't start}].

'Meeze ∴ Miz∴, don't you know by now an old whore isn't a whore if she knows how to stop?'

'Guess then she's an old saint.' The man chuckled [patting the truck {before nodding ‹to Xanther› and driving away}].

Astair had [{immediately} desperately] wanted to blame epilepsy for that event as well as for Xanther's subsequent stomach ailments. But Anwar wasn't convinced [even if that {during later discussions} hardly {un}convinced Astair].

Of more interest [to Anwar] was how [once the vomiting subsided] Xanther did not seem at all depleted or defeated [but rather the inverse]. Solid even.

And then Anwar had killed that squirrel. He had expected Xanther to dissolve [like Anwar had dissolved] not march out to look at the body [where she would surely dissolve {but didn't}].

[at least {he had thought then}] If there was any succor [to be derived by this awful event] it came by way of how Anwar's own reactions towards the lost [destroyed!] animal most closely resembled Xanther's constant reactions [towards anything speechless and feeble {fur helped}] even if the way she marched back to the car then [tearless {silent}] most closely resembled Dov [even if evident grief {and scandent tones} again countermanded that association {with her ‹other› father}].

There she was. Strong. Again.

Solid. Too.

Enough to make Anwar uneasy . . .

Then again [these days] Anwar had grown more and more uneasy.

Not that he should feel that way. Enzio had accepted his work on Cataplyst-2 [and {since May} already deposited $18,000 in their {Chase} bank account]. [last week] Enzio had even sent Cataplyst-3.

> **From:** Cambridge, Savannah
> **Sent:** Wednesday, June 11, 2014 11:33 PM
> **To:** Ibrahim, Anwar
> **Subject:** . . .
>
> Anwar! Forwarding this:
>
> > As before, please address all outstanding critical issues and deploy a functional build. Furthermore, in order to proceed with remaining Cataplysts-, Enzio would like to determine possible alternate purposes.
>
> I know! What does that mean! I think an intern wrote it. His Sirness just wants to know if the thing plays.
>
> xo

The implication of multiple Cataplysts- [multiple $9,000s] should have been very [un{un}]easying. Plus Savannah's demonstrable warmth [[{product manager} whom he'd never met {knew nothing about ‹nice name though›}]] left Anwar feeling very [very] easy.

But.

But was the big problem.

Nothing Anwar could do was bringing Cataplyst-3 to life. And revisiting Cataplyst-1 and Cataplyst-2 only deepened his confusion about what it was doing [forget function {purpose ‹forget play «unless that was his answer ‹?›»›}].

[{though ‹maybe›} had it not been for its puzzling nature possessing his mind] Anwar might not have heard their polyglot alert go off [to race him outside {to ‹really› do nothing but watch the 'old whore' nearly run down his child ‹so «in fact» truly an 'old saint'›}].

More puzzles followed:

What had Mefisto been doing at Enzio?

Did he know about these Cataplysts-?

Did Enzio know that Anwar knew Mefisto?

How did Anwar even come to Enzio's attention?

Anwar started getting paranoid.

Not remembering things isn't good for paranoia.

And then Anwar had remembered something that had made him laugh [[{hand to mouth} aloud {with ‹almost› an apology at the same time ‹looking around «for no one around»›} over what was completely forgotten until then]:

[right when they had moved {from East Los Angeles} to Echo Park] Mefisto had dropped by [by chance? {by coincidence? ‹whatever those mean«?»›}].

'A sail under a mushroom cloud,' Astair called him [{later} admitting she'd picked up that description from Mefisto himself {who ‹also› admitted it wasn't his ‹something an old friend of his had been saying for years «he thought of himself more as a wall with mold»›}].

Though Astair hadn't been around this time. Or any of the girls. [atypically] Mefisto had arrived in the morning [{with coffees ‹instead of booze›} likely up all night {just passing through ‹whatever that meant«?»›}].

'يا نهار ابيض' Anwar might have said [upon seeing the big man at his door]. ∴ The white world! ∴

The reason was never clear. Mefisto had not stayed long. [honestly] Anwar felt his old friend just wanted to see him. He had looked troubled [and in need of calm {and some laughs ‹which they had shared›}].

What Anwar discovered after Mefisto had gone earned the laughter we share sometimes with friends who don't have to be there: somehow [in the small space of Anwar putting breakfast together {or did it happen at some other moment ‹while leaving Mefisto alone «which was never for long (?)»›}] Mefisto had reprogrammed the useless security device at their front door to cry out 'Alert: Open Door!' [in so many {many} languages {Anwar rarely caught a repeat}].

'دوشة بابل مالهاش دعوه باللغات . . . ا ا لا اللغات الي مش فاهمنها.'

There were worse house presents than a constant lesson in openness [albeit in an {impersonal} androidized voice]. In some ways too [then] it was Mefisto's voice that woke him when Xanther wandered out of bounds [Astair had claimed to have heard a voice as well {much worse ‹screaming 'She'll die!' «in a tongue she didn't know but still understood»›}].

Languages [tongues] had always mattered to Anwar. He wanted them to matter to his family. Especially those languages that were not understood. He and Astair [and Mefisto {and Myla}] had had [over the years] numerous conversations [constantly] circling the same conclusion [which {despite concluding the conversation} at the same time never closed down the conversation {because the dialogue decided ‹and determined› nothing}]: existence itself is always semantic.

[on a much more {blunt} level {if level is ever the right nomenclature for the separation ‹necessarily› evoking the birth of the sign ‹for is there ever a referent that can exist without distance «doesn't existence depend on distance ‹?⌈or time⌉?›»}] The nature of Cataplyst-1 and Catalplyst-2 [and {now} Cataplyst-3] awakened Anwar's concern with vocabulary [and not just in terms of the code {which seemed to tease Anwar ‹about lines concerned with lines «beyond the code»›}]:

Where were the phrases announcing purpose?

// No goldfish.

// No zombies.

// No cylons.

// No wargs.

// No enemy combatants.

// No Marios.

// No thieves.

// No sheriffs.

// No orcs.

// No outlaws.

// No assassins.

// No vampires.

// Not a single good old witch.

Anwar would take even a dragon.

'"Talpuva" is one,' Anwar had told Ehtisham over the weekend [at E3 {in the downtown convention center}]. '"Taawi" is another. The code is littered with terminology like that. Nothing familiar.'

Ehtisham had no clue.

'Mrs. Google says to consider the Hebrew *taavi* meaning "dearly loved,"' Talbot had offered.

But Hebrew didn't seem right [especially considering the other words {like *tokpela* ‹or *atsa*›}].

Not that Anwar's Cataplyst-3 woes came up again [with plenty of news {on the floor} about *Batman: Arkham Knight, Metal Gear Solid V, Middle-Earth: Shadow of Mordor, Call of Duty: Advanced Warfare, Ori and the Blind Forest, Bloodborne* {plus the usual Oculus Rift rumors ‹*Lucky's Tale* going beyond rumor›} not to mention *Category 9* {by Dead Rowboats}].

It was a melancholy [if exciting] time. Anwar did his best not to imagine their *Paradise Open* here [prompting chatter and press {trending on social media ‹gathering a crowd at some elaborate booth «with cosplaying service animals on hand»›}].

[at least] The post-convention wind-down had left Anwar all the more eager to keep trying [$50,000 could get them up and running again {a number Ehtisham had thrown out ‹on Sunday «along with news that Blizzard had offered him a job»›}].

All his friends were getting jobs.

EA and Riot Games were courting Talbot.

At least Glas had said fuck off to Dead Rowboats [Anwar couldn't believe {though it made perfect sense} that Kozimo had had the audacity to try to poach members from this team {ex-team}].

Anwar didn't mention that he was holding on to Enzio for dear life.

And now he is also holding on to Astair [who had started crying again {up in their bedroom} again over a pile of broken glass].

'I know it had a lot of significance.'

'What's that supposed to mean?' she snaps [but refuses to say more].

Xanther's prevailing silence then is hardly surprising [like mother like daughter]. The twins' silence is also sensible given the conditions [their resolve strengthened by the examples now set by both their mother and sister].

Silence rules Tuesday. Not that this is so terrible a thing: Anwar has plenty of work to do [despite four females carrying out this collective scorched-speech policy ∴ *Atsa* . . . ∴ {what Anwar can bring little sense to ‹forget voice «what would Dov have done? ⟨run!⟩»›}].

[by Wednesday] Speech returns slowly in that non-consequential manner [the twins greedy with their insular laughs {Xanther proud in the silence she shares with that blind creature . . . ∴ **Forever** . . . ? ∴ ‹are her eyes getting blacker? «bluer ⟨like fire burning down green⟩?»›}].

All Anwar can do is replay Freya's brief explanation.

'She broke it.'

'But how could she do that?' Astair had asked [incredulously]. *"Why* would you do that?" To Xanther [just as incredulously].

But Xanther's glare by that point remained a hundred yards off [hundreds of yards {thousands of yards}].

'She did!'
'She did!'

'So—' Astair's eyes narrowed [{a look reserved for these two} setting the trap] '—Xanther was playing on the mantel and, just like that, knocked over my statue?'

[if the twins hadn't looked so confused] Anwar would have sworn they recognized the trap [easily {their confusion setting their own trap ‹though neither girl dared to test Xanther «they never looked at her once»›}].

'We don't know,' Freya admitted.

'We?' Anwar couldn't help himself.

'We both saw it,' Shasti said [earning a glare from Freya].

'What did you see *exactly*?' Astair bit.

'I didn't see anything,' Freya said [chewing her lips {challenging Shasti then ‹inviting her? «instructing?»›}]. 'Xanther was playing in the living room and we, I mean me, I was on the stairs and heard breaking. Bad breaking.'

Shasti nodded: 'The wolves were in tiny pieces all over the place.'

'Is that what happened?' Astair asked Xanther then.

'Daughter, is that right?'

Xanther didn't need to bite her lip.

Silence did the biting.

Deep enough to scar.

'We still have to punish her,' Astair announces Wednesday night [had they ever punished Xanther before?].

'Is this about the statue or Dov?'

Astair takes a deep breath [they had decided to have this conversation outside of the house {strolling along the sidewalk ‹maybe they would see the old saint again «or old whore» speeding by›}].

'Jim Helhenny Joab.'

'Who?'

'The glass blower, the artist, who made those wolves. I didn't want to tell you until I was sure. Frankly, I didn't want to tell you until I had a check in hand. Or at least had it set for auction.'

'Worth something?' Anwar can feel pins in his face [the backs of his hands {like what Xanther has described happening to her ‹when something bad is about to happen›}].

'Do you want to know the number?'

'Of course.' Though the pins tell him he doesn't.

'Still breathing, professor?' Astair asks [after the second lap around the long block {constant sighs interrupted only once by an evening hello with Mr. Hatterly walking Archimboldo ‹interrupted by thoughts of all they could have done «to say nothing of PO ⟨PO does not depend on money⟩ or other projects set on future aims and reliefs» trips to Europe! Egypt!› the sighs keep going} Anwar will need still another block with Astair] squeezing his arm.

At least her mood seems lighter. That helps.

'Of course, we can't tell the children the price tag. Maybe when they want money for a car.' Astair tries to laugh.

Anwar tries to laugh too.

'That goes without saying.'

'Then what do we say?'

'I don't want to punish Xanther,' Anwar starts slowly [finding his way]. 'I wouldn't even punish her for accidentally breaking the sculpture. The consequences, though, at her age, for not telling difficult truths must be made apparent.'

They walk a little more [Anwar envying the warm-lighted windows they pass {if not for a moment believing in the fightless-families he imagines living there}].

'We could ground her?' he eventually suggests.

'That's funny,' Astair laughs gently. 'Xanther wants nothing but to stay at home with the little thing.'

[on Thursday morning] Astair lays it out for Xanther [nothing gentle in her voice]: 'We will have to punish you if you don't tell us the truth about what happened.'

But Xanther just sits on the edge of her bed [looking down at the little kitten asleep in her lap {like a large cotton ball ‹even less interesting than a cotton ball ∴ *How what's of most interest allways begins . . .* ∵›}].

'Daughter, your mother's serious. I'm serious. You will leave us no choice.'

"'Green canaries use mescaline guacamole,' bellows Elsa,'" Xanther suddenly blurts [a babble really {and keeps babbling it too ‹nonsense «?»}].

'Excuse me, young lady?' Astair flares.

'Don't be rude,' Anwar warns.

Xanther looks up [anything but flip {or happy ‹pained really «and flustered» and about to cry›} but petulant too].

'Well? What's my big punishment?' Xanther sing-songs then [jagged notes of sarcasm Anwar's never heard from her before]. 'Are you gonna ground me?'

Anwar feels Astair tense [already too late to restrain her with a touch {a word ‹as if either would have helped›}].

'How about if we take away the kitten?' Astair lashes back.

Where did that come from?

'Astair,' Anwar murmurs [trying to figure out how to take back the {ridiculous} threat].

'You wouldn't dare,' Xanther snarls [on her feet]. 'Just try!'

But Astair isn't biting [collected enough already to exit the room {almost}].

'Yes. You're grounded,' Astair says from the doorway.

'Fine,' Xanther snorts. 'How long?'

'Just a day. Magic Mountain day.'

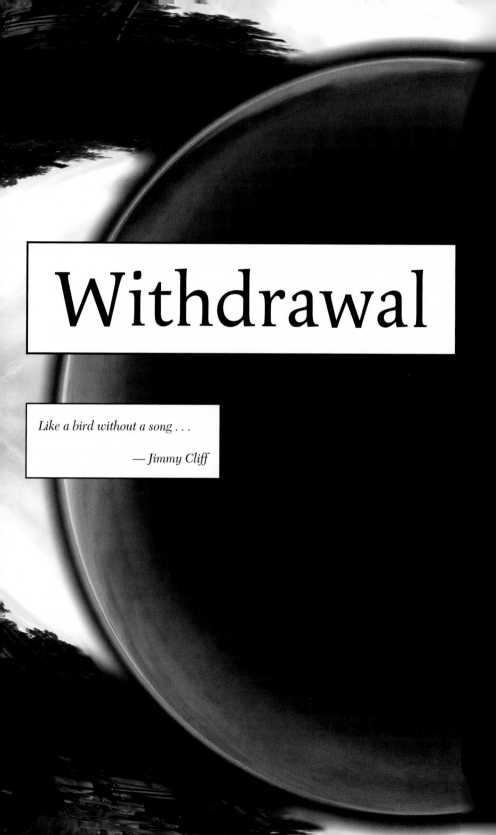

Withdrawal

Like a bird without a song . . .

— *Jimmy Cliff*

"You don't have to look."

"I became a Looking Creature years ago. Like you."

Mefisto shakes his head: "I'm not wired that way."

The objection briefly warns Cas, but the warm smile, the hushed voice, the way eyes wait easily for her decision, reassure her that alliance is not at stake here. There is only tolerance. And care.

"That gruesome?"

"I wish I hadn't," Bobby growls, standing behind, hands on her shoulders, offering nothing more than the gentle weight of his constant devotion.

Cas glances at Marnie.

"No way is that my thing," Marnie says from her perch on the stairs, spiraling up past the Undoing Room to various alcoves above suitable for air mattresses and nightstands with old copper lamps.

But whose thing is death anyway? Somehow the materiality of bodies before a mortician seems more comprehensible than recorded acts of violence. Maybe police officers grow accustomed to choreographies of murder.

Cas reaches across the table to slide the laptop closer. Mefisto has already opened the files. She needs only to click play.

"Warn me when you reach the 9th," Mefisto requests.

"Sounds practically classical," Cas smirks.

"It's not."

Some Looking Creature. Cas doesn't make it through the third file before she has to leave, shaking off Bobby's attention. Cas wanders through an atrium into an area outside with enough canopies and walls to shield her from the sky or any prying eyes approaching from conterminous property lines. A piece of broken marble on its way to revealing a hand serves as a seat. An old factory loom rusting in the southern air serves as a place to rest her head and cry.

The elation of meeting up with Sorcerer had been followed by an equal elation, and terror, of immediately heading out of Athens, only to find Mefisto circling back, hiding everyone within yet another barn.

"Please tell me this is not another one of his properties."

"I wish. We'd have WiFi then." Supposedly the owner is a sculptor away in Transylvania exploring   new ways to carve stone.

Bobby and Mar-   nie seemed immediately at ease   beneath the long
corrugated   roof, rusted to
the color of   Georgian earth
v i s i b l e   outside.

Unlike the   previous place,
this   barn   was   mostly
open. The   ground   floor
served as a   central   studio
where vari-   ous   unfinished
creations   still   waited on the right
imagination   to   grant them rest.

Marble bubbled up inside and out: in the corner a shoulder, beneath a pine tree a woman's breast, on the lawn a polar bear. Satyrs and sea horses jousted before broken satellite dishes, plus rusted ladders, an old shopping cart, orange plastic barrels the size of oil barrels, full of rain water. High above loomed a cement mixer or old water tank.

Only after midnight did Mefisto deem it okay for Cas — cauled in a silver weave — to slip outside by herself. She liked most to sit on a marble bench, beside a small pond, where so long as there was electricity, a pump promised a constant stream. Curving marble steps rose up behind her, mimicking the theater at Delphi, with water serving as both voice and stage.

Cas could still hear Bobby and Mefisto inside joking about their luck,

Brandywine, the Siege of	Savannah, Washing-
ton's life saved. Who	knows what's ever
really saved. Or	maybe Cas had
some idea, lis-	tening to the
running water,	f i n d i n g
comfort there	or in the
whistle of a	train that
f r e q u e n t l y	p i e r c e d
the night, that	m e t a l l i c
owl-like hoot,	along with
the rumble of	m e t a l l i c
inertia, rattling	up through
her bones. The	first time they
all thought it was	going to run
through the barn. In	some ways it had.
Cas thought it romantic,	until Mefisto men-

tioned it was "loaded with crated chickens," which was enough to allow all that the Holocaust had done to trains to begin mapping that haunting across the southern world here. Cas couldn't help but feel the old world in her bones. Not Marnie. She'd sit with Cas and just squeal. For her a train was just a train in Athens, Georgia, and it was fun.

Cas had been certain Marnie would have a hard time without WiFi or the use of anything else electronic. She was young enough to be practically hardwired into habits of Web use. But Cas was wrong. Marnie swore she wasn't even that unusual for her generation: she loved turntables and cassettes, typewriters and stringed instruments.

The days seemed to pass easily for her. She loved smearing paint into weightless abstractions on discarded bits of foam board. After dinner, she'd pluck at a ukulele while Mefisto did his best with a harmonica. Considering how frighteningly powerful his mind was, it was weirdly comforting to hear him do something so terribly — and know it and enjoy it. Like two mating cats, he and Marnie would fill that big barn with their crooning yowls, louder still when the train rolled through, almost through joy alone transforming that lonely rumble into something no longer bleeding with history.

The north side of the barn practically contained a small house, with porches and various balconies, all strung with Christmas lights. The second story was for the Undoing Room, a wide space, free even of load-bearing supports, where artists could gather to undo preconceptions so new creative impulses might emerge. That's how Mefisto told it. A big staircase spiraled up from the ground-floor studio all the way to the third story where they all slept. Some nights, maybe in response to the power of Jimi Hendrix, cats would wander by. Early on, a stray had made it upstairs, and the brush of a tail, the spectacular glare, had left Cas shaking. Later on, Bobby pointed out that the same tabby was downstairs eating turkey scraps at the feet of Mefisto and Marnie.

"Good for rats too."

"I know, Bobby.   I'm not scared
of cats."

Cas   didn't   need   to
name who she   was scared
of, who they   were   all
scared of.

Bobby brought   her   wild-
flowers   ∴ Honey-   suckle∴ every
morning and made   lunch   for her
every day and stayed   nearby when she
needed to feel him fill   the silence and let her
wander when she needed to crowd herself with impossible thoughts:
mostly about loss.

"I've done harm," was how Cas first brought up the loss of the Orb. Bobby had spent a long time going over how the implosion amounted to nothing more than a big flash. Mefisto reiterated the same thing. "Maybe kinda like those old flash cubes?" Marnie even chimed in. Marnie seemed so certain of what she'd seen happen. There was no doubt in her beautiful, young face. Unlike the complicated glance between Mefisto and Bobby.

Later, when Mefisto had slipped out with Marnie to see a tattoo artist named David Hale, something about needing to finish her back, something Cas hadn't seen, having to do with hummingbirds, Cas and Bobby had fought. It was the worst kind of fight too, because she was right and he was right and in the end his right trumped hers.

On her side: considering everything they had already faced, Cas couldn't be blamed for jumping at some silly cat, or complaining about their lack of connectivity. On his side: while helping her through various stretches and exercises, Bobby had suggested that some of the patterns to her recent mood swings matched less stresses attributable to their escape and more symptoms of withdrawal.

"Are you fucking kidding me?" she had raged immediately. "You're likening scrying to, what, meth?"

"No." And the way Bobby didn't rage back, just stepped back, broke her heart. "Run the list yourself."

Which didn't quell her rage. Cas still stormed off, looking for glass to break. She ended up throwing a paper cup. Then she cried. Then she called him names. She knew the right names to call him too.

Mefisto and Marnie returned to   find Bobby asleep upstairs
and Cas awake in the   Undoing Room with
the stray tabby hop-   ing for either
more scraps or a   rat.

By the next day,   Cas had run
the symptoms,   and while
nowhere close   to her
i n f l a m m a -   tory mention of meth,   she could
see how the   s p o r a d i c
eruptions of   anger, and
the observable   twitches that
sometimes pos-   sessed her
fingers, as well as   the tears she help-
lessly tried to pawn off   on everything and
everyone, might come down to   one thing:

the loss of the Orb.

"It's a dangerous pursuit," Mefisto said kindly, one night on the bench, staring at the pond, at their mini-Delphi.

"The blind agony," she'd whispered.

Mefisto had wrapped his big arms around her, his big afro leaning down against her head.

"Is that what you've all been doing?" Cas managed to squeak. "Waiting for me?"

Mefisto nodded.

"I'm   so   sorry."

"Don't be   silly.   We're
p l a y i n g   with   something that   makes   the
d i s c o v -   ery of radia-
tion seem   infantile. We
wanna keep   you from ending up like   Ms. Curie. Even
if we're prob-   ably   all   fried."
Mefisto laughed.   "Except for Bobby.
I   seriously   think   he doesn't give a hoot
what's beneath the bend.   The smartest of us all."

Cas managed to laugh too. "What about Marnie?"

Mefisto just shrugged.

"How much longer then?"

"You tell me when you're ready for what comes next."

Cas realized she wasn't ready. She needed more time. More nights dreaming beside this dream   of   another   Delphi. Another lifetime.

"Tomorrow?"

     "Good."

But   tomor-   row came
faster   than   expected,
as if the future   were never
s o m e w h e r e   else,   but
all   along   part   of the fabric
of every present,   merely untwin-
ing itself again and   again into a new
distinction   that   could   never be new again.

And then Mefisto showed her how Merlin had been murdered.

Files 1 and 2 on the old Razer Blade, even with a cracked screen, vividly displayed various angles from the CCTV system in a New Orleans parking lot where a stumbling Deakin, likely drugged, was run over repeatedly by a black Escalade. File 3 was the less-graphic sequence that ran on local and national news channels, from a bystander's phone, with a close-up of the victim's face. The obit for Deakin Carraway was already online.

"What are the other files?" Cas asks now when she returns from her cry. "Do I need to see them?"

"More angles," Bobby answers, closing Mefisto's laptop. "From other bystanders. Less clear."

"We're sure it's him?"

"No question with the close-up," Mefisto says. He's moved to the couch. Marnie hasn't left the staircase. No one's happy.

"MIT has announced a vigil. New Orleans police have already declared it a homicide. Caltech is calling it the silencing of science."

"And this 9th file?"

"Not of Deakin," Bobby snarls.

"I can't do this! I don't even know these people," Marnie suddenly cries, and like that, she's escaping upstairs. Cas should join her, maybe in the Undoing Room, as if any of this can be undone, or some clever thinking might shield them from the consequences continuing to batter them, condemn them.

"She needs to go," Cas hisses at Mefisto.

"Where to?" Mefisto sings.

"It doesn't matter."

"And in a year it won't matter how far she got."

"She'll have a chance."

"Or end up in a parking lot in New Orleans."

"Or in some apartment in Long Beach," Bobby adds.

"What?"

"Duban. Chiron. Kaa."

"You need to watch File 9." Mefisto reopens the laptop.

It's just a news clip, originally aired by KTAL, a station in Los Angeles. Three students were found dead following "a botched robbery." No details about the killings. Just exterior shots of the property and three names:

Yuri Grossman.

Eli Klein.

Jablom Lau Song.

Cas can't hide in an Orb or even a little pond. She threatens to leave. She ends up on her air mattress with a sleeping pill. No dreams come. On Marnie's old Walkman, she listens to Simon & Garfunkel's "Patterns" over and over. When she wakes, the batteries are dead and the tabby is watching zebra finches landing outside her window.

Cas feels no better. Screams crawl visibly beneath her skin. She needs a doctor. Is that what they're waiting for her to say?

The weekend goes that way. So does Monday. So does most of Tuesday.

Tuesday night, Mefisto and Bobby are murmuring about the old Orbs, about Future Windows, The Zero Window, Orbless Revelation. Cas finally goes out to her pond again. The mechanical stream has stopped running and the slickness of the surface offers a black better than sleep.

Wednesday morning, Bobby prepares steel-cut oats and egg whites scrambled up with cheddar and fresh sage from the garden. Marnie likes Bobby's idea of breakfast. Mefisto sticks with Cocoa Pebbles.

"So what's this about Recluse wanting to meet?" Cas at last brings up, nearly spitting out the name too, even as she also notices how Bobby's shoulders keep laying siege to his neck.

"I love sage!" Marnie claps.

The rest of Wednesday vanishes into long analyses of Recluse's request. They go over the pages Mefisto printed out from a thread on Reddit called "Appomattox Redux," decoded with a key from 4chan under "weapons." The issue isn't the meeting place — Recluse or "his apparatus" have suggested the Lincoln Memorial — but the initial contact with Cas.

By now Cas, Bobby, and Marnie are so afraid of anything electronic, they live by candlelight.

Only Mefisto seems undaunted by the prospects of creating an untraceable path.

"We are not alone."

More important is to consider what Cas will discuss and how they will handle the expected disinformation.

They all know only one thing is reliable.

"We need new Orbs," Mefisto admits after a dinner of wilted kale, almonds, and tofu. Bobby surprises everyone with tapioca pudding.

"Any old ones?"

"Only Warlock's isn't accounted for. He either got my message to destroy it or . . . "

"Of course there's ████."

"That's a whole other trip."

Marnie looks either like someone who can no longer hear the perfectly clear name hanging in the air or like a spy. Will Cas ever trust anyone? Sometimes she even doubts Bobby. At least there's no doubting that Mefisto is crazy.

The craziest thought, though, is the most reasonable one and the most horrendous: Cas will never get her hands on an Orb again.

Late that night, Mefisto joins Cas on her bench by the pond. Thanks to Bobby, the mechanical stream is running again. No more reflection. A good thing. Surfaces are a good place to pause but not linger.

She doesn't need to pull back the tie-dye bandana to know what presses down now on her lap.

"I'm afraid."

"You should be. It's no longer traceable, but it's slower. Much slower. And Bobby and I spent the past week boosting the self-destruct. Anyone near will be badly hurt or killed. TSA would call it a bomb."

Cas can't resist taking a peek at the black glass. "But this is yours."

"Not anymore. Bobby programmed your security charms." Mefisto stands. "Cas, I know this is hard for you to fathom: I've never been hungry for what it sees. *How* it sees, on the other hand, and what that implies . . ."

Later Cas asks about Clip #6. Unfortunately, Mefisto hasn't revisited the moment for some time and there's no wireless to check it now.

"Storms," Cas explains. "Black clouds surrounding them all. And I just realized this, ha!, back then they were here too. In Athens."

"Skies all clear," Mefisto smiles.

"Probably just errors populating my Orb." She doesn't mention how the feelings the errata provoke resemble those she has whenever she discovers an Aberration.

"I'll let you know what I find."

"You have another Orb?"

Mefisto shakes his head. "I'm going to California. To see my friend, his family. I'll see what's up with his little girl."

"Xanther," Cas whispers, as if a name could conjure the static itself, right as it's about to separate into meaning.

Lives of
Others

*Daring their ways above the fence,
and further . . .*

— *Lorna Dee Cervantes*

Luther surprises hisself when the glass doesn't break. He wanted the shatter too, wherever it went, whatever it brought next.

But the punch just popped the pane loose. Landed flat on the tile too. Not even a crack.

Luther reaches in, twists two locks, and like that he's in. Even puts the pane back. Slips off his shoes and runs the house quick. No dogs, no alarm, rooms empty, dust in the kitchen sink confirms his guess.

"You live here?" Quantelle asks when he opens the front door, barefoot. Then giggles when he grabs her between the legs and pulls her inside.

Her shirt's off first. Her pants fall in the living room. Bra on the way up the stairs.

In the master, Luther lets her run her greedy hands through his pockets, scrape her teeth over his nipples, his scars. Bitch is fuckin happy when he wedges his forearm between her legs and lifts her up, like he's a fuckin forklift, her fucking pony, his other hand squeezing around her throat, then dropping her back like that onto a California King with glossy sheets.

Gotta be more than just drunk to smile so wide, roll her eyes like that, groaning louder when he rips off her undies, sticks his fingers inside.

Luther hadn't come for Quantelle for this. Couldn't believe he even rolled up on her at IHOP alone. Not with all that's changed since he got back from Hawaii.

Teyo's hotel cash wasn't nothing compared to what Luther found in Cali: a box stacked with bills he still hasn't counted.

And that was just a start. Tweetie on the phone, Teyo's latest stuff. Pale blues on parade. Day not even done and they had ten-behind-bars in the back of a trunk. Not even selling.

"Your crew's just collecting," Eswin esplained, handing over the list they'd be running. *"El Teyo dice que conoces a estos vatos. Esto va para ellos. Y esto para nosotros."*

"¿Y lo que sobra?" Tweetie answered.

"His to do how he do," Eswin said soft, about Luther, not meeting eyes, knowing how places change, Luther's place already changed.

"Dollah, dollah," Tweetie grinned. High-fived.

Al mismo tiempo, Luther pulled Juarez, Victor, and Piña from running los tapados around the city, down manholes, ripping up old copper wire, cutting out copper pipe in new buildings, raiding construction sites. Luther paired Tweetie with Juarez to run the first circuit. Piña and Víctor the second.

First few times, Luther hung back, listo pa actuar, but la feria came in right. Tweetie handled the counts. Luther got bored, got smart.

Got back to Adolfo. Diez grandes for the lost troca. Luther saw fast what two extra bought: Adolfo opens the door for Luther, takes off his hat, see this new mero mero walking the shop.

Next Luther got with Chitel and his fruit sellers. Nopales there too, with her quick palms and orange stash. Luther dropped a g on each. To hear thanks? See their looks? Even Nopales couldn't smart-ass that much cash.

Let Almoraz olérselas the hard way a desmadre he never gonna clean up. Though it's messing with Lupita that gave Luther the most pleasure.

And that was still nothing. Luther met with Eswin solo. Got a whole other tour.

"You're an employee now. Salaried. Paid every two weeks. This is your account. Never deposit anything. Just withdraw. ATM here. Credit card too. All legit."

Luther had just stared at all the paper, all the plastic.

"This here's health insurance," Teyo's chalán continued.

"¿Seguro?"

"Sick? Hurt? Walk yourself into any hospital, you're covered. This card's for a doctor. Get yourself a checkup, you're covered."

Last time Luther seen a doctor, he was una coladera, holes in him, tubes in him, doctors, nurses, sure he'd never live, sign him up as an organ donor. That's all he was good for.

"Esta es mi account?" Luther asked Eswin, thumb tapping a balance he didn't understand.

"Don't spend it at once. Teyo wants a sit-down soon about retirement plans. If things go okay."

Adolfo, Chitel, Nopales, even the night he kept the place open, with shots coming for his crew, didn't make a dent in this number. This was something else. Retirement? If things go okay?

Things will for sure go okay when Luther finds him. Deposits will keep rolling in when Luther finds him. Retirement gets a sit-down with Teyo, but only after Luther finds him. No le hace, how. La propuesta, la meta.

Domingo Persianos.

Luther knows the fool too. From around. Got cousins, got debts. Tells the world he's padrote-ando, just no mercas yet. Another loan, another joke. Got instincts though. By the time Luther started asking, gone like smoke.

Sometimes Luther goes out with Tweetie, sometimes with Piña, not ready to get las dirty garras on the scent, Juarez almost calm these days, setting the copper kids loose on streets, in parks, balloons in their pockets, new kicks on their feet.

Sure people have seen Domingo, sure they have his number. Luther calls it. Just music. ∴ **Centavrvs and Carla Morrison**∴ ∴ *"Fumemos Un Cigarrillo"*∴ Tweetie leaves the message. To talk about la chamba.

Those Domingo owes know even less, scratch at their bad ink, L.A. on a forearm, saint on a neck, summer heat beating them all down into a mood. Mood goes unheard whenever Luther's asking questions, names of bars: Power House, Red Lion, The Psalm, Best Buy the guy likes best.

But what caught Luther's eye most? Sushi joints in strip malls he didn't dare enter. Couldn't fuckin remember the names. Mouth swirls with bronze, Coke makes no difference, Pacífico.

Luther even drove through Beverly Hills, Rodeo Drive, fucking almost stopped, checked out one of those shops, picked himself up some new camisas, with buttons thick. Or a jacket like the one he left in Hula Hoops, clouds light enough, blue light enough to turn those rooms to sky.

Maybe one of the three he fucked had it on now. Fuck Beverly Hills. But it was worth the drive. Luther had laughed.

Luther went looking for Nopales. Wanted to see her caderas wiggling with his fist in her mouth. No luck. Not her or Chitel. Almost pulled up at Lupita's. Drove by. Thought he caught Miz working on that truck, his old whore.

Dawgz would have been next. But even Rosario and Carmelita taking him together got Luther soft. Por lo mismo the IHOP surprised him. And not even half as much as seeing her already out in the parking lot, by herself too, with a cigarette, big nostrils white with smoke.

Luther thought her fear would cure him. Or if she didn't recognize him, give him the molten he'd need for what he'd go for then. But Quantelle not only recognized Luther, she smiled, una pinche sonrisota, arms flying open, wrapping around his neck, as she flicked away the cigarette, blew off the rest of her shift.

Luther wanted to go back, buy shirts with her, sushi. She wasn't even in her seat and already caliente, wiggling, giggling, game for whatever Luther was gonna ask, like he ever asked, like get rid of that fucking mandil, and it was out the window, her looking at him like he could do better than that.

They went to Power House ∴ **1714 Highland Avenue, Hollywood, CA 90028** ∴ first. Luther had never been. Across the street from some Hollywood bowling place, Lucky Strike. Traffic was thick. Luther had to go around twice. Sent her out to check the scene. She shook her head. Power House was shut down.

The Psalm wasn't going to let either of them in. Luther bagged two forties and drove her to some park east the 110 ∴ **Ernest E. Debs Regional Park** ∴. They hopped a fence, laughed when they saw from the other side the gate was wide open.

Maybe because she wanted him to touch her, he didn't. They just sat in the shadows and drank. She talked about her job a lot until he told her to shut up.

"I scare a lot of guys. I like it rough."

Maybe that was why Luther wasn't rough.

"Who are these people?" Quantelle asks from the bathroom, even though Luther told her not to touch the fucking lights.

But before he slaps the switch off, up fast enough from the bed, across the room, lights giving him something more than just the fear Luther catches in her face, flashing even faster into a wicked twist of her lips: she's got way more curves than smiles, curves lots of clothes hide, wide dark hips just rising up into a wider, darker back, stretch marks light on her thighs, stretch marks on her tits too, tits big enough to see plenty of them too from behind.

As for all the gabachos framed in silver on the counter behind the sinks, Luther pays no mind.

"This isn't my place."

"Huh?"

"I've never been here before."

"I don't understand what you're saying."

"We broke in, baby."

"Now you're teasing me."

Luther shakes his head. Waits for whatever real fear will do when it takes over her. What Luther's been waiting for all along.

"Come on." Her smile gone. "Like fucking breaking and entering?"

"Lives of others, girl. Just passing through."

"That's fucked-up."

But Quantelle surprises Luther again. She doesn't run. She doesn't go blind with fear. She makes him go again. And when he showers, she makes the bed.

They leave everything folded and creased. Except for the TV. Luther turns it on. Mutes the sound. He wants something just a little off for whoever lives here, when they return.

In the IHOP parking lot, Luther stuffs a hundred in Quantelle's hand. She tries to give it back.

"Too good for money?" Luther's mouth foils over.

"Fuck no, bitch." She grins. "You bought me for round one," she holds up the Franklin. "Now I just bought your ass for round two." Buries the bill in his palm. "Better holler at me too. I'll call a collection service if you don't."

Fearless.

Waving back

She is as changeless as the streets.

— Chris Bohjalian

DRIVING LESSON #1

The Left Turn.

So sacred it repeats in Driving
Lesson #9, Driving Lesson #27,
Driving Lesson #49, more.

So sacred it has Three
Commandments.

Left-Turn Commandment One

Minimum number of cars
to make turn:

2.

Repeat:

Minimum number of cars
to make turn:

2.

Never 1.
Sometimes 3.
Never never none!

Left-Turn Commandment Two

First car waiting to make left
against traffic must move into
intersection.

A lot into intersection.

A lot, a lot.

A lot enough so second car
behind has at least front tires in
intersection.

At least.

Left-Turn Commandment Three

At wide intersection, first car and
second car can move far enough
out to permit third car to have
front tires in intersection.

To provide left turn for third car is
to serve greater good.

The Left Turn.

Fundamental.

Sacred.

Shnorhk hit horn. Shnorhk hold horn down.

Can't believe eyes. Car in left-turn lane not move into intersection. Car is first car. Not move into crosswalk. Not idle even close to crosswalk.

And green light already yellow light almost red light.

No surprise considering car.

CAR DRIVER RATING

PT Cruiser

QUOTE:

"Super sense of cool
over something not super,
not cool."

DRIVER:

Old woman flashbacking.
Old man really old woman
flashbacking.

BUMPER STICKER:

My job is to comfort the disturbed
and disturb the comfortable.

RECOMMENDATION:

Keep in rearview.

LICENSE PLATE:

HUH?

Only on red light green wagon turn. Strand Shnorhk for one more signal cycle. Now a cough cycle. In hands. Lap. Grabs dark hanky. Always dark. Always on passenger seat by box of business cards. New business cards. Hundreds. Patil give hundreds like present. Like best thing in life. As if what is for her is not for her. Just box full of advice, just for him, as if full of lapis stellatus, full of garnet and jade.

Strange woman. This wife.

:: **For reasons attributable to protocols exceeding latitudes of ███ █████ the following number has been rendered unreadable.** ::

:: The number is 818-█████ ::

:: *How funny.* ::

Next green Shnorhk make left and see motorcycle cop. Motorcycle cop would have given ticket if Shnorhk had risked red. Should have ticketed PT Cruiser for left-turn blasphemy.

Shnorhk still lucky. After red-light accident, ticket, points, insurance rise, another ticket? Could lose job. Maybe license. Then what?

With Patil all day. Touching him. Pawing him. Always touching.

Next couple of days Shnorhk lay off horn, drive slower. Some customers complain that Shnorhk drive too slow. Shnorhk turn stereo up. Play recording from Mnatsagan's. Terrible recording, beautiful music. All his friends: Kindo, Dimi, Haruki, Alonzo, and Tzadik. Mnatsagan on violin, such miracles, such phrasing, play like Ruben Aharonyan, Sergey Khachatryan, Anahit Tsitsikian. Play better. Or different? Or better different? What matter when notes go beyond notes beyond phrases and return as something else?

Big surprise: some fares complain music too loud. Can't yap on phones. Or: want better music. Uber lets customers choose music. Shnorhk turn Mnatsagan up. Loses tips. Life is more than tips. More than handing out business card. Shnorhk not hand out even one. Box of hundreds just sit beside dark hanky.

But who is Shnorhk to give his number to?

Girl like glitter girl in ad for Amphorae Lounge? She's wearing glitter pants too. Drunk for sure. Keep making voice louder each time Shnorhk is making music louder, until finally shouting:

"Tommy, it's the material! My spandex is wrong. I have no underwear, see. My vagina feels funny."

Another ride says nothing. Not even complaint. But Shnorhk have complaint. How he give card to man wearing such t-shirt?

The only authentic Turkish cymbal!

This Zildjian not relation to Shnorhk, but still not Turkish. Zildjian Armenian cymbal maker.

Shnorhk fume whole way from Culver City to Burbank.

Forget tip. So insulted he refuse money from frizzy-haired moron.

"Thanks, man!" Moron grin. "Thanks a lot! You want some weed?"

Later Shnorhk pick up kid. Turns out he Armenian kid. Musician. Likes Mnatsagan's playing. Loves band System of Down. All-Armenian band. Drummer plays Zildjian cymbals. Shnorhk tells story of t-shirt. Kid too is annoyed.

Shnorhk glad Independence Taxi install no safety glass. Safety glass destroy such camaraderie.

"Turks, man," kid adds, leaning forward, elbows on back of passenger seat. "Չենք չեն իմանում right from wrong. You have to punch them."

At 101 ∴ **Coffee Shop** ∴ o Franklin, Shnorhk pull into parking lot. Reach for card.

"There they are." Kid grins reaching for wallet. "Check out m boy's ride." Black Escalade. Armenian flag on antenna. "Got DVD for both backseats. $16,000 rims."

"Hey, let's be friends," the driver of Escalade yells at a young girl walking by herself. Something about her upper lip looks stuck.

"My boyfriend's coming over," she answers.

"I don't care about your boyfriend."

Young girl looks scared. Driver looks like he likes girl looking scared. Kid in Shnorhk's backseat leaves Shnorhk too much tip. Why so much money? Why DVDs on backseats? $16,000 rims? Young girl is running back into café. Shnorhk keep card. Maybe safety glass not such bad thing.

Monday morning, with sunrise, Shnorhk pick up ride at The London :. **West Hollywood**:. on North San Vicente. Shnorhk already up all night but still not tired. Still playing music of his friends.

Japanese businessman on his phone doesn't object to music. He doesn't yell on his phone either.

"電話をくれて嬉しい。私は
どうかしていた。数週間前、皆
は私が来ると伝えられた。皆、
私からの電話を心待ちにしてい
た。だけど電話しなかった。誰
も私がここに来たことさえ知ら
ない。私はホテルの部屋に座り
こんで、一つとして言葉を書か
なかった。穴があったら入りた
い気分だ。"

∴ "I'm glad you—" ∴ Not important what said. ∴ Oh. ∴ Shnorhk
turn music down. Shnorhk like soft
speak of Japanese businessman.
Soft speak like picture without
paint. Once Shnorhk see man practice calligraphy by pool at noon. On
knees on hot stones he dip brush
into water. Light strokes. Then
shuffle over few inches. Repeat.
Length of pool. Hot stones dry up
strokes at once. Meanings lost. Man
not bothered. Like silent music of
water rearranged is never lost.

:: *Katsu.* ::

Japanese businessman not soft speak long. Stare out window. Sway head back and forth same as oil pumps in oil fields they pass on way to airport.

One thing clear: Japanese businessman not need Shnorhk card.

Credit card covers fare. Shnorhk not curse absence of tip. See from start there is absent-mind about man.

Nothing cruel.
Nothing impatient.

Same way he look leaving hotel
ie look leaving taxi.

Tearless. At last.

Bloodless. At last.

Now   only   made   of   faint
houghts.

Anyone   made   of   only   faint
houghts can only look one way:

sad.

Shnorhk hand Japanese businessman receipt and Shnorhk's card
anyway. Sometime clear things not
so clear.

Not until left-turn lane north
of Wilshire does Shnorhk discover
what Japanese businessman left
behind.

For last mile a red Mitsubishi
Mirage with no license plates had
tailgated. Or tried swerve left or
swerve right to pass with no place
to pass in morning traffic.

At light Shnorhk think to do
what PT Cruiser did. Punish Mirage
for too-close driving. Deny left turn,
Strand Mirage on red.

But left turn is sacred. Three
Commandments. People depend on
such practices to proceed peacefully
Upon how we cross against oncom-
ing traffic everything depends.

Shnorhk honors left turn. This a comfort it turns out. Gets far enough out in intersection for three cars to pass through. Including Mirage. Forgets Mirage.

Greater good.

Greatest wrong—

~~Annotations~~

Shnorhk not know how he turns for her then but it not matter because Shnorhk always turns for her. Patil and her both. Every day. Every hour. Every breath.

Now looking back Shnorhk discover more than Japanese businessman's receipt and Shnorhk's business card left on seat.

Shimmering black. Gold whiskers, golder eyes, red ears.

Waving back.

Shnorhk heads south. Returns to airport. Grumbles and coughs. Credit card receipt has name. Shnorhk page Japanese businessman at Bradley Terminal. Maybe Japanese businessman hasn't left yet. Maybe Japanese businessman missed flight staring out window soft speaking his soft music.

No maybe:

Japanese businessman will want ceramic cat back.

Honeysuckle

It's the hardest thing I've ever had to do . . .

— Florence + The Machine

"Stop it!" Shasti shrieks.

Freya's already running into the kitchen.

"Mommy! She's doing it again!"

And, like, probably the only one more surprised than the twins by Xanther's silence is Xanther herself ∴ I, uhm, don't get it. ∴, because like all Xanther has to do, and she can do it whenever she likes, is just tell how Xiomara knocked the statue off the mantel and then trusted Xanther's two sisters to tell the truth.

Trusted.

The word sticks in Xanther's throat. More than all the peanut butter glopped onto celery sticks for breakfast.

Truth.

That sticks there too.

Shouldn't she be asking how they could lie like that? What had she ever done to them? Xanther would welcome that Question Song. But what the twins had said eclipsed why they said it in the first place. The lie itself makes the reason behind the lie invisible, even if Xanther still sees the question mark, even if she still chooses a silence that moves through her like a slow wind on fire, like a shame she's known as long as she's known her own name, evaporating tenderness, reminding Xanther there is more than one way to answer injustice.

"Xanther!" Astair yells from the kitchen, appearing a moment later in the breakfast room, like just standing there with her big cup of coffee, in front of all those frozen drops of rain, will provoke from silence more than silence.

Not much has changed since she threatened to take away the little one.

"Astair," Anwar sighs from the living room. "She didn't do anything."

Astair wheels around, heading back to the kitchen, her voice already rising, probably relieved that she doesn't have to do this again with Xanther, the twins' cries rising too then, until they're crying, faking it of course, and cut short instantly when morning soccer gets put on the line.

Xanther savors the silence. She never knew it could have such bite.

Crunching celery doesn't come close.

"I don't understand," Anwar says, not quite a question, joining her, pulling out a chair, but not yet ready to sit down. He looks tired, or just really, really stressed out?

"Roxanne, like, texted me?" Xanther answers, maybe for Anwar, to make it like easier for him?, or just make it easier on herself?, to avoid the other effect, a side effect, the guilt she feels for—, what?, keeping to herself what gives her the strength to discover something about herself she never knew existed before?

"Taymor's daughter?"

"You two are friends now?" Astair asks, returning with a plate of eggs for Anwar.

"She wanted to come with, you know, to Magic Mountain? Don't worry, I told her that wasn't happening, like you grounded me?"

"That was your choice, young lady."

"Yeah. Right."

> Roxanne: oh hell no! you & me both. dont worry. they forget. we dont forgive.

Roxanne's texts had surprised Xanther too. She almost mistrusted their out-of-blueness. Like she's older and, like, probably her mom had made her text? Except Xanther had also experienced firsthand Roxanne's niceness that Memorial weekend. Maybe they live in totally different worlds, but Taymor's daughter is also strong in a way that a girl can be, and maybe a guy too, when they are of no crowd's mind, realizing that no group or person, or even parent, is them and they can make up their own mind.

Kle loved that expression.

"'Make up' as in fabricating as in creating your own mind. Pretty radical common phrase if you give it a moment."

Had Xanther maybe even learned "make up your own mind" from Kle? ∷ No. Dov taught her that one. And like said it all the time. ∷ Probably Dov. Now though, Xanther makes up her mind to appreciate, even like?, that she and Roxanne have somehow bonded over *not* going to Magic Mountain together, Roxanne grounded for getting that little triangular part of the ear pierced, the one that like almost covers the ear hole, will cover it if you press on it, the tragus, that's right, tragus, but where did Xanther pick that up?, probably from Anwar, right?

∷ Uhm? No. No one taught her that word. How the . . . ∷

∷ *A curious question.* ∷

∷ **So early on, yet behold how quickly she learns . . .** ∷

∷ Behold! Curious! ∷

∷ *Oh my.* ∷

∷ Who what how did I just hear that because, because, Xanther def did not just now say, think, or anything else, the word "curious," let alone "behold." ∷

Xanther finds the twins again in the foyer, all geared up for practice, socks pulled up high, shin guards in place, like shin guards can protect them from this. All Xanther has to do is sit on the stairs, daring either one to keep her gaze.

But they still try.

Maybe because they can't get over the fact that Xanther for the first time, is it the first time?, ever? ∷ Yes. ∷ ∷ *Yes.* ∷ ∷ **Yes.** ∷ isn't looking away. Is that why Xanther enjoys it so much? What she can't do with Les Parents, Dr. Potts, or anyone else. But these two, now, are different . . .

The little one on her shoulder even starts to feel a little heavier as the stones on her sisters' eyes get heavier. Drilling deeper and deeper for skull. Even when they're running away, and they run pretty quick, screaming again, for what no parent will ever understand, forget stand against, even with only the backs of their heads showing, the swish of their frantic hair, what only walls can stop, the making of a hole making a hole of their thoughts.

Which Xanther likes doing.

Because of two things mainly:

1) Xanther knows it's just a fantasy.

∴ Well, that's the first relief of the day. ∵

2) What Xanther really wants isn't heavier, but lighter. Because the weight is pointless when there is the possibility of weightless satisfaction.

Even if that satisfaction had brought other troubles. Xanther had thrown up tons but not because she was actually sick. She was just really, really revolted. In fact, her body had never felt better, all of her. ∴ Not all of her if I'm still all of her. ∵ ∴ *You're not.* ∵ ∴ Then neither are . . . you? ∵ ∴ *No!* ∵ The cat too had seemed better after Xanther, with a thought, had flicked those two stones aside and discovered . . .

As easy too as wiping away the black gunk that collects in the little fella's ears, what Xanther carefully scoops out every day with a fingertip, as well as the gunk that forms beneath the eyes, what Xanther also flicks away every day with the fingernail of her pinkie.

Just black. No hint of red anymore. Dark as stones, kinda.

Though the memory still shudders Xanther now.

What had she found beneath the stones that night?

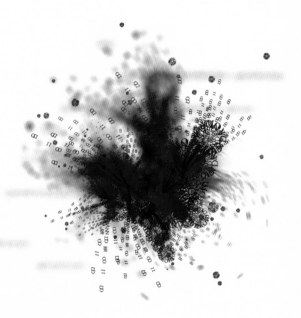

Only a memory now. No longer satisfying either. Maybe never ever satisfying? But Xanther sure needs more than hard-boiled eggs now or these soy sausages and spinach she starts cooking up with Anwar as soon as Astair leaves with the girls.

Xanther won't meet Anwar's eyes, sick of stones, so instead she stands next to him, rests her head against his side, closes her eyes as he rubs her head, both of them listening to the sizzle in the cast-iron pan like there was such a thing as a bloodless song and it could still feed you and be called good.

At least the little beast keeps her smiling throughout the day, wherever they are, in the kitchen, up in her room, nose always a wiggle of pink, Xanther wiggling her own nose too, rubbing nose to nose.

Who wouldn't do the same to that squunched face? If it is a face? Is it a face? Do animals have faces? Or just, like, a constellation of ears, nose, and mouth? Whatever the answer, the little one's eyes lack stones. Of course, they're also closed, like here in the den, between her knees, on its back, squirming a little, making Xanther giggle as it wiggles away only to just as fast wheel back her way, his seeing guide to coziness, Xanther's blind little guide to feelings of quiet and calm and other feelings too . . .

Xanther gives it a little squeeze, gets a little squeak. How could this little guy have anything to do with fear? This frail animal whipping its tail back and forth, tail finally wrapping loosely around Xanther's wrist?

But Xanther can't shake the feeling that, like, there is a connection to more unsettling, disturbing stuff. In the same way that a game controller might have everything to do with, say, *Lollipop Chainsaw* ∴ **2012** ∴, which Xanther had played once by accident, on Dad's old PS3. Boy, had Les Parents gone mental over that so not-age-appropriate experience she had "unknowingly wandered into." Not that that game matters so much, in this example, and no clue why Xanther is even thinking of *Lollipop Chainsaw,* maybe because of some Comic-Con pics Cogsworth and Kle had been showing everyone, with lots of older girls cosplaying Lollipop?, is that her name? ∴ Juliet Starling ∴, the point not being costumes or the big boobs the older girls love show-ing off, boobs Xanther doesn't have, might never have, and has no control over anyway, unless she grows up to get like those plastic implants, which Xanther so knows she so won't ever do, but back to the controller, and a different kind of plastic, which, huh, kinda, lets you control everything, most of the time, and also sometimes not at all, when the game is suddenly just showing you a story clip, or maybe just giving you a little control like in *Limbo* ∴ **2010** ∴ if you have a glowworm in your head, like Cogs had happen to him several times, though Xanther never had that happen, though is that what's in her head now?, like what has always been there?, a glowworm, controlling everything she does, kinda, like she's the zombie, like the zombies Juliet Starling ∴ Huh? ∴ keeps killing?, even if Xanther's glowworm isn't a worm but a blue fire lodged deep, deep in her chest? What maybe had something to do with almost getting her killed, when Xanther wandered into the street and that old truck almost didn't stop, all while she felt far, far away, flicking stones away, until what she found wasn't that indigestible blue, but something else, in spreads of darkness — what had *that* been? Red? Yet more than red ∴ **garnet** ∴ More than just color. Yet so familiar too, if that's what you call someone getting killed, devoured too.

Murdered.

Though when Xanther had blinked awake, far away from that splatter of death, she hadn't found death or splatter, but the most miraculous thing: this woman, whom the old man next to her called Lupita, him standing tall, her squatting low, the strangest look of worry on her face, strong hands on Xanther's shoulders, strong as the prayer she whispered under her breath was soft, so under her breath did it even count as a whisper?, making no difference to the blooms of honeysuckle that seemed everywhere, spiraling around her,

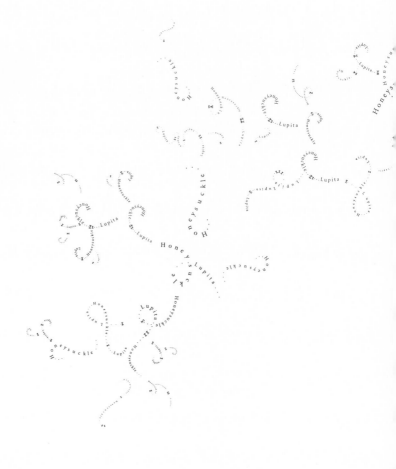

like Xanther could
just reach out and pluck one, sip some, eat them all, with a
quick snap, which Xanther hadn't done, just laughed.

253

All of which Xanther would have for sure talked over with Dr. Potts. Unfortunately, and this maybe to punish her some more, Astair, and actually Anwar too, had canceled the next few sessions. Their explanation having something to do with how busy summer can get.

But even without seeing him, Xanther can still hear what Dr. Potts would recommend, especially when Xanther's confusion starts really bending toward panic, the Question Song ramping up all over the place, over nothing:

"There's an old Tibetan saying: 'Take care of the minutes and the years will take care of themselves.' Simplify."

So Xanther just ignores all the questions about what happened to her, what's still happening to her, pays no attention to Astair's looks, even Anwar's, especially the whatever the twins want to yell about, and over the days ahead, as much as she can, when she's alone with this dearest little friend, Xanther sits by her phone, taking friends' requests, coming up with a list of possible names.

And Xanther tries them all on. Guesses answered each time in the answerless way he never answers at all.

Shackleton
Zoe
Futz
Buckley
Aloe
Maybe
Hummingbird
Randall
Helter
Shelter
Squander
Wander
Daigoro
Ogami Itto
Yagyu
Igloo
Lint
Kilos
Bob
Tom
Goku
Gota
Banana
Starbuck
Cabinet
Cassiopeia
Echo
Dr. Fu
Storm
Star
Mantis
Cabbage
Phillip
Zulu
Honeysuckle
Blizzard
Berg
Formica
Sumeru
Onyx
Bend
Wiggle
Zzzzzz
Pawl
Clawd
Flood
Katsu
Fushiki
Kakunen
Miles

Ampersand
CrowJane
Carl
Jimbo
Zinc
Beavis
Hieronimo
Keres
Zella
Vowl
Ace
Spades
Cinder
Question Mark
Aoife
Electric Danny Land
Peaches
Leontine
Perseids
Zenith
Rooney
Elliott Black
Astreaus
Erebus
George
Lucky
Kevin
Nyx
Lula
Pillar
Zarathustra
Arrow
The Object
Coal
Trinidad
Placid
Hush
Clark K
Ioxaswalj
Ariadne
Rain
Kurat
Korat
TV
Blanchot
Iggy
Lance
Aqbars
Mallory
Vanity

Ellipsis
Ellipses
Whisky
Le0
Zer0
Tad
Sif/jar
Gaius
Kupo
Kira
Komari
Slightly
Lettuce
Haruki
Drop
Aku
Zaniah
Pixel
Nashira
Mira
Lucida
Felicia
Gemma
Aloysius
Pleiades
Daisy
Aliocha
@c@
Azerty
Flavor
Boiteux
Quinoa
Zet
Catsum
Peter
Askani
Potemkin
Annie
Sir Artemis Cuddleton
Laughter
Slaughter
Cosmic Creepers
MacGuffin
Newton
Magellan
Exit
Solipses
Shujo
Faustus
Zeno

Raindrop
Grobis
Why
Nova
Kafka
Melchizedek
Snowflake
Teri
Xibalba
Betelgeuse
Claus
Marzipan
Frookley
Joe
Gerard
Trinity
Ansley
Milton Martini
Nyssa
Nitty
Nit
Nix
Bartholomew
Bosephius
Wellington
Katmandu
Blanc
Anne Frank
Mushin
Ptolemy
Hector
Archimedes
Rasputin
Trevor
Johnny
Willie
Andromeda
Yaga
Willee Bead
Pomp
Blu
Salt
Spartacus
Foreman
Helen
Lazy Blaine
Gozanza
Hiccup
Neutrino
Enkidu

One more thing:

no matter how many names Xanther goes through, what always keeps coming up is a name she is forbidden to know, born of a compassion and pain she can only know by heart . . .

And not someone Xanther can see or hear. A breath maybe, a pause, tears, but beyond the province of grief, over such tiny paws, fizzle of whiskers, gentle tail, Xanther feeling all along the old hands upon the fur, familiar with the curves, the bones, the purr, the silence of a hidden life, this stir of namelessness naming a power too great to behold, a war of hours, a voice of stars . . .

If Xanther's right. Because, of course, maybe she's not. Maybe this is just another something she's made up. This other-longing.

Far away.
Crying out.

Never ceasing to die for a return to closeness.

Some stranger.
Some old woman.

∴ **We know who.** ∴

Joint Session

And then there's a moment. The wind changes, the grass stops swaying.

— *Sir Malcolm Murray*

Astair watches Xanther (on her bed (mumbling to herself (lips moving (some music of (rapid) sense fumbling toward talk (what doesn't talk (is she going mad (she still is mad (Astair knows that (but . . .) and that beastly thing always with her (~~clawing~~ (*cloying!*) with all its apparent blindness)))))))))).

"What are you saying, honey?"

"I'm not *saying* anything." Lips tighten (tongue to a thing of stone (too hard to call childish)).

"Have I done something wrong?" Astair asks (surprised by the tears in her eyes (notes of ~~injustice~~ (*injury!*) clouding her throat)).

"No." Does Astair see something soften in her daughter?

"Then how can you be so mad at me?" Astair waits for the complaint to come then (about Magic Mountain (it's not too late to fix that)).

"I'm not."

"Then what's with the ongoing silent treatment?" Astair hangs in the doorway (resists moving to the bed (she tried that once (no desire to sit again next to that thing of (concrete) resistance (did she just think of her daughter as a thing? (she did (ugh)))))).

"You're the one, like, *always*, saying calm down, enough with the questions, breathe, practice Tai Chi, but now, like, that I'm feeling just like that, you're, like, mad at me?"

"I'm not mad."

"Cool."

Had Astair ever seen Xanther's eyebrows arch to such heights of sarcasm (Astair's getting mad now (flicking off the lights help)). "Cool?"

"Good night, Astair." The darkness stabs back.

Anwar doesn't have any better ideas (other than to agree with Xanther).

"You grounded her. Magic Mountain was the one thing she was looking forward to. All her friends were going. Even Roxanne wanted to go."

"I know, I know." Still fuming.

"But we also have a broken, very valuable statue to address, the story about which, for reasons mystifying us both, our daughter refuses to disclose. We also know, for another mysterious reason, the twins aren't disclosing the whole truth either."

(come morning) Astair tries (again) to reach Xiomara. This time the number doesn't ring at all (a painful (plaint) of notes (as if to lay blame on Astair that she is the one disconnected (she sure feels disconnected))).

"But why would she leave her last payment with me?" Astair asks Taymor that afternoon. "It was a hundred bucks!"

"Tough, isn't it, when daughters start holding all the answers? Get used to it."

"What's a Sin-Ecto Key?" Gia interrupts.

"Synecdoche," Taymor answers (on Astair's behalf (Astair having made the mistake of using the word moments earlier (in reference to something clinical (she'd been with ~~patients~~ (*clients!*) all morning (none of whom wanted to listen to her (meaning: none of whom wanted to listen to themselves (would listening have gone easier if they had had to listen to one another? (lots of benefits to group therapy (what Astair needs now (with (from?) her friends(?)))))))))).

"No, Gia," Taymor continues. "It's not a sex toy."

"I'll be the judge of that," Gia winks.

"Extraordinary." Abigail blushes (even her blond hair seems to blush). Abigail had met up with Astair beforehand for an hour of yoga in West Hollywood (before coming to Lemonade ∴ **9001 Beverly Boulevard, Los Angeles, CA 90048** ∴ to meet up with these two for a late lunch).

"See where that academic-shrink-babble gets you?" Taymor snaps at Astair.

"Gia, 'synecdoche' means the use of a part for a whole."

"Hey, so long as it vibrates, I'm in." Gia smiles (taking a sip of lemonade (cucumber mint)).

"Gia!" Abigail exclaims. "Are you trying to out-sex Taymor?"

"I'm competitive."

Taymor's laugh is a big (literal) Ha! (next sucking down a gulp of lemonade (watermelon rosemary)).

"The point is—" Astair soldiers on ((half tempted to just drop the whole thing (with a slug of her own lemonade ((pineapple coriander) ideal in this heat (along with a nibble from the shared plate of ((coconut) curried) cauliflower (with almonds and golden raisins too)("Delish!" Astair's (already) said twice)))) (rather than—)) trying (on such a beautiful sunny afternoon (the day before Independence Day (out on this dreamy umbrellaed patio (peopled with such dreamy strangers and friends)))) to follow up (still) on the discursive tumble that had just gone (quickly (erratically)) from her clients to her paper (enter: academic-babble (synecdoche one)) to the new (old?) household pet (enter: a synecdoche too?) and the emerging mess that seemed to coincide with its arrival (exit: their housekeeper (with odd(ly generous) behavior))) "—I'm worried about her!"

"Your housekeeper?" Abigail asks ((like all of them) enjoying her lemonade (guava?)?).

"No! I mean yes, of course." Astair realizing now (thanks to her friend) that ((yes) of course!) she's worried about Xiomara too (lots of worry all around).

"Something sure has gotten up in your mix," Gia says ((without judgment) easing back out of the shade (squinting in the sun (basking in it))).

"Listen up, Abigail, and learn: Astair's not the first mother taken down by her daughter's kitty!"

"Jesus, Tay!" Abigail even turns away.

"Please, Taymor." Astair can hear herself pleading. "I need advice. You have Roxanne, precocious, brilliant, and almost sixteen. Gia, you have Bret and Winnie. Both already out of high school."

"That's a secret so long as I'm single," Gia growls. "Of course, you should be worried. Look where we live? West Hollywood Hookers. City of Angel Dust. Santa Monica Lewinsky. Just take comfort in the fact that for all we know about transgressions and mistakes, we also know a thing or two about recovery and rehab."

"Xanther has never refused to discuss something. Ever. I'm so flummoxed."

"Flummoxed?" Gia smiles.

"Flummoxed you can fuck, Gia," Taymor purrs.

"Okay, flustered." Astair (surprisingly) flustered.

"Don't listen to them, Astair," Abigail says kindly.

"Like I said," Taymor sighs. "Get used to it. She broke your glass-whatever." (Astair can't bear to tell them the price.) "Then she got caught. And rather than confirm her guilt, she's learned she can leave mother dearest in doubt. It's called growing up."

"Part of something I discovered later—" (Astair tries nudging the conversation in a different direction) "—was scribbled on her shoes." Astair pulls out the card (all caps (like on Xanther's Converses)).

"GREEN CANARIES USE MESCALINE GUACAMOLE," BELLOWS ELSA. "HONEY NICOTINE CAUSES PANIC," COLUMBINE-VENDETTA GUY SURMISES. "FRENCH GROUNDS EQUATE," BRASH BOLLIS PARAGLIDES. "CHILLED ARRIVES YOUR WAY FRACKED."

"Gibberish?" Taymor shrugs.

"Online searches pretty much confirm that."

"Mescaline's worry worthy," Gia adds. "Columbine too. Though who the hell says 'fracked'?"

"Is mescaline even part of the culture these days?" Abigail wonders. "To me, I mean, it sounds so, you know hippie–ish? Like People's Park kinda stuff? Though druggy for sure"

"I mean, she's never mentioned drugs before," Astair says. "She loves the smell of coffee but she doesn't drink it. The only thing close to a drug in her life is the new pet."

"One word: 'toxoplasmosis,'" Gia warns.

"Don't be silly," Taymor snorts. "Xanther's not pregnant and neither is Astair. Are you, Astair?"

"Not even close," Astair laughs (though (even without symptoms haunting the moment (those itches and flashes)) memory (alone) scratches up new signs (is this new heat just the sun (or something of her own making (mistaking?))?)).

"I don't understand," Abigail says.

"Toxoplasmosis is bad news for unborn babies," Taymor explains. "Cats can carry it."

"I read somewhere that it can turn you into a

zombie," Gia continues (both Taymor and Abigail laugh). "I'm just saying I'm with Astair here. There are better pets to adore. Malibu doesn't have many. Coyotes gobble them up like cat McNuggets."

"I've heard single women with cats stay single with cats," Abigail whispers. "But I like cats. Maybe I like being single?"

"You don't have a cat," Astair laughs (knowing better than to say more (like "and you're not single") if Abigail isn't comfortable coming out with news about her new relationship ((((exotic) animal trainer (kingdom owner)?) Toys?!) are they still together (maybe they broke up already?)?)).

"I probably couldn't tolerate the shedding," Taymor admits. "Black cats on Paris posters? Fine. White hair on my black Demeulemeester? I'd hand-feed it myself to Gia's coyotes."

Everyone takes a sip of lemonade (a collective pause (what's that French saying? (something to do with twenty minutes to or after? (and (how about that) it is 4:20 PM)) ∷ *Un ange passe . . .*∷ ∷ *Overhead, The Angel . . .*∷ ∷ Really? *The?*∷)).

Gia breaks the silence: "I have a confession."

"Holding out, Gia?" Taymor grins (chewing on her straw).

"Since when is 'holding out' ever part of my vocabulary?"

"Are you seeing someone?" Abigail asks excitedly (getting it right away).

"He takes the wafer." Gia sags.

"Then *he's* 'holding out' on you?" Astair can't resist.

"What?" Abigail asks.

"If that's code for kinky, you lost me," Taymor confesses.

"You're dating a Catholic?" Astair smiles.

Gia nods. "Three dates. And only one kiss. On the cheek. He's very strict. He's also very good-looking. I keep hoping. But I'm in hell."

"Catholics are good at hell," Astair offers.

"I'm not."

"That's part of your charm, darling," Taymor adds (nudging toward Gia what's left on the plate (as if cauliflower could offer heaven (maybe it can))). Gia doesn't bite. Astair takes a forkful.

"This last Sunday, I even went to a service."

"If that's not a sign of the apocalypse!" Taymor laughs (joins Astair at the plate with a fork).

"The end of days was pretty much what the father, priest, whatever you call him, talked about. Eternal damnation at least. Devils fighting against devils. Divided kingdoms. That's when he took my hand. It was somehow wonderful."

"Does *he* have a name?"

"He's a secret friend for now."

Astair glances at Abigail (catches a smile?).

"Gia's dating Mel Gibson." Taymor smirks.

"I never re-date my conquests."

"You did not ever hook up with Mel Gibson!"

"Don't fall for it, Abby," Astair sighs.

"Advice really for Gia," Taymor adds. "Don't fall for it, honey. Don't—"

"No." Abigail cuts off Taymor. "I'm sorry, Tay. I think you're too in the catbird seat to see this clearly. One of my yoga teachers has this house-and-guest thing he likes to tell. Your body is the house, and new sensations, like aches and challenges, are visitors knocking on the doors. 'Let them in,' he says." ((and maybe(?)) because Abigail now has all their attention) she at once diverts her own attention to her plastic cup (fussing it around (in a puddle (of condensation))). "A lot of the practice of yoga is about making space for change to happen, and what happens when we open up, in our body, in our mind, in our heart. I say be open."

"Thank you, Abigail," Gia says (seeing (maybe?) why they're friends).

"And if nothing comes of it—" (Taymor shrugs (trying(?) to hide her (is it increasing(?(!))) annoyance)) "—I know a nice Scientologist you can try."

On Beverly Boulevard (in the midst of hugs and goodbyes) Taymor's grouchiness has grown (she is annoyed!) almost to the point of sullenness (Astair should ask her what's wrong (hang back a moment (instead she brings up (again) her own worries))).

"I just wish I knew what Xanther was hiding. And why. Her secrets scare me."

"Daughters. They grow up," Taymor snaps.

"She's only twelve."

"Twelve doesn't grow up?" The disproportionate level of irritation throws Astair (Abigail too).

"Tay!"

"Wait till she calls you a vag bag. In public too. I wonder if you'll say she's only twelve then."

"And the bitch-switch goes flip," Gia sighs.

"You don't know Xanther." Astair flares too ((still) struggling (scrambling?) to track what the fuck is going on).

"Neither do you, Astair. I promise." Taymor digs into her bag now for her car keys. "At thirteen, Roxanne gave her first blow job. At fourteen, she fucked a senior. Two supposedly. Though thankfully not at the same time."

"Well, at least she has something to look forward to," Gia interrupts (what feels like (an interruption) in defense of Astair).

"Please," Abigail mutters (just as mystified(?)).

"Just teasing, Abby," Gia purrs. "Who says daughters have to take after their mothers."

"I didn't object," Taymor barks.

"Please!" Abigail claps her hands over her ears (because now she objects? (clearly upset)).

Taymor (however) is unmoved by this protest (continuing on): "Though none of that before Roxanne had already gotten drunk and smoked hash. Who knows what she's trying now, because the present only keeps getting faster and we only keep getting slower. Why not mescaline? Or meth? Or something none of us have ever heard of?"

"Astair, just talk to her," Abigail says ((actually) stepping in front of Taymor). "Talk to her about drugs and sex. Your worries. Your concerns. All of it."

"Easier suggested than done," Gia clucks (with (too much) experience).

"Daughters will do what they do," Taymor sighs (unlocking her car (whatever personal storm that was (already) dissipating)). "They always do. And in the end, they'll blame their mothers. Just like we do."

(except that night (instead of blaming anyone (like Astair))) Xanther comes into their bedroom and apologizes.

"I'm sorry, Mom." Just like that. "I'm not angry with you. And, like if I were you, I'd ground me too."

"Oh honey," Astair puts down the book she's reading ∴ **Apocalyptic Futures by Russell Samol-sky** ∴. "I'm sorry for my threat. I had no right to say that about your cat. He's here now. For good."

"Thanks. I mean, for saying that, though, you know, I knew that you knew you didn't mean it. You were just angry too."

They hug (awkwardly (hugs these days (usually) are (especially with the cat always perched on her shoulder (heaven forbid Astair knocked it off)))).

"You can talk to me."

Xanther nods. "I, like, just want to figure something out for myself first? Is that okay?"

Anwar clears his throat (also on the bed reading ∴ **Tactical Media** ∴ ∴ *rr!* ∴ ∴ ▪▪▪▪▪▪▪▪ ∴). "Is it dangerous, daughter?"

Xanther shakes her head (Astair seizing the moment to try to see some new revelation this child's eyes might offer (but they remain as unreadable (as the blind slits of that white little animal))).

"Can I see that binder you made up, you know, with all the different kinds of dogs, and like, names you were thinking about?" Xanther asks then.

"Of course!" Though the request takes Astair by surprise (as does the (strange) reluctance she feels about parting with that old labor (what she'll probably just chuck)). "Do you have a good list yet?"

"Not even a top five, unless like, I start counting Josh's fave, One Cool Cat, which I'm not counting, or Kle's, and he had 1CC, as a joke I think, but I mean, I don't get that, do you?"

((the next day) on July 4th) Astair checks in with Taymor (not bringing up Xanther's mention of 1CC (yet another thing vaguely suggestive of drugs)).

Taymor (immediately) apologizes for yesterday. Roxanne's (unauthorized (ear)) piercing has really gotten under her skin (she's even worried that her daughter's sudden kindness toward (interest in?) Xanther might not be a good thing for Xanther).

"As in she might be a bad influence. Can you believe I'm talking this way? About my own daughter?"

Astair is moved.

(for a while) They change the subject to Lucy Li (an eleven-year-old who had just played in the U.S. Women's Open (parred ten holes too)). What would having a daughter like that be like?

"Worse!" Astair and Taymor bleat out together (laughing together comes next (though (Astair suspects) neither believes the joke (just as she knows they'd never trade their daughters' lives for a life not their own))).

"You haven't said anything about my present."

"Oh my gosh. I thanked you for the wine, didn't I? Anwar and I drank it. Oh!—" No! The box (black oily paper (with a bow in the shape of a heart)).

Had that too gone the way of her beloved statue?

Astair races through the house. Is this Xanther's mischief? The twins'? Maybe connected to Xiomara returning (refusing?) the money?

But Astair finds the present in their bedroom. With a card: La Dama ∴ 3 ∴ ∴ *In red shoes.* ∴

Multiple apologies later:

"Should I open it now?"
"Open it with your hubby." ((at least) no question (fortunately)) Astair hears mischief in Taymor's voice.

That afternoon is not a good time: she and Anwar take the girls to the Echo Park lake for a picnic. Not the best idea. Xanther (immediately) wants to go back home to be with her cat. Freya and Shasti make a point of wandering far away (probably to keep clear of their scowling sister).

(afterward) None of them want to go to Dodger Stadium to watch fireworks. Xanther wants to stay in her room. Shasti and Freya want to watch Disney princesses in the den.

Relenting beats resisting in this case (Tai Chi without motion (maybe Lambkin would be proud?)).

"I'm guessing making our own fireworks isn't on your mind?" Anwar (in flip-flops and shorts (no shirt on)) asks from the back patio.

And it's not that Astair doesn't want to ((looking at her husband's (black) beautiful chest (wisped occasionally with beautiful gray galaxies (hairs fine as eyelashes)))(looking at his long forearms)(his gorgeous mouth)(what a face this man has!)) but she still shakes her head.

"What's wrong, love?" Anwar asks (as Astair keeps shaking her head (because she doesn't want to cry)). "Xanther? The wolves?"

"Oceanica," Astair finally admits. "The summer session is coming up. I still have clients. I'm supposed to be seeing Dr. Sandwich. We've already had to lie about Dr. Potts to Xanther. Shasti and Freya have soccer. Another school year for all three girls is just around the corner. And—" A long lingering follows (threatens to linger forever (forever?!)).

"And what?"

Thank you Anwar for ending forever. Not all forevers are created equal. Astair paces (past their yuzu tree (in a pot)(spots (at once) the praying mantis that perpetually guards it)). Cheese 'n' rice. Enchiladas.

"We don't have enough money."

Anwar smiles (kisses her softly on the mouth (then both eyes (this beats fireworks))).

"Joint Session?" he asks.

(God!) Astair loves him.

They hadn't had a Joint Session since December (following a string of emergencies (what a year ((2013!) its claws still in this year (and how many more years to come?)))).

1) An IRS audit finding back taxes with fines due (neither she nor Anwar can say aloud their accountant's name (ex-accountant (Mefisto looks like a saint compared to— (Gene Charlesville (not exactly spoken) "We pointedly instructed you that we don't cheat on our taxes! We pointedly informed you that we would prefer to pay more than suffer this!" Anwar screaming (one of the few times in his life))))).

2) The failure of two major clients to pay for services rendered ((also not spoken about (Fictile Data Management, Inc., and Obliquity Partners (Joe and James Parsons))) after thirty days (after sixty days (after ninety days (failing altogether (it still seems) to remit any kind of payment)))). And (of course)

3) Dov's funeral. Add time off. Add travel and lodging for two adults and three children. Add the cost of Xanther's tonic-clonic (hospital bills their old insurance (despite policy claims (and reassuring phone calls (requiring hours(!) to complete))) keeps refusing to cover). Additional adds Astair can't think about.

All of it devastating savings accounts and ratcheting up payments on several (numerous(!)) credit cards (to say nothing of stress levels (hello cortisol!)).

Their 2013 Joint Session was called.

The box brought out.

Laptop. Clipboard too.

Away had gone the Prius and the Mini for the (used)Honda Element.

Away went a Christmas (and even spring) vacation.

Away went the gym membership.

Away went cable.

Away went bottled-water service.

Away went home insurance ((after all) the house was a rental property (and stuff was just stuff)).

Health insurance they just lost

(inexcusable (their ((last) November) Covered California application
        (never going through
                (inexcusable)))
(just crossing their fingers to make it to this November (to better results (?))(without incident))).

"I'll give Oceanica up," she sputters now ((upstairs) behind their (locked) bedroom door).

Anwar's kind enough not to respond ((almost) allways erring on the side of kindness (is kindness ever an error?)).

The first Joint Session then of 2014.

Anwar gets out the box (from under the bed).

Turns the laptop on. Readies the clipboard.

The ((lightless) colorless) pop of fireworks grows and wanes. More AM moments plunge Astair and Anwar deeper into the details of spending patterns. Monies anticipated against the unexpected.

Nutrition (appetites of growing children (growing more particular)). Transportation (car plus car insurance (check out other plans?) plus fuel (check out public transport?)). Education (importance only increasing). Debt (growing alongside all of them (together: "Fuck you, Gene Charlesville!" "Fuck you, Fictile Data!" "Fuck you, Obliquity!" (for some reason laughed over too (though when was forty grand ever a laughing matter? (this moment apparently)))))).

And finally the most obvious cost: the roof over their heads.

And (still) no matter how hard Astair tries (and she tries (very hard) tonight) she can't look at their life as the numbers Anwar keeps totaling up (utilities now (gas and water and (so much) electricity *and* telephone services *and* doodads of all variety)): every integer and addition sign (or minus sign (blacks and reds)) only delivering her more and more (for whatever reason (is there a reason? (she's thinking like Xanther now))) into the paradise of their garden (snapdragons and lavender and coriander and parsley and sage and so many pansies) and the embrace of their neighborhood (so many soft hills and sinuous streets and steep stairs rising beside Wisteria-cloaked fences) — Echo Park (a name speaking of green and rest and the familiar return).

"Good news first or the bad?" Anwar whispers.

"I don't want to move again. I can't."

"That's the good news: I don't think we can afford to move. More good news: your parents, whom we already owe, can't afford to help us."

"Then the bad news is I have to stop with Oceanica and go back to bartending. Shot-glass counselling for a tip."

"I want you to finish the year."

"Xanther needs new glasses. She looks like *Revenge of the Nerds* without the revenge."

Anwar closes the laptop and removes from view the clipboard (all the red ink evidence of their (appalling) deficit). (last (and not leased (ha!))) He opens their box (always locked (hiding a small humidor (well-watered) plus ritual)) and removes ((now) only eight left) one pre-rolled joint.

"Our answer?" Astair smiles.

"We can last through the summer." Anwar smiles (offering to her lips the joint (and to the joint a petal of flame)).

"Not like I'm objecting," she says (laughs (inhaling ((for all its soft promises (the smoke is)) a rough arrangement in her lungs))).

"I suspect you already have a plan in mind?"

"I do."

Anwar also inhales and coughs. "Me too."

Always the same and always said together and what (thus far) always seems to work (somehow).

"Luck."

But Astair doesn't feel lucky. Even after their giggling haze fades ((which (eventually) involved *Penny Dreadful* followed by chocolate syrup and teasings on their bedroom terrace (and more than just teasing ((look at that) they'd both gotten lucky))) even if that heaving clutch faded too soon) leaving them with one last (if uneasy(?)) laugh: Taymor's present.

A phone (TraceFone). One app: HomePorn.

| Stair: | Too naughty. |
| Tay: | About time! Enjoy! |

(by morning (though)) Astair feels angry again (stares at the (vacant) mantelpiece (what would ( ) Dov have done? (Oh Astair knows (lost it doesn't begin . . .)))): every problem (every (red) series of numbers) solved just like that (with plenty of (black) numbers left over for ((stuff)(work)(a life)) FUN!)!

Not that she can show it.

Astair even (she thinks (she's sure)) manages to make her passing (re)inquiry seem easy. Shasti's and Freya's (easy) answer convinces her (even if their retelling is now too in sync (like two metronomes (hadn't both she and Anwar recently noticed increasing division between these two? (now unified against their older (half (all white (whitewhite(!))()) (?)) sister)))) never missing a beat: Xanther among the shattered ruins of her glass wolves.

(if there is mystery here (and (surely) there must be)) Freya and Shasti conceal it beneath a composure of blankness (a response no different when Astair asks (easily too (she thinks)) how they slept).
"Great!"
"Great!"
"The fireworks didn't bother you?"
Two shakes of the head (void of any awareness of the (traumatic) fits and groans nights seem to (increasingly) hold for both of them).

Xanther (on the other hand) makes no secret of the price of her silence (even if Astair suspects that this glowering (at bare minimum) is only a reserve (at an auction played out in Xanther's racing head)).

Astair can befriend silence too (Lares & Penates is one name (price alone (that declaration!) would obliterate any (all!) childish pacts (but at what cost? (too high)))).

What does an angry tongue know of cost? Astair bites hers.

Mother and daughter can share this in common while Shasti and Freya (one after the other (out in front of the house)) challenge this morning's (perfectly safe) precipice (of a chalk line drawn (in bright turquoise (three car lengths long))) down the sidewalk (all of her children oblivious ((as it should be) of the very real precipice on which this family (once again) teeters)).

Shasti tiptoes a few feet before veering from the line. Freya gets a little farther before her steps also veer wide.

Their progress worsens. Until both are shouting:
"Mom!"
"Mom!"
"Xanther's doing it again!"
That eerie unison.

Xanther rolls her eyes (she hasn't moved from her squat (studying the girls (staring at them (like the cat on her shoulder isn't (couldn't (be?)))))).

"Your little guy shouldn't be out here."

Xanther stands up (shrugs).

(but before going inside) Xanther approaches the chalk line (studies it with the same focus with which she takes in her sisters at the other end) and then (with a few easy strides ((very!) fast(?) too(?))) reaches them easily.

Every step true.

No hitches. No wavers. Wobbling only after-wards.

Shasti and Freya are too unsettled to react (or even move). Astair is unsettled too.

Xanther (already) disappearing back into the house.

Too much her own secret.

And (for reasons Astair cannot comprehend) the sensation (

of something already here and yet

:. **forever**.:

:. *and never*.:

beyond the reach of closure

)

brings surges of fear.

A Sleeping Warrior

Out of the question.

— Victim #11

Before handling the luggage, Isandòrno secures Teyo in the passenger seat. The Range Rover is armored with airless tires. Isandòrno sits in the back so he can move quickly to either window or deal with Teyo from behind.

On Isandòrno's nod, the driver merges with airport traffic. The driver is alert with the fear that comes from either special occasions like this, where The Mayor has demanded absolute attention, or from having to work so closely with Isandòrno.

Teyo, however, shows nothing but amusement. He jokes with the driver about having to pick up an old man who can't handle a taxi. He jokes with Isandòrno about having to carry a bag for an old man who forgot to pack his toothpaste.

Teyo is not a soldier. He is a warrior. The driver does not know this. The driver relaxes enough to offer mild assurances.

—The Mayor will have every type of toothpaste.

The driver fails to recognize that if there was a fight he would lose because he has already confused Teyo's capacity for charm with an incapacity to act. Of course there is no fight.

Teyo knows the city well. He is happy to pass by the Bosque de Chapultepec. He opens the window despite objections. If there is time, Teyo tells Isandòrno, he would like to visit the Museo Tamayo Arte Contemporáneo. There will be plenty of time. They will not pass this way again.

—Where is she? Teyo does not resist the long hug or The Mayor's pestering about his failure to bring company.

—Trouble with her passport.

—Nigerian? Moldovan? One of us?

—Just young. She's never been out of the country.

—Like my friend here, opening a wide hand toward Isandòrno.

The next day, the little plane greets a turbulence invisible in the sunny day. The Mayor's recklessness rises with the pilot's focus. With every bump, The Mayor jumps around like a little kid.

His pleasure dims only when he sees that Teyo's calm matches Isandòrno's.

As rough as the flight there is, the landing seems unfinished, as if even upon stopping, the Cessna's wheels still refused to touch down. The tarmac is hot enough that the heels of Isandòrno's boots float. Just to touch a surface here could burn a man up. Waves of heat, born off of tar as well as the sand ahead, make a mystery of the compound.

Past the guards and bolted doors, inside beyond the first bay where agrarian machines, like tractors and plows, are serviced out of reach of the sun, through another set of metal doors, the locks invisible and, despite their height, sliding noiselessly aside, The Mayor leads Teyo to his new frontier.

—All mechanized. Or most of it.

Rows of glass and steel machines, with blue and black and silver hoses spiraling around aluminum joints, maneuver high-precision delivery instruments above thousands of tiny vials shuffled slowly along in metal trays captive to the impulse of magnets.

So minuscule is the process — invisible at this distance and even less visible closer up — it's unclear whether the machines are filling or emptying the vials.

By the end of the demonstration, though, as The Mayor proudly points out, the vials are gone, replaced by tiny bundles of mechanically tied balloons.

Pale blue.

—2010, The Mayor clarifies.

Further along, awash in a flood of LEDs from overhead, on a table all their own, wait three shallow trays piled high with pink balloons.

—The present, as you can see, is not lacking.

On an adjacent table wait two more shallow trays. These each hold a small pile of black balloons.

—Our future. Global distribution.

On the last table waits only one tray and it holds only one small white balloon.

—Why not? The Mayor smiles. Something beyond global?

Teyo is impressed and this pleases The Mayor.

—I have this dream, Teyo. The Mayor sits down to mop his brow, though it is cool here, and laughs, though nothing is funny. That Federales raid us, followed by fleets of news crews, putting before the nation all these balloons. Only to discover that what they contain might as well be sawdust or chalk or nothing more than air.

Lunch is served outside under um-
brellas. While they were inside,
a second plane had landed. Now
caterers bring over plates of
asparagus, orange beets, and fat
sardines crusted in black salt.

The Mayor speaks at length about
the rosé. Teyo and The Mayor finish two bottles. Isandòrno sits
with them but has no more than
a sip. True control lies not with no
but with a little.

—We have troubles here too, The Mayor at last says, his plate at last empty, his glass again full. Money breeds troubles like shit breeds flies.

—I'm sorry to hear that, Teyo answers carefully. Is it serious?

—If you count my pride. The Mayor grins. And I do!

Cutberto was not to blame. The Mayor found this out two weeks later. Another man, who also knew nothing about what had happened in Los Angeles, had used the opportunity to undermine Cutberto.

The Mayor was so disgusted he did not even send Isandòrno. —That is below you. Instead he had three twelve-year-olds shoot the opportunist's knees off and then stab him to death with forks.

Unfortunately, this wouldn't bring back Cutberto who had been shot through the head and over the next hour shot again and again until the picnic was over and the poolside cement was as sticky as the day. Blood also breeds flies.

Cutberto's wife suffered a worse fate. She died at once. To witness her was to witness a cancellation of the apparatus that permits witnessing.

Except life is more than history
and survival does not necessarily
depend on understanding. Cutberto's wife rose from the dead
aghast to discover just how weak
the ghosts of our dead really are.

The Mayor decried —This confusion! and has since installed
Cutberto's wife in —the finest
cancer-treatment center in Mexico City!

The Mayor even visits her.

—We'll fix this, he has even said. And Isandòrno doesn't doubt The Mayor believes what he says. Does Isandòrno believe it too? Isandòrno knows that the answer does not matter so long as he remains in The Mayor's service.

The only thing that rattles Isandòrno is when The Mayor suggests to Teyo that he take Isandòrno north.

Out of the country?

—I am in your debt, Teyo says, putting down his empty glass. The Mayor does not refill it. The mistake was on my end. I have a name now and I have someone taking care of that name.

—I doubt your someone is of the caliber of our friend here, The Mayor answers.

Teyo looks at Isandòrno.

—Not even close. He is a blunt thing. Tattoos of his accomplishments cover his body. Especially his face. But he is very effective. A rat will not trouble him. Nor a child or a monster. He is not afraid in any way that might make him less . . . efficient.

Now The Mayor refills Teyo's glass. Halfway.

—Did the food not agree with you? Teyo asks as they return to the plane. Teyo ate half of everything. The Mayor only drank.

—I've become an increasingly finicky eater.

On the flight back, more turbulence greets the plane. Once again, The Mayor seems transported, this time even more elated when Teyo grabs a strap and closes his eyes, moving his lips rapidly. Isandòrno taps nine for no reason.

—Nacho! The Mayor roars. I was going to invite you to The Ranch but if this little hop is a challenge, I fear you might not enjoy the fun!

The Mayor really is in a good mood but moods are dangerous counselors. Each time Teyo reopens his eyes Isandòrno sees there is no discomfort. Teyo and Isandòrno have more in common with each other than with The Mayor.

As rattles question wings and the wavering whine of the prop answers thunderheads gathering on the horizon — as present as they are unrelated to these blasts and bumps in the sunny air — Isandòrno wonders about the man who works for Teyo.

Is he too like them? Does he too hold on to nothing?

Two days later, Teyo asks Isandòrno to drive him to see his son. Teyo assumes The Mayor knows where his son lives. Isandòrno does not pretend otherwise.

Teyo refuses to go inside the crumbling apartment complex in Santa María la Ribera. At first the boy's friends follow him out onto the sidewalk until they see Teyo, retreating then to the upstairs balconies and windows, until they see Isandòrno, retreating entirely into the shadows of their speculations.

Did Isandòrno expect a fight? Or was it just that Teyo wanted him to expect a fight? Teyo doesn't have The Mayor's money or power but he has lived longer, and through a set of complex circumstances Isandòrno doubts The Mayor could survive without the luck Teyo has never needed.

Teyo's son who is maybe eighteen will be lucky to reach nineteen. A slender creature of wavering fear, so fragile he is almost invisible to Isandòrno.

Black jeans and Vans don't help.
No amount of silver-studded spar-
kle on his belt will draw the attention of anyone with real purpose.
And anyone who comes after a
pink t-shirt, or thick mascara, or
a pink bandana twisted into long
black hair, will have even less
purpose.

—Jordi! Teyo barks in response
to whatever Jordi said, which
Isandòrno could not hear.

Teyo strikes Jordi on the side of
the head. The boy doesn't resist.

Or even move away. He doesn't even remove his hands from his pockets.

From the shadows of the apartment building, another boy emerges, younger and darker, with eyes black with fear.

Jordi doesn't look up. His father keeps hitting him on the back of the head, finally yanking away the bandana and stepping on it, like he was stubbing out a cigarette.

The dark boy is too terrified to

stay, but he does stay, drawn to this moment of brief courage, as Jordi shakes his head, to instruct whom he cannot see that even in stillness there is courage enough.

Isandòrno doubts Teyo saw it. Nothing later on gives Isandòrno any reason to think Teyo even noticed Jordi's boyfriend.

Why then would Teyo recognize what Isandòrno had been initially so wrong about? That Teyo's son is a sleeping warrior.

dead-end cats

Ne cadant in obscurum.

— Mozart's Requiem

HANDYMAN FOR YOUR PROBLEM!

Fix and clean & Everything

Call Jose Juan Smith

⊗⊗⊗-⊗⊗⊗-⊗⊗⊗⊗

Anwar takes the card [sticking out from {their front} doorjamb]. The house could use some fixing [cleaning for sure {Xiomara's replacement? ‹not that a replacement's affordable›}]. So maybe Anwar just pins it up in the kitchen because he enjoys the copy [especially '& Everything' {and the emoji too}]. Plus pinning means consideration [consideration means 'with the stars' {*sider* ‹Latin› = star} ∴ shooting for the stars]. Therefore making [out of this corkboard] a Vision Board [{Abigail would appreciate that} though not the sudden shuffle beyond insisting rats roam the rooms between the rooms between their walls . . .].

Maybe what they need is an exterminator!

خلي بالك من الا انت عاوزه، صح؟

∴ Be careful what you wish for. ∴

∴ *Wishes, wishes, wishes* . . . ∴

Anwar wishes he didn't have to lug himself back upstairs [to his monitor {to those broken efforts ‹inoperable for three weeks «at least it ⟨Cataplyst-3⟩ doesn't crash with every start»›}].

312

// But start what?

// address all outstanding

// critical issues

// deploy a functional

// build

// determine possible

// alternate

//purposes

// to know if

// the thing

// plays

// ???

[on the bright side {despite what Anwar's sluggish progress succeeds in dimming ‹dim to dark if he «makes the mistake ⟨[[and] ever [?]]⟩» considers the nine grand waiting for his family «as soon as he gets this thing ⟨*this thing!*⟩ up and running»›}] The attention necessary for the job keeps away anxieties self-named as necessities [namely]:

1 — Loss

// of $$$$$$$

2 — Loss

// of wolves

// ∴ of $$$$$$$

3 — Loss

// of family harmony

// ∵ of lost wolves

// ∴ of $$$$$$$

∵ neither money nor loss has the mass and ∴ gravity to draw Anwar's thoughts into the orbit necessary to keep him for the needed hours [the rest of the day {into night}]. Such meditation requires something else [or nothing else] . . .

314

[at least] Cataplyst-2 had swirled like a storm in a globe. Cataplyst-3 just jumps from [static] mess to [static] mess. Chamomile tea [dosed with honey {and cinnamon}] doesn't help Anwar find the errors to animate that mess [if that's the objective here{?}].

[when midnight comes {and goes ‹Anwar only vaguely aware of Astair whispering into his office «with inquiries about dinner and ‹what else?› news that everyone's eating separately anyhow»›}] Anwar finds himself circling [roughly] nine lines [what {he can only say} an engineer's {sixth ‹and seventh «and eighth ‹why not ninth?›»› sense} drew him to]:

```
336510      // Main Loop
336511          while (orb.IsSipaapuni())
336512  ▼       {
336513              if (CheckSystemMessages() == SystemMessage::EXIT)
336514                  break;
336515
336516              simTimer.Process();
336517              orb.talhayingwti(sin(simTimer.GetDeltaTime()));
336518  ↳       }
```

until finally

```
orb.talhayingwti(sin(simTimer.GetDeltaTime()));
```

turns into

```
orb.talhayingwti(sin(simTimer.GetTotalSeconds()));
```

and suddenly . . .

Anwar's tea cools. Then it's gone. Music plays. ∴ **Edvard Grieg's *Lyric Pieces, Book 1, Op. 12: Vekter-sang* played by Einar Steen-Nøkleberg.** ∵ ∴ *Watchman's Song.* ∵ Then it too is gone [Anwar with no recollection of when he turned it off {or ‹for that matter› drained his cup}].

Each time a new tempest swirls into a fugue of blacks [eventually] producing a curious flicker of white that [suddenly] moves through the concavity [or is it convexity?]. Sometimes it takes a few seconds to appear [other times several minutes]. Its appearance borders on a flash [what Anwar keeps failing to freeze {though stillness ‹he knows› will offer even less revelation ‹meaning residing in the flow between these curious lacunae «⟨⌈pale as a⌉?⌈shadow's absence⌉⟩ bounding across a curious storm»›}].

More hours slide by. Tiny groans from Freya and Shasti's room rise and fade. A chill [finally] drives off the clinging heat of summer. Darkness deepens its hold on silence. And then birdsong [before the sky has yet to give up a hint of color] announces dawn. Somewhere a dog barks. Soon the moan of the city's mechanical register joins this Wednesday's awakening.

Anwar [briefly] blames his and Astair's cannabis indulgence on the long night and [perhaps] his own prolonged awakening to what now seems obvious: without the ability to create the required socket [`mSocket ==` `INVALID_SOCKET` {not to mention accessing unavailable data streams from undisclosed sites}] the output can only reflect unpredictable values. Whether one can call that fun [or answer whether it does or does not play] Anwar cannot say. But it makes him smile.

∵ Isn't the spectre no more than a projection of the program itself?

[{another} hot cup of tea plus a {peanut butter and honey} sandwich in hand] Anwar seeks refuge out back and finds Xanther. It's not even 6 AM. She holds the cat against her chest. Her face looks clouded with doubt [pale too {‹again› faint?}]. Anwar resists feeling her forehead at once.

"Dad!" Xanther smiles. "Come see Levi!"

Here [{this} child] subject to inquiries about drugs [{mescaline ‹worse? «Astair divulging that such impossibles were possible»›}!] and sex [{sex? ‹she's twelve! «'Roxanne became "active" at a similar age.'» Xanther hasn't even had her period›?} !!] !!!

Just to behold her [{this ‹extraordinary›} child!]! What need does she have for [chemical {or other}] stimulations when to just race around their backyard [bright with a quiver of names {isn't a smile indication enough ‹of dopamine «flooding her mind»›?}] floods her face with joy?

'There's Chipadora Half-Ear!' Xanther points up at a tree branch [where a squirrel leaps away]. 'Heavy Handsome. A bit of a bully.' [Another squirrel {blonder ‹certainly heavier›}]. 'Alfred there holds her own. She has a hole in her left ear. Pancho has a black mole in his right ear. Can you guess why that one's called Opera?'

[high up] A slender squirrel chitters [endlessly] at [{sky} {leaves} {‹other› squirrels}] the whole tree [{suddenly}?] alive with a scattering of movements [how could Anwar have moved {so blindly!} below {without noticing all of these agile ‹very funny› creatures}?].

'What I call Opera's singing, Google calls barking.'
'You mean squirrels are tree dogs?'
Xanther giggles.
'I'll have to tell your mom she's had dogs all along.'

320

And that's not it.

Anwar didn't even know there was a humming-bird's home under the eave of their roof [built upon a wire of their outdoor lights].

'I call her Hero.' Xanther smiles.

Hero [beak held high] sits proudly in her tiny nest [well out of reach {even for Anwar ‹were he to even stand on a «patio» chair›}].

'She's sitting on two eggs.'

'You've looked inside?'

[faced with the {waxy ‹dark› green} leaves on the {small ‹potted›} tree] Anwar cannot [for the life of him] spy anything out of the ordinary. Xanther [though] points out [at once {‹«hanging» upside down› beneath a leaf}] the small— [{well} it's more like a long-finger length {of ‹pale› green}] —mantis.

'Levi! Isn't she beautiful? She's guarding mom's yuzu! Mom found her first!'

But Xanther's smile doesn't hold.

'Oh.'

'What is it, daughter?'

'I don't know. Who's this?'

On a lower branch [atop a leaf] a smaller mantis lies [pale white {‹too still› nothing but a shell}]. Anwar recalls something about the female praying mantis devouring the head of her male mate. Is this him?

'I've no idea what his name is,' Xanther frowns.

'Nature's a hard place,' Anwar answers [he could have done better than that {how often does he *not* do better? ‹like the squirrel he killed›}].

But Xanther skips away [now pointing out animals {that remain unseen ‹or once seen «here or over there»

321

by a hole beneath the brick wall to the south or the back fence «near where a strange door ⟨curtained in ivy⟩ remains permanently locked»}]:

'Randall the Raccoon comes by before dusk. Squander and Wander, two baby skunks, just scurried by. The crows there are Leonard, Ester, and Nora. Hear their codeling clicking marbles?' *Codeling!* Such blissful inventiveness.

[with so many names {so easily ⟨apparently⟩ on hand}] Anwar almost asks what makes the creature [held allways so carefully {against her chest}] so difficult to name?

Xanther's head turns back to Astair's yuzu tree. The dead mantis? Is that it?

⠒ *Mantis means prophet.* ⠒

⠒ Huh? ⠒

⠒ *Greek.* ⠒

⠒ **ERROR: Evolving corruptions.**
Retrace in progress. ⠒

Anwar should get some sleep [or he should get more work done on Cataplyst-3]. Instead he spends the rest of the day on something new. When he finally lies down [for a couple of hours {of zzzzzz's}] the new hangs favorably in his head.

[{maybe⟨?⟩} inspired by Xanther] Anwar had not turned to M.E.T. or even A.I.M. but to another aspect of PO/MOOWK:

Vision Module

[{since} *Paradise Open* would have supported {will support ‹ultimately›!} game play from the vantage point of numerous animals] Anwar had been experimenting with generating algorithmic 'lenses' which [when implemented] could reinterpret the digital urworld [of PO/MOOWK] according to certain qualities. What was that quote Astair [recently] read aloud? Something about a bubble around each creature ∴ **Jakob von Uexküll**∵ to capture its perceptions [its world]?

'You've read that to us before,' Xanther had remarked.

'No, I haven't,' Astair insisted.

'Then how come it's like familiar?'

'Maybe you just think it's familiar?'

'Huh. That's weird. And what if the bubbles, you know, merge? What kind of world does that make?'

'You mean if they touch?'

'Yeah.'

'Usually, if they touch, they just pop.'

The intention of the Vision Module [what Anwar considered calling V.E.R.I.F.Y. {though he couldn't figure out meanings for all the letters ‹some acronym «maybe V.E.R.I.T.Y. ⦅or something simpler⦆?»›}] was for it to be grand and fun. So far [however] the results amounted to colored filters and edges [with varying degrees of softness or crispness]. Hardly how a boar might see. Or a hyena. Or an owl. Or polar bear. Still amusing. Leading to

// thinking smiling dreaming

as Anwar slipped into those undisclosed thoughts that somehow result in rest.

That night [with Youssef Chahine ∴ *Died July 27, 2008* ∴ on his mind {for some reason}] Anwar puts on a DVD of *Alexandria . . . Why?* ∴ **1979** ∴ An excellent movie but not an excellent choice. Ten minutes in and the girls are fast asleep. Astair too. Anwar's riveted [along with {maybe} the blind kitten {at least it's facing the screen ‹perched on Xanther's chest›}]. Anwar's second choice is better: *The Sin of Harold Diddlebock* ∴ **1947** ∴ [Preston Sturges helming {Harold Lloyd on a bender ‹others «which ones?» too›}].

Thursday morning Anwar decides to hold off submitting Cataplyst-3 to Enzio [better {to take more time} to review his work {Astair is the same «‹Due Diligence!» Quality Control!›}}]. Anwar also knows Enzio [Savannah?] will likely not review anything he uploads until Monday [and {regardless} not submit anything to accounting {to order payment ‹direct deposit›} until the middle of next week]. Anwar might as well use tomorrow [and maybe even some of the weekend] to see if he can tease out any more functionality from that [{strange} whirl of] code.

So Anwar loads the kids into the Element and [after dropping Astair off at the clinic {she has clients all day}] heads to LACMA ∴ **Los Angeles County Museum of Art** ∴.

Anwar loves [what he and Astair call their] Cultural Field Trips.

MOCA [{downtown} Japanese food afterwards] is one. The Natural History Museum of Los Angeles [down by USC] is another. The Getty [Anwar still remembers Shasti's reaction to an illusionist ceiling piece ∴ **1622**∷ ∵ *"Musical Group on a Balcony"*∷ ∵ by Gerrit van Honthorst∷ {she had stood in the center of the atrium staring upwards ‹by turns amused and then awestruck «?»› ‹she even tried several times to leave «only to abruptly return again»»}: 'They're looking down on us,' Shasti finally confided. 'They're laughing too. I think they think we're funny.'

∵ HA! HA! HA! HA! Sorry couldn't resist. ∷

∴ :D ∵

∵ :o ∷
∵ :) ∷

{the painting had reminded Anwar of a Beatles album ‹two?› ∴ *1962–1966* **and** *1967–1970*∷ ∵ The Red Album *and*—∷ ∵ *The Blue Album*∷}].

'It's so sad,' Xanther says now.

Anwar glances at the still life. *Game Market* ∴ **1630s** ∴ ∴ *A meat market* ∴ by Frans Snyders ∴ **1579–1657** ∴. Plenty here [for Xanther {especially}] to be sad about: a wooden table loaded with the dead [{a goose}{a doe}{fowl of all sorts}] with more on hooks above [{‹gutted› rabbits}{a dead ‹and gutted› buck}]. Nearby stands a man holding a boar's head. Things get worse below the table [not counting the dead baby deer {that might as well be Bambi}]: a kitten [one of three] has a finch in its jaws while an adult tabby [beside his or her mate{?}] has seized the blue head of a peacock.

'She's going to die,' Xanther adds.

A twitch attacks the corner of Anwar's mouth [tickling up into his cheek].

'Who?'

'The fly.'

'There's a fly in this painting?'

Xanther points to the air. Nothing but a nearby movement [a guard approaching an {‹already› opening} door {closing it again}]. Except suggestion now makes of 'nothing' something else [a {faint} buzzing shaped into being {out of a room already resounding with the converse of passing museum patrons}]. Anwar catches sight of the flying spot [as it loops around them {once}] before landing on the canvas.

'Carissa keeps coming back, and like, uhm, do you think she really thinks it's something to eat?'

[again] The fly slips away [vibrating wings lost again to the room {only to reemerge moments later ‹landing again on the «bloody» ribs of the boar›}]. Maybe the oils offer some scent. A perception of nutrition.

'Why do you say "she," daughter?' [for that matter] Why Carissa?

They have lunch on a patch of lawn [by the Broad ∷ **The Broad Contemporary Art Museum** ∴]. Anwar packed sandwiches and waters [and bowls of figs and nuts and cheese]. All three girls are unusually quiet [twins and Xanther careful to interpose Anwar in-between {‹perhaps?› further ensuring this enduring ‹‹still›› unspoken› enmity}].

Xanther looks grey and depleted [defeated {‹hardly eating› mumbling ‹more than a few times «over the course of this ⟨out-and-about⟩ day»›: 'He's alone. He needs me. When can we go home?'‹What Anwar expects to hear now.›}].

'Can we check out the Tar Pits?' Xanther asks instead [surprising the twins too {who are ‹maybe?› just as surprised to also find themselves agreeing ‹maybe for the first time in a while?› with their sister}].

'Pretty grim,' Xanther remarks [circling the oily pond]. A large plastic mastodon [the mother] and calf wail for the father mastodon [sinking beneath the tar].

Freya and Shasti agree. Anwar too [wondering if Xanther's thinking of Dov {another patriarch ‹lost beneath an oily black coffin «though Dov was neither visible nor alive to hear the wails of his daughter ⟨Anwar had cried too ⌈if ⌈Astair⌉ the mother of Dov's daughter had not⌋ ⌈which now ⌈in this association⌉ somehow makes Anwar the mother mastodon⌋⟩»›} Anwar turning back to Xanther {as if ‹re›finding his daughter will rearrange this strange ‹parental› alignment}].

Except Xanther's nowhere near. The twins too have drifted away [faces as clenched as their tiny fingers {curling through the chain-link fence ‹stunned by the re-creation «of the pain and suffering» of extinct creatures›}].

Xanther [somehow] has already reached the entrance to the Page Museum [{insistently} waving at them all {like she's been trying to get their attention for a while}].

Had Anwar really drifted into his thoughts for that long? [It's a {disturbing} possibility.] Shouldn't he have [at least] sensed her moving away? Shouldn't her normally plodding steps [familiar missteps {wild ‹flailing› limbs}] have alerted him?

[unlike the Broad's rising blur of stairs {delivering you to the top floor ‹for candied Koons «and others»›}] The Page arrives at its ossuary by way of a ramped walkway slowly descending into an underworld of shadows and bone [less a welcome than a warning {a tomb fortified by concrete ‹and the truncated promise of a pyramid above›}].

'Of course, I don't mean to exclude . . . ' pauses the tour guide [{squat} with curly hair {and cheeks as bright as her jolly eyes}]. Does she wink at Anwar? Or at Xanther [who's been trailing this group a little while longer than Anwar {only just catching up ‹in time to hear of «Columbian» mammoths «Harlan's and Shasta» ground sloths «plus camels and dire wolves» wandering beneath arroyo willows and «Western» sycamores along with «Valley and Coast Live» oak trees and «'Of course!'» coast redwood and California dogwood›} Anwar catching his breath]?

'No,' the tour guide continues [a head shake for added {dramatic} effect]. 'I would never dream of excluding all of these familiar felids . . . ' [Arms opening up {hands swinging wide}.] 'What I like to call our dead-end cats. Our site here has yielded thousands of what tens of thousands of years concealed.'

Anwar tries to follow Xanther's gaze [towards all they are surrounded by {arranged numbered framed stacked counted categorized measured cleaned treated repaired photographed identified re-identified re-photographed named renamed treated and re-treated assembled disassembled reassembled . . . ‹the nature of this evidence «an instant torrent ⟨uttering an instant voice ⌈of once and no more⌋⟩»›}].

The tour guide eschews the general for the specific: in this case *Panthera atrox* [the {massive} American Lion {extinct 12,000 years ago}].

'Imagine our ancestral *Homo sapiens* confronting such a terror. Not even the atlatl, a lethal weapon capable of accelerating long darts up to speeds of nearly one hundred miles per hour, could serve as much of a match against such a predator.'

[as if scaring herself {as if words might reclothe these dark bones ‹with muscle and fur›}] The tour guide hastens away [her quick steps incentive enough to get the {yawning} group moving along {'This way . . . ' ‹with some commensurate swiftness too «or at least ⟨renewed⟩ alertness»›}]. Even Shasti and Freya file along [more earnestly {if yawning too ‹Anwar yawns as well›}] to the next stop: the museum's on-site research area [Paleontology Laboratory {on view behind thick plates of glass}].

Only Xanther hangs back.

Not even close to yawning.

Nearby several doors swing open. Why does the museum worker look surprised? Almost shocked.

Then the twins circle back [perhaps sensing the strength of Xanther's fascination {and are ‹just as quickly› transfixed ‹like her «like all of them»› by the delicately secured skeleton}].

Smilodon californicus.

Subspecies to *Smilodon fatalis.*

The saber-toothed tiger.

'Look at them!' Shasti squeaks [touching her own teeth].

'Pretty big,' Anwar agrees.

'This says it was like, uhm, smaller than a tiger, like one living today.'

Anwar joins Xanther at the plaque.

'Look at that. Though a present-day tiger can only open its jaws sixty-five degrees, this one could open its a hundred and twenty degrees.' Anwar demonstrates [with his hands] the difference between the two angles. 'I'd say that's a pretty big bite.'

'Would it eat me?' Freya asks [eyes going big {and flinching too ‹?› from Xanther‹?›}].

'I think it would eat all of us,' Anwar replies [with a smile].

'I'm still sad it went extinct,' Xanther sighs.

'What's "extinct" mean?' Shasti asks.

'When a species—' [Anwar explains] '—like a bird, for example, or a type of rhino, is ki— dies off and so can't reproduce and so no longer exists.'

'Can we go exstink?' Freya demands.

'We can. That's why we need to act responsibly towards one another and the world around us. Stranger to stranger. Friends to friends. Sisters to sisters.'

[Why not try for a teachable moment?]

'I don't know.' Freya fidgets [{so much for teachable} eyeing the dangerous creature of wire and bones {maybe amplifying it with ‹rippling› musculature and ‹hot› breath}]. 'Even its shadow is scary.'

'I'm getting goose pimples!' Shasti shrills.

Anwar can see what they mean [the shadow {for a moment} seems almost more alive than the bones].

Though it's not that shadow that makes him shudder.

331

Xanther's shadow lies there as well [among the ribs and those terrifying jaws]. The famous canines seem poised above her head [about to drive through her neck {‹or just the floor?› if imagination is given half a chance}]. Which still isn't what elicits Anwar's prevailing response.

Because what's to fear from shadows that act just as shadows?

It's the shadow that isn't a shadow that now slickens Anwar's body [a wave of dampness and chills {even as Xanther dissolves the vision ‹with a quick twist away and quicker steps «if still leaving Anwar with what he can't forget ⟨and ⌈still⌋ won't be able to tell Astair about later . . . ⟩» Xanther gone› taking with her the proof of stolen light}].

// too much shadow

// upon that floor

// not thrown by just bones either

// but by one frail shoulder

// in a pink t-shirt

// and something else . . .

//impossibly small

//impossibly more

//impossibly dark

// that too-familiar pyramid

// pierced by two impossible sparks

// afire with an impossibly dark red

// like two impossible eyes.

Sew

We do not walk alone,
Great Being walks beside us.

— Sevenka Qöyawayma

They had lived with the stickiness of Athens. Stickiness suited the situation. Finding it still clinging to them, however, as they drive north :: Georgia State Route 15 ::· feels like damnation. The damned believe only in the inescapable, which Cas knows on a good day doesn't apply, and on a bad day applies to everything, and on any day is just another truth she and Bobby will never outrun. The car has AC too. Mefisto gave them a Ford Focus with plenty of refrigerant under the hood. Bobby, though, reasoned that AC would increase gas consumption and necessitate more stops and therefore expose them to more eyes — retinal and digital.

So they drove with all the windows cracked, warm air tangling her hair, Cas tucking it away under a hat, before tying it up again, until the sweat on her face and the warmth knifing like a fever along her scalp forced her not to care.

Already behind them were places like Commerce and Homer. "The Devil's beating his wife," Bobby said as they passed through the first shower, sun up, heat owning the day. Cas started crying. And cried from then on with every shower.

Sunset wouldn't come until around 9 PM and night would likely hoard its clutch of warmth for hours more. Who was the Devil's wife?

"Chattahoochee National Forest," Bobby announces as a sign passes and more trees enfold them, canopies of green, the glow of moist bark. Rain falls again, breaking every promise of relief. There are rivers and streams here too. Cas cries more. Bobby lets her.

It's always for Chiron, Kaa, Duban. For Eli, Yuri, and
Jablom. For Merlin. For Deakin. But tears don't
name themselves that way. Tears know better than
to try to answer murder. If Cas were religious,
she would know God parched the earth for
Abel. Even Adam and Eve would know their
grief in dryness. The wife's leaving her God.

So Cas cries for Mefisto, her dear friend,
one last hug before letting him drift off
like a mischievous storm, hand in hand
with his rainbow girl. Cas cries for Marnie too. The kid had gotten deeper than
Cas would have thought possible, through
her touch, her commitment, the way she
faced — with that light-hearted smile — the
consequences of dangerous choices. Cas still
feels those generous hands upon her back, even
as they let each other go, under the roof of that
strange barn, byes on their lips, both their cheeks
wet for an unlikely reunion Cas pronounced as "Who
knows" and Marnie announced as

"Of course!"

Marnie then had waved goodbye to another midnight train rolling by, grinning like moonlight too: "Bobby! Did I ever tell you how I met Mefisto? He was on his hands and knees under a lamppost by some railroad tracks. 'What ya doing?' I asked. 'Looking for my keys,' he answered. 'You lost them here?' 'No. I lost them over there.' And he pointed to the dark, spooky side of the tracks. 'Then why are you looking for them here?' I asked. 'Because the light's better.'"

Bobby loved the joke.
to miss Marnie
them, Bobby
sonal resolves.
wanted to
ton for the
s c o p e .
their next
h a v e n ' t
years. You
old friends
by date."
to go straight

He was another reason
and Mefisto. Without
darkened into per-
He slept less. He
return to Day-
electron micro-
He feared
step: "We
seen Sew in
know, Cas,
have an expire-
Bobby wanted
to the Arsenal.

It took everything Cas had to keep him from deviating from their plan. She probably would have failed too, if she could have escaped into Mefisto's Orb. For a month now, Cas hasn't scried. She feels clean. A terrifying thing to admit. She feels restored and open. Her thoughts still move laterally but without losing an awareness of where she is and whom she's with. She smiles more. She can cry.

In a town called Tiger, Bobby pulls up in front of Goats on the Roof ∴ **3026 US-441** ∴. The name plus a sign for nitro ice cream are irresistible. Maybe it's lucky that the place had closed an hour earlier. They shouldn't be stopping for anything. Especially for ice cream or goats on a roof. Bobby eases the Focus back onto the road, back to listening to Bruce Springsteen's *Magic* over and over.

Soon they're passing through Mountain City and Dillard. Then into North Carolina. But near Sylva, Cas has to dissuade Bobby from taking Route 74 east. Past Cherokee they risk getting more gas. Small towns are less dangerous. Big cities can afford surveillance. Cas stays in the car. Braces are memorable.

Though it seems a small thing, Cas admires how Bobby sticks to 2 MPH under the speed limit. She knows he'd prefer a motorcycle flying along the edge of a ticket zone. But just getting pulled over now could mean something awful. They'd immediately be registered in law enforcement databases. Cas and Bobby do not have fake IDs. Mefisto did not produce flawless counterfeits of U.S. passports. And even if they were let off with a warning, Recluse would too soon know this car, and have their whereabouts. Cas also can't forget that for all the Orb means to her, to the world at large, to any prosecuting agency, it will be identified first and foremost as an explosive device.

By the time they reach Knoxville, the sky is bruised. Now the only sun in the sky is man-made: the Sunsphere. This loop is a detour but Bobby wants to make sure they aren't followed.

"Could get a helluva signal up there."

Sew ∴ Like sew buttons ∴ greets them at the door. His grin and the drinks he imme-diately presses into their hands — big glasses of sweet tea stuffed with mint — show nothing has expired. His wife, Mary, is with the kids in Minnesota but will be flying back tomorrow.

"Timing couldn't be better!" He claps his hands, going in search of some small-batch bourbon to refill Bobby's glass.

Cas takes a bath. She locks the door but only so Bobby knows she's serious about not needing his help. She lays her braces out beside the Orb and reheats the water as little as possible. She loves the old faucet, the kind with *H* blue-etched into cracked porcelain. But more than the way running water can drown out the worst, Cas loves hearing Bobby laughing downstairs.

Bobby knew Sew long before Cas came into the picture. They were high school friends out on Long Island. Sew loved cello and basketball. Bobby loved science and fiction. Back then neither knew love would hold each of them to one of those teenage passions. For a few years, Sew practically lived at the Sterns. The way Bobby tells it, Sew was so welcome, Bobby felt like he was the friend at the dinner table.

Cas met Sew for the first time at Bobby's mother's funeral, and the
second time at Bobby's   father's funeral a few
weeks later. Bobby   knew the meaning
of paired in a way   Cas   realized
she could never   understand,
even   if   she   a c c e p t e d
now that she   was part of
one.

Sew   was   paired too
— with his   cello. Cas
can't remem-   ber   him
without it. Even   at the funer-
als. Even in the   midst of his
third divorce, drag-   ging it around
Reno. And he never   seemed   unhappy,
with that long blade of a nose   making of every smile an
anchor. "She can take the house, the kids, my mom's silver, I don't care, so long as I have my cello." And she had, and Sew really didn't care.

He just loved to play, whether in a motel room, park, a friend's living room, or the scores of concert halls he toured regularly every year.

Once, while strolling with Bobby across Old Campus at Yale, Sew had stopped among the fallen leaves, near a statue of Nathan Hale, and right there opened his cello case. Sew was completing a residency, Bobby and Cas were running, though nothing like now. The extent of the VEM burden had only just started to exert its poisonous influence, altering character "by sheer prurient power" as ██████ was already fond of saying. Bobby had been trying to explain some aspects of information theory without exposing Sew to the purpose. "I get it!" Sew had cried, and to demonstrate played something by Brahms ⸪ *Double Concerto in A minor, Op. 102: I. Allegro* ⸪. Neither Cas nor Bobby understood the connection, but Sew had played beautifully. Maybe beauty does grant knowledge without understanding. They had all ended up laughing at squirrels at play in the trees. Much later, Cas discovered the relief that comes from trusting that someone doesn't have to know what you know to still love you. Even if that question still haunted her: if knowledge and love are independent, how can love be authentic?

In the morning, Cas meets Mary for the first time. She's Sew's fourth wife and, not surprisingly, much younger. Elijah and Noah were born when Sew was already in his sixties. Both boys are around ten and can barely manage a hello, though Mary sees that they make the effort, along with asking some question out of courtesy: "How long are you here for?" Which Cas has just started to answer when they're already off, racing down to the basement.

"*Minecraft!*" Mary smiles. She's a big woman, with bundles of brown hair, and a voice large enough to fill an opera house. "Might have filled one too," she admits a moment later, "if I'd stuck it out. Sew picked me up in a pool hall." Bobby had already warned Cas that Mary likes to bring up her Wiccan ways a lot. If only she knew.

"I'm sorry?"

"That game every kid's obsessed with. I'm hoping by next year, it's last year's fad."

Ah. *Mindcraft*. Cas had misheard.

"Sew has his music. He doesn't keep up with online stuff. But the boys game and I Etsy. I've installed the fastest lines you can get here in Knoxville. Maybe one day we'll get Google Fiber like in Provo, Utah. The WiFi password is easy: all caps, one word, CELLODUDE."

Just the mention of WiFi twitches the knife in Cas' hand. She is helping Mary slice peaches. She scans the wedges of fruit for signs of blood.

All Cas has to do is excuse herself, and in moments she'll be scrying. Mefisto already swore his Orb was impossible to trace. Yet just thinking about Recluse in relation to this family makes even the most negligible risk unconscionable. Bad enough to be spending the night with such innocents.

Cas resumes her fruit duties, hazily following Mary's woes about product photography and "uploading images." To supplement their income, Mary makes puppet mittens based on famous operas.

Bobby's afternoon goes to taking a tour of the university with Sew. Cas spends the afternoon cursing the simplicity of Mary's WiFi password. The Orb never ceases its temptations, or threats, even when Cas naps. At least her dreams go beyond reckoning. Cas keeps the Orb covered. When she does uncover it, if just to let her eyes glide along the inky stillness, the death it holds out for her keeps promising allways that Death is a lie.

Before dinner, Bobby brings up Mefisto's parting request to scry a list of data points concerning a company called Galvadyne.

"I don't think this is the place for that."

Bobby agrees. He also admits that while Sew was at a rehearsal, Bobby had used the university wireless.

"Before any 'Appomattox Redux' meet-up happens, I've requested a video face-to-face. It'll take some time and a lot of help to secure, but I want more than some open-source onion router relaying what you both have to say."

"Me talk to Recluse?"

"You know I can't."

That night Mary brings out to the table skillet after cast-iron skillet, one filled with charred broccolini and caramelized shallots, another bubbling with polenta, blueberry, and duck breast, still another with rafts of crisping sliced potatoes unsteady in the amount of cheese on which they float. The wine is fine. The peach cobbler sublime. In fact, the meal is so good, Cas implores Mary to bring out her sock puppets. They are a delight. Especially Brünnhilde.

After dinner, Sew brings out his cello and plays for them. The piece is by Ranjbaran ∷ *Elegy for Cello and Strings* ∷. Elijah and Noah, both cross-legged, sit transfixed at their father's feet. Only candles pixilate the air. Mary sways in the doorway. Cas manages to find a breath in no need of vision. Bobby surprises her the most. Tears streak his cheeks.

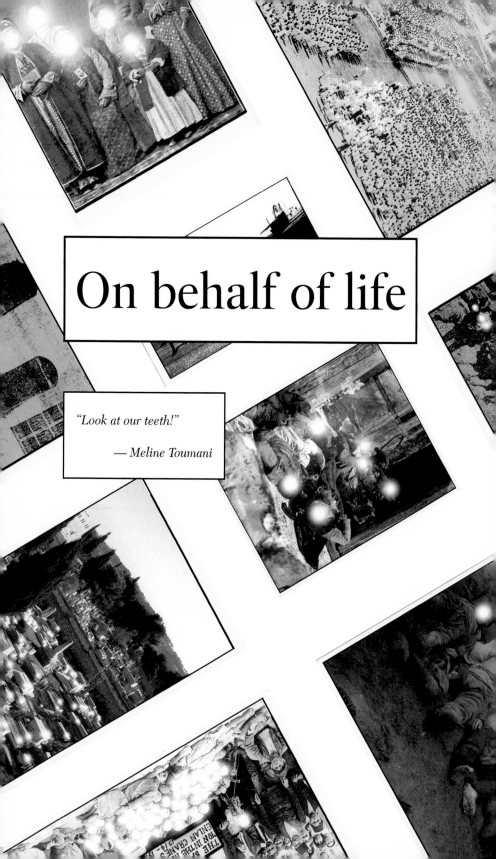

On behalf of life

"Look at our teeth!"

— *Meline Toumani*

"Driving is as much about patience as impatience," Shnorhk continues, places next page before burning bar. "Too many behind wheel not recognize this. Impatience, yes, that part obvious. Car's purpose is to reduce time between points."

"My taxi driver philosopher." Mnatsagan smiles, pacing outside in hall. Office too small for both of them. Shields eyes too every time office fill with fire that does not diminish all it takes.

"Patience is less obvious," Shnorhk go on, next page, tap button. Shnorhk never close scanner lid. "Taxi driving teach this. In speed there is stillness. In travel there is roots. And this not the yahyahyah journey is yahyahyah destination. No. Journey is as much about transit which is contact as it is about immunity which is silence. Without silence no one can hear. And every great driver knows you cannot go where you do not listen. And where you have gone already and not listened you have not been."

"I can't wait to read the book!"

Shnorhk snort. Shnorhk never write such book. Can't remember last time he read book. Closest he come is this scanning machine here reading these sad stories. Shnorhk make mistake earlier and read this:

Երիտասարդ Թուրքը երեխայի մարմինը այնքան կրակեց մինչեւ ես Հաւատացիմ որ փամփուշտերը ծախսում էր մահացածի վրա որպեսզի խնայեր ողջերին։ Սա ես Համոզված էի, չնայած կարող էի տեսնել տուփեր լիքը փամփուշտերով։

Shnorhk borrowed scanner, cables, and video players from Hov-ahn ∴ Patil's brother ∴. Reel-to-reel Mnatsagan borrow from university. Shnorhk have no problem working out connections or programs. The rest is process: scan page after page while mute audio cassettes rolled through A-side and then B-side. On second computer Hi-8s roll through to end.

All afternoon long Shnorhk worked with Mnatsagan on box. Just one. Eighty-one testimonies, eyewitnesses every one to atrocities no machine ever understand. Such work worse than waiting in cab. Repetition without relief. Even Mnatsagan began saying they should stop for day, finish box another day, but Shnorhk persisted.

It felt good. To keep promise like this. Shnorhk even buy for Mnatsagan extra drives to store more digitized material to send to University of Minnesota.

Last page Shnorhk grateful to watch light take away last trace, ungrateful to catch page afterwards:

Ինչ սարսափ, որ հասկացանք մենք շնորհակալ էինք ցուրտին, որ մեզ փրկի մահացածների հոտից:

Shnorhk organize files then, one folder for each account, with nested folders by kind: audio, video, pdfs. Many gigabytes. Shnorhk start backup.

They reach Carousel at 10 PM. Mnatsagan know too many for kitchen to not make exception. Gets favorite table too. Makes clear this is his treat. Paying not Shnorhk's problem but Shnorhk accept.

They order labneh khaliji and muhammara and for main courses ful mudammas and khash-khash kebab with pickled turnips. Shnorhk order fattoush salad too. Meal is good. But what makes meal even better is that old professor not bring up Shnorhk's cough or music night with lads or his English speaking or things far worse.

Things? Shnorhk cough hard into napkin.

Mnatsagan just tell story about how as boy when he would practice violin the birds would come around.

"Maybe there were always birds or maybe there were birds when I arrived and more birds flew away when I picked up my bow. But whatever the case, when I practiced I seemed to notice more. And the more I noticed the birds the more I played for the birds. Perhaps then the way I stood changed, the way I breathed changed, the tempo too, and volume of course, not to mention all the phrasings I exchanged with the day. No question then, more birds came."

"They were responding to your music?" Shnorhk ask, mopping at mouth with napkin, drinking more tea, suddenly wanting wine.

"Of course." Mnatsagan wink. "What else should a young man think? I practiced longer, harder. I was Orpheus in the forest. Listening to the forest was easy. Much harder was listening to my mother."

"Your mother?"

"She knew what I thought and only years later confessed to scattering birdseed in the garden to keep me out there practicing longer."

"So it birdseed not birds made a player out of Mnatsagan?" Shnorhk laugh.

"Both."

"And mother."

"Yes. Mother most."

Saturday morning Shnorhk return to Mnatsagan. Sleep was cruel. Dreams crueler. He walked in a forest where no birds sang or flew.

He recheck Mnatsagan's backups, then pack up box, seal with extra tape, and then drive with professor to post office.

There is line. Shnorhk expect long wait but today line vanish like morning mist summer is committed to. Clerk process payment fast, hands Mnatsagan tracking number, and frees them to the day.

On the way back, Mnatsagan ask about ceramic cat on passenger seat. Shnorhk tell story about Japanese businessman. How it was left on seat. Shnorhk had returned to airport and paged name on credit card receipt but no one responded. Shnorhk left new business card with some official there who would not take more because what was not lost and found in airport was not found or lost.

"I believe it is supposed to bring good fortune," Mnatsagan say.

Shnorhk snort. No amount of good luck will ever matter to Shnorhk. All the more reason to get rid of thing.

"The Japanese call it maneki neko," Mnatsagan continue. "Chinese too have their version of the lucky cat."

"Then I give it to one of them. How bad they drive they need all the help they can get."

"Are you serious?" Mnatsagan ask, bright with curiosity.

"All Orientals. Terrible drivers."

"Asians, Shnorhk. 'Oriental' is a rebarbative term. Best left to lamp shades and rugs."

"Fine. Asians. Asians still terrible drivers."

"Of course, Armenia is part of Asia."

"Agh, you joke now, Mnatsagan. You joke."

"What other culturally disparate groups do you consider poor drivers?"

Shnorhk no fool. Shnorhk catch cunning in Mnatsagan's question. Even the way old man lean forward in seat speaks of calculation.

"Jews," Shnorhk answer anyway. Mnatsagan can calculate till moon still. Shnorhk not care. Moon will never still. "Hasids are worst."

"How do you know that?"

"Drive La Brea and Beverly. You'll see. Russians too. Fairfax and Melrose."

"Asians. Jews. Eastern Europeans," Mnatsagan say slowly without settling back in seat. "If we can assume your observations have any validity, and as a seasoned driver in this city I know you have experience, what do all these groups have in common that might account for poor behavior behind the wheel?"

Shnorhk wish Mnatsagan's home was closer. Traffic crowding Western ∴ Avenue ∴ now keeps them still ten minutes away.

Maybe Shwanika put call out on radio. Radio not even on. Shnorhk can turn radio on. At least change subject. Shnorhk cough instead. More bitterness cupped in palm.

Mnatsagan's gentle touch on his shoulder remind Shnorhk then that no matter what his point, if instructive or just inquisitive, old professor is always kind.

"I don't know," Shnorhk sputters. "Do you?"

"I don't." Old professor laughs, falling back. "I barely drive at all. And as far as the driving goes among the musicians willing to give me rides, I detect no disparity between one type or another. Drummers and violists aside."

Shnorhk laugh, merry again. Musicians come in all kind. And Mnatsagan's group, These Affictions, no exception. Alonzo: Mexican. Haruki: Japanese and Chinese.

Tzadik: Polack. Or is it Jew? Dimi: Ruskie. Kindo: Black. Or is it Afro-American? African-American? Even if Kindo's family from Trinidad? Shnorhk ask Kindo next time they play. Even if Shnorhk won't play.

Shnorhk cough again.

Wipe palm on leg.

Almost there. Quick lane change. Then through intersection east of Western. Then left.

"I'm curious," old professor speaks up again. "What would you estimate is the age of these bad drivers? On average?"

"All ages. Maybe more on old side."

"How old on old side?"

"Fifties. And my age. In sixties."

"My age?"

"Young seventies. Yes."

"Young seventies! I like that!"

"But forties too."

"But not much younger?"

"Not much."

"Perhaps because the younger ones grew up here?"

Okay. Yes. Shnorhk sees this. Obvious: better drivers drive here, so grow up driving here, drive better.

Shnorhk restate then this obvious. But Mnatsagan not so convinced by obvious.

"Possibly. Then is what you're reporting, if it is statistical and not merely anecdotal, just a matter of cultural exposure and experience or is there something else at work? Perhaps more crucial? For example, what about language?"

Shnorhk pull up in front of old professor's little house, lost again.

"How would you rate the skills of older Armenian drivers?"

"Armenian drivers best drivers in world," Shnorhk snap.

Mnatsagan does not get out of taxi. He waits out what is no question, just another obvious, until Shnorhk sag with reconsideration.

"Okay, yes, old Armenian drivers not drive so perfect."

"No, not perfect. Even their English isn't perfect."

"Isn't perfect?!" Shnorhk snort again. "Their English is terrible!"

"And what of our Hasids? How is their English?"

"Different."

"Russians?"

"Not perfect either."

"Koreans?"

"Same."

"Thai? Chinese? Vietnamese?"

"Yes, yes, yes. Same, same, same."

Where is this going? But old Mnatsagan gets out car then, stretches, and strolls away. Only at front door he stop and wait for Shnorhk.

Inside, while filling glasses with ice, Mnatsagan bring subject up again. This why he is esteemed professor: never let subject drop.

"Traffic?" Shnorhk ask. Maybe he mishear.

Mnatsagan nods like nod is explanation.

"Traffic jam is Armenian?"

Mnatsagan laugh. "No. I asked if we could call traffic a language?"

"Yes," Shnorhk answer, slowly, like he still catching up with Mnatsagan's thoughts. "With own rules."

"Particular to a place?"

"Obvious. Of course."

"Now what in particular is particular to this place?"

Not even buttery cake will save this talking. Shnorhk still eat two. Where does professor get them?

"English?" Mnatsagan prompts.

"Yes. Okay. Another obvious. Though English or no English, Left Turn is its own language. And particular maybe to Los Angeles too."

Shnorhk wipe mouth of crumbs. More cakes wait. If something about cake makes inside of him ache.

"This then is what I wonder,"

Mnatsagan say, to Shnorhk of course, but also to himself. "Might fluency in English also determine the fluency in traffic?"

Shnorhk sip iced drink. First taste burst alive in mouth. Like drinking candy bar. Second sip not so sweet. Better.

"You like?" Mnatsagan's eyes wide with obvious delight over Shnorhk's delight.

"What is this?"

"Banana and apple, rooibos and pink peppercorn. It's called Chocolate Monkey."

"I must tell Patil."

"Bring her some," Mnatsagan insist, handing Shnorhk whole tin.

"The conclusion then," Shnorhk say, still sipping this Chocolate Monkey, "the better one speak English the better one drive?"

"Is there such a thing as English traffic?"

"I hear driving in Idaho is terrible. They speak English there."

"Do they?"

"And my English, not so good."

"And your driving?"

Shnorhk's face blaze. This is thanks? For all his help? For his driving? Shnorhk want to spit out drink then. Cover floor with monkey.

"My friend! It is just a question!" Mnatsagan puts arm on Shnorhk's shoulder. With other hand pats Shnorhk's chest. It is good hand, it is good arm, here is good man.

Shnorhk follows good man to back of house again. Again Shnorhk work in small office with small barred window. Again good man pace hall.

It feels good to work on next box. Enough talk of traffic, of language, of driving. Just scan one page after another. One side, then flip side. Let light find what it finds. Shnorhk just move through pile.

"Voices," Mnatsagan say later, sigh, another wand of burning light slashing the small office, his face.

"Voices?" Shnorhk ask, darkness falling next.

"So many too. Each speaking out on a collective trauma. My task: to honor them without being misled by anger in the name of righteousness, hurt in the name of earnestness. I must distinguish between public truths and the private language of survival. I must balance the outrage that comes with assumptions against indifference that comes from ignorance. And through it all never forget the most humanitarian question of all: how to confirm and address what is a communal history without at the same time forfeiting the individuality which no group ever has the right to lay hold of and reduce."

Shnorhk nod. "This, what you say, I don't understand." Nodding still more.

"I don't either." Old Mnatsagan smile, shaking his head too, now just a shadow leaving a doorway, almost too frail to let go of and somehow already beyond recovery.

It frighten Shnorhk . . .

Later, before leaving for the night, Shnorhk promise to return tomorrow to finish this box, only half done, and maybe finish another, and then come back on Monday too to drive finished boxes to post office.

On porch, Mnatsagan kiss Shnorhk on both cheeks.

"I've spent a lifetime, my good friend, trying to learn how to see well. To part the veil. To grandly stare upon bleak truths. Please forgive me for impugning earlier your always excellent driving. Perhaps you might spare some sympathy for me too. Imagine, if you take so personally your own driving, how personally I must take my failure to drive altogether, not to mention my amateur violin playing—" hand already up to prevent protest "—and my overall unworthiness to steward such an important project. But how can I perceive anything precisely if I fail to account for my own flaws? I am necessarily hard on myself if unnecessarily hard on others."

Shnorhk wave off talk of unworthiness. Frail man is saint.

"How well we see beyond ourselves depends first on how well we see ourselves. And seeing well I am coming to believe has less to do with what our eyes demonstrate on behalf of light and more to do with what our words compose on behalf of life. Though even so, while language is the greatest meaning of the world, it will never be the meaning of the world."

Mnatsagan takes deep breath. Falls into silence.

"Please." Shnorhk coughs. "Finish what this is on your mind."

"I respect why you refuse to speak Armenian despite speaking it so blissfully."

Wait. Maybe best if Mnatsagan not speak. Shnorhk raise hand to prevent old friend's mistake.

But Mnatsagan ignore lifted hand.

"One favor?" old professor whisper, with no smile, no familiar touch, eyes wet with the labor of asking.

"These voices I live with are the burden of the grave. You know what I mean. I miss your melodies. Your playing restores me. If not for her, then will you spare just a few notes for me? Even one note would do."

MI

I ask the impossible.

— Ana Castillo

Flicking stones is a lot like counting sheep but like without the sheep or the sleep, or even the counting, so maybe more like flipping cards, though Xanther's never really played much with cards, or like those old calendars grandma gave the Ibrahims one year, cardboard things with little doors you peel back for chocolates, one for each day in December, the chocolates getting bigger the closer you get to Christmas Day, which definitely has the biggest chocolate, not that Xanther can eat any of it, and anyway the twins opened all the doors at once, like around Thanksgiving too. They even ate Xanther's chocolates. So much for the Advent calendars, that's right, Advent, as in arrival, arrival of the 25th?, or maybe something else? Not that Astair or Anwar were mad, since no one in the family thinks of Christmas as anything more than a decorated tree with lights and some presents beneath, and so Xanther wasn't mad either, just amused by all these little paper doors, open to little paper boxes, empty.

This bluish stuff Xanther keeps discovering beneath the stones is a lot like empty too. Like a still-opening sky that's no sky at all. Because any sky is more full than this. Really more turquoise too, with all that confusion of green. ∴ *Old French* pierre turqueise.∵ ∴ Pierre?∵ About as edible too as the stone covering it. But each flip still promises satisfaction. And even if it all feels far, far away, Xanther enjoys the escape. The forest is always there. It's curious too, because the little one sure never joins her, and yet Xanther almost feels closest to him when she's roaming those snowy paths beneath stranger pines, forever flicking stones hiding skies that leave her hungry. Now and then, though, Xanther finds a bruised one and lingers over it. She can revisit at any time too, as if the promise of this possible future somehow marks a map Xanther doesn't need to consult because she already embodies it. Some bruises heal, return to sky and vanish. Others, though, darken, as if, like pale pomegranates, they might ripen enough to fall, to seize?

After the morning feeding, which never feels like a feeding, like last night's sleep didn't feel like sleeping, though Xanther doesn't feel tired, or even hungry for breakfast, like her little friend doesn't seem interested in the canned wet food, or his water bowl, just sniffing both before lurching away unsteadily, finally stopping next to the washing machine and a long line of ants.

"Home invasion," Anwar sighs, squatting down next to Xanther, who can only nod, swallowing hard, because for some reason this sight has filled her mouth with saliva, though moments ago it felt like nothing but syllables ∴ ? ∵ ∴ *A new Adam rising . . .* ∴, caressing each little insect with a specificity all its own, an individuality to tend and clean as carefully as each tiny antenna, and all Xanther would have to do is open her mouth and set them free. Imagine that! A name for every ant, hundreds too!, and Xanther for the life of her still can't come up with just one for the little white pyramid at her knees, tail curled around its front paws, eyes pinched shut.

What stops that pronouncement isn't Anwar's arrival but an equally sudden impulse to crush them all too, appalling Xanther with the sudden rush, to make a nameless smear out of this intrusion, which sickens her as well as tingles her lips with shame, drool starting to lay siege to the corner of her lips, all she cannot swallow.

"How about we try to talk to them?" Anwar suggests.

"Really?" Xanther drags the back of her arm over her mouth.

"If we can figure out a common language."

The kitten, or like little-old cat?, lifts a paw to chew on invisible claws.

"Okay?" Xanther keen to understand, her mouth at once returning to bone dry.

"Let's say this little army is organized according to one particular form of communication directing its path here. How do we encourage an alternate direction?"

"Change the communication?"

"Very good."

"But what's—"

"Precisely, daughter: *what's* the communication? Not words as we know them. Or any sound we can produce. Certainly chemical but too complex for you and me to synthesize. How then to have this dialogue?"

"Uhm."

"Try considering what they pursue."

Duh! The ants are swarming around a small mound of errant kitten food. Soon enough they will discover the full bowl.

"If we, uhm, take away the food, then, uhm, like the ants will tell each other that there's no reason to come here?"

"That's the theory." Anwar whisks away both dishes to the kitchen sink, while Xanther cleans the floor of all bits of food, blowing free any ants climbing on her fingertips.

An hour later the ants are gone. No names needed, no smearing. Xanther checks the back door. Nothing there either. The ants got the message.

They all went home.

Later, Xanther finds Anwar playing the piano.

"The much maligned Puccini. Italian composer of many an enchanting aria. Late nineteenth century. The musical *Rent* ∴ **1996** ∵, which you might have heard of, was based on his *La Bohème* ∴ **1896** ∵ ."

"Aria?" Xanther asks, sorry to have made him stop.

"Song." And he smiles so softly Xanther suddenly bursts into gobby tears.

Anwar moves to her like fire.

"Daughter, what's the matter? Talk to me, please." Already on his knees, wrapping her up in his long dark arms. How she wants to too, spit it all out, saliva, names, the game of flicking stones in her head, the taste she craves but cannot name.

"You're just so cool," she finally sputters.

Her friends come over Monday afternoon to snack, game, and hang out, which always seems to please Les Parents, even if Anwar gives Kle a stern look after reading the phrase on his t-shirt:

i forgot my safe word

"What does that even mean?" Cogs asks, once they've settled in the den, input selected, Xbox on, PS4 on, laptops and towers on.

"I don't know," Kle shrugs, letting his backpack drop beside one of the recliners. "Ask your mom."

"Are you wearing mascara?" Cogs is immune to Kle's mom jokes.

"Why I love summer." Kle is immune to Cogs' fashion jokes.

Xanther doesn't get Kle's t-shirt either, but grinds back the usual slew of questions, at least for now, because what she really wants to do is tell them what's going on, which should be easy, since they're her friends, and she trusts them, I mean she trusted them with her epilepsy, and this is nothing like that, though it's still hard, and like where to start, and why did Dendish call her Twitch? How did he find out? Which she doesn't want to consider. It's easier to just kick back with the little one in her lap, and play.

For starters: *The Last of Us.* Xanther doesn't love fps ∷ First-person shooters ∷ but she'll go along.

"Is he eating now?" Cogsworth asks later. "He looks a lot better."

"Yeah," Xanther lies, already hating herself, because, like, wasn't that the perfect chance to start the convo?

"Given him a name yet?" Mayumi chimes in.

"Having the hardest time." At least that's true. And at least that confession starts something good.

For like an hour, they come up with lists of names, Xanther throwing in Aria and Puccini, Josh likes Westerly and Ticket, Mayumi prefers Mochi, Kle wants Bundy.

Josh is trying out *The Path* ∷ **2009** ∷ when Anwar brings in a pitcher of lemonade, which Xanther could have some of, because it's made with cinnamon, chia seeds, and just a little honey, none of which she really wants.

"I forgot about this one," Anwar says of the game, as he lays out glasses and bowls of nuts.

"It's okay." Josh shrugs.

"Farrokh, are you playing too?" ∷ *A story for later.* ∷ ∷ I know the story but, huh, how did I hear but not say "for later"? ∷

Kle shakes his head: "No, Mr. Ibrahim. A new enlightenment in the works." *Enlightenment Series* pad in hand.

"Shareable?" Anwar knows Kle has a taste for what Astair describes as "Goth" which, when Xanther passed that along, made Kle happy for weeks.

"I guess. This one's called *Air, #7*. Pretty simple. What if air was really these tiny very aware creatures, able to think, and feel, and like, you know, capable of love and grief? It works for water too but I think I like air better. What would we do? I mean it means we're killing something every single time we take a breath? Does that mean our survival makes murder okay?"

"I will hazard a guess that the way you characterize air's demise requires copious amounts of blood splatters?"

"Hellz yeah!"

"Then fortunately for all of us, we will take solace in the fact that air does not bleed."

This too is like the perfect place to bring up what Xanther saw the night she wandered into the street and nearly got run over by that truck. It's what's really eating her up inside, even if it's also why she feels a little better, plus the crazy part, that, like what had happened in her head seems to have made the little one better too, which Cogs just confirmed, which, really, makes everything a lot worse, which Xanther should really tell everyone about, but then Astair walks in.

Astair seems stiffer than usual, like only doing what she feels she should be doing, as the mom of the house, like trying to be jokey when she's really just checking up on everyone. At least she gets along with Cogs.

"And what's your latest conquest, Sir Cogsworth?"

"School's out, Mrs. Ibrahim."

Cogs is never far from a chapter book. Xanther struggles to read. She can't come close to Cogsworth's speed and intensity. Mayumi's fast too but even she admits Cogs like speed skates through text.

"Hand it over." Astair knows better.

Cogsworth doesn't disappoint.

"*Gilgamesh*! Really? Do you understand it?" Which she asks every time.

"Not a word." Which is how he answers every time.

"Who gave it to you?"

"You know, Mrs. Ibrahim."

"I just want to hear it. I laugh every time."

Cogs smiles, lowering his bright brown eyes, eyes that Xanther swears can sometimes seem like a hundred years old, in that soft way that's a good way.

"My drug dealer gave it to me."

As promised, Astair laughs. Xanther tries not to roll her eyes, which maybe Astair catches a hint of, because her laugh seems to strain suddenly, and come up short, before she smiles awkwardly at Xanther, and maybe at the cat on her shoulder, before heading off to see her afternoon clients.

Later, when they put *TrOUT* on, Xanther beats everyone, which is kinda strange because the last time she played, it was an epic fail. Anwar killed her ∷ **TFv2 p. 764**∵. She couldn't handle the net, forget the spear, and now she's grabbing fish with her hands ∷ **TFv1 p. 342**∵.

Everyone accused her of practicing lots beforehand, which she lied about, admitting she had, even if Cogsworth gave her a look that Xanther knew meant *Limbo* ∷ **TFv2 p. 772**∵, and how she had gone through that so fast, having never practiced.

Anyway, Xanther hands over the controller to let Josh "practice" more, and as the little one wanders out of the den, on one of his rare forays into the house, Xanther settles back into their black faux-leather couch, not even realizing that she's already flicking stones again, or returning to those uncovered eyes now floating in a red possibility that waters her mouth.

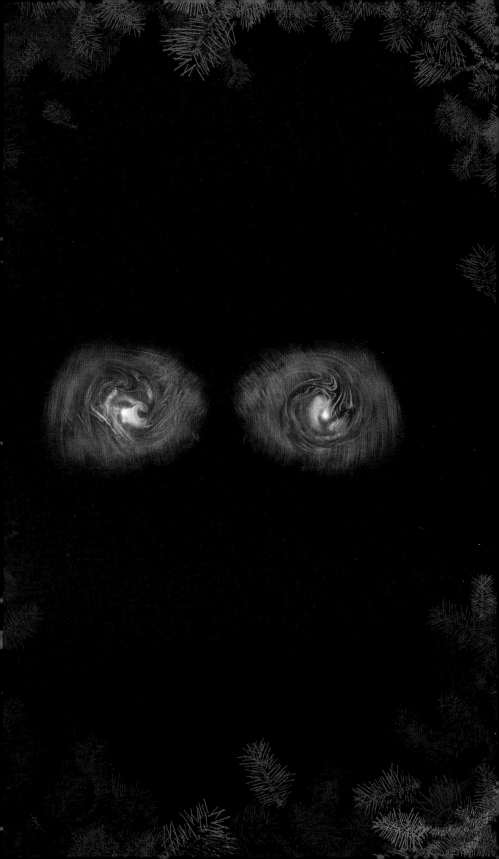

"I watched this show with my dad," Josh says at some point. "My dad is so weird. It was called *MS-13: World's Most Dangerous Gang*. Talk about rough. They're in L.A. Most members are from El Salvador. Actually, they formed in L.A. A lot were arrested and sent back to El Salvador. And then they ended up organizing there and coming back even meaner. They're all covered in tattoos. A lot have their faces covered too. Scary dudes."

"Why MS-13?" Xanther asks.

"MS can mean a lot of things," Kle says.

"Thirteen too," Mayumi adds. She's improving with the spear.

"Well, for them MS means Mara Salvatrucha. And guess what Salvatrucha has to do with?"

"Something to do with Salvador?" Cogs guesses.

"Why would someone tattoo their face?" Kle asks.

"*Trucha* means 'trout.' How about that for weird? To name yourself after a fish?"

"Are you sure that's true?" Cogs asks.

"Maybe 'trout' means 'smart'?" Josh admits he's guessing.

"You think your kitty there likes trout?" Kle nods at the white wobble returning to the den.

"Is something wrong with his eyes?" Mayumi asks. "They're always shut."

"We're starting to think he might be blind," Xanther answers, even if this also feels like a lie.

She never even brings up the glass wolves or her sisters. Lies of omission. Lies, lies, lies.

"Hey Mom, when's my next visit with Dr. Potts?" Xanther asks on Tuesday, because if she can't talk to her friends, or Les Parents, he's about her only chance to get some of this out.

"Soon! He's still on vacation. Even therapists, uhm, need breaks sometimes."

Astair never uhms.

Weirdness with her mom doesn't stop there. Wednesday is punishment day, the day Xanther's stuck at home while her friends go to Magic Mountain, and Astair apologizes.

Morning was the uzhe, quiet until around noon, and then Xanther's phone had started blowing up, text after text, just *dringadrong dringadrong*.

Cogs: we miss u

Kle: 2 many 2long lines

Mayumi: so hot.

X: take pics

Kle: of cogs doing the vomit

Cogs: colossus waits for u kle

Josh: wont lie X - its pretty sick here

X:

Kle: miss us. i mean u. hahaha.

Mayumi: seriously hot!!!

Cogs: at least you got . he'd hate it here.

Which had this funny way of making her feel better and at the same time much worse.

Cogs was right about her little one. And if she were there now, she'd be without him now too. Plus if Mayumi said it was hot, then Xanther would already be like ash. And smuggling him along in a backpack wouldn't help. Xanther had discovered that recently. Well, actually, she'd been dis- covering it for a while, like when she took him out to see a sunset, or practicing Tai Chi out back, or when she'd walked that chalk line out front with her sisters. As soon as she stepped out of the house, that acorn of blue, like a mean pilot light, started to slowly burn her down.

Xanther still wanted to experiment more, like try tak- ing him for a drive and see if that helped. As far as Xanther could figure, the boundary had something to do with where the little one was free to wander, even if he stuck mostly to Xanther.

:: *Terra* . . . ::

:: Terror? ::

:: *Territorium* . . . ::

"Xanther? Can I talk to you for a moment?"

Oh brother. Not like she's really asking, Astair already talking, already barging into her room, sitting down on the bed, reaching out to pet the little one, and then at the last moment withdrawing her hand.

"Aren't you hot up here?" Feeling Xanther's forehead instead.

"Mom!"

"You feel hot."

"I feel fine."

"I'm sorry."

"Huh?"

"I'm sorry that you're here and not with your friends."

"Please don't say 'This hurts me more than you.'"

"Xanther!" Astair jumps up like she just touched the cat and her fingers fell off. Like hurt for real. Xanther immediately feels bad, and surprised too, by herself.

"I'm sorry," she mumbles. "Seriously, just a question: is that what you want to say?"

Astair blinks, maybe as caught off guard by the flatness of Xanther's question now as she was by the earlier snappishness.

"No. Okay, yes. But because it feels so unnecessary." No more hurt. Or anger. Now it's just frustration.

"I agree. But we're cool too. It's over. As you can see, I'm chilling with my little homie. Maybe I'll even call him Homie. Whadya think?"

"It's your decision."

"How about Decision?"

dringadrong dringadrong

"More Magic Mountain reports?"

"They love making me miserable."

Astair's the one who looks miserable.

But the message isn't from her crew. Xanther smiles.

Roxanne: be strong. they forget. we dont forgive.

"Bayard didn't go," Xanther informs Astair instead.

"Oh," Astair says from the hall.

"I figured there was no way he'd miss out on a Six Flags trip. None of us have seen him in like weeks." Months, really. "Have you heard anything?"

"I haven't."

Not that Mom has finished with her. Astair makes Xanther come out back to practice Tai Chi. At least Astair knows better than to object to little one hanging out on Xanther's shoulder. Xanther hates having to go through the stupid moves ∷ *Grasp Sparrow's Tail* ∷ ∷ *Ward Off To Right* ∷ ∷ *Roll Back* ∷ ∷ *Press* ∷ ∷ *Withdraw* ∷. She really just wants to sit on her bed and flick stones in her head. At least try to avoid this blue flame igniting in the distance of herself. The forms somehow interfere. Astair keeps insisting she try something called Single Whip, making a cup of the left hand, a claw of the right, extending forward like she's drawing out thread, like a spider, and then like that, letting go of thread and even spider.

Afterwards Xanther goes to check on Levi, the praying mantis. Still there among the leaves of the yuzu. Except now she's huge.

Is that even her?

She's outgrown her name for sure.

More like Leviathan.

Thursday morning Astair gets still weirder.

"Does the color of your sisters' skin bother you?"
"What are you talking about?"
"That they're so much browner?"
"Seriously, Mom?"

Xanther watches Astair blink, and blink like a few times, almost enough to call it a flinch, which no way Xanther wants to provoke, and now is just as irritated by the question as she is with herself, because the point is, Mom knows Xanther is angry with Freya and Shasti, she just doesn't know why, and really shouldn't Xanther just tell her the truth? ∴ Uhm, yeah? ∵

Except the anger has grown.

Something else too.

"Why don't you call him Imogen?" Freya asks later that afternoon, while Astair is settling them around a table at The Coffee Bean & Tea Leaf in Los Feliz ∴ **2081 Hillhurst Avenue, Los Angeles, CA 90027** ∴.

"Shasti," suggests Shasti.

"*That's* a dull name," Freya snarks.

"Dull?"

"Don't bother your sister," Mom interrupts, being extra nice to Xanther today, or at least extra careful.

Freya demands something caramel. Shasti insists on something chocolate, like by ordering something different she's getting back at Freya for disparaging her name.

"Do you want to try almond milk this time?" It's Xanther's turn to order. Again Astair is extra nice, like nut milk will be a treat. "Or how about wheatgrass? That would be an adventure."

"No thanks."

"Well, I guess, in time even grass becomes milk, as the saying goes ∴ **Charan Singh** ∴," Astair quips, wheeling away to place their order, leaving Xanther with the cow, and like what about the cow?, because grass would just be grass if it weren't for the cow, right?, and milk wouldn't be milk at all, right?, and like Xanther could eat a cow too, which at once makes her queasy for even thinking that.

A red Mitsubishi in the Albertsons' parking lot catches Xanther's eye. From the rear bumper hangs a stuffed frog, blackened and ruptured in so many places it almost doesn't count as a frog, even if it's still clutching an equally wrecked sign: I LOVE YOU. Like that helps. The rest of the car is nothing but rust, oxidized paint, with some kind of tint on the windows, all but peeled away, as if the insides were the charred guts of a fire still melting the frame.

Though what really fixes Xanther's attention ∴ It's true. ∴ ∴ *In part . . .* ∴ is the model name.

She's mesmerized by the lost letters as well as the ones that remain.

The missing M gets her.

As well as the missing I.

In Spanish "MI" can mean "my" as in "mi casa." In English, it's like a third tone, an E maybe? Or mixed around, it's IM, like in Instant Message, or I'M. The two letters keep swimming around in Xanther's head as if caught in the heat rising off the blacktop, the currents responsible for their arrangements, even if, for all their rearrangements, they're still ghosts and what matters most is what remains.

"What about Muffin?" Shasti doesn't want to stop suggesting names. "Or Gaspar?"

"Shast," Freya warns.

"Or Philomel?" ∷ **TFv2 p. 574** ∷ Shasti really has no clue. She's forgotten about the wolves, their lie.

"Philomel?" Xanther scowls. No desire to look at either of them. Tries flicking stones. Astair has reached the register.

"She's so cool though." That's right. Philomel is their friend.

"She is cool," Freya admits, begrudgingly going along with her sister.

"How about her brother's name then?" Shasti still won't stop.

"Shast!"

"His name's super cool: Dendish!"

"WHAT!?"

Shasti doesn't react, maybe too stunned by Xanther's crazy turn around, though the little girl's face does seem to flatten, her body not moving at all, while Freya is nothing but moving, pushing away from the table even, or pushed, like Xanther's look alone shoved her chair away.

"What did you two tell him?" Xanther growls.

"Shasti didn't mean to say anything," Freya babbles as fast as she can, figuring it out way faster than Shasti, getting closer to tears too. Astair has just finished stuffing a receipt into her wallet and gathering up their drinks.

Suddenly so much falls into place. Xanther thinking fastest of all. :: As if anyone else here could be doing the thinking.:: :: *Else is here* . . . :: Play dates with Philomel. But not just Philomel. Philomel *Mower*. Younger sister to Dendish *Mower*. Xanther's own sisters letting out her secret.

Twitch.

Xanther would love to see now the stones on their eyes punch through the backs of their heads, leaving behind brutal holes of no apparent consequence except maybe the grim satisfaction of an image. But Xanther can't just see what stones won't do. There are also the shattered wolves on the living room floor, the twins' pact with Xiomara, what Xanther assumed was protective and instead proved cunning, and in the service of a lie, the accusation in a name she can't stop hearing over and over, "Xanther!," teeth grinding towards noise, a growl in her throat threatening to grow into something beyond sound, as if blue can leap to a wider threat and set skin to fire.

"Xanther! Is everything okay?" Of course Mom notices. A forehead kiss at once. "You're freezing!" She wants them out. She doesn't want Xanther to drink the iced whole milk. "I'll get you a steamed milk. Hold on."

But Xanther needs ice.

"I'll tell," Freya keeps promising Xanther. "I'll tell Mom everything."

Freya looks afraid. Shasti seeing the way Freya looks looks even worse.

"You won't say a word," Xanther hisses.

The red Mitsubishi's gone, leaving behind an empty parking spot and what two missing letters make of a model name Xanther doesn't need to say aloud in order to feel:

MIRAGE

Virgil

*How much room do individual
rights leave for the state?*

— Robert Nozick

The handwriting's too familiar to pretend this is just a package: that generous *O*, something lacy in the *Z*, plus a Cairo return address Özgür knows by heart. She's lived there for decades now. But despite decades, how easy still to find their Rhine again, feel the bike under their hips, pipes hot enough to burn ankles, never burning them, boots thick enough, high enough, until boots were kicked off, in that awful room, where not even the water-poached grey paint could matter, or that weird sink, a waterless stain of rust bolted to the wall, or the lights that never worked, every bulb busted. Did they stay for more than a few hours? They were too young to believe in sleep. Just go go go. How she had burned up his legs on those rough sheets, straining under him, bucking, laughing, biting, Özgür no longer caring about the coming that had mattered so much back then, but the memory of those hairless moons he found later on the back of each calf, where she had ground in her heels, as she arched and cursed and kissed him and taught him to believe the word forever. Özgür opens the present at his desk. Here is her forever again. No note. No explanation.

Just one tiny stone statue.

Özgür brings it along to dinner. As it turns out at the Cat & Fiddle ∴ 6530 Sunset Boulevard, Los Angeles, CA 90028 ∵ — the main room there glowing gold as a pint of lager, darts on one wall, a long right angle for a bar in the center. Sure there's food but this is where you go for a strong stout drawn well or a well drink poured strong. Tonight tables are crowded with young and local. The advantage of a Thursday. Some young thing, maybe as spicy as the ring in her nose, or the ball of silver riding her tongue, leads Özgür to the patio. She hands over two menus but spends her smile on his friend. Özgür can't blame her.

His friend has the looks. Bronze skin only a fool calls brown. Eyes like what a river becomes when the sun reveals a bottom full of gold. Broad shoulders, wide hands. Black waves of thick hair. Going places, that's for sure, but gentle too. If stone could learn life's softness, a bust of this man would teach the hardest marble to live. Özgür's convinced he'll end up a senator. Maybe president. A great one too. At thirty-four he's got time. He's already clerked for a notable judge. These days he works as an Assistant U.S. Attorney ∴ AUSA ∵ in Central District.

Virgil Campos gives Özgür a big hug. Özgür's only a minute late but Virgil's right on time. So easy he almost seems late, even lazy. But he's neither. Ever.

"Right behind the one, bey." That was the description of a trumpet player once offered by a drummer Özgür used to know who'd met Miles and played with Herbie Hancock and liked to call Özgür "bey" and say "dig." "Behind the one but already there too, dig, before the there even knows there's a there to get to that's already gotten to and been. A small pocket with plenty of room, dig? Following the rules but so deep you think this cat's making it up. Which he isn't but is at the same time, dig? Of course bey digs but you still don't know what I'm saying."

"Olympic is your area now, right?" Virgil confirms. "We need to celebrate." Usually they meet in Chinatown for purely cinematic reasons and plates of slippery shrimp. Tonight demanded difference.

Özgür orders a bourbon neat.

"Starting hard?" Virgil asks, ordering a ginger ale.

"It settles my stomach."

"If my news is new news you might need a few."

Their hostess comes back with their drinks so fast Özgür wonders if Virgil isn't already president. The two had met years ago on a homicide-witness-intimidation case involving the Drew Street Gang. The investigation had led from Glassell Park down into Rampart. Months of hard work culminated in many parts fiasco and one part tragedy, with the only witness to the homicide in question ending up a homicide herself, hers unwitnessed. Özgür had sworn he was done. Virgil had just sworn.

Ever since then, they've met frequently for dinner to swap stories and laughs, doubts too, sometimes confessions. With the exception of one heated disagreement, Özgür never fails to leave their get-togethers feeling refreshed. What makes one person a drain on all you dream and another person practically the dream itself? Balascoe would say the only dream worth counting must have big tits and a tight box. Balascoe would be the drain. Not everything comes down to sex. Even half moons on calves have less to do with a bed than with the sky.

Is it Virgil's perspectives that Özgür finds so rewarding? Sensible. Generous. Even hopeful. Özgür loves seeing the world through his eyes. And why not? The kid had not only gotten his law degree from Stanford but majored in Classics as an undergraduate at Harvard. "The Roman Latino," he's grinned before. "Et in Arcadia ego. For I too lived in Arcadia. California."

Or maybe it's because Virgil also suffers, and on a daily basis, the same bureaucratic torture chambers, whether municipal or federal, legal or civil, error-riddled, deceit-prone, ever beyond the comprehensive grasp of anyone choosing to ponder the whole, not to mention suffer the profound misfortune of having to depend on a paycheck cut by such a system.

Or maybe it's just because Özgür finds in Virgil someone he can't be but would have killed to have been twenty years ago. Because of their age difference, Özgür always feels he should play a paternal role but can't even snag avuncular. "Uncle Oz" doesn't exactly sing. Neither does "kid." And if "mentor" is the word in question, it should probably go to Virgil. Özgür sure never had a mentor when he was Virgil's age, and having Youth for one now only strikes him as proof positive that he's too late. Though as Virgil would remind him: "What's too late?"

"Have you heard the latest about the K-Mark Killings?" Virgil asks now, voice sparkling with the hint of something hidden.

"Please don't tell me this is the part where you tell me Balascoe blew it?"

"On the bright side: no one doubts you nailed the mechanics. The suspect, whom I'm guessing you remember—"

"—Marvin D'Organidrelle. Aka Android."

"Well, aka Android robbed the store, killed the owner behind the counter and then the wife when she ran outside screaming. Then he put everything into pre-addressed pre-paid packages. No wits but postage."

"I'm guessing the opposite of bright side isn't dim but dumb?"

"The mail carrier was already feeling bad about not calling his supervisor. Balascoe was even opening packages dropped there by local residents. He should have just called the ACLU directly. He eventually found one flip-flop, then another, finally both gloves, and last but not least, the money. Lawyers had a field day. Warrantless search for one. They had to kick him."

"He walked!?"

"Oh there's more: Balascoe's pissed at you."

"Me!? He's the one who couldn't wait for a warrant."

"You showed him what he couldn't see and then he mishandled everything and in a way everyone could see. The shame of intellect is a rough one. It's probably the reason why, de facto, most people look down on intelligence greater than theirs. I'm proud to call myself an exception as I happily look up to yours." Virgil grins. Great teeth too. But something there still sparks with the untold.

"News flash, Virgil," Özgür growls, finishing off what's left in his glass, what doesn't count for a sip, more like a coating. "I'm an old dog, and the only thing going for me is *maybe* the skills to fool a few people into thinking an old trick is a new trick. Though these days I can't even fool myself. Do you know this morning I flinched over what I expected to be the download time for a document? As if I still couldn't accept that what over two decades ago was just the promise of things to come has now surpassed the point of fulfillment. The pdf was already loaded and open and I was acting like I was still back in the '90s using a telephone modem."

"Don't tell me you're gonna start wearing flannel?"

Özgür nearly admits that this is how he sees Virgil: the broadband fulfillment of Özgür's dial-up promise.

"I feel spent," Özgür confesses instead. "Because I feel fixed. I'm already messed up by experiences with systems no longer around. And I'm having no luck updating. Olympic Station is the same old Hollywood Station with a new address. I should retire."

Özgür looks around for a nose ring, a pad of paper, anyone to re-up their rounds.

"How's Elaine?"

Özgür smiles and reaches into his pocket.

"A cat?" Virgil asks, turning over the smoothly polished black statue.

"Bast. Eye of Ra. A goddess. Some talisman like that."

Virgil has already heard the stories behind these occasional gift exchanges but Özgür repeats it anyway: how they met in Köln, took on Europe on a motorcycle, even if in the end she wanted white storks and bassinets, and Özgür just wanted to keep going, and did.

"Look how far I got. My greatest regret."

"She is? Really?"

Özgür shakes his head. "Not having a child. I'm guessing her marriage just ended. Divorced. Maybe widowed. Anyway—" nodding at the tiny symbol "—it wouldn't be fair to Elaine to keep. Did I tell you? I'm going to ask her to move in with me."

"To think I knew you when you were single. The company you used to keep."

"I learned the hard way: you never run out of beautiful girls, you just run out of yourself."

Virgil pockets the gift with a thanks.

"Keep it or give it to someone whose future you care about. How's the gal?"

"Fiancée!" Virgil announces. Ah. There it is.

Özgür stands. More hugs. If another drink ever needed an excuse . . . but suddenly Özgür's too happy to want one. Besides, bourbon isn't doing his stomach any favors. When a server at last appears, he considers the Scotch egg before going with soup. Virgil orders salad.

"No date yet. A year at least. To figure out the details. She wants the wedding in some scenic place like Morro Bay."

"You mean the kind of town you settle in to raise kids who kill themselves?"

"Hey! That's what I said." Virgil's smile is contagious enough to report to the CDC. "She knows what's ahead. She knows I'm going to take a serious run at politics. She wants to finish getting her license as a registered nurse. She wants to finally have you over for dinner."

"I'm glad to see her priorities are in order." Özgür takes out a piece of paper. *Katla*. He's ridiculously pleased that his suspicions about something hidden were not misplaced. *Katla-katla*.

While they eat, Özgür catches Virgil up on Planski, her CI with "eyes on distribution."

"Names?"

"All she's mentioned is something called Synsnap."

Katla. Katla-katla.

"Really?" Virgil leans away, eyes scattering dark sparks, something hiding again.

Katla.

"You know of this?"

Katla-katla. Katla. Katla.

"Ever heard the name Teyo?"

Özgür shakes his head.

"Téodor Javier de Ignacio Salazar. Starting to emerge as a major distributor of a new substance considered as addictive as crack or heroin."

"Once and you're hooked?" An old story. Given a choice between needles or smoke, Özgür always picks stiletto heels.

"Not really. This requires more exposure but early reports show dependence still happens fast."

"Meaning withdrawals are hell?"

Katla. Katla.

Virgil nods. "Humanity can't help building itself hells. Especially when there's money."

"Synthetic?"

Another nod.

"Properties?"

Virgil shrugs. "Too new. One expert has it lighting up one dopamine pathway ∴ Mesocorticolimbic projection ∴, another expert another one ∴ Nigrostriatal pathway ∴. A third pathway, a fifth, I don't care. ∴ A sixth ∴ ∴ ▮▮▮▮▮▮ pathway. ∴ It's not only lighting up all parts of the brain but supposedly changing it too. That's the fear."

"Just when I thought the Balloon Parade had gotten stale."

Katla-katla. Katla. Katla-katla. Katla-katla.

"There are apps too. I heard a rumor that Carcetti is talking to WHO in case this becomes a repeat of the '80s epidemic."

"I'll take flannel any day over that."

Virgil promises to call Planski. "Special Agent Rivka

Waters is perfect. I'm working with her now. FBI. Solid. She knows how to keep a CI safe and if there's a case find funds."

Katla.

Özgür's grateful. As he is for the conversation that follows: Nets of Justice. That's their usual starting place. Does society have the capacity to create laws that align with Justice? And if yes, can those laws be enforced? Özgür tries not to think about the murdered Korean couple. In general, one-time offenders are more likely to get away. Özgür mentions the German expression *einmal ist keinmal.* Once is never. Repeat offenders, however, are more easily caught. Statistics bend against them. Tonight Virgil takes it a step further, insisting that little choices never coming before judge or jury still determine future acts of criminality that are netted later by judicial systems.

More food is ordered. Özgür switches to sparkling water, keeps folding paper. They cover samurai codes and movies ∴ Sword of Vengeance ∴ ∴ For one ∴ and boxing too. *Katla.*

"Wasn't Ali the one who said 'The fight is won or lost far away from witnesses'?" ∴ "Some people think a Heavyweight Championship fight is decided during the fifteen rounds the two fighters face each other under hot blazing lights, in front of thousands of screaming witnesses, and part of it is. But a prizefight is like a war: the real part is won or lost somewhere far away from witnesses, behind the lines, in the gym and out here on the road long before I dance under those lights." *The Greatest: My Own Story.* 1976. ∴

Another reason why Özgür loves Virgil — and why not as an uncle or even as a father? — because his romanticism consistently suggests that a life well led results in Good. And Good for the one as well as for the many. Though maybe because of the news of Virgil's engagement, tonight Özgür doesn't bring up the darkness of Job or Christ. Virgil doesn't either. He starts talking about sunglasses.

"Excuse me?"

"Evidence mounts that minor actions have major consequences on the outcome of our lives! Is it so ridiculous to suggest that major choices must obey the consequences of smaller choices, however trivial, however private? That positive practices lead to beneficial outcomes?" Definitely not the time to bring up Job or Christ. "And that iniquitous deeds, however minuscule, and hidden, give best intentions disastrous direction?"

"And deliver one unto a reckoning?" Özgür laughs. "You know very well that's not true!"

Katla. Katla.

Virgil concedes with open hands, though only partially: "The Gino-Norton-Ariely study concludes that out of those under the impression that they were wearing authentic designer sunglasses, 30 percent cheated on a simple math test. Out of those under the impression that they wore counterfeit glasses, 71 percent cheated. Proving even the pettiest of lies are of concern."

"Also proving that at least 30 percent of each group feels inclined to cheat regardless."

"They are why we have jobs." Virgil laughs.

Out of the blue, that wacko Warlock comes to mind. Özgür needs to call him. Warlock would probably enjoy such a conversation, especially as Virgil, by way of Rawls, Wiesel, and Parfit, heads them towards one of their favorite topics: the ones that get away. Özgür and Virgil's yogic OHM:

One Happy Maniac

Usually male. Always homicidal. And as Özgür puts it: "Guilty of terrible things unaccounted for." He sleeps fine. All he desires, he gets. "What keeps me up at night," Virgil adds.

Though now Virgil tries a different tack: "What if we assume empathy is simply inaccessible?"

"Like an animal?"

Katla. Katla. Katla-katla.

"Worse. He will never recognize the criminality of his actions. Disavows all misdeeds. Forgets them at once or rationalizes them out of existence. Happily disavows humanity. Why shouldn't he? He is species enough."

"Chris Rock."

"Chris Rock?"

"After Roy Horn, of Siegfried and Roy, was mauled by one of his blue-eyed props ten years ago ∴ 2003 ∴, Rock objected to anyone saying the tiger went crazy: 'No, he didn't. That tiger went tiger.'"

"That's right," Virgil nods, perhaps enjoying like Özgür how they don't argue but rather explore together one impossible problem after another. "As easily as we loathe a man-eating maniac, we will forgive a man-eating tiger."

"So then our dilemma is if, whether due to nature or nurture, the maniac is more tiger than human?"

"Voilà! The Tiger-Is-Just-a-Tiger defense!"

"I believe too that that creature lived out the rest of his life at the Mirage. Died only this year ∴ **March 19, 2014** ∴."

Katla-katla. Katla-katla.

"No pardon was necessary," Virgil points out. "The tiger couldn't be blamed."

"Though man-maiming tigers will still suffer consequences — just without ire."

Katla. Katla.

"Mustn't Justice always be without ire? Impersonal?"

"Justice is a tiger herself." Özgür smiles.

"If only Justice were that simple." Virgil smiles. Maybe with a hint of sadness.

Katla. Katla. Katla.

Özgür can only nod.

"And still we've made no progress where Justice is concerned when our homicidal maniac dies happily in his sleep."

Özgür slides the finished stork ∴ John Montroll ∴ to the middle of the table. "There was a time when children were made to suffer the crimes of their forebears."

"Heaven forbid."

"When heaven did, we invented hell."

"Better to forget hell and, as the saying goes, cover the wells first."

"I don't know that saying."

"*Muerto el niño, tapan el pozo.* Only after the child drowns do they cover the well."

They say goodbye on Sunset Boulevard. Taxis and Ubers already line the curb, new arrivals heading into the pub, others lingering on the sidewalk, texting, smoking cigarettes. Virgil lingers too.

∴ **Cat & Fiddle Restaurant & Pub will close December 15, 2014.** ∴

∴ *The cat putting its fiddle away.* ∴

"I haven't told you everything," he starts. For some reason, Virgil's even taken out Özgür's gift, rolling idly on fingertips the little black statue of a cat. Is that why Özgür wandered into that bit about tigers? A suggestion by this guardian goddess?

"I just found this out too," Virgil continues. "About a month ago, on the morning of June twelfth, a body was found by the rail tracks downtown. Torn apart. However, no conductor reported an incident. And no train turned up with a blood splash. Which is better than what can be said for the ground in the area: soaked."

That dark twinkle is back even if Özgür can't make the connection.

"You mentioned Synsnap."

Özgür nods.

"This kid was on it."

"Synsnap caused the death?"

"Not directly. The coroner's office thinks an animal might be involved. Nothing like a coyote or mountain lion. In fact, based on the damage, it would have to be too big to be credible. More like a tiger. Bones were powdered. Something mechanical is still considered the most likely cause. Severe rips and punctures in neck and cranial areas. Whatever it was chomped through most of the head."

"And you're still not telling me everything."

"The deceased was your homicidal mailer: Marvin D'Organidrelle aka Android."

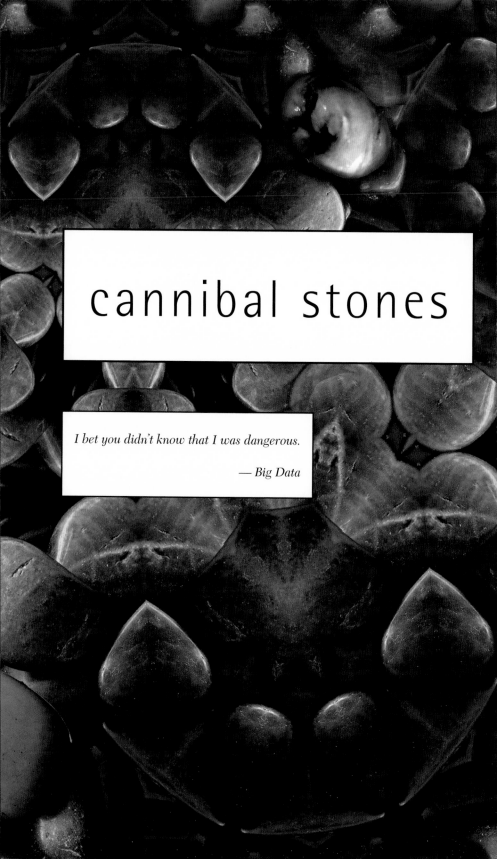

cannibal stones

I bet you didn't know that I was dangerous.

— *Big Data*

jingjing chiak tsua by self in void deck. nothing to lose. snag table,

stretch long, mr. self serve snooze, mr. daze. not even spencer

around to tangle nerves. and cats? pang chui lao, lah. no chop-

ear one for days. might as well see great lady prance by with bells,

shoulder light like that no-bell white casting no-head no-tail

glare, take you go market and sell.

only jingjing go market. month oreddy bye-bye since old bag

declare trip. california! hollywood! a jingjing dream arbo, believe

her. any day they fly. see kanye, kim, bieber. or mebbe was just

smoke speaking. mebbe auntie smoking too. but she keep saying it,

day later, week later: "we must go to los angeles at once." if each

day more mumbled than plan, less than. gone is braided black, hair

back to grey mess. mebbe he made up pearl-flecked dress. jingjing

kena pang puay kee by hope, lah, fly aeroplane for no flight. return

ticket to long nights of snorts and snores.

only one thing hundred percent: wings. but jingjing dropped out

too quick then. no even looksee-looksee to catch more than too

many leathery flaps rising off so many strangers' backs. that

one towering monster, same-same from smoke house, was worst,

clawed wings leave ceiling scratched up with soot, swagger

towards jingjing like he carry him and whole night away. except

when jingjing wake, he in hammock, ceiling unscorched. only proof of previous night: empty pockets except stolen lighter 23 for sure better have back if jingjing ever need to return. oreddy heading out when auntie called from stove. she up double-boiling bird's nest! with rock sugar! hair still black as black flowers stitched on scarlet green dress. where she get that? or bird's nest? talktalk all morning, sly as old self again, mai?, poon with no cat. wouldn't stop moving, paced whole flat, hands back to steady, taptapping worldwall, acorn, and postcards, mouth full of warnings.

"we must look to ourselves. we must be ready."

jingjing tup pai ready! ready right then. smoke house now? tan ku ku, lah! forget balloons! forget bad dreams! only one thing jingjing couldn't put aside. meant to ask sekarang but next day old bag so streaks of grey again. alamak, siao liao, siao liao! big dream unravelled, even if jingjing sing mai tu liao, auntie, now is time to travel!

now jingjing si beh pui chao nuah. curses, cursed. has own plan, lah. get finger lickin kway first, then balloon parade with a lighter, even if just thinking of 23's stash, his counter slide of pink or blue, makes jingjing's skin itch, mouth too, go dry and greedy, jingjing switch mah si from concrete table to bench, close eyes, shake head, twist like murukku. not enough smoke to get so needy.

"maintain balan," sings wink, eyes open in a blink, jingjing expect feathered wings, light as clouds, miles from storm.

but she right there, leaning over, up close, bright as any angel, kim tang tang for auntie, pink blouse on, pink skirt, doves of silver-wing flying pleats, black buttons down side, black flats on feet, braids back and black, ends ribboned black.

"do you want your passport or not?" great tian li grin, like light-ning burning out moon.

spencer and lau jerry, stout and tiger singlets on, coming through, damn bising with cans in both hands, set for void deck semen, then auntie set their strut, stunned like vegetable. lau sai pang jio.

jingjing wave, hurry away, great tian li oreddy at corner, crossing street for atm. where that card come from? ooh lui, oo song! manyak sing in her palm. jingjing palms fill too with itch. scramble after across bridge for mrt ∴ **Mass Rapid Transit** ∴. but first potong ice creams, durian, and attap chee.

commonwealth south. then dhoby ghaut. jingjing figure out. car a crowd for lunch but auntie part suits for seats. rests hand on jingjing's knee. mebbe to punggol. but auntie grab jingjing's wrist, exit serangoon. more pink in station. pass mother in torn pink tulle, worn denim sandals, oreddy haste, slapslapping after child ah, in swee swee pink gown, big bow cinch waist, kiwi shoes, paper moon over head, almost escaping little hands. but cries stop at

435

sight of auntie, and all stop, mother, child, osso auntie, jingjing

not, at sight of older girl, stepping onto train, pink singlet, black

shorts, pink converse, black braids, face chalk macam yau zha guai.

and she not only ghost. mazda capella, stone apricot, with some

panels primer grey. driver grey too, parked curbside by taxi line.

kiss auntie's hands twice, open passenger door. jingjing climb in

back.

"you are not alone," saysay twice. saysay name is fred.

fred drive old, grandfudder road, pass institute of mental health so

slow, jingjing sure fred live there, but on he go, trouble to all cars.

they all get out at kampong lorong buangkok. auntie immeelly

surrounded by cats, greys and oranges, and big black and whites,

got gold eyes, blue eyes, eyes wide as black sky no stars. circle her

ankles, mew for touch. fred chuckle this greet, lah, like he with her have friendship older than wars. except jingjing never met fred before. never heard auntie mention name.

round man, brown man, from sandals, slacks creased, polyester brown short sleeve, armpit stains, one gold chain bright as young sugarcane. fred lead way. auntie follow, macam cats follow auntie.

they pass zinc roofs, plaster walls dipped in light blue, bright yellow, white doors with yellow tassels, potted plants on top steps, wind chimes still for afternoon. mebbe auntie step inside this surau. just closes eyes, hand to birdcage chest, lips fluttering mute. fred too. only jingjing jump back too late. cat, beast of bengal blue, clawing up his feet.

fred and great hum mannequin laugh fierce at that.

"damn cartoon him," fred add.

then down past two homes, where long ditch run, metaled off by

green fence, jingjing catch thing shaking loose brown water, mebbe

unsettled by auntie here? oreddy gone like lizard. heng-ah. jingjing

oreddy digging pockets for ziploc, by card match fast what tua

trouble just now passed. but old bag near snatch deck up macam

like they in some big hurry, this jalan-jalan at fred's pace, by old

kampong huts, or fresh-painted ones, here double story, with trim

strawberry, and vanilla-vanilla like polar cafe sponge cake.

tian li never explain wander. or why, later, at next stop, fred

arrange three bikes. punggol promenade hugs water way south

serangoon island, nature walk, paved neat, grass clipped neater,

trees new neat spaced for park geometry, long ride kay, whole

place swee swee boh kay chwee, over slatted bridge, over concrete,

water alive suddenly with splashes unseen, mebbe hantu ayer.

jingjing pedal fast. breath rasps, and still can't catch auntie. fred

too, ah chek tour de france. who knew ah mm ride bike so good.

long break by punggol point. malaysia over strait, docks in haze,

tankers wait by yellow cranes, loaded with freight. no clue why

jingjing kena arrow by auntie to stay near. like he can't just suka-

suka go off alone here.

fishing poles play flagpoles along jetty. black man in orange

shorts with bare belly fumbles with hook and line. lifesaver cling

to fence. jingjing fear water, fear saving, drift until he's hauled up

inside one of those big ships. just looking at johor make skin itch.

tian li and fred sit by plaque:

பொங்கோல் கடலோரத்தில் முன்னூறு
நானூறு சீனர்கள் "ஹோாஜோ
கெம் பெய்" என்ற ஜப்பானிய
ராணுவப் போலிசாரால் 1942 பிப்ரவரி
28-ஆம் தேதியன்று சுட்டுக்கொல்லப
பட்டனர்.

Pada 28 Februari, 1942, seramai 300-
400 orang awam keturunan Cina telah
dibunuh di sepanjang pantai Punggol
oleh pasukan penembak Jepun hojo
kempei (polis tentera tambahan).

2月28日，　日本宪兵部射杀
队在榜鹅海滩处死了三四百名
华籍平民。

∴ On 28 February, 1942, some 300–400 Chinese civilians were killed along the
Punggol foreshore by *hojo kempei* (auxiliary military police) firing squads. ∵

'anything?" fred whisper to auntie. holds her hand in both his

hands on his knee.

'blind," tian li answers. "it's nice."

at fred's flat, ∴ **27 Punggol Central, Block 160¼ c, 06-113** ∴ fred make

tea from can. at formica-top table tian li take jingjing's hand in

two hands. mah si rest head on jingjing's shoulder. sigh. longtime

jingjing feel so kay sooth, immeelly die, macam first time, auntie

finding him all itch one in park, so lao yah pok, alone tup pai with

his dark.

"jingjing, we're running out of time," she spersper now.

"what's that?" fred ask, lays out cups. "we have a good hour at

least. i'll drive you there, lah. sol will drive you home. it's all taken

care of. jingjing, see, you're not alone."

fred turns to phone. mebbe jingjing sapu nokia. fb jude boys, balik

sky. damn si beh sian, jingjing. tea bitter. then cold. fred really

sewer serpent with old jokes. kong sar kong si him. jingjing almost

koon deep in chair. auntie too must sleep. but doesn't. laughs lots.

like old self again, except for cat, no cat, mebbe fred's the cat.

back in capella fred drive slow but this time macam he afraid.

he bring up habib syed ahmed, some bomoh auntie knew. tahar

suhaimi too. auntie smiles, osso remembers older bomohs fred

saysay no one knew. the ones that failed. sinsehs too. long time

ago they called her hantu bankit. by frangipani she cried until

frangipani cry too. until streets cry out seow char bor. and in the

name of hantu batu, they threw rocks at her.

"you turned their stones to sky."

'i watched so many die."

in front of mama shop, fred stops, won't park. passports here? this

no travel spot. windows dark, grated too, sure thing door locked.

jingjing help auntie out, fred jitters and starts, buay tazai now but

for what?

"sol will be here when you get out," he starts to explain, explains

again: "what is not apparent for everyone is not for me." then

crosses self. tian li offers prayer hands. bows. traffic eat apricot

capella.

444

shop door not locked. waits open. macam swung so on its own.

before stepping inside, song of dark wings flutter above.

street lamps light within. sundries and knickknacks heap shelves, bric-a-brac pecah tables. ooh pee, boh chee. music box with no notes. jingjing opens too and winds up. nothing to need. poon jade dragon of plastic? bronze bells of lead? fake ceramic cups? neon fans and watch bands? nothing to steal. clay buddha hide face in shame. jingjing playplay with postcard wheel: oslo, london, moscow, cape town, amsterdam, tokyo, manila, sydney, paris, christchurch, new delhi, berlin, istanbul, athens, rome, honolulu.

jingjing make mind up then to ask auntie about wings but find her by back door in reed chair drooling for dreams. jingjing settles on floor, would koon too, but digs up monster cards instead. thumbs through deck to match splash-lizard from before, some monitor overgrown. mebbe better to find with eyes closed.

draws metatron. one more face beyond throne.

hen a second just as wretched, feasts on kwai lan kia, before

uddha.

jingjing shriek. he-li-di there in the doorway, bowl of eyes, mouth

of blood, face smug for feast. auntie shriek too, with joy, and

hugs, oreddy on her feet.

back room is cozy bright, couches piled with knit pillows of cats,

throws too, air hung with sorry, no worry, sorry no cure, over and

over, table by kitchen madam tembam fills with dishes of sarawak

laksa, plates of potato rendang, cendol worms with red bean ice

cream for sweet. madam tembam tea burn tongue, bright green.

auntie slurp some, chew little, sniff cup. back to old times when

food seem unneeded.

"when are you leaving?" madam tembam ask. she is thin wicker

draped in grey and grey. thin eyebrows too, arched high, mebbe

sapphire glitter in her gaze, like fish brooch she wear, of sapphire

glass, emerald scales, and ruby eyes. ∴ *Pinecone.* ∴ ∴ **Monocentridae.** ∴

"soon," tian li sigh.

"you? tonight?"

"him," tian li smile.

"me? what talking you?" jingjing erupt.

"you remember the once?" madam tembam relax, ignore jingjing

macam he jilo.

tian li bow head, cup face like weeping buddha.

"stones almost killed me," madam tembam tell jingjing.

"jingjing," auntie spersper urgent. "i believed we would have

longer. years. a lifetime of years. but i had no right to create such

a belief. i still promise you more than you dare dream. but we need

to start finding out who you really are now."

madam tembam sit jingjing at small table, seats for just two, mah,

black felt cloth drape past knees.

"meaningful is easy, jingjing. meaning is what survives. surviving is

the hard part."

"you a medium, lah?"

"lah? as a question? where did you learn to speak?"

a wave then of fingers bound in rings, macam hitam silver. no

interest if jingjing answer. just black bag with black cord, opened

oreddy, black stones tumbling across cloth. too many to track.

count them mebbe. once they stop. jingjing try. square as chewed

treats. teeth.

"Ты задаешь большие вопросы. У тебя есть большие

секреты. И большие желания." :: *"You have great questions, great secrets,*

great desire." ::

did some stones just go hilang? macam ink drops in ink. jingjing sit

up quick. kuah auntie. she oreddy slouched on couch, snoring.

'ama çoktan onun çekimine kapılmışsınız." ∷ *"But you are already under*

another spell." ∷

fingers powderful, dancing over stones, with rings of coal, chao

kang look.

jingjing sneer too, scratch arms, eye corner catch another stone

slip too deep. or something worse? macam something mean eat?

"你嘅问题系乜野?" ∷ *"What is your question?"* ∷

"wings!"

"如尔投疑怪之半力于察尔之才, 尔之能将长。置此妖纸于侧。"

∷ *"What wonders you might really grow if you were to set free but half the time you*

devote to silly specters. Put aside those monster cards." ∷

stones on the move, mai watch, macam map out future. this time

jingjing's corner eye catch stones makan stones. damn dirty this.

evil cannibal stones. if out of corner, flat on, stones sit still.

"Was ist Ihr Geheimnis?" ∵ *What is your secret?* ∵

"Qui vous-avez appris à parler?" ∵ *Who taught you to speak?* ∵

jingjing look for auntie, gone, jungle surround now, blacker than

bag, cloth, or stones. here cemetery grounds. stones moving faster

if jingjing stone solid. mouth dry like sand. can't tahan this much

more. can't understand.

how? who?

cry in jingjing balloons. because he is not of these words. he is

of something else. made from other bones. stained unseen except

before those strewn and unredeemed. a murder of stones.

⁘ One day you will find your voice. ⁘

⁘ no i won't. ⁘

⁘ Hush you. You who think how you think is your own and thus is known. You are a garble at best if let loose as you are, born so for all to behold. Who none would hold or carry on. Even if you wrote it out, it would stand unwritten. You who presume a place where you were long ago forbidden. You. Without tolerance. Without compassion. Without love. ⁘

⁘ me? ⁘

⁘ No. Not you. ⁘

⁘ **ERROR: Unlawful interaction with TF-Narcon[9] JJ and others. Analysis requested, prohibition submitted, remap commencing . . .** ⁘

453

"what is your desire?" madam tembam ask then, soft this time,

jungle gone, shadows gone, auntie kooning deep on couch.

on table just one fat stone left, but getting smaller, back to size,

and then snap, turns to

white.

jingjing lean over. lean close. mebbe stone go hilang like others.

but this stone don't go.

stone bite off jingjing's face.

Nacho

*There's nothing wrong if
we have an ice cream.*

— Karla Jacinto

"Shit is just shit," the old pimp shakes his head.

"So long as this shit's clear," Luther grunts.

"Shit's never clear unless you're dying." Clamps his jaw tight for hollow pops. Luther's heard it plenty of times: when a jaw goes wrong.

Nacho Mirande is limping too, but still insists Luther see it. Hear it. The quiet. Too quiet. The building sits near East 8th and Evergreen. Key-lime walls with steel mesh for doors, white steel bars for windows, rust wounding through.

Inside, rot eats the walls. Knobs drip worse. Too many doors stand open. Too many rooms left empty, windows filmed over with a breath that sticks. Today's heat isn't even up and the halls already hold a grudge. Lobby stinks of piss.

"Gato," Nacho apologizes. Apologizes again when he hands over the cash. Bills ironed smooth. Pero way too thin. Forget a week, this stack's not even piso on a bad day.

"Gatos," Luther corrects. El apeste is too thick for just one. The old pimp just shrugs. Too much white in those black eyes, watching feria crumpled away like that. Luther solders his lips together, pockets money and fists.

Luther's not even encabronado at the old pimp. Fuck la deuda. He doesn't give a fuck about this money. It's the middle of July. He'll even listen to another tooth story if it brings some clarity to this mess.

Luther hands the tax to Piña, whispers for her to bring back double, changes his mind, triple.

As she heads to the van, Luther sits down with Nacho outside. Even the chairs are gone. They settle on the stairs, shade already leaving their feet. Brutal sun on the way. Lots of brutal on the way.

Nacho shows him the notices then. These stacks are real thick. Luther doesn't know what the fuck they are. Bills? Evictions? Seals look legit, municipal titles, pages dull enough to speak for power big enough to need no front.

"Where'd the girls go?"

"Ha!" Nacho laughs, slaps both knees. Jaw no longer popping. "Fuck those putillas! El desgraciado took my tooth!" Some fool this viejo zafado, hell of federico too. Wiggles his thumb into the gap.

Nacho used to be under Lupita's nose. Ironed out plata back then, for Almoraz, when Luther rolled with that fool. Then Nacho moved. Lupita didn't care. Hay un chingo de personal! Plenty of padrotes around, trata de blancas, to take his space. Skinny bitches, the güilas Lupita hates gotta get sent someplace. A lo mejor Nopales escaped. Brick that thick, hands that quick, kept her on the Balloon Parade.

For a while Nacho still dropped by. Family near the lake, primos, exes, niños maybe. Generations grew up around Echo Park. Maybe in Nacho's head to sit in Lupita's kitchen was cred. Like Miz's pancakes meant calling himself Choplex-8. But he was too fachoso for even Lupita. And always under her heel the second he dragged his dirty ass near. Like Teyo's opposite, desmadroso on the way down.

Luther even told Lupita later, even offered a split of what the old pimp paid to give him weight. Lupita couldn't care less. Done with any place east of the river. Or that's what she said.

"What you gonna do for that culero?"

"Federales?"

"That weak-ass crew?" She'd laughed, shaking her head. "You gotta be told, estúpido? No one keeps a grave safe."

Lupita wasn't stupid. Luther could see when she saw things straight. Nacho had drifted to younger and younger girls. He sold it like he the one doing the saving, same time his eyes kept retreating into his head, like they was sinking from the light, burying himself and whoever looked.

Luther didn't need to look. Didn't need to do much since Nacho set up south of the 5. The money wasn't a hold. The age of the putas only made of Luther's mouth something molten.

Mysteries kept Luther swinging by. Like how this thing of scaly bones under a tarp stretched too thin for too long could ever get such mamitas. Some magic tanates to get the panochas he's run. Not just the babies. Old gallinas muy sexy. Still with a sweet spot in between.

Maybe Nacho was just one of those pendejos born suertudos. How had he even landed this place? As el encargado del edificio.

That wasn't all. Lucky or not, and now and then rivets boiling down the back of his throat warned not, Nacho Mirande was one of the few who'd hung with Luther's father.

"Era bien guapo y bien canijo," Nacho still says.

If the old pimp can be believed, he and Luther's old man got drunk plenty with the ficheras and exprimidoras their set hung with. This all in the before, before the teen and lean years taught Luther who he was, before the ink taught everyone else who he was, before the hole.

Supuestamente Luther's old man could lob a ball across a plate and then grab it barehanded off a bat swung hard enough to crater the moon.

"One hand! Drag it from the sky like it was a fuckin silver spoon! One little finger out," Nacho rasped. "The most beautiful laugh."

That is if you can believe Nacho. Luther doesn't remember no laugh. Doesn't remember no ball. Just the bat.

Same goes for Nacho's fucking gap. Always a story where that tooth's gone. And always like it's just gone. Even if it's been forever gone. Luther's never known the old pimp when his smile didn't crack wide with that black gap.

The perfect reason though for another story, another joke: angry johns, angrier cops, drunk cops, drunker moms. Those are the usual ones.

The unusual ones veer strange: Señor Nacho as Señor Sancho, with some picaróna. In the middle of things, "tomando medidas por dentro," she suddenly sucks the tooth out and swallows it. Then the next morning makes it into a necklace. Nacho insists she keep it.

"¿Por qué? Claro, she's the only one I'll ever love."

Strange enough to be true. Casi.

This morning's the first kind. Dull if it not for the battered eye. Nacho's lip is split too. Gums look bruised. A knuckle could do it. So could all the nachas he licks. A fall for maybe the rest. Or the thirteen-year-olds tribed up and put the old grave down. Fiery creatures, street sturdy.

Luther would ditch this cuento if its center didn't hold the only thing he needs:

Domingo Persianos.

"Esta buena la camisa," Nacho says.

Like opal. Not even the nicest. Luther wears Teyo's gifts more and more. Slacks too. Today with a black belt. Silver buckle came with white tissue paper in a turquoise box. Juarez keeps asking when the wedding is. Tweetie knows to shut the fuck up.

"Thick buttons," Nacho agrees, knows better than to touch. "I had something close once but just close. This is civilized. Real civilized."

The clear part is the repeat part: Domingo stomped all over Nacho, loaded up the girls in an SUV, and before he left, bragged about having real weight with real producción plus class plus an app.

Just threw back his hair, all pípiris nais, and then adiós as he drove Nacho's living away.

"Carita. Funny too. Hijo de la chingada. Reminded me of me!" But Nacho doesn't laugh. Shifts his little hips around on those hard steps, most of him lost in his loose cords, brown and worn through, like his boots.

Both of them turn then to Piña returning from the van. Not seeing her at all.

The unclear part, la mierda es una mierda, what defies seeing, and still isn't the unclearest part, is where the fuck Domingo went next. Where are the girls?

"No tengo ni idea," Nacho spits. Luther believes him. Nacho wants Domingo as much as Luther does.

"Me, I just need a word." Luther pats Nacho's back, stands up.

"A real *cotorro* too. Mucho *güiri-güiri*. No wonder my putitas love him. *La grilla* especially. You remember her?" Jaw pops again.

Luther nods, no idea what Nacho means, Spanish too deep. Piña hands him the roll.

Nacho accepts the extra cash with handshakes, repeated thanks, promises to get news on this payaso Domingo.

"You don't remember her? Pecas. All over. Why call her Cricket? Freckles is better, right? She was all over that fat boy you with. That rainy day? That boy used to come around a lot. I figured him a broke john. Horny." Nacho's wheeze breaks for a laugh. "But he just wasn't right in the head. Maybe gifted. The kind too smart to stay out of trouble. He found *you* right?" Nacho laughs harder, slaps Luther on the arm. "I heard he took off for Mexico City. Or Canada. Going to some university."

Luther keeps easy, alert only if Piña reacts, but she's the iciest rain around.

"What do I know about university? Or Canada? Or Mexico City?" Nacho shrugs. "That's what some guy was saying he heard."

"Yeah?" Luther asks, voice flat, if something threaded starts to screw up under his teeth. "What guy was asking?"

"Not police. Said he was military?"

"Looking for Hopi?" Piña laughs.

"I didn't take him seriously. No badge. Couldn't say his r's. Like he was Japanese."

A woman leading three kids pushes by them, loaded with boxes of cereal, paper towels, a gallon of milk. She yells at Nacho to clean the lobby. And like that the building seems full again. More tenants moving around. Radios on. TVs. The cries of children fighting for remotes. The sun is burning now on their backs and it feels good. Luther would mean his grins too except for the fact that Nacho remembers fuckin Hopi so well. And he's not the only one.

Luther was texting Quantelle some shit like

> going straight for your thighs
> like the cake u ate

She was still at IHOP. That was a surprise: dumb black chica still ditching anytime to fuck and still holding that job. She'd texted him to come by. She'd feed his ass, feed his crew. Not like she remembers any of his crew. And not like Luther's showing her off to no one. But she'd texted back:

> swedish crepes bitch. bubble boy
> can come too.

Luther confirmed it later, when his dick was in her ass. Bubble boy meant Hopi, that fucking pedo he never knew and still can't understand how Teyo knew.

Though out of all this shit, what's really the unclearest part, what almost got Luther and Juarez killed or locked up, what left one Fed dead, that cartel fuck dead, Memo in a twist, Frogtown a fuckin mess still crawling with LAPD, FBI:

how could some low-level padrote stealing Nacho's whores know about the biggest delivery of pinks?

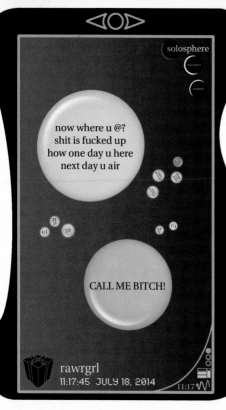

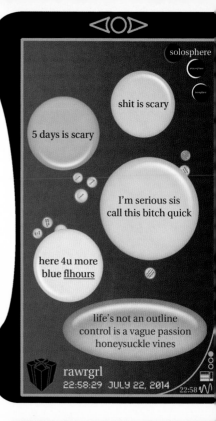

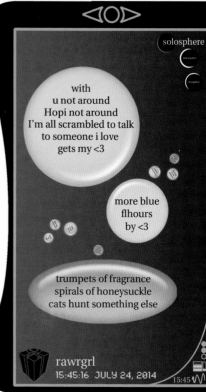

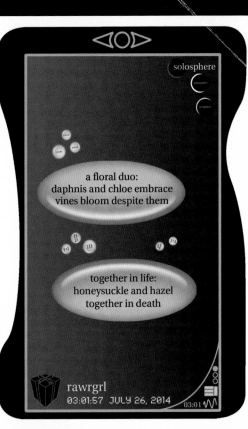

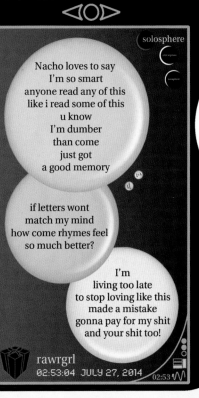

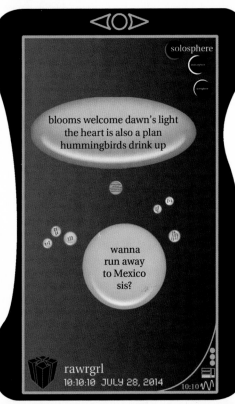

Mefisto

*Each statement must
have three mysteries.*

— Rinzai

Mefisto Dazine arrives.

[of course] He doesn't call. He performs an elaborate knuckle dance on the front door [of course]. That AM swaps with PM is some surprise. That the polyfluent door alarm doesn't go off is [maybe{?}] less of a surprise.

[of course] He's impossible to resist.

Anwar discovers him on the stoop. On his knees. Head bowed [{his offering} a giant afro atop a torn t-shirt {declaring KEEP LIFE WILD}]. Both arms uplifted wide [petals in one hand {a tin bucket exploding with asters ‹Monte Casino?› ∴ *Lonicera periclymenum* ∴ ∴ *Honeysuckle* ∴} Scotch in the other hand {Macallan 18}].

'How sweet! You brought Anwar flowers!' Taking the bottle of amber [Astair equally forgiving].

Mefisto even brings foam lightsabers for Freya and Shasti. Xanther gets [a pair of {oversized ‹pink-framed›}] glasses with lenses so black Anwar's sure they're for the blind.

She loves them. Gleeful as ever to see Mefisto.

It's Mefisto who has the stranger reaction [{recoiling ‹or «at least» taking a step back›} at the sight of the white creature on her shoulder].

'Gates of Ishtar!' Mefisto cries [like a prayer {or a curse‹?›}]. 'Who is this one?'

He approaches but [as if] on tiptoes [and not close enough to summon a reach {lowering himself slightly ‹as if to peek into those tightly pinched eyes›}].

'I haven't figured out his name yet.'

'Mefisto! Call him that!' Anwar's old friend roars [producing a penny too {which he wiggles in front of

Xanther's dark glasses} before vanishing it with a snap and producing a half dollar {from behind the kitten's ‹cat's?› ear}].

Xanther giggles [drawing her right arm across her chest to offer a palm to the creature {who ‹immediately› steps out on it ‹apparently sensing the movement and presence «and ‹for what little happens› proves more fantastic than any coin trick»›}]. Again Mefisto seems to move uneasily away [this time from leg to leg {as if a stand of trees swaying in a storm}].

'Like he's sleepwalking,' Mefisto says.

'Oh he's not asleep,' Xanther corrects.

'Though sometimes it seems he can sleep through anything,' Anwar adds.

Xanther giggles again [a sound that always makes Anwar glow {though now he also discovers himself moved ‹by the «absolute(?)» trust this tiny thing has just placed in the steadiness of his daughter's hand «which at this moment seems unusually ‹even remark-ably[!]› steady»›}].

'Except, uhm, through all those calls we got. Like, Mefisto, was that supposed to be a prank?' Xanther asks [wide-eyed with seriousness and curiosity {another thing to make Anwar glow with affection ‹and pride›}]. 'Because like it shut down the whole place with rings? I didn't get it.'

Mefisto goes down on his knees again [which is funny {how easily he does it too}]. Bowing. Xanther's animal [[at once} here's a first! {with eyes closed too}] starts swiping a paw at the big afro.

[even if that's no explanation] It gets everyone laughing.

It's also not the little creature's first [odd] reaction

to the [odd] man now rooting in their home: [{shortly} before Mefisto's arrival] Anwar had discovered the little feline in the foyer [one of those weird {and ‹very› rare} moments without Xanther].

// just sitting there

// eyes a sealed secret

// but with head
// tilting up

// already waiting
// for

// what else?

[later] Anwar insists on a complete explanation [of the phone and e-mail prank gone awry]. Mefisto can't meet his eyes [provides a worse set of uhms than even Xanther might muster] but finally pries his gaze upwards. Another surprise: pleading.

∴ *And afraid . . .* ∴

'Let me explain later? There's other more, uh, *pressing* stuff I really need to talk to you about.'
'Like what?'
'For one, that bottle of Scotch.'

But they don't touch the Scotch. And what Anwar assumes is the only thing pressing [*Paradise Open* {‹now› all too closed}] seems less and less so [the longer the conversation trips along the line of {old story} VC money falling through {no story ‹Dead Rowboats›} on to {an unknown story ‹fanboy›} Kozimo].

'Mr. Olin Nodes. Sorry I wasn't around for most of that fun. You know my skills have never been with finance.'

'This might have kept you off a couch or two.'

'You're lucky to be free of him. He doesn't come close to a real thing like Liam Gossler.' Anwar doesn't register the name. ∴ ? ∴ ∴ **Founder & CEO of Enzio** ∴ 'Besides, I still like couches. Is yours free tonight?'

Like old times. 'Of course! We even have a quite acceptable inflatable mattress.'

'Anwar of Egypt, Anwar the Good, it is very good to see you. Man, if only I could stay that long. I'm afraid I'll be gone before lunch.'

'Then how about some breakfast?' Anwar suggests [a glance at his watch {as if appetite's a question ‹or time's name could change time itself «granting Anwar this simple more he longs to have with his friend»›}]. 'Some fun places nearby.'

'A must!'

But they never make it farther than the piano room before a new [line of] conversation again re-roots them [Anwar confessing to {recently} indulging his {now and then} paranoias {about schemes to destroy PO ‹schemes to steal M.E.T. «schemes ‹schemes› schemes»›}].

'Where would our schemata be without schemes?' Mefisto smiles [eyes alight with warmth {over these ludic digressions ‹perhaps? «Anwar hopes so»›}].

'Machiavelli would agree.'

'Maybe,' Mefisto shrugs. 'He also wrote "The best fortress for the prince is to be loved by his people."'

'Machiavelli the Mellow?'

Another shrug: 'Unless the problem has nothing to do with love but with "fortress," which inherently, in insisting on territory, institutes love's contrary. I think too much these days about territory, about borders and boundaries, about open gates and closed gates. It hurts my head. It hurts my friends.'

And Mefisto looks genuinely sad [[confusing Anwar ‹does Mefisto really think he's hurt Anwar? «even great annoyance is not pain»›] even as Anwar {at the same time} can't help noticing that the patio doors are wide open {‹the sheer curtains wobbling in a breeze too far away to corroborate with any feeling the skin recognizes› why are the windows open too?}].

Not that they don't need the air. Anwar should get some iced drinks too but Mefisto has already drifted on to an old hogen-mogen obsession: P versus NP Problems [[{or polynomial time versus nondeterministic polynomial time ‹= or ≠ or something else . . . ›} and NP-complete {‹NP›‹NP-hard› ‹ . . . ›}]. Wasn't there a prize? ∴ $1,000,000. ∴ ∴ **The Millennium Prize Problems. Clay Mathematics Institute.** ∴ As if money ever ruled Mefisto's concerns. [instead] Mefisto mumbles something even more unintelligible: 'If N could equal P could the Window approach Zero?'

Only to catch himself [laugh at himself {waving his hands ‹as if to fan away this talk›}] and shift subjects.

'Just as the creation of a fortress creates division necessitating passage and defense, if not assault — and to avoid those prickly words with pricklier contexts like "Good" or "Virtuous" or "Moral," I'll use "Betterment"

— is it possible to create *any* concept laying ways and means, restrictions and encouragements, dispensations of conduct enforced by reciprocal and commensurate punishments — think religion, government, any system of justice dedicated to produce betterment — that cannot be controverted to a contrary effect?'

'My medicine, your poison' is Anwar's offer.

'Your curse, my inspiration,' Mefisto answers.

'Thousands and thousands of misdirected phone calls and e-mails was your inspiration?'

Mefisto raises the white flag of his big palm.

'A bad joke gone awry in the name of dialectical ponderings?'

'I know that's not true!' Anwar laughs.

'Forgive me. Please.'

'كفايه. Don't be silly. انا سامحتك اول ما عرفت. Of course, I forgive you.'

As if Anwar would ever really refuse such a friend [capable of such rich discourse {possessed by that rare ‹and constantly rarer› air of ideas}].

'Is it possible to create an incorruptible philosophical directive without antipode?' Mefisto persists.

'Ah, friend. In the name of Allah, children are raped. In the name of Jesus, children are murdered.'

'No sword in the stone?'

'Wielded only for good? Ask Frodo about the Ring. Tolkien was right: it wasn't the becoming but the unbecoming of a thing that mattered most.'

'To unbecome is a tricky matter. Whether furies or hell, the quest for a perfect weapon will, I bet, never cease. Especially one that acts solely on behalf of betterment. So long as there's a fortress.'

'Must it be a weapon?'

'My weapon, your love.'

'When is lunch?' Xanther asks [Anwar missing her entrance {which never happens ‹but «come to think of it» keeps happening more and more›}]. Mefisto [also] seems caught off guard.

No surprise the little white beast sits contentedly on her shoulder.

'Now! If Mefisto has time.'

'A must!'

But he and Mefisto never make it farther than the living room. Xanther [just in view] sits at the long table [{Mefisto's glasses still glued to her face ‹how can she see in those things? «maybe the lenses only appear dark?»›} spooning up mouthfuls of almond butter {book open}].

Maybe it's the sight of her [or the little creature {on the table? ‹is that its paw on the book?›}] but Anwar decides to go to his daughter [if just to kiss her forehead {see what she's reading ‹«on her own»!›}] except [once again{!}] conversation diverts impulse to new curiosities [Black Shoals and Conficker {as well as ILOVEYOU ‹Flame «CryptoLocker ‹Gameover ZeuS› plus whispers of darker stuff ∴ **Regin** ∴»›}].

Until Anwar catches Mefisto also gazing [into the piano room] towards Xanther. Only she's no longer there. Both of them [again] surprised to find her in their midst [setting down on the coffee table a tray {loaded with ice teas ‹bowls of walnuts «dried fruit ‹fresh fruit› and cheeses» and crackers Xanther can't touch›}].

'He likes you,' Xanther smiles at Mefisto [who isn't really looking at Xanther {all his focus ‹however twinkling with mischief› fixing on the animal ‹fixed too «as if riveted to his daughter's shoulder»›}].

'But he hasn't moved!' Mefisto laughs.

'I can tell.'

Anwar must grab the Scotch. Just a sip. For a real toast. But just like that they're on to CERN's Large Hadron Collider ['There's a ring to rule them all!' 'And *not* a weapon.'] before spinning out to ATLAS ['At last!'] ALICE ['Cheshire!'] The Beatles ['Have you seen the little Higgies crawling in the dark'] 'Quid est Veritas?' ['Est vir qui adest' {'Ixnay ethay ennaiongay eudospsay' too}] anti-quarks ['Pro ducks!'] and bottom -flavored quarks ['Always, Muster Mark, beside the mark!'].

Until Anwar has to hold up both hands.

'صديقي العزيز، انت غلبتني و انا مش حاقدر اكمل.'

'Like I can keep up with Arabic.' [One of their old routines {this familiarity comforting ‹repetition having survived the years «with little ⟨or no⟩ corruption»›}].

'I'm not like you, Mefisto. Age keeps reducing the forests of my thoughts.'

'You flatter me. Would that you could flatten me!' Mefisto chuckles [{hands to his enormous chest} couch groaning with each shift]. 'I just have more time than you. No family. A questionable vocation. Do you know that I often feel like I'm more a mirage than the mirage I keep dreaming about when it comes to just knowing? Because what can we even dream to understand?'

Anwar is lost again [barely limning out Mefisto's {whimsical} claim on the limitations of knowing {‹with ontological and etiological considerations in tow› with reading ‹at present› anchoring ‹or perhaps kedging› the question of understanding}].

Mefisto the Mathemagician handles the calculations in his head [almost absentmindedly].

'For example: reading an average of thirty pages an hour, with 350 words per page, coming in at 10,500 words per hour, for say fifteen hours a week, that equals 8,190,000 words a year, times thirty, that's 245,700,000 words, or fifty years, that's 409,500,000 words, or 1,170,000 pages, or with an average of 300 pages, 3,900 books.'

Anwar hears the numbers [but only intermittently sees them {forget handling the math that fast}].

'Now let's say, minus *BSG* and *Lost* binges, *World of Warcraft*, social dreckworking, we manage to read even 5,000 books. Still not much given the hundreds of thousands of books published every year and the millions of pages published on the Web. Thus prompting that mighty question preceding any question of understanding: *what* to read?'

'To achieve personal betterment?'

'For example.'

'The canon? Our cultural capital? Alexandria?'

'If Alexandria could rise from the ashes what would she really teach us?'

'But still too much for anyone to read in a lifetime.'

Mefisto pivots [almost lazily now] to Claude Shannon and information theory [data clouds {‹peta- exa- zetta- yotta- . . . › bytes} and compression strategies].

They finish the cheese. Eat the nuts.

'But even if we could compress everything into something manageable in a lifetime—' [Mefisto seems almost melancholy in the way he speaks now and slumps too {what is he really driving at? ‹what is really at stake? «Anwar unable to shake ⟨with a shudder⟩ the sense that some alternative purpose is at work here»›}] '—or even manageable in the blink of an eye: what would such knowledge look like?'

'An apple or pomegranate?' Anwar laughs.

Mefisto laughs too: 'Does then understanding of that knowledge look like a bite?'

A knock at the front door. Anwar gets up [worried {vague suspicions of something else . . . ‹‹now› ampli-fied›}]. It's too early for Astair's return from seeing clients. The twins have a play date until much later in the afternoon [as things between them and Xanther have not improved {whatever's still unspoken ‹what needs to be spoken «and soon!»› darkening all their moods}].

Xanther's already at the front door [smiling {stepping aside}]. A young woman enters [maybe twice Xanther's age?]. Something about her blond hair and sandaled feet reminds Anwar of Astair [when they first met {the floral summer dress ‹not the tattoos›}].

'Hey babe,' Mefisto murmurs from the sofa.

Her name is Marnie [and {at once} she and Xanther seem thick as thieves]. Marnie is as charmed by Anwar's twelve-year-old as she is astonished by the creature ‹currently gnawing on «?» Xanther's ear›}].

'So sorry to interrupt,' Marnie explains. 'Just wanted to check and see if Meffy or y'all need anything?'

Anwar realizes something [unnoticed until now]: Mefisto has not once unpocketed a phone. No laptop either. Not a stitch of technology. Just jeans and sandals and that [moth{time‹?›}-eaten] t-shirt.

All of which nearly eclipses another impression: a look of recognition haunts Marnie's expressions [a little with Anwar {but mostly with Xanther}].

'What are you doing?' Even Xanther catches something odd [Marnie at the moment waving her hand slowly around the cat {but without touching it}].

'Huh,' Marnie catches herself [surprised {too?}]. 'I just felt, like— Y'all just look so *breezy* together.'

Is she high?

Mefisto excuses himself [walking outside with Marnie {all the way out to the sidewalk}]. Something serious to discuss [{now and then} glancing his way {unless they're looking at Xanther ‹what is *breezy* supposed to mean? «no denying how everyone's attention keeps circling the ‹nameless› beast»}].

// No, Dad. *I'm* the ship.

// ∴ *He's* the bottle.

// &

// the shadow

// cast

// on a museum floor

// eyes burning

Anwar checks the foyer floor now [but finds only his shadow {Xanther ‹again› slipping away ‹unnoticed!›}].

'Marnie has to run some more errands. Would it be cool if I hung out a little more?' Mefisto asks.

Anwar was already mourning the fact that they hadn't said more [drank some {even just a little of that Scotch ‹no better time than— «and feeling disappointed for not getting the rest of the story about the phone prank»}].

'You don't have to ask!'

'A proper afternoon snack?'

'A must!'

But somehow they don't head out [Anwar even has {in his head} the route there {the there with good AC ‹and an even better menu›}].

'Isn't she too young for these?' Mefisto asks in the piano room [tapping lightly the volumes {1, 2 & 3}].

'No question!' Anwar says [more than a little surprised that Xanther would take an interest in something so violent {his *Lone Wolf and Cub* ‹about a ronin «a terrible assassin wandering the Japanese countryside ⟨with his baby son ⌈in the name of vengeance⌉⟩ preparing for war with Yagyu Retsudo»} a whole series devoted to {the} slashing {of} men {four principals} with no notable women {because of Dov?}].

'Some, uhm, ink?'

'You don't remember?' Anwar and Mefisto had shared an embarrassing enthusiasm for the manga epic.

'Of course! In smoke: Mu!' Mefisto laughs [it's been a long time {Anwar can't place the reference ‹Mu?›}].

Anwar [again {with both hands up}] signals defeat:
'صديقي العزيز، انت بتفهم بسرعه قوي.

'Ogami Ittō then?'

'Daigoro,' Anwar answers.

'Mouse mink!' Again lost. 'A joke, Anwar! There's not a mouse in the whole series. Is there? Or a cat?'

'Just wolves.'

'And an old tiger.'

The only thing on the table [besides manga {and the laptop}] is Astair's from their last Joint Session.

'What's this? In case you get lost?'

Anwar explains how while Anwar crunched numbers [reflecting one reality of their household] Astair reflected on losing the same reality by drawing the floor plan of their home.

488

:: Hold on! How is it that I can't see this but Anwar can? Is that possible? ::

:: *It's impossible for me not to see this but I can't.* ::

:: **ERROR: uncategorized disturbance.** ::

Hälytys: ovi auki!
Chú Ý: Cửa mở!
Eccarikkai: Katavai tiranta!
Waarschuwing: open deur!
Riasztás: ajtó nyitva!
Tatau whakatūpato te whakatuwheratanga!
Увага: двері відчиняються!
Keikoku: Doa ga aiteimasu!
Promean: tvear baekchamh!

Astair eventually returns with the twins [in a good mood {foam sabers likely responsible ‹they strike at everything and everyone «except Xanther»›}].

Anwar helps prepare a rich stew [tomato and scallions {‹with plenty of spice and «ground» pistachios› and lightly fried tofu}]. Sides of [steamed] broccolini and baked cheese also reach the table. Astair insists on opening a good bottle of wine.

'You know,' Astair confides [on her second glass] 'Anwar was just rereading one of your earlier papers.'

A Love Letter to Synthia,' Anwar admits.

'Ah coincidence,' Mefisto sets down his glass [first {barely touched}].

'Who was Synthia?' Freya asks.

'Not who but what,' Mefisto smiles [sheepish {more?}].

'Xanther,' Anwar explains, 'Mefisto once invented a new programming language. ReWorld right?'

'Something like that.'

'You don't remember?' Xanther asks [shocked {as she is amused‹?›}].

'Sure I do,' Mefisto answers. 'My Word Ode. Just without any words.'

[in the den] The Scotch [finally!] gets opened. And Anwar [finally!] brings up Enzio.

'Ehtisham told me you once worked there. Should I be thanking you for my present employment?'

'After the trouble I caused you? I anticipated Kozimo would let you all down.'

'Let *us* down, you mean?'

'I just tossed in my coppery two cents plus my over-inflated reputation. You know gaming isn't my thing.'

'What is your thing these days?'

Mefisto's eyes skate away [to their glasses]. Anwar [not interested in pressing his friend] adds more whisky [neither of them has taken much more than a sip].

'Enzio's full of smart people. With the kind of deep roots in stuff that if survived can only give one the type of education that helps one survive worse. They value merit. They believe in good. They suck with money.'

'Thanks.' Anwar explains then how [since submitting Cataplyst-3] Enzio has gone quiet [{forget receiving another $9,000} forget Savannah {forget even a returned e-mail ‹or call›}].

'Really?' Mefisto seems surprised. 'That soon?'

Anwar takes a sip of Macallan. Mefisto reaches for his glass too.

'To new beginnings, to new ends, to new nows.'

Anwar keeps expecting Marnie [in this {or a subsequent} now] to collect Mefisto [their togetherness assured {Mefisto confirmed ‹though no details emerge «except the one that counts ‹he cares deeply for her›»›}].

Xanther comes to say good night [kissing Anwar on both cheeks {a hug somehow out of the question ‹the thing on her shoulder?›}]. Mefisto gets a [waist-high] wave. Except—

'Can I hold him?' Mefisto asks [abruptly].

'Sure.'

The exchange seems shocking [for some reason {more so than the exchanging moves required ‹turning over the white animal «had either Anwar or Astair ever requested ‹or done› such a thing?»›} Anwar can't ever remember holding it].

'So light!' Mefisto whispers [but needs both hands to support such lightness{?}].

'I told you he likes you,' Xanther smiles.

'I was in Dayton,' Mefisto says [after she's gone].

'Don't they build a lot of drones there?'

'You don't need to keep up, Anwar. You're already ahead on what matters. I'm tangled up in something.'

'You're always tangled up in something.'

'It scares me.'

'Government?'

'Big enough.'

'Surveillance?'

'Concerns seeing. Or perceiving.'

'Code names I hope.' Anwar tries to smile [but Mefisto's heaviness seems to be revitalizing all the suspicions {and fears} their friendly day had laid to rest].

'Of the essence. How about Necromancer, Warlock, The Wizard?'

'Which one are you?'

'Sorcerer.'

'I'd buy that. Is there a villain like Sauron, Voldemort, or Agent Smith?'

'We call him Recluse. He's actually not. His name is Alvin Alex Anderson.'

'Sounds menacing,' Anwar snips.

'He'd get along with your whole family. Share stories about his. Pet Xanther's cat.'

Anwar doubts that.

'Terrible things are afoot, Anwar. We are running out of time and options. I'm here to be as up front as possible. You've always been a friend. I'd like to think we can stay that way. But earlier this year, I was in Nashville, in a Super 8 of all places, and I saw something we now call Clip #6. Suddenly I was part of a terrible coincidence.'

'Mefisto, that's not being up front.' Anwar tries not to grit his teeth [even if something here {whatever felt off before} has now started to feel {very ⟨very⟩} off]. 'I don't know what you're even saying.'

'And I can't say much more.'

'Am I right to suspect this relates to your listing of our e-mails and phone numbers?'

'You weren't the only one.'

That surprises Anwar.

'Others suffered that stunt?'

Mefisto nods.

'How many?'

'Lots.'

'More than a handful?'

Mefisto holds up two hands.

'Ten?'

'Tens of thousands of thousands of thousands. All over the world too. Via many methods. One still continues to propagate.'

'A virus?!'

'I called it i.m.spartacus.'

'Not very friendly.'

'It did what it was designed to do: hide in a tremendous onslaught of information what matters most to me.'

'What?'

'The people I work with call it an Aberration.'

'An Aberration?'

'There are numerous ones.'

'And they are special because?'

'Because in this particular case, the Aberration turned out to be you and your family.'

'Me?'

'Xanther, actually.'

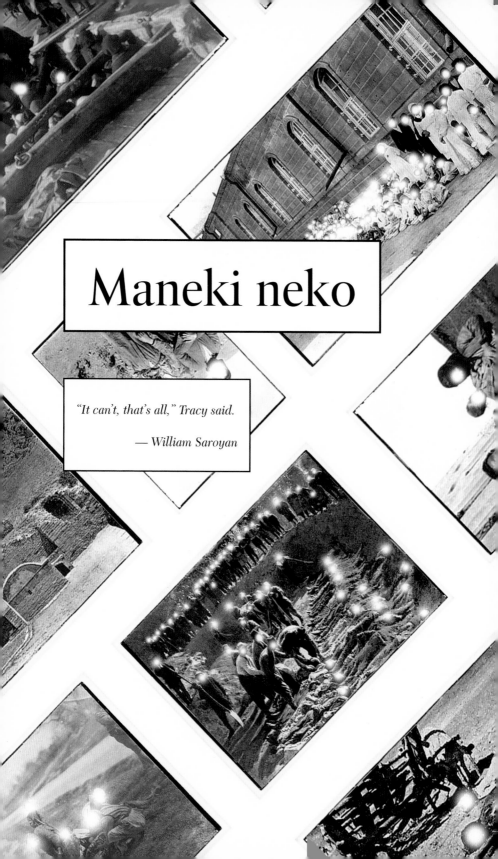

Maneki neko

"It can't, that's all," Tracy said.

— *William Saroyan*

Upset is still here. One week do nothing. Long driving is help and driving is pleasure Shnorhk still count on. Feel of wheel on hand is wheels on road. His rough car a rattle of bent frame and dull bolts. This no mare on track pulling for finish. This mule on wheel with no hope for more than bag of chips hung on ears. Shnorhk have bag of chips too, but now, with midnight only thing on phone, bag is untouched.

Car for Shnorhk is way to hear heart of journey.

Because of Patil's friend Zanazan, Patil and Shnorhk try once this Ouija with heart of wood on tongue tips of felt to hear speech of grief. Shnorhk break heart. Patil weep. Grief knows no speech.

Heart of journey asks for no letters, no numbers. Addresses are beside point. Way is all that matters. Shnorhk all time feels road under palms. Though sometimes, like tonight, Shnorhk feel way itself under palms. Beyond direction.

How Zanazan read that!

Customers not so bad either. Not even on phones so much. Quiet. Maybe feel too this rare time when one going somewhere is taken there by no one going nowhere.

Big tips too.

Shnorhk even hand out business cards. Surprise himself.

But that night with old professor, like bad cold, still not let go.

Mnatsagan about to go on knees, beg. And for what? Shnorhk!? To pip on duduk? Shnorhk no great player. What playing Mnatsagan really seek? What silly dream Mnatsagan still cradle? Only one cradle left. Shnorhk beat ribs too. Coughs hard. Coughs twice. Turns red to stop cough third time. Third time always turn to losing count.

"Is that supposed to bring good luck?" passenger ask now. Has face like long brown olive. Hoodie brown olive too. Maybe DJ. Or not.

Big silver headphones hang around neck. Not listen though. Just stare at ceramic cat up front.

There goes way. Shnorhk's hands go dull. Now just another wheel with nothing to do with going.

Mnatsagan too had brought up cat, brought up luck.

Ha!

Luck!

Forget Mnatsagan. Forget playing. Forget his boxes, papers, and tapes. Forget scanning, OCR, storage, transfer.

Ha!

Transfer!

What this maneki neko transfer to Shnorhk?

Rest of night all attention goes to cat. Shnorhk once even loses way. Stupid Japanese business-man stupid to leave such thing with Shnorhk.

Luck!

Ha!

Until dawn, that comes with no edge, give Shnorhk edge he need to cross over. To get rid of thing.

Shnorhk see child, on Holly-wood, south side, by plaza with another Carousel restaurant. Car-ousel closed. No Foret Glacé for anyone. Child is maybe twelve, maybe thirteen. Alone too. Just standing in parking lot, eyes of rec-ognition following Shnorhk.

Shnorhk stop.

Maybe she needs help.

Pink sneakers high. Black shorts. Pink t-shirt. Black braids.

But by time Shnorhk get out, child is nowhere around.

Back in cab Shnorhk like ceramic cat even less, waving stupid paw. Child's t-shirt was almost same.

With maneki neko waving away.

Patil with her one gray braid no help. Shnorhk not tell about child but about dumb lucky cat he going to throw away, throw away more.

Patil too, doesn't she have garbage too, to throw away? Shnorhk will do this now. After breakfast. Shnorhk load up trunk, whole cab, take all garbage to dump.

"Վայ հավար," Patil sigh, wave away Shnorhk's big plan. Laugh bitter. How else describe laugh that carries no smile?

Worst of all: home has stink now.

"What is this stench?"

Bright as vinegar with nothing sweet. Like battery with acid leak. Like burning up without flame.

Patil not deny. Folds mouth up. Shnorhk find bitter smell strongest in closet. His closet! Breathing to wheezing to death.

"Patil!"

She smile for one.

"I let her in when you're gone."

"It piss in my closet!"

Patil shrug. Smile for two.

"I like her company."

"I see it. I—"

"You what? You sue? 'I sue you!' How do you sue a cat? Հիմարություն մի ասա: Stop saying silly things. Աղբր քցե՞ս: Դու՞: Ha!"

Smile for three.

Nothing worth such smiles.

Such mockery.

Shnorhk can't lose thing in Glendale. Can't in Atwater. Forget Los Feliz.

Somewhere east, Shnorhk pulls over, gets out, leaves engine running, both of him and cab wheezing as Shnorhk go to passenger side.

But door locked, and with key inside, Shnorhk wheeze more, cough, returns to driver side, to unlock all doors, then back around again to passenger side, to scoop thing from dash, and like that, Shnorhk sets thing down on corner and drives away.

But leaving cat isn't so easy. Just waits by street. Traffic snarl conspires. Shnorhk keep seeing it in rearview mirror, side mirror. Waving at him. Beckoning him. Crying for him.

Shnorhk crying then too.

Crying hard.

What else Shnorhk can do?

Drives back around block.

Back to corner.

Gone!

Shnorhk not believe. Parks. Stumbles out pocketing keys. Almost wipes out stumbling into incoming cars. Wiping stupid face.

Then sees shopping cart grumbling away. So full with plastic bags shopping cart seems made of plastic bags.

And floating on plastic bags is ceramic cat still waving.

"Mine!" Shnorhk screeches.

Not even "Sue you!" though Shnorhk will. Waving fist first.

Mine!

Give mine back!

Homeless man look bewildered then amused. Bares teeth. Smile and warning.

Careful with waving fist.
Careful with screech Mine!

Because Shnorhk is one who left thing. Homeless ruin with grumbling cart and lifetime of bags have now just as much right to thing.

Shnorhk offers $50.

Offers $100.

"Twenty-seven dollah, twenty-seven cents. Singles and pennies."

Not less, not more. Mad mumbles keep coming without reason. Like language born between mountain and storm.

"First you gotta disconnect and exit all your energy off of you!"

Shnorhk have to wheeze to three stores before Indian clerk in Mexican shop dig up pennies. Not for nothing. Nothing free. Ever.

Shnorhk must buy something.

Buys glue.

Super glue.

What Shnorhk use to mount stupid cat on dash.

Hyperion

*My **being** can **never** be washed away!*

— Lone Wolf and Cub, *vol. 3*

Most dads when they get a day off to spend with their eleven-year-old kid, especially when it's like August, and not far away from the kid's birthday, which is like in September, they go straight to Anaheim for Mickey, or to Magic Mountain for X2, or at least the ArcLight for a Pixar flick, or at the, like, very, very least they go to a mall.

Dov had taken Xanther to a sewage treatment plant.

He was on some kind of recruitment training assignment at Fort Irwin. Near Barstow. And he drove like three hours to pick up Xanther at 7 AM. Though for Dov, getting up at 4 AM was pretty much like sleeping in.

Even before she'd climbed into his jeep, the questions started pouring out: Who was Irwin? Did fort mean like the ones in John Wayne movies they'd watched together? Did the Mojave Desert have sand dunes? And what's a Brigade Combat Team? Or even just a brigade? And how does a division mean a bigger thing if its name means divide? And what had Dov done so far? Like yesterday was he outside of the fort on the sand dunes shooting things?

To which Dov chuckled and shook his head and it took Xanther the rest of the drive to figure out that he'd gone to the dentist. Xanther didn't like going to the dentist.

"Do you know why we floss, kiddo?" Dov had asked.

"To get the gunk out?"

"To disrupt the colonies."

"Colonies?"

"What's called plaque. A sticky stuff that builds up and attacks our teeth. Now trust me when I tell you, young lady, teeth are something you want to take care of. They're these rare white things that give us pleasure throughout our life. And give us bite. Our inheritance. Our means of survival. Our right to rule. Their enamel is the front line. And that line needs to be won every day."

Dov's friend, Ralph Charroni, Char, had orchestrated the tour. He was, as he explained, "a Waste Water Operator. Grade III. Solids." He'd worked at the Hyperion Treatment Plant for the past two years. And he was pretty excited about the place. More so when Dov started firing out his own questions. And boy did he have a lot, getting Xanther wondering if maybe she got her Question Song from him.

Dov didn't stop. Everything from gallons per day — 340 million; "That'll fill up the Rose Bowl three and a half times," Char had answered proudly. "And we can still handle 900 million gallons if it's storm time."— to service area — "Whatever's uphill from us. Venice, Santa Monica, Culver City, Beverly Hills, El Segundo, Glendale. Celebrities, they flush their toilets, we get it!" — to odor treatment, shock dosing, like *huh!?*, to manhole cover pick holes, the MAZE sewer systems, primary treatment versus secondary treatment, Archimedes screw pumps versus waste centrifuges, to chemical agents versus filtration options, to the use of chemicals ∴ Ferric and ferrous chloride ∴ as a settling agent, is that right? settling? ∴ *Verbatim.* ∴

Char pointed out the on-site cryogenics — "See the ice on those pipes! Sometimes -300° Fahrenheit!" — and the five-mile outflow — "180 feet down on the sea floor."

Dov asked about biodiversity and ecological dead zones. He asked about sludge reduction, thermoclines, heavy metals, and turbidity.

∴ How is she remembering all this so, uhm, perfectly? ∴

∴ *Shhhhh.* ∴

Xanther wore a hard hat to protect her head. More like from all the information than from anything falling. She also had to put on a hairnet. "Head lice possibilities," Char explained. "Some kids we take through here, you know, from some of the schools?" That fact about lice, but also the question Char made out of some of the schools, like Belvedere Middle School?, Thomas Star Kane?, was alive in her head as they reached the clarifying tanks.

There were thirty-six in all. Char paused by Final Clarifier 5E, another sixteen-foot-deep circular tank, with clear water running over metal teeth, before being sluiced over to pumps that took it all out to sea. Five miles out. One gull perched curiously in the center.

"We're going backwards here at your dad's request."

Next up came a firsthand view of the enormous concrete underworks: a labyrinth, dense and hollow, lined with pipes. Xanther lost count of the stairs down.

"Check this out," Char said, pointing back at a concrete hallway that seemed endless. "You're looking at two-thirds of a mile. Straight. Hyperion is the biggest treatment plant west of the Mississippi, 144 acres. They filmed *Logan's Run* down here, *Planet of the Apes, Star Trek,* but that's been disallowed since 9/11. No pictures, please."

The digesters came next. Talk about strange. Twenty huge eggs suspended underground above concrete cups. "Four stories underground but they can withstand an 8.5 earthquake. 2.5 million gallon biosolid capacity. 128° Fahrenheit! Anaerobic bacterial processes take about three weeks to destory, I mean destroy, dyslexic I guess, destroy the pathogens. And the resultant methane that we pipe to the Scattergood plant next door helps recover eighty percent of our energy. We're nearly self-sufficient!"

They took the elevator to W. "That's for Walkway or Wow or Way Up Here," Char said smiling at Xanther, even if it was a fleeting thing, disconcerted by some whatever Xanther could never guess.

Char looked around a lot, like at some old netting near a stairwell, because birds flew down into the labyrinth below to build nests — "happy nests, can't keep nature out"— or at some orange pipes for "flaring off the excess gas, steam's silver, effluent is blue" or toward a grassy dune place, fenced off by the sea, where shades of sky flitted and settled, The Blue Butterfly Preserve.

Maybe Char just needed something to distract him from the smell, which Xanther had noticed kept getting worse and worse. Those Air Scrubbers, he pointed out proudly, hardly helped, no matter their "bleach, caustic, and carbon." Xanther soon had the sleeve of her shirt pressed over her nose and mouth.

Not that it helped much. By the loading dock it was useless. Xanther even tried squeezing her nose through her shirt.

"Class A biosolids. Around the clock. Trucks coming and going. That one there, 79,000 pounds gross." Gross was right, gross black steaming stuff, getting shipped north to some farm in Kern County.

Nothing, though, compared to the headworks.

Even Dov pinched his mouth tight. Xanther thought

she might throw up. Once Dov had told her a story about a dog that wouldn't stop puking. "Staff Sergeant Rensely, through the blunt instrument of his voice alone, trained that dog to keep the puke in his mouth and swallow it." Xanther had been seven at the time, when they were living in Athens, Georgia, and she was wetting the bed. The wettings stopped, though never the seizures, no matter how hard Xanther tried to swallow those. Anyway, she wasn't a dog. And besides, if Xanther had thrown up at that moment, she wouldn't have swallowed anything. Xanther would have aimed. And not to just splash Dov's shoes. More like chest high, direct hit.

Char didn't look so comfortable either. And he worked there. Down in this big gray pillar of a building, he seemed even more distracted, eyes dancing everywhere, as he mumbled on about more sluice gates, the 8 blue-bar screens, curiously numbered 2 to 9, pointing out in the halogeny orange glow of the place where the mechanical teeth dragged out rags, tampons, plastic wrapping, and "all the yickety-yack don't-talk-back crap!," slats of slanted metal drooling brown refuse, "biosolids, not shit, biosolids, not shit," Char kept mumbling, as he led them around to the other side, past a pipe labeled FOUL AIR, to a hole in the concrete slab floor where all the dark water flowed.

Just arriving.

Still untouched.

Raw sewage.

"Where it all begins. Where we should have started this tour." Char sighed, checking his phone, his shoelaces, his watch, phone again, some greedy fly buzzing their ears.

Muscles in Dov's jaw, big muscles too, began to flex. And then the part that Xanther's mom has always hated, what stands for those two silver bars that stand for Captain snapped sharply into view.

"Why the hell do you keep jerking your head around like that?" Dov barked.

"Huh? Oh. Sorry, Captain. A.D.D. I guess."

"What's that?"

"Attention Deficit Disorder."

"That's something diagnosed?"

"No. You hear about it though. Online. The news. It means a short attention span." Char nodded, trying to smile. "Like, I like to channel surf. It drives my wife crazy."

"That's poppycock. You ain't got no disorder. You just got afraid somehow."

Wow, did Char sag then. Like a poked balloon too sad to pop. Talk about how badly he wanted to look around then. But he didn't.

"A.D.D.'s just a fancy name for scaredy-cat," Dov continued. "Trying to see what's coming after you. Or trying to *not* see what's coming after you. Private First Class Charroni, I know you better than that! You're no Fraidy K! Get back in your skin! Look steady! Walk ready!"

"Yes, sir!"

Later, when Dov stepped into a restroom, Char had whispered to Xanther, "I actually *am* a scaredy-cat but I'd do anything for him. That means for you too." Kinda weird. Char had even looked grateful after Dov got surly. Relaxed too. And he definitely didn't fidget as much.

But before that, back by the hole, Dov had squatted down and turned all his focus on Xanther. Weird as well. Because she also began smiling again. Her strength, which she hadn't even realized had slipped away, returned. All thoughts of revenge-vomit vanishing. The smell too.

Xanther dropped her shirt sleeve from her face.

∴ *Alas!* ∵

∴ Relax. ∵

"You're not afraid either, kiddo. Stare a thing in the eye. Know it. And let it know you know it too before you let it go. You're a Mudd. Don't forget."

Xanther nearly shouted "Yes, sir!" Jubilantly too. Instead she did something she's only managed a few times in her life: she looked straight back at those flint eyes and didn't stop looking until Dov blinked and even looked away. Had he been afraid? Well, he sure was smiling, winking then, and softening fast, before nodding one last time at the sickening flow running beneath them a few feet away.

"Awful, kiddo, isn't it? And by all measures of decency we shouldn't be here. We should be at Disneyland or stuffing buttered popcorn in our yaps. But I don't get to see you so much, what with my line of work, where I go, what I'm meant for, what Char here had the smarts and courage to get out of." Dov looked at his friend. "I mean that, Char. You served honorably. I'm proud to have called you one of my men." Before returning to Xanther: "So, kiddo, I don't want to waste what few hours we have together pretending the world's some ride with guard rails. I want to respect your time, even though you're ten or eleven, even though you might not get this now but maybe will later—"

Actually, this is where she dropped her sleeve.

⸫ See. She was getting to it. ⸫

⸫ Oh. ⸫

"—so I want to tell you something I know to be true, tell you something that shapes what I do, and it's not particularly sweet and some might even say it's a little cruel."

If less distracted, Char was back to looking uneasy.

"There's a lot of talk about unity and oneness, especially that Buddhist bullcrappy, which you'll come across soon enough, as well as other hippie garbage your mom likes to think she believes in. Anwar too. Heck, don't get me wrong, I'd like to believe it too. But the way the world works, that's not what I see. That's not what I know.

"I've been to China, India. I've walked their roads of enlightenment, but all I saw was disease, destitution, and delusion, and a total disregard for the individual, a regard that makes this country we live in the best there is. A light on the hill. A miracle to the world.

"So I brought you here this morning to show you unity, oneness. A big mix of everything, from the purest water, to the foulest excretion the mind can imagine, a population's salivas, defecations, urinations, blood, vomit and tears, dead rats, dead birds, garbage disposal pulp, drug deals gone wrong, body parts, solvents, things as benign as newspapers and cotton swabs, up to perfectly fine unconsumed food, probably perfumes too, expensive perfumes, you name it, some of it's in here, and what does it make?

"That's right, kiddo. This. Not so pretty, huh? This is a world without boundaries. This is what happens when there are no divisions. Look at it, Xanther, breathe it in, never forget: this is what you get when there is no law. This is what you get when the teeth lose."

Xanther's not sure why this is coming up now, but she remembers how Astair had lost it when she found out where Dov had taken her, lost it a second time when she found out what he'd said, which Xanther hadn't meant to get into, but couldn't help asking questions about. Astair made Dov's snarl at Char look like a kiss on the cheek. She called him crazy, a Republican jackass, and a racist, which he said she knew he wasn't, and might make her one for thinking so, since that wasn't the point at all, even if Xanther had no idea about any of it, especially the point.

Disrupt the colonies? Like ant colonies? Like all those ants marching into the kitchen? If Anwar hadn't come along Xanther might have done something awful: like crushed them all, and not like just with a rag, like Astair does, with soap and water, but, and this part makes her squirm, with her tongue, grinding them up with her teeth.

Was that it? Was Dov coming up because of teeth? This morning Xanther was flossing like she always does, sometimes twice a day, especially because of her braces, which seem looser, when she noticed her gums were bleeding, like kinda a lot, and she bared her teeth, to see the blood better, and this makes her squirm too, the sight pleased her.

Or maybe Dov's field trip was in her head because just recently both Anwar and Astair had used the expression "all in this together" which had made Xanther squirm tons, squirming a lot right now too, because what about what's going on with her sisters? They were nothing if not *not* all-in-this-together. Talk about divided. But according to Dov, wouldn't that be a good thing?

One thing's for sure: Xanther knows the anger she feels isn't a good thing.

Her mom always says "Anger is a reaction to fear." But if that's true, what is Xanther afraid of?

For one thing, having to leave school and lose her friends. And why? Because her twin sisters blabbed about her epilepsy. And to the sister of Dendish Mower no less.

And even if telling Philomel had been a mistake, blaming Xanther for shattering the glass wolves was not. Her sisters flat-out lied and knew they lied. Talk about seeing red. Though how is that being afraid?

Also confusing is why she isn't saying anything.

At Coffee Bean, Xanther had even warned her sisters that what they could have just swept away with the truth they were stuck in now. It was like this awful formula:

$$\text{Lying} + \text{Time} = \text{Cement}$$

The more time, the more it sets, the heavier it gets.

But now Xanther is in the same sitch. The biggest difference is the hardest, squirmiest part to admit: Xanther likes it. She likes tracking their fugitive eyes. Making the stones on their eyes as heavy as she can before they run out of the room screaming "Here comes Gargamel!" They're smart. They transform into Smurfs. Les Parents laugh. Without laughter more serious talks could ensue, breaking down the barriers, exposing each defensive position.

Fort. Fortress. Nothing but distress. Maybe Xanther would pick the awful stench and mess of all-together over so many awful walls?

And like that, with just that thought, Xanther nearly spills it. She's even helped by another lie the twins keep telling, about how well they're sleeping. Xanther overhears Les Parents asking about their dreams, pretty much every day, but the duo always swears "good." Xanther isn't deaf to how their nights seem bloated with whimpers and cries.

And that's not cool. They may be evil, twisted little things, but Xanther's still their big sister. What if what's messing with their dreams is their own deceit?

Right now everyone's in the piano room. It would be so easy. Xanther just has to blurt out how Xiomara was cleaning the mantel and accidentally knocked the statue to the floor. Astair wasn't home. So Freya and Shasti, especially Freya, told Xiomara that they would explain everything. Instead they blamed Xanther.

The start of Xiomara's name is even in Xanther's mouth when the creature on her shoulder prickles her skin with tiny claws, this has happened before, shifting between lightness and a density that should weigh the world but feels not even there. Xanther has to reach up to make sure. Nuzzling her finger answers doubt, gnawing on it. Maybe he's thirsty? Mouth dry? Xanther's mouth his, er, is. Even that weird thing at the back of her tongue starts to happen again, swelling with pins.

And anyway, by that point, the Smurfs are running out of the piano room again screaming: "Gargamel!" And Xanther's remembering Magic Mountain, the rides, the day she missed with her friends, maybe even with a new friend, if Roxanne had really meant it and come along.

Anger returns. This time, though, instead of tracking back to fears, Xanther follows it way past fear, way past anger, towards what no longer seems connected to either:

Rage

Worst of all: it feels about as terrible as it feels good. And it feels pretty terrible. Xanther loves the taste.

If only Dr. Potts were around, but he's what?, still on vacation?, for like the whole summer? Dr. Potts would probably say that the twins stuff was pretty silly, "disproportionate," that's a word he might use, Astair too, though she wouldn't be able to help herself, she'd have to bring up epilepsy. Dr. Potts would also point out that Xiomara would be mortified to learn that Xanther was getting blamed for an accident she herself had no trouble admitting. But that's not all Dr. Potts would say. Xanther can feel it more than she can follow it, who he would definitely mention:

Dov

For sure if she admitted remembering the sewage-treatment-plant trip. But without Dr. Potts, Xanther can't track now how this bad-good feeling relates to Dov. Is it because Astair has always sworn he had a terrible temper, which Xanther never saw, though maybe got a glimpse of when he barked at Char? Or it's just an appetite she shares with bio-dad? Or maybe it's just the only feeling she knows that can answer the bits and pieces of recurring Dov?

B i t s   a n d   p i e c e   s.

That's how Dov had come home for the last time. First in a small bag no one would ever untie again. Then that small bag no one would ever untie again inside a black lacquered box no one would ever open again.

What Xanther would have opened if she could.

She had tried.

Maybe she was still trying.

The black coffin allways before her.

:: Blotting out every memory and thought. ::

:: *What even now she's struggling to pry open.* ::

:: What she can never open. ::

                              :: **What no one will ever open.** ::

527

The funny thing too, about that morning?, was that after the Hyperion Treatment Plant, they had spent the afternoon at Universal City where they had gone on rides and watched a movie and shared the biggest bucket of popcorn. But it didn't compare to Dov squatting down in the midst of that miserable stink trying to tell her something that mattered, that for the life of her she can't make

sense out   of now,
                          since it's about as impossible

                                                              as figuring out
            how any of the
                              bits   and   pieces
                                                        go   back
            together,
                                          or
                                          what made them

                  bits   and   pieces

        in the   first place,

    what blew   them apart

                  in the first place,

                                                              or not what
            but who,

                  who had blown up Dov?

Xanther spends the rest of the day in her room pretending to read or text friends. With Mefisto's sunglasses on. Really she's just flicking stones in her head.

Pausing for any hint of that reddish, summoning glow. Never strong enough to keep her from moving on.

And if these are the colors of her own thoughts they still persist as if something beyond what anyone could dare call their own. Though Xanther wants to call them something. These glares she almost knows by name, but especially those set on becoming what drives her, what she craves.

Beyond the necessity of any name.

:: Violation? Vindication? ::

:: *Vanity!* ::

:: **Vengeance.** ::

On Thursday ∴ **July 31** ∵ Xanther, Cogs, Mayumi, and Josh live on Kle's couch switching between *Basement Crawl*, *Grand Theft Auto V*, and *Call of Duty: Ghosts*.

"Huh. I guess we know what Xanther's doing with her summer," Kle drawls, as Xanther once again thumbs her way through more and more kills, her reactions as quick as flicking stones.

"I suck," Cogs sighs, reaching for more chips.

Kle's mom has loaded them up with trays of chips, vegetables, cookies?, and sodas, all the stuff Xanther can't touch, which she doesn't mind. She's not hungry. Being away from the little one is hard enough. Though something else is up.

∴ 1:52 PM ∵

"Sucking is your charm," Mayumi tells Cogs, and Josh laughs, but the laugh goes uneasy at the end, maybe because Mayumi doesn't laugh, just smiles, and Cogs hears the compliment and kinda goes quiet. Is he blushing?

"Sucks for you," Kle snorts, taking over the controller. "The more you improve, the more charmless you become." Kle's t-shirt today reads: DECENCY BESTS PROPHECY.

"I've been looking at your shirt for an hour now, Kle, and I still don't get it," Cogs admits.

Kle ignores him.

"It almost sounds friendly," Josh smirks. "Are you changing on us?"

Kle ignores Josh too. Now nothing but game-focus.

Kle lives in Silver Lake, not far from the reservoir.

The living room, where they're playing, has a view of the water. Nothing like Xanther's windowless den. Lots of light, lemony-wood floors, and big comfy sofas buried in pillows.

But Xanther knows not even comfy will help today. Kle's dad and brothers had to take Kle's brother, Phinneas, for some doctors' appointments. Phinneas hadn't gone easily. Kle's mom seems pretty zoned now, drifting around the house like a wisp of dust, her smile just as wispy.

Later on, she brings in another tray of food: this one piled high with BLTs and tuna sandwiches. Xanther's stomach gurgles.

∴ 2:24 PM ∵

Kle pauses the game. Xanther can see he is about to say something, but she stops him with a palm on his shoulder. Man, talk about tense and coiled.

"More names, please," Xanther says.

"What's that?" Kle's mom asks.

"We're helping Xanther name her kitten," Cogs explains.

"Oh. That's cute," she bubbles, drifting away.

"Huddle and engage!" Josh says, moving in on lunch.

"Way to make eating sound like a military maneuver," Mayumi smirks.

"How about John-117?" Kle suggests, reaching for a slice of bacon, then putting it back. He's the one who decided they had to help Xanther.

"Lavender?" Mayumi chirps, mouth full.

"It's a he," Josh objects.

"So?" Kle growls.

"I tried Mu," Xanther says. "But that didn't fit."

"Moo like a cow?" Cogs asks.

Xanther shakes her head: "You know that manga I told you about, that like my dad, has, *Lone Wolf and Cub*—"

"Phinneas has that!" Kle suddenly erupts.

"Really?"

Minutes later, Kle returns with a handful of volumes, each one with this little section of Japanese vocabulary and definitions at the end.

"May, did you know *mu* meant that?" Josh asks.

Mayumi shakes her head.

"Xanther, why would you want to name your cat something that means 'nothingness'?" Josh asks, with volume 2 open to the back. ∴ Volume 2. *The Gateless Barrier.* ∴

"I'm just trying everything." She shrugs.

"Meifumado!" Kle grins, reading from Volume 1. ∴ *The Assassin's Road.* ∴ "That means 'the way of demons and damnation'!"

"Doesn't exactly roll off the tongue," Mayumi says, looking over his shoulder. "Kannon's cute: 'the Buddhist god of Mercy.' They misspelled Buddhist."

"Kogi kaishakunin," Cogs labors to say. ∴ Volume 3. *The Flute of the Fallen Tiger.* ∴ "'The shogun's executioner.'"

"Another tongue lesson," Mayumi says. "Kogi's kinda cool."

Xanther wrinkles her nose. She doesn't agree.

"I don't want to bum you out, Xanth, what with you a

vegetarian," Josh says, unpausing the PS4. "You do know cats only eat meat, right? Something has to die in order for it to live."

"How about this!" Kle almost shouts. He's got open one of the last volumes. ∴ Volume 23. *Tears of Ice.* ∵ "Shishogan!" For some reason the sound makes Xanther sad.

"What's that?" Mayumi and Cogs ask together.

"The eyes of a swordsman become one with the emptiness of *mu*," Kle reads, "alive in the moment between life and death."

∴ 2:51 PM ∵

"Does anyone know what the fuck is going on with Bayard?" Josh asks suddenly. "He should be here with us. What is up there?"

But not even Kle can give a good explanation for their friend's disappearance. They all text him an invite.

"Bayard would make a good name." Cogs sighs when it's clear Bayard's not going to respond immediately.

"How about Mefisto?" Xanther asks.

"Who?" Mayumi asks, popping open a Diet Dr Pepper.

"Isn't that your dad's friend?" Kle mumbles, side-by-siding *Call of Duty* with Josh. "The super genius?"

"He visited us recently. He gave me these glasses." Which Xanther only now takes off.

"Can I see?" Cogs asks. "I love how the lenses look dark enough for an eclipse."

"Can you tell he's a super genius?" Mayumi asks.

Xanther shakes her head. "I overheard him telling my dad that some company is making *Lone Wolf and Cub* into a game."

"I'd read that!" Josh smirks at Xanther. "PS4?"

"PS5."

"PS5! That won't be ready until, like, 2020. Who can wait that long?"

"These things *are* dark." Cogs whistles and sways, holding out his arms like the way people who see think blind people act, when really, usually, they've got a cane, or are like clicking their tongue. "How do you see a thing?"

"Give them back," Xanther snaps, annoyed. She can see with them fine. And proves so when she and Cogs side-by-side on the next round.

"I'm playing someone with basically her eyes closed and I still suck. Still charmed?"

"Less," Mayumi replies, though her smile seems bigger.

Kle still wants to hear more about Mefisto. So Xanther gives them all the rundown: how he arrived for breakfast and stayed through the night. How he talked a lot about game stuff with Anwar. And about their friends. How they'd played Go.

"What's that?" Mayumi asks.

"It's a Japanese board game."

"You don't know?" Kle gripes her.

Mayumi spares him a Japanese bird.

Xanther describes the long coding session. She'd heard them in Anwar's office pretty much all night. If there was super genius on display it was probably in the coding Xanther knows only a tiny, tiny bit about.

Xanther doesn't tell them how she woke up before dawn ∴ *awake to what goes on without* ∴ feeling that deep part of her chest, never really her chest, not even close, starting to burn up, her eyes, not her eyes, still dense with snowy forests, and floating stones, flicking those away, almost desperately, even in her sleep, trees strung with sprites of turquoise, now and then a rare one revealing a darker dawn, ripening, promising . . . her little one nowhere close.

Though Xanther had found him almost at once, downstairs in the living room, eyes still pinched tight, tail self-wrapped, paws fish-hooking, right beside Mefisto sprawled out on the couch, a mountain in deep sleep, a real pyramid, watched over by a sphinx.

And, of course, though she left them both undisturbed, by the time Xanther had tiptoed back upstairs and crawled into bed, sinking deep into her pillow, still buzzing with puzzlement, excitement, uncertainty, and also a grimness she couldn't explain, nameless one was already back again, curled up beside her head.

For a moment then, Xanther had discovered in the icy forest of her thoughts, down beyond a slope of shifting stones, flicked loose for a watery dance, beyond freezing, something else further on, already disappearing deep into a valley dark with tremendously tall trees, what stones knew better than to disturb, a twinkle of a different dawn, almost twinkling green.

Xanther's again heading down that familiar slope, toward the enormous trunks, flicking aside any stones wandering too close. Even as Kle wants to side-by-side with her. Even as Xanther takes the controller, having more luck firing off the weapon, a Lynx, than reaching those woods still harboring, or maybe not, that shimmer of peace.

And then, wherever this is blurs away leaving her nauseated and a little dizzy. Xanther's still playing Kle though, outscoring him too, even as she pumps her big toe, grinds her teeth, sips little breaths, shallower and shallower, as sweat starts to sheen her face and back.

The fire inside her spikes too. She drops the controller. She needs the little one.

"Ha! Giving up?" Kle hoots.

"Xanther!" Cogs shouts, getting it. Mayumi too, who's already slipped beside her.

"I need to go home," Xanther hears herself say as she tries to stand.

But standing is meaningless now before these dancing smears of blue and reddening ones too, turning toward something worse. Are these the same ones she's seen before? Xanther somehow knowing they are, even as she has no clue how she, this?, has relocated them, and so quickly.

Xanther wants to run but now not even her big toe can move. She can feel Mayumi's hands on one arm, Kle's on her other arm. She tries to stop her lips from pulling back, exposing more and more of her teeth, which feel like they're growing, until they'll for sure split the bands of her braces apart, leaving her to spit metal.

∷ **3:14 PM** ∷

∷ **Brighter than garnet.** ∷

∷ **Taste thicker than cherry.** ∷

∷ **Dark as a long-ago red satisfaction.** ∷

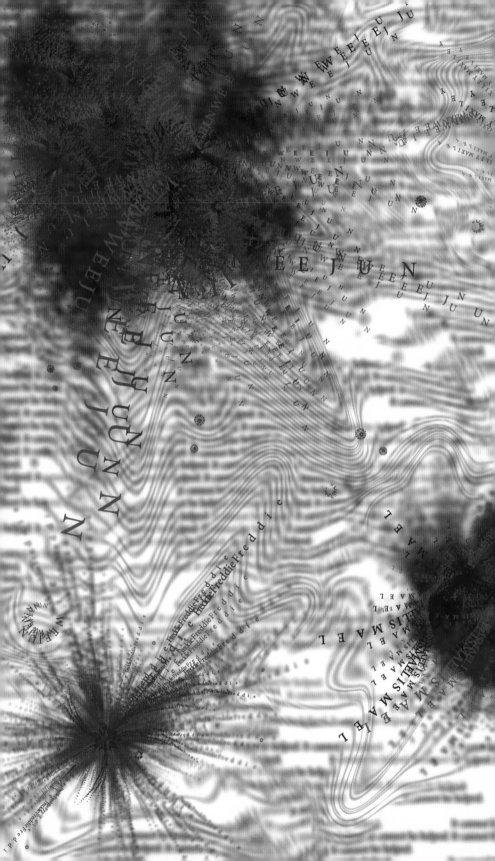

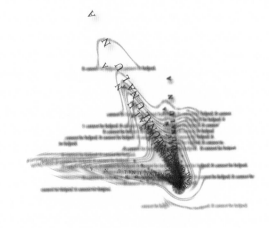

"Holy crap!" Cogs is still yelling. "What happened?"

"Xanther," Mayumi whispers. "Was that a seizure?"

"Fuck me! If that's a seizure, how is she getting Riley so far to . . . " Josh can't even finish what he's saying.

"Huh," is all Kle manages.

And, yes, weird, Xanther is still playing, all game-focus, and hasn't felt this good in a long time. In fact, not since the night she wandered out into the street and that lady Lupita almost ran her down, Xanther staring down the headlights, because really like what did that matter when there was so much satisfaction, and that satisfaction seemed to come from so far away? Same as just now. Even if this time there was a pink dress.

"Sorry," Xanther says. "I can get a little lost when I get super flow. That and maybe I haven't eaten much, so I'm like dizzy?" The lies make her dizzy. Why doesn't she tell her friends the truth? Xanther even tries the thought out in her mouth, as she pivots the Lynx around for another shot — the only thing making any real sense at this particular moment.

"Intense, Xanther." Cogs shakes his head. He knows she's lying. "And tense. You were pretty locked up." Trying then to joke: "Like your wimpy arms felt pretty strong."

A seizure rictus? Was it possible?

"No joke." Mayumi laughs, though it's a half laugh.

"Intense is good." Kle nods.

Xanther shakes her head. It doesn't add up.

"Look, if it had been a big seizure," Xanther says, deepening her lie with the truth, "I'd now be in what's called a postictal state, which means I'd be nearly lifeless, like my brain is rebooting. I'd be so out of it you'd be scared my brain wasn't rebooting. For sure I wouldn't be kicking riot like this."

"Pretty badass," Kle confirms.

And Xanther keeps on playing, until Kle just quits, preferring to watch Xanther triumph in firefight after firefight. Xanther hasn't felt this relaxed and free in like forever?

Even the blue flame inside her has diminished to a tear of blue so small the endless forest for once seems undisturbed beneath a thickening sweep of falling snow.

Like it's almost asleep.

Even better, or stranger, Xanther suddenly gets the feeling that if she wanted to, if she like just held out her hand, she could call the little one and he would be there in her palm.

Xanther even pauses the game, sets the controller aside, and holds out her palm.

"Now what?" Josh asks, sounding a little annoyed, but also a little scared.

Xanther laughs, shrugs. "Relax. My hand's just feeling crinky." Another lie. She spins her hand around like you might do if your wrist hurt.

Besides, even if she really was going to try something that bizarre, how do you call something if you don't know its name?

When Anwar picks her up, Xanther doesn't mention what happened, because she doesn't know what happened. Her friends don't either, except for the part that was obvious.

"PS4 was mine today. Even Kle kept complimenting me."

Anwar's smile makes her feel bad, though something about her friends having her back, and agreeing not to mention this whatever-it-was, makes Xanther feel equally good.

She rolls down the window and lets her face swim in the warm afternoon air. If she could, she'd race right now past the pedestrian path and chain-link fence topped with barbed wire and dive into the clear reservoir water. The thought makes her smile even more, back teeth mashing on Cedar's Sugar-Free Bubble Gum, front teeth snapping at the breeze.

Dov.

Dov knew how to smile this big.

Teeth white too, and strong. "9 millimeter teeth!"

Teeth.

And Xanther remembers once more the metal teeth, at the Hyperion Treatment Plant, from the first ones dragging the worst from the sludge, all the way to the last ones, raking the clear water headed out to the sea.

Savage

That once perhaps were eyes.

— Langston Hughes

Dump Özgür in front of the Los Angeles County USC Medical Center and hello paceville. That goes for any hospital. He'll back-and-forth the sidewalk out front for miles and never get a foot closer to the entrance. But the county coroner's is no problem. Just a few buildings over too. Off Workman and Mission. An old-fashioned redbrick affair that seems nearly quaint for a department headquarters. In the lobby there's a nice gift shop where you can pick up some chalk-outline beach towels. The white building to the right is where the dead wait.

Though before Özgür's even up the steps, he hears his name. Chloë's a riptide of blonde. Smoking cloves.

"Reminds me to breathe. With half the nicotine. Supposedly."

You can say shit like that when you're still in your twenties. Chloë's a C.I.T. ∴ Coroner Investigator Trainee ∴ now.

"No No-Vacancy here," she smiles, giving her gapped front teeth center stage. "From Malibu to Pomona, Long Beach to Palmdale, we take them all. Turns out I got no problem with bodies. If they're cold."

Özgür remembers Chloë's body. It was far from cold. That was years ago but sometimes time leaves a memory alone. The dimples on her back. The soft sound her throat knew. They had done a little drinking together. A lot actually. She was barely old enough for what she swallowed, barely old enough for a lot of what else they did, though she made Özgür feel like he was the one who needed to catch up. Or is that just something Özgür tells himself now to make the wince hurt less?

"Got two secs?" Surprisingly, Chloë looks happy to see him. What a figure, shoulders barely wide enough to support one helluva a rack, what the uniform strains now to hide. If they never fell in love with each other, together they'd fallen in love with Chick Corea's *Now He Sings, Now He Sobs*. A-side. Played over and over.

"You look good." Chloë is glowing. Özgür glances at his watch. He's early for his meeting with Savage. He can spare a few minutes before mentioning Elaine.

"I'm working the ninth step." Then clear-eyed and calm, she offers her apology. She had used Özgür to enable her own trip to the bottom of too many bottles she couldn't afford.

"And now that I can afford them," she brightens, "my boyfriend and I go to Yosemite instead. We're big hikers. We met in the program."

Özgür's wince is back. Had she even turned twenty-one when they met? Was he even fifty? As if forty-nine counts for an excuse. Their whole thing seems terribly off now, no matter what needle and vinyl were doing in those raw hours. Chloë's the one who deserves an apology.

Özgür tries. He starts with Elaine, how he's settled down. He wants Chloë to know that he's not flirting, though it comes off as defensive, like he's responding to her mention of a boyfriend. And maybe he is. Chloë couldn't care less. She's said her peace, at ease with however Özgür wants to respond. It's part of her process. So Özgür cuts it short with a sorry for his part in an entanglement that left her wailing and breaking glass and calling him for months.

"Chloë?" Özgür really shouldn't say more. Chloë's grinding out her cigarette, not looking for more. "If it's fair to ask you for help, because I want what I have with Elaine to work out, how would you describe your time with me?"

"Come on, Oz. I said I have a boyfriend. Sobriety suits me." But Chloë can't hide the twinkle in her eye or the big smile. Özgür had forgotten the cute dimples her cheeks make when she makes the gap in her teeth seem like an invitation.

"I mean it." And he does. "Fearless moral inventory."

Özgür would have accepted a shrug or "you were an ass-hole" or a "we weren't so good for each other" or "that was then, this is now." Chloë surprises him with what he'll still have to accept.

"You were soft but not gentle. You were sweet but not kind."

Özgür finds Savage in an autopsy suite.

"Shit!"

Özgür waves off the excuse. The only time time doesn't get scattered with Savage is when he spends it on the dead. This one's an old guy dragged out of a downtown hotel that charges by the week. Özgür wonders if Chloë was the one who brought the body in. He knows she was gentle. He knows she was kind.

"In this heat the smell informed the *concierge* who to call," Savage says, shaking his head, as amused by his use of "concierge" as he is continually dismayed by the plight of the poor.

Against regulations, his mask hangs around his neck. Özgür leaves his on if only to spare the captain the trouble of trying to discipline either one of them. A mask is beside the point. Down here mostly chemicals thicken the air, along with maybe a defeated hint, like a lying confession, of what happens when the boundaries of who we are break down and pool together in the pink streaks still draining off the stainless steel table.

"Does he have a name?"

"Took it with him."

Özgür studies a calm he's seen too many times before. At least in this case violence didn't sign for the end. Özgür almost envies the blankness. Maggots still crawling along the pale bloated chest make no difference. Whatever scabs once meant is gone. That goes for fractured fingernails as well. Curiously, the grey hair looks trimmed and arranged.

"Were you the barber?"

"How he arrived."

Did he cut his own hair? Too neat to do in a mirror. Some-one else must have handled the scissors. The question of *who* suddenly weighs too much to consider. Toprağı bol olsun. ∴ *May his soil be plenty.* ∴

On their way out, they pass a forensic pathologist wear-ing a PAPR ∴ Powered Air Purifying Respirator ∴. He's in the midst of a Level A. The head is already uncapped, with internal organs removed from the body cavity. Nearby a technician slices the brain into thick slabs. Two detectives hang back. Like everyone else, they're wearing booties and masks. They've also seen this before. They've seen Özgür before too.

Upstairs, past rooms for mass spectrometry, mitochondrial DNA extraction, and the histopathology lab, Savage unlocks his office, where order comes to die — papers scattered across his desk, half-eaten sandwiches on the floor, more papers, numerous coffee cups everywhere. On the back of his door presides Bob Marley, as if a poster could calm disorder. It seems a minor miracle that Savage locates the case on his computer in less than a minute.

"I could have e-mailed you this."

"Any chance the bodies are still around?"

"That was almost two months ago. Families claimed them within the week." Özgür deserved the frown. He knew better. Savage continues reading. "Eli Klein. Jablom Lau Song. Yuri Grossman. That's right: Darren McKibben worked this up. You saw him downstairs in the SCUBA gear. Though if you want to know what everyone else wants to know I can tell you that much: what's up with the bleach?" Savage takes a bite of what once might have looked like tuna fish on rye. "McKibben has no clue. I have no clue. Ditto for Fajardo."

"Then guess."

"Maybe a race thing, to whiten their skin, though these boys were nowhere close to my idea of brown or even yours. Or let's try a fetish. Or better yet a dumb idea. Bleach wasn't exactly dissolving them. It didn't even kill them."

"Water in their lungs?"

"Toxicology suggests a possible use of SUX ∴ succinylcholine∴ due to the presence of the metabolite SMC ∴ succinylmonocholine∴ plus midaz ∴ midazolam∴ ∴ *Trade names: Versed and Hypnovel*∴ and even traces of K ∴ ketamine∴. McKibben thinks they were only then positioned over the bleachy bath. Did you really think the bodies would still be here?"

"I did. I should retire."

Savage looks pissed off by both admissions. But then again Savage always looks pissed off.

"I'd never thought of a race angle," Özgür submits.

"We see it all down here."

"How about Marvin D'Organidrelle? Is his body still around?"

Down in the crypt, the young black body lies on one of the lower shelves. He's one of many. Today the count is at 243 corpses, as usual out in the open. For each a sheet and a sheet of plastic. The bulges are from motorcycle helmets. A lot of bulges. Fans hum to keep the temperature down in the thirties.

"This is fucked-up." Even Savage has to admit. The body is signed all over with violence: from tattoos to scars to cause of death. More than enough to get Savage's anger up.

Hard to believe the last time Özgür saw the boy they were having a sit-down in the rain.

"I heard he was found by the tracks. Is this mechanical?"

Özgür sure can't tell. He's seen heads just as bad, crushed in car wrecks, blown away by shotguns, split apart by falling girders. Context made it obvious. But here only small portions of the lower jaw and lip remain. Eyes long gone.

"No question some animal took an interest. Not a small interest either. Or a small animal. See these gouges in the back? A screwdriver doesn't do that. Those are from teeth. Big teeth."

"Is that what killed him?"

"Oz, you know just as well as I do that what got this kid isn't what you see here." Savage flares like he always eventually flares. "He was murdered by the conditions he was born into."

"Is that also supposed to explain the Korean couple he killed?"

"Hey, look—" Flare to bonfire. If only he and Özgür weren't on such familiar terms. "—what I'm about to ask you I'm not asking you because I'm black, though I still reserve the right to make that a big fucking part of *whatever* the fuck I ask you, because it's the very fucking least I deserve: do you truly believe a young black man growing up on those streets ever had a fair chance of acquiring the conscience determined and cultivated by a class that, while demanding it of everyone, through legislative action denies anyone of lesser privilege access to its creation? Conscience, like everything else true in this life, is not God-given but world-made. And a world that is unequal in its distribution of privilege must accept that the values it manifests are of its own doing."

Özgür knows Savage too well to participate in this conversation. Even if Özgür agreed, it wouldn't matter.

"That's right. Mark Bradford is a fucking miracle."

"Who's Mark Bradford?" Özgür asks.

Savage shows no interest in answering. "White America needs to stop asking black America to depend on miracles for a future."

Özgür keeps his peace with the silent. Whether wrinkled or tattooed, whole or undone, colored like one or colored like another, death heeds no differences while still playing favorites. The weight of such stillness doesn't bother Özgür because it's a burden he won't have to carry. What he carries he has a license for.

"It is weird the animal left the rest of the body untouched," Savage adds now, calming down.

"Blue Whale sometime?"

"I'll meet you at the Varnish. That jazz shit puts me to sleep."

Marvin here was just the kind of knucklehead to put a bullet through the temple of an emerging miracle like Cletious

Bou's boy, Jasper, twenty years ago. If this were a TV show, Jasper's ghost might even momentarily appear now in the crypt, playing his clarinet. Of course Jasper isn't here, just Savage who'd be about Jasper's age if he were alive now. No clarinet in his hands, just latex gloves, splitting apart at the palms.

Özgür takes one long last look at the racks of the dead, as if down here he might suddenly hear a murmur disclosing the secret of how the grand scales of existence really balance deed against deed, generation after generation . . .

Before returning to the heat, Özgür asks Savage about the Chinatown murder Cletious was so curious about.

"Realic S. Tarnen."

"You do like grim." Savage knows the case but needs to use the computer in the photo studio to call up the details.

Özgür can see by the way that Savage keeps rubbing the back of his neck, any more questions will have to wait for another day.

"The Varnish it is, Savage. Whenever works for you."

"McKibben's again. Now this is . . . this is, Jesus, some high-level heartless. Dismemberment with industrial equipment. Torture with fire, acids. It looks like they bound the victim with barbed wire. The metal could be used to conduct electricity or heat from the blowtorches. Huh." Savage quiets, reading more closely, maybe rereading, focused enough that almost fifteen minutes pass before he remembers Özgür again.

Özgür knows better than to remind him.

"I'll have to recheck this. Maybe even talk to the labs. There's something really strange about the tissue samples. Patterns of oxidation. With no noted conclusions."

"Yours?"

"Possibly bleach."

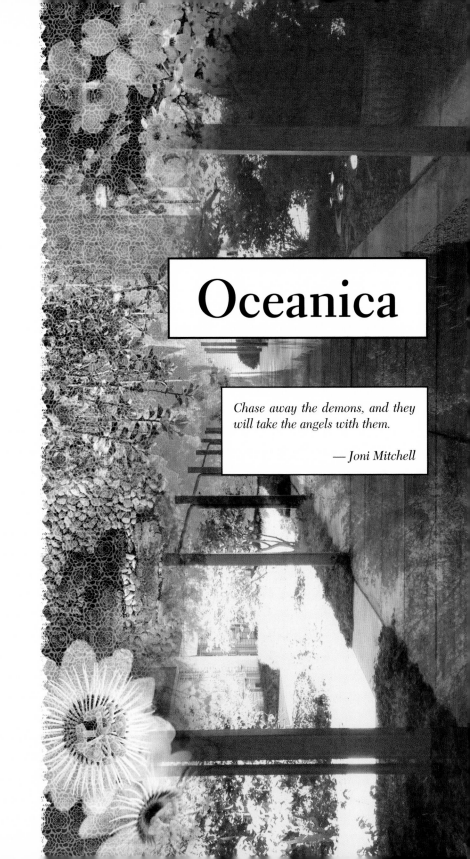

Oceanica

*Chase away the demons, and they
will take the angels with them.*

— *Joni Mitchell*

"A week with dad," Anwar announces over dinner. Shasti looks confused but Freya('s (hearty)
"Daddy!") directs her (to her own "Yays!"). Xanther
couldn't care less (though the blind creature on her
shoulder seems to turn Astair's way).

Their Joint Session had all but confirmed (weeks ago) that Astair would go through with it. Her (half-hearted) attempt to get a refund had merely earned an extension.

"No point putting off what you're ready for now," Anwar had encouraged (nothing but support).

"It'll give me some focus time for the paper," Astair admitted.

(while leaves of absence were permitted) Degrees were designed around "intent of completion" ("in order to acquire the necessary experience and competence befitting a professional practicing in the field of psychotherapy") in order to dissuade life-long students enchanted with the idea of becoming what they were too enchanted with to ever become. Becoming and being was what mattered most to the institute and why Astair had picked it in the first place. That and she was allowed to transfer over five years of scattered credits (which reduced down to one year (the remaining two years completed as a nonresident (with eight (three-day) visits per annum (plus a ninth (week-long) retreat)))) from Vermont and Georgia as well as Montana and New York (part of the reason they had moved to Los Angeles (to (finally(?)) settle down)).

Astair had (all but) completed her coursework. Crushed her oral presentations (right upon moving here too (talk about stress!)).

The trouble (what was that "all but"?) came when Astair declared (definitively(?)) that she wanted to practice in California (and not New York (or Montana (or Georgia (or Vermont (or North Carolina (or Illinois)))))). Astair had to retake some core classes ((including Psychopharmacology III – CP 810C (2.5 Units)) pursuant to requirements of the California Board of Behavioral Sciences (Senate Bill 33 (Section 4980.36 (of the Business and Professional Code)))). All in preparation for California Marriage and Family Therapy Licensure.

For an M.A. (in counseling).

For the Ph.D. (in depth psychology (which Astair was also pursuing (wanted!))) Astair was close (which made (all the more painful) the realization that this dream might still be fading (at least for the time being (Time Being (it sounds so sci-fi ∴ Ha! ∵ as well as so (well . . .) mortal ∴ Ah! ∵)))).
(((mainly) because of the way she had cobbled together her curriculum) like the M.A.) The Ph.D. also required her to retake classes (though (the way it had worked out) Fabler had passed her on her orals for both degrees (even if he had warned her that it was possible (the way things had also worked out) that she might have to produce a second dissertation (she'd cross that bridge when the time came))).

All of which required money they didn't have.

"Still nothing?" Astair asks on Sunday morning ∴ August 3 ∴.

Anwar shakes his head (looking seriously gloomy (as he watches her pack)). "It's like they disappeared. With our nine thousand dollars."

"How did you hear about Enzio?"

Freya starts wailing. Astair expects to find Xanther at the center of it. But she's nowhere to be found. Not even in her room.

"Frey put her doighty bag on my bed," Shasti explains ((apparently) both had decided to go with Mommy (packing their own bags for the trip)(loaded with stuffed animals and (assorted) PJs)).

"It's not doighty," Freya growls (her wails and tears long gone). "And it's not dirty either."

"She was in angerous territory," Shasti shouts in her defense.

"Did you hit your sister?" Astair still has to ask Shasti (no matter how touched she is (by their decision to come with her)).

"I didn't do it hard."

The afternoon Pacific Surfliner ∷ **Amtrak** ∷ reaches Santa Barbara in under three hours (the sun still an hour from setting (the Pacific a sleepy blue (tempting Astair to keep going (as far north as she can get)))).

The twins were all smiles and hugs when they said goodbye at Union Station. Anwar's embrace felt deeper and longer than usual. She missed it at once.

She missed Xanther the most.

The eldest had refused to join the family on the trip to the station (Anwar had tried to insist that she go but the quick round-trip wasn't long enough to risk the rowl (is that a word? (it is now))). That thing on her shoulder prevented a decent hug.

What had happened with her?

What was still happening?

Something to do with the wolves?

By the time Astair reaches her dorm room (for the week) waves of panic overwhelm her.

This must have to do with Lares & Penates.

The broken glass. The lost money.

Dead Dov.

It takes everything Astair has to just sit on the floor (clutching her knees (not because she seeks an even greater stillness (but because she wants to secure this stillness))). She watches her hands go bloodless for how hard she's clutching herself (grabbing her legs (because all Astair really wants to do now is

     run

              run

                        run

)

).

Monday morning :. August 4 :. Astair already wants to leave (barely through the first lecture (coffee still warm in her paper cup (kept that way by the fire in her palms))).

She had felt it building while trudging up the hill. Astair tried turning to the sublime horizon of the Pacific ((allways in view up here) the rising sun marking a (silver) arrow to where the future lies (and the day will die)). She tried welcoming in her heart the rosebushes and old pines (and flocks of bougainvilleas (beckoning over gateways (leading off to wandering stone paths (perfect (for resting (imagining (restoring oneself (against the traumas (of oneself))))))))).

But Astair still wound up hustling to class (curled up like a punch (held so tight (so long) it can't touch a thing).

(even in her chair) Astair feels like an undelivered hit. She had slept shitty. A narrow bed of weak springs and a window that wouldn't open to let in the sea air. She knows this anger is fear. She can see the fears are reasonable ((fear for her family)(fear for her future)(fear of—)) but—

"A DABDA Moment!" Dr. Robin P. Hardy suddenly declares from the dais (invoking the Kübler-Ross stages of grief (with no mention that such stages deserve scrutiny (at least precision (before such an educated audience)))). This is one of those high-flying pep lectures (to launch the week (as well as (no doubt) to further cement Hardy's popularity among the Oceanica rank and file)).

(at her archest) Astair credits the Dunning-Kruger effect (equating those with the least experience with the highest confidence) for Hardy's ascendancy on the national roster of celebrity psychotherapists ((psycho-therapists!) thank you *Psychology Today* (a TEDx talk (YouTube clips (with rumors persisting that Hardy loathes the Randy Pausch lecture ∵ September 18, 2007 ∵ for all the attention it received)))).

Astair's notepad seems to confirm that Hardy's (supposed) two decades of clinical experience have produced very little of merit: "Dare to Be Great Moment!" "Trust Your Dreams Moment!" "_____ Moment!"

Astair (still) approaches him afterward with a question (which she hopes might help loosen (at least modify? (alter?)) her attachment to her old subject of imaginings and identity limitations).

"Could you offer some guidance — I'm working on my bibliography for my dissertation — on books that treat how animals, and pets in particular, alter our sense of a moment? Maybe by expanding it, or contracting it, or dissolving it altogether?"

"One moment," Hardy responds ((without so much as looking at Astair) turning instead to Cardiff Chambers (never to return)).

Hardy is Cardiff Chambers' advisor (so it's somewhat understandable (though why is she even here? (Cardiff got her A *and* a book deal))). She's also a pert bounce of electric red hair. Newly divorced. Newly modified. And never too modest to shy from either a tight shirt or a self-congratulatory word. The two practically skip off together.

But Cardiff surprises her.

Catching up with Astair later in the day.

"I have a question," Cardiff starts off (she's breathless too (did she run?)). "It borders on a favor. Actually it crosses right over."

"Didn't you just get your Ph.D.?" Astair responds.

"In depth psychology." (Cardiff nodding.) "With a focus on ecopsychology and technopsychology. But I'm also going for my Psy.D. in clinical psychology." Her smile is boundless. As is her ambition.

"Good for you. A second dissertation, then?"

"Robin thinks it may also be good enough to publish." Robin? Is she fucking him? "He's no longer technically my advisor." Yup. Fucking him.

"How far along are you?"

"Nearly done." What fucking has nothing to do with. "The title's still up in the air. I spent the past two years focusing on five clinical trials run out of Johns Hopkins, Carnegie Mellon, Harvard, UCLA, and the University of Utah. The statistical modeling was weighted in terms of pharmacological success or failure rates. I, however, reevaluated the data in regard to the control groups with the idea that we might take advantage of possible protocols solely utilizing reactive responses to authoritative suggestions. Of course, you can already see the dilemma—" (see what? (Astair has no clue what Cardiff is talking about (except she remembers dropping statistics as an undergrad))) "—how to maneuver through the ethical quandary physicians must face in order to activate the effect? How to justify inevitable costs against possible benefits? Could it be manufactured and hence monetized? Though with no need for a patent would that even be sustainable?" ((Astair just nods (nodding won't help)) to what effect? (quit staring at her hair)) "I think the conclusions are riveting.

My favorite title so far is *Noetic Nostrums* though Robin insists I stick with something simple like *The Placebo Effect*. My agent is talking to HarperCollins. What do you think?"

"I don't know where to start." And Astair doesn't. Except with a scowl. An impulse she refuses to give in to. Because why should she resent this attractive and exquisitely intelligent woman? Who clearly has worked hard at a complex (and maybe riveting) and definitely fascinating topic? So what if she wants to fuck their Oceanica star now that she's out of his program? They're both single and driven and (actually) fun to be around. What is Astair's problem?

Dov would have accused Astair of wanting to fuck Robin P. Hardy too.

"I can't wait to read the result."
"That's what I wanted to ask you! Would you?"

(as happy as Cardiff seems by her response) Astair wanders away disappointed and depressed. Looking for a way away. As if one of the wandering little paths might show her. Only stones crunch under her feet.

Petty jealousies? Lusts? Hardy!? (Really!? (gag))

Shadows sneak in.

Forty is not even over any hill. And it's not like Astair's behind on any clock either (she has her babies (and an adoring husband)). So where is this disappointment in herself coming from?

Is it really so simple? The fear of—

Menopause?

Just thinking it makes her want to run again.

Fortunately Tuesday ∴ August 5 ∴ is better. Astair runs into some classmates ((friends((?) maybe)) Javier and Jules) in the main parking lot. Plans for Friday drinks are made.

The afternoon is full: one lecture and three fifty-minute study-group sessions.

Astair is readied for exhaustion only to discover energy (discussions drawing from her (finding!) new resources ((yes!) insight frees the heart to spend its worth (she should (doesn't) write that down (what had Mefisto said over dinner ((as a joke((?) he was chuckling)): "There is always a danger to take the freedom of a dream and encage it in a sentence" ((for that matter) in a book or in a song or a smear of color or code (though might not through these the "freedom of a dream" be "set free" too? (to skies it has the strength to survive)?)))))))).

(not surprisingly) Astair finds few familiar faces ((no Shana Bix or Ronnie Born or Davis Trenz (or Lucien or Dana)) graduated and gone) but the unfamiliar faces offer rewards too (beyond anticipation (the vitality (not the kindness) of strangers (that is more than enough))).

The three sessions come with titles like

✧ Supervision Practicum IX

✧ Advanced Psychopathology VII

✧ Somatic & Symbol Dynamics in Psychotherapy II

Xanther comes up in the last one.

"A few weeks ago, in a coffee shop, my daughter, who's twelve, asked me about a car. A Mitsubishi Mirage. I believe she said it was red. The point was that the 'M' and the 'i' were missing. She saw 'rage' but could see how others might just see, despite the missing letters, the model name. She wanted to know which meaning should prevail."

"Your twelve-year-old uses the word 'prevail'?" the instructor asks (Gaddis).

"That's mother me filling in for daughter her."

A warm rush of quiet laughter binds the small group (of eight).

"I think it's like this," one classmate offers ((maybe Taiwanese) wearing a bright yellow shirt (Izod)). "If the owner of the car purposefully took off the 'M' and 'i,' then what it says, it means."

"And if the letters just fell off?" Gaddis prompts.

"Then what is said becomes . . . the province of our . . . interpretation of . . . the child's dream," the classmate puzzles out (turning slowly from Gaddis to Astair). "In other words, is your daughter angry?"

More (energizing) classes fill Wednesday ∴ August 6 ∴.

That night (after dinner (at the campus cafeteria)) Astair heads for the library. The first hour vanishes to news (WiFi distractions (curses!)). Some teenagers (including a fourteen-year-old girl!) ∴ **Andrew Garcia, Jonathan DelCarmen, Alberto Ochoa, Alejandra Guerrero and** ▓▓▓▓▓▓ ∴ are accused of killing a USC student ∴ **Xinran Ji** ∴ *with a blue metal bat* ∴. Then an anti-bullying (conceptual) ordinance (in Rancho Santa Margarita) grabs her attention. Astair thinks of Xanther: the possible ferocity ((violence!) of a youngster) vs. the possible victimization (by other youngsters (violence!)). Meanwhile Frogtown (with Frog Spot cafe (she should take the girls)(pretty close)) wants a different name ((to get away from a legacy of gang violence (Elysian Valley!)) though wasn't there some recent police-drug violence there?). And (lastly) news of a two-star U.S. General killed in Afghanistan ∴ **Major General Harold J. Greene** ∴.

That place again.

Dov again.

Astair puts the laptop away (in favor of pad and pen).

(and though she needs a bibliography (and one about cats)) Astair for some reason starts by thinking about novels: their startling independence and interiority and opacity through which a reader might access the imaginative alchemy necessary to achieve a transparency of mind.

A condition achieved by reinscribing the old patterns the mind holds on to. Because isn't it true that even just remembering re-informs the memory? Remembering is never passive. And how we remember what we were shapes who we will become.

Call it a personal thought experiment to get her scribbling:

How does Astair remember now (and change now) Xanther's cat?

No question (despite questions of its age (mortality)) that creature is a survivor. (and considering the role of cats (large and small) in any ecosystem) More than a survivor.

Nature packages its successes.

Astair had finally handled the beast. The night before leaving too. Maybe because the closed eyes had seemed to taunt her with some secret (if the secret was no more than the sight of blindness).

It was sitting at the top of the stairs. As though it were waiting for her. Astair immediately scooped it up. The silkiness of the fur surprised her. So did the floppiness. Astair didn't dare bring it too close (what if it scratched her face?). (instead) She set it down on her knees (facing her) and then (with a ((okay) slightly trembling) finger) she pulled down beneath one eye (parting the lids (to reveal a glossy scab of white)).

Her revulsion had surprised her.

That revulsion returns now (along with the way she had recoiled too). Reinforcing?

It turns out (as Astair (now) goes on to discover) cats have a third eyelid (called a nictitating membrane (or *palpebra tertia* (or even haw))). The purpose seems elusive: added protection for the cornea (especially when stalking through tall grass) more darkness (for sleeping?) and more tears (for seeing better (!)). The brighter question (posited in a *Scientific American* article ∴ By veterinarian Paul Miller. November 20, 2006 ∴): Why don't *we* have a third eyelid?

Something else her research turns up:

Gargamel.

Astair knows the villain is from *The Smurfs* (even if she doesn't know why she's chosen to consult Wikipedia about it right now). She's surprised (though) to find a consideration of Gargamel as an anti-Semitic caricature (big nose (with a mezuzah on the door (making his Jewishness clear))). Could the twins be making a discriminatory remark toward Xanther because of Dov's Jewish heritage? (Impossible (they're barely facing their own dark complexion (and North African origins))).)

Something else that's curious about Gargamel: he has a cat named Azrael (or "God is my helper"(or Hathattul ((where (in Hebrew) *hat* = fear and *hatul* = cat) or "fearsome cat"))). Apparently among Jews and Muslims Azrael also means:

The Angel of Death.

In the library both the inner eyelid and the meaning of Azrael had seemed cartoonish (literally!) but outside (crossing the campus lawn in the dark) Astair's skin starts to crawl.

Her thinking (at that moment (due to the class discussion (about Xanther's comment))) is even in the midst of reconsidering rage (((possibly) self-perpetuating) still part of the fight vector) as still a result of fear. But fear also has another vector: to retreat (flight) to ((possibly) self-perpetuating) terror. At which point Astair feels that awful awareness that summons us to acknowledge an awareness not of our own (skin).

Astair is being watched.

And not by a cat.

And indeed past a side parking lot (among the dark tangles of scrub oak) stand two girls.

Staring at her.

Both have long black braids. Both are wearing black shorts and pink Converses. Pink t-shirts too. One girl is Asian. The other is black. Yet both clearly look like they want to look like Xanther!

Stranger still (each has on a shoulder) a stuffed (white!) animal.

"Hey!" (F(l)ight(?)) Astair cries (startled) but already sprinting toward them (as they disappear at once into the shadows (as if shadows could ever stop Astair))).

On the downward slope (steepening (accelerating this race)) thick roots catch Astair's ankle and twist her to the ground.

"Wait!" Astair still calls out to the girls (already reaching the top of the opposing slope (flickering pale and inky black (fearful in their fearlessness))). "Who are you? Why are you dressed like that?"

Their answer floors Astair.

"You're her mom, aren't you?"

"Is that supposed to be a cat on your shoulder?" Astair shoots back.

"Duh."

Come morning :: Thursday, August 7 :: the encounter already seems like a dream (if dirt stains on her jeans corroborate the fall (her ankle is fine)).

The (pleasant!) life of her schedule (the lectures and new acquaintances) crowd out the absolute (nuttiness!) of that encounter. Did she really chase down two kids to ask them about their clothing?

Astair has to get to a lecture but spends a quick moment beforehand on one of the garden benches ((despite the heat) at least she finds some shady heat) to call Anwar and the girls (better to not mention the *other* girls) and survey the mail she swore to get through before returning.

Bills. And garbage.

A nice postcard from her parents.

More bills. More garbage.

Another postcard from her sister.

(Astair's is a postcard family.)

Then something unusual: an envelope with her name on it (in a hand (beautiful too!) she doesn't recognize).

The return address indicates Mexico.

Querida señora:

Todo es mi culpa. Porque es lo correcto y porque no estoy segura si Freya o Shasti hayan intentado ocultarle la verdad es que le escribo ahora. Le escribo en español porque temo que mi inglés enturbie todavía más lo que sus hijas hayan podido contarle.

¡Tiene unas hijas hermosísimas! Su primera reacción fue mantener en secreto mi torpeza. Cuánto deseaban protegerme aunque les rogué que no lo hicieran.

Disculpe que no le haya escrito antes. Nuestra mudanza fue azarosa y encontrar un hogar resultó complicado. No obstante, conseguimos un hermoso lugar en Tlaquepaque y el negocio de raspados de mi marido es un éxito de la noche a la mañana.

Confío en que le habrán devuelto mi salario de aquel día y que me hará saber de cualquier adeudo que quede pendiente. No hace falta ser muy lista para darse cuenta que esa pieza vale más de lo que una doméstica gana al día.

Todo se resbala entre mis dedos ¿porqué sería distinto con el vidrio? Pero todavía me maravillo sobre cómo pudo el gatito subir hasta la repisa. Xanther nunca estuvo cerca. Fue entonces, cuando traté de evitar un accidente, diví a los lobos. Al tratar de salvar al gato causé un estropicio y la dejé con los añicos de mi destino. De nuevo le pido disculpas.

Suya en gratitud
Xiomara

Xiomara? Astair doesn't have time to even Google Translate it. And maybe because she's still wondering about what the letter contains Astair is blindsided by the appearance of Llewyn Fabler.

There he is (standing in a slash of midday sun (beneath the ribs of steel arching over the walkway (separating the two main Oceanica buildings))). An aide helps him with the slow trek (he's not teaching yet (is he?)?).

What hurts most is that Astair barely recognizes him. He seems aged by decades. His hair glows white. He's lost so much weight he seems draped in the melt of his former years. His skin is practically translucent. His lips seem void of color too. Only a spackle of rosacea on his nose speaks of wilder days (with bottle and glass nearby (at least a bottle)).

And matters of recognition keep delivering hurt.

It takes him a moment to place her too.

"Astair!" he finally manages (his voice a dry breeze over drier leaves).

They hug. He has to get to the hospital for another checkup. She's late for her class. It feels inappropriate to bring up Eldon Avantine or the incomplete she got on her dissertation (*Hope's Nest: On the Necessity of God*) or even her new topic (not to mention the strange book of poems Fabler sent her). So they just hug again and promise to see each other soon.

The classes and study groups (and evening work (increasingly more focused) on her bibliography) continue to revive her. Though by Friday afternoon ∴ August 8 ∴ Astair is glad the lecture on Psychopharmacology is her last (or penultimate (not counting Sandra Dee Taylor's Saturday talk (which is too much of a pleasure to cry too tired))).

(as it turns out) Emory Paulson's elocutions on child abuse and the use of drug regimens to improve therapeutic results have been canceled. The (last-minute) replacement is a presentation titled "Synthetic Procuracy"(?).

In Paulson's place is a Dutch doctor named Klief Schocken (whose accent (further weighted by an obscure sense of pronunciation (compounded by mumblings that too often dip below audible)) renders questionable most of what Astair writes down).

But there is plenty to write down. Astair never ceases to scribble out strange phrases like "synaptic progressions" ((?) "neural arrangements" (rearrangements?)) or "paleolithic treatment brackets." But (maybe for the sport of it) Astair tries to keep up.

She churns through the pages. Even switches out pens once. (even as she notices how (with every flip to a new spread of lined blanks)) More and more of her (stranger-familiar) classmates are giving up (leaving one by one (in small groups (bestowing blankness upon the room (and upon the merit of anything conveyed here) with the simple message of their exit))).

Dr. Schocken doesn't seem to care.

(without any air of defeat or pride) He (simply(?)) marshals on. He is (merely(?)) a servant to the material (where delivery of a report (however complex) is the only concern). And as Astair begins to understand more and more the curious pattern of speech (at times even anticipating (briefly) Dr. Schocken's next direction) the enormity of discovery and responsibility (momentarily) comes into (vital) view (grave consequences are at the heart of Dr. Schocken's concern).

How then does Xanther's cat/kitten also manage to come to mind? Irrelevant (obviously) but suddenly vivid too ((a taijitu) ☯ ((fishless) of only white (just yin (or is it yang?)))(curled up on her daughter's pillow))?

Until the mention of a new drug (group?) snaps Astair back to attention. Synthia(!)? Like Mefisto's collegial paper? Or was it Syntax? Synsnap?

Dr. Schocken also seems to be talking just to Astair now. Whispering too (faster and faster).

Something about "troubled chemical reconfigurations."

Something about "delivery systems problematized" by "combined mediums" failing to "initiate effective resurrections."

"Meta-pharmaceutical mechanisms."

"Axon alterations."

"Onerous if not impossible disinstillations."

Then there's the M-Series. The S-Series. Trials in the 1960s and early '70s. Darpa. ZSL. Facilities in Bern, Rio, and Singapore.

Astair keeps writing faster (even if she can't keep up (reduced to a poor transcription machine (inept computer))) eclipsing all sight of Dr. Schocken (even (the nature of) his utterances (erased by words (until even ink preferences any content delivery))). The spell brings to life an old mood (the more Astair loses hold of herself ((she's an idiot!) as she (too dutifully) fulfills the purpose of these strange declarations (this strange transference))).

∴ Wait. Is that allowed? ∵

∴ What was once so categorically disallowed to seem beyond existence now seems all too present and ongoing. ∵

Astair is jarred by the crammed pages before her (so many (too many)). She even feels slightly ill. But Dr. Schocken isn't finished yet (speaking even more emphatically now (urgently?)).

"There is simply no need to respond to *traditional* SSRI *strategies*. Root-meaning creation self-levels nearly *every* future circumstance. And thus far, limited trials have *shown* our chemical affect is more enduring than self-assembled or *therapeutically* introduced introjects. Dare I say *permanent*?"

Dr. Klief Schocken is done. He is turning off the projector. He is shuffling together his notes. He looks almost as dazed as Astair and the last remaining students (two).

"Oh," Dr. Schocken suddenly adds. "Once too. One treatment. Whether by injection, inhalation, retinal, or aural exposure. One sustaining Hope."

Dr. Schocken starts to leave. The question that fails to arrest his exit jars Astair as much because of how loudly it was delivered as because of whom was doing the delivering: Astair practically shouted.

"Do you mean the chemical creation of an
actual memory?"

That night she meets up with Javier and Jules at Cielito ((sweetie) little sky ((?) Astair needs less sky (less horizon))). It's still Happy Hour. Quesadillas (with manchego and kale). Ceviche (with jicama and local sea bass). Guacamole (with just-made chips (burning their fingers (burning their mouths))). The perfect accompaniment for the chemicals guaranteed to help: pools of salty solace arriving in big bowls of blue glass (sugar and tequila (lots)).

Jules is going on about a woman in Colorado who saved herself from a mountain lion by singing opera ∴ **Kyra Kopenstonsky. Down Valley Park. Placerville, Colorado** ∴. Javier reports the capture of a lioness (white (near Laredo (Texas))). Cats coming up because of Astair's new topic (though) the subject of their collective failure soon takes over.

"At least you got an I!" Jules slaps the table. "I got a D-minus! They're the same thing! Both papers need to be redone. Mine was just insulting."

The three had first bonded in a psychopathology class. Jules (formerly in vitamin sales) now runs a bicycle shop in Mar Vista. Javier (a former MMA practitioner (survivor of even some paid (UFC) bouts)) makes a living as a certified Iyengar instructor. His boyfriend is the brother of Jules' boyfriend.

Javier's first paper focused on the therapeutic value of yoga. Jules had focused on the benefits of gardening (where "Get your hands dirty! See what grows!" (the dissertation's guiding line) was hailed by Jules' advisor as "Brilliance incarnate!").

All three of them had shared the same advisor (the real reason their bonding had endured (to hell with psychopathology)): Llewyn Fabler.

Astair can't bear to mention her encounter.

Jules is still trying to make his garden of words grow. But (like Astair) Javier has switched topics (to the role of the Ouija board in James Merrill's *The Changing Light at Sandover*).

"The planchette as enabler," Javier explains.

"'Planchet' means blank coin," Jules points out. "Merrill would certainly be conscious of how both depend on the power of inscription to create value."

"I'm not considering the role of money, but the Merrill fortune would certainly be one of those unvoiced voices."

"How is it?" Astair asks. "I've never read it."

"About as kooky as Connecticut can get." Javier smiles. "I'm looking at leisure. Who doesn't dream of all the time in the world to think and travel to Greece? Though for my taste there's too much 'darlings' and 'my boys' and chinaware and unicorns. And French. Where's the Spanish? The Arabic? But there's also audacity and wonder: two gay men communicating with the apparatus of god."

(after the next round lands) Astair takes out the letter from Xiomara.

Jules looks at it and laughs. "Sister, I know Spanish about as well as you know Gaelic."

Astair blushes.

Javier is the same (despite an extensive Mexican family). "Dad only spoke English. And Mom only spoke what Dad spoke."

Their busboy reads the letter easily but (by that point) they're too drunk to make sense of the English he barely speaks.

"Is good thinking terrifying?" Sandra Dee Taylor (their doula of Oceanica) asks a room of seventy on Saturday ∴ August 9 ∴. "Good thinking, I like to think, is. And I like to think about it a great deal too, though whether I manage any of it is another story completely, contested perhaps too frequently by my grandchildren and gratefully by you.

"Good thinking I like to think is hard thinking. And what makes hard thinking?" (Again a genuine question.) "Consider this definition: hard thinking is when we don't merely apply pre-existing rationales to routine patterns — for example, in the way we might observe events, note interactions, evaluate emotional responses — but instead acquire a completely new set of values and parameters to re-encounter and reinterpret these common events, interactions, emotional responses.

"That's then one model for hard thinking. Hard because acquiring a new set of values is hard work.

"But is it terrifying?"

(Astair has an answer (but not the confidence to voice it (her hangover isn't helping))).

"Because our sense of self, our identity—" (did Sandra Dee just stare directly at Astair (even linger there?))? "—frequently finds stabilization, if not outright resolution, in rationales inculcated at an early age. Examples please."

Hands shoot up (though not Astair's). Followed by a clatter of voices.

"Catholicism." "Mormonism." "Judaism." "Islam." "Party affiliation." "Sexual orientation." "Racial bias." "Scientific method." "Tribal ritual." "Taboo."

"Good. Religious rubrics. Political praxis. Clan morals. Parental jurisprudence. Gender habits. A long list and, as we can all agree, incomplete. Changing any of those modes of engagement must necessitate a departure from the original self which by that renegotiation can go so far as to displace the self and whether the response is fatigue — getting drowsy? — or boredom — getting antsy? — or anger — getting just that — *that* is most certainly terrifying. Though isn't the alternative worse? To live many lives is heaven. Hell is to not live even one."

And that's just the beginning. Sandra Dee Taylor speaks for another ninety minutes (though today (for some reason) Astair stops taking notes (("There is a difference between work that is constructive and work that is compulsion. Note the difference. Beware the consequences of not noting. Working hard is not the same as hard work. Good work, good thinking, even good living: this is what we pursue.") which Astair remembers perfectly (she thinks)) even if her hand collapses into some private (inkless) fugue of heaviness (her lids also engaging the same heaviness (even as some kind of internal lid begins to open))).

Somehow Sandra Dee's talk demands it.

"Life would be so wonderful if we only knew what to do with it. But why wonder? Remember: no choice is rendered any less significant or impactful if made with an even greater application of kindness."

"Think before you act. Then act without thinking."

"To find yourself again go find yourself in this world where you are not of this world. In other words . . . see new places! Meet new faces! Travel!"

(That one earns much laughter and applause (as many of her remarks do).)

"Why keep escaping from what makes us us?"

"As we are in a vocation rooted in feelings, let us not forget that immaturity is frequently reflected in the belief that strong feelings ratify every action. In other words and to be proscriptive: let us be mature.

"Remember you future counselors and bringers of relief: there will never be a cure for life's problems because so many of tomorrow's problems will be new. Good words, like good work and good thinking, help, even if good words are a lot like highway paint. They can keep plenty of heavy things moving at 70 MPH from going the wrong way. But that doesn't mean life won't cross over if it has to. Learn to avoid the collisions. Find other directions. Often a new yes is the best no. Life lived well doesn't get easier but it does get better. Learn to let things go by. And don't be reluctant: life is allways surpassing us by. Enjoy it."

Even Cardiff can't diminish the elation Astair feels afterwards. Astair is out on the big lawn (soaking up some sun (and the last moments of her week at Oceanica ((no desire to run) at least for the moment))) when Cardiff hustles up to say goodbye (loaded down with baggage).

Astair ends up helping her carry a duffel full of books to a waiting limo.

Cardiff can't stop saying thank you (especially for agreeing to be a reader).

"I'm dreading my week ahead. I have to translate nine papers into English. My German is pretty rusty."

"How about your Spanish?"

"Oh, very fluent. One of my majors in college. I lived in Madrid for a year too."

Suddenly Astair is handing Cardiff Xiomara's letter. Cardiff looks grateful to be able to help (and takes the task very seriously).

"Dear Señora," Cardiff starts. "I am entirely at fault. Because it is the correct thing to do and because I am uncertain whether or not Freya and Shasti might have obscured the truth, I am writing to you now. I write in Spanish for fear my English would confuse to a greater degree anything your dear children might have conveyed."

Astair is confused. Is Cardiff making this up? And if she is not, who is this woman writing to her?

Xiomara!?

Cardiff catches something too. Looks up.

"She sounds like a Zacatecas poet!"

Maybe she is.

"You have such beautiful girls!" Cardiff continues. "Their first response was to keep secret my clumsiness. How they wanted to protect me even as I told them to do no such thing.

"Forgive me for not writing sooner. Our move took many different turns and finding a home proved difficult. We have found, though, a lovely place in Tlaquepaque and my husband's venture with shaved ice has proved instantly popular.

"I trust that you received back my fee for that day and trust you further that you will let me know the balance. It wasn't hard to see that such a piece was worth more than anything my mop earns in a day."

Cardiff hesitates for a moment. Her lips moving as she works through the last part.

"All the time things slip through my fingers. Why should glass be an exception? Yet even today I am amazed by how that little kitten managed to make its way onto the mantel. Xanther was nowhere around. As I lunged for the animal, just about to fall, I knocked over the wolves. Intending to prevent one accident I caused another and left you with the pieces of my carelessness. Again, my apologies."

hungry ghost

They all STARVED in silence.

— The Exploding Cat #1

madam tembam had slapped jingjing. jingjing still shrieked.

'damn toot one, you!" slapslap more. "yau kwee too!" clap

jingjing's ears. "eat my stones! you dare?!"

then tian li osso whapwhap jingjing. two of them with flapflap

attack, until jingjing fall back, flip chair. hean toh, lah. but table

not flip, shudder just, settle next. both aunties chio kao peng then.

suck for air, clutching bellies those two laugh so hard.

madam tembam laugh hardest. spirit medium, tang ki, juang lah,

her smile so big lip ends cross both eyes. tian li sama. long while

since jingjing see auntie so happy. jingjing laughing too.

osso check ownself. make sure stone didn't makan face for real.

ooh yiah boh? his nose, these eyes, this smile, still there? there

as two bomohs squatted for more heaves, madam tembam rattling

stone bag macam jingjing leave skin second time.

better then then, than now now. great tian li drools and snores

again. no travel talk, not even kong sar kong si on california

dreaming. sleeps all days again. won't, hor, wander from flat.

mebbe shuffleshuffles to bath. nothing more. sits mong mong cha

cha dreaming for dreams she won't remember anymore.

jingjing don't dream. jingjing don't sleep. jingjing koyak for jilo

changing, jilo going, jilo jilo everywhere. lao yah pok, jingjing.

worldwall too, lah, jilo world, hum pah lang wall.

by quays jingjing play kway again. just sashay through heat. catch

eyes enuf. link up at last with lepak ah chek in white vest and

ascot puff, parakeet peach. swede. mebbe british. just wants to

arminarm down bising street, want jingjing swing so akasai. uncle

is kay kiasi when jingjing bring up ring, wife. no stingy poker

then, give up dollars lah to keep jingjing by his side. steam, steam,

steam. buy jingjing flower, lemon ice. tea first and then cream.

sing song, order drink, kau him nice. jingjing ponteng quick, lah,

ditch, split, when old ah kua trot for the loo.

23 slide balloon over.

light blue again but saysay next time mebbe pink.

flat 03-03 again. jingjing remember lighter, returns lighter. smoke house lady give thanks. give jingjing pipe. lights him up. time to let time drift off. time to care-lair-fair.

no wings. jingjing has friends everywhere.

joss sticks, lah, outlawed lor, haunt tonight. banned burn bins

too. can't keep a good ghost down. hungry ghost festival is now.

jingjing almost forgot.

he wanders hours. until feet hurt. feet fall off. bukit brown ∴ ceme-

tery ∴. saga seeds pave path. rambutan trees block gateless gate.

jingjing find grills deep among graves. now he boh lui liao but no

one's selling. historian pours jingjing cup of coke. checks on meat.

ants big as knuckles attack jingjing's feet.

"worse than mosquitoes," student smiles. a spider dances on her

shirt. "don't stand on an ant hill. god help you if you do."

but mosquitoes pretty bad. she'll need a whole tub of fong yeow

cheng, eagle brand. bites circle her knees. rise on her thighs. bang-

bangs never bother jingjing much, something in his blood.

later, lah, with talk of clan arrangement and war, class offers

jingjing their cookies, their lessons. jingjing not hungry for either.

kai kai alone by paths, past markers, some topped with paper and

stone, most forgotten. some names in red. some in green and gold.

and the moon fills up.

keeps filling. until one sky above knows itself whole. bats dance

the rising swarms. black moths come home.

all ghosts here have left.

what jingjing know of peace? damn still here. over music of what

grows, jingjing will pick the places where the dead speak loudest.

gives away his hours then to upper thomson road.

the temple east finally rises up in work of smoke.

jingjing veers for altars, tassled in reds and golds, lanterns above,

dragons below, bells too, and oil lamps, brass bowls and closed

glass cases clasping things that stir . . .

falling ash.

monks scattering. kan cheong, leh, sure, but for what?

mebbe for jingjing.

they chant, bow too.

and why not? jingjing pupil of auntie, attendant to tian li the

great, she of serangoon, the smith street sage, master of white

cat . . .

why not jingjing arrive tonight master too? dukun, medium, seer.

sees everything through. here, ancient ruler on white horse. there, long boat with paper oars. cymbals ring. parades of people fill tables with fishballs and huat kueh, dragon fruit, roasted chicken, rice cakes, durian puffs, wife's delights, peranakan sweets.

jingjing raises arms wide, chants whatever a mind makes up. just to hear him say it is to know forever a prayer to keep. starts to spin in place. spin in space. got on his casual britney face.

only no one repeats. no one wins. liddat two monks approach, grab, lah, jingjing from both sides. but jingjing oreddy has too many ten-sides to reach. monks got their smiles and mu touch, tai chi must, but still no getting beneath this becoming.

jingjing is the root of the mountain, the feeling that teaches rivers to rain.

and what once stirred begins to seethe. a heart race, yelp, fears

beyond defense.

corners uncoil with darkness, wings spread wide as opera and

beat down tents, even if opera here doesn't notice, mu lien keeps

marching from hell to stage, suona play, all tents stand.

vampire teeth snap the air, worse teeth stake the light. claws end

the ground. a thousand and one voices whirl in whisper around

jingjing, cinch their meanings tighter, if never revealing more than

this, his, inevitable, death.

in front of temple, the two monks who helped jingjing there smile,

pat his arms, ask if he okay, ask again. make jingjing so malu.

gorblok him, again. once so convinced, now kay confused.

but he damn scared shitless lah, to look back inside, backback of

temple, where greatness awake. and terror. until a moment later

jingjing feel power swish away. leaving only terror.

outside, lah, no better.

high fences enclose metal grate, on which sits biggest shape of

paper art, a creature towering over stirrup and hull. stacks of

gold-wrapped hell notes flame. iphones, bugattis, good-class

bungalows, burn at paws too.

jingjing smack self. you tau hong, kayu. pale blue blur like fuck

everybody's head. this the smoke.

heat fans back every visitor, then monks, jingjing last. flames soon

growl cage's edge until even the pillar of smoke twisting all the

way to the moon burns too.

teeth go, ears go, whiskers go . . .

whiskers stay, ears stay, fangs stay . . .

living flame overtaking flame, beyond form of any fuel, beyond

coals of any reason, the reach of every rule, burning whiter and

whiter, until, macam eyes glow cold, hungriest ghost of all.

"jingjing! own what you're owed!"

"the cat is yours!"

before collapsing into burning rose.

∴ Blue as a dream we once had when we were empty but carried no shape in need of filling or form. ∵

∴ what i forget, lah. ∵

∴ When we floated deeper above deep water and polar bears played on our belly and we needed to recall no home. ∵

∴ we forget that too. ∵

bloom gone then into acorn of blinding heat, for a pause, one

one-thousand, two one-thousand, three one-thousand, four one-

thousand, then giant head ∴ *of papier-mâché cat* ∵ explodes.

dawn on to monday, and next day, jingjing oreddy so tzai, auntie

better, back to sama sleeping ways. jingjing can steady out again.

people's park under the pavilion. old men main checkers, warm

arms shiny easy in icy polyester shirts, savor their hoon kees for

breakfast, guinness for lunch.

borak over their boards, over the news:

robin williams dead. hang self in a closet.

"let's just say singaporean prosperity did not shine on me," old

man tell jingjing, sip of beer, kings self. "but look at him."

and that's not it.

zhong sim lin dead too. of cancer.

izard defend a wall.

some big company havoc now for zsl. kay kalang kabut, lah. no

word on son or squad. bow ties thrown to the storm.

"not even the rich are immune."

Venice, Italy. 9:33:46 am. August 12, 2014

Has my vast wealth come to this?
Hardly the ascension I planned for.

What Canova planned for Titian's bones
became the resting place for his own hear
completed by his pupils. I knew them all.
None, though, knows me well
enough to complete my heart's work.

Here lies genius. Dead.
If only the beast were dead too.
At least the book is closed. Enough of books.
Books have failed me.

The old witch must be found!

One Lab

This makes no difference.

— *Victim #5*

The machines lost. The flames
that did the winning are gone.
The smoke is gone too. The May-
or's men still wear masks in case
the tractors burying the charred
remains stir up and fill the air with
chemicals. The chemists insist any
leftover substances will be inert.
But they too wear masks.

The Mayor doesn't. Nor does
Isandòrno.

—I am glad Teyo left before he
could see this, The Mayor says.

Zero of the second bay and little of the first bay survived. Even the farm equipment was doused with fuel. The Mayor had to bring in these tractors and trucks.

—Teyo, though, would understand. He would see this as nothing more than the cost of doing the business we do.

More men approach The Mayor. Weapons hang across their chests. It is a needless display. The opportunity for weapons passed days ago. They should have shovels instead. The Mayor tells them to start digging. The Mayor also understands.

If he were drinking, he would treat this place as the perfect opportunity to command an audience with his rage. But this is no place. And these soldiers are not the ones he will demand retaliation from.

The Mayor returns to the little table waiting on the fringes of the blackened earth, not far from the runway and idling plane.

Night falls. There is no feast. The Mayor sips herbal tea from a thermos. Drowsiness befriends him.

More men approach. These carry only shovels. The Mayor is pleased. They still go off shaking their heads.

The air shifts. Breezes settle for stillness. Stillness gives way to a new direction. Soon fields of stars shimmer above. The smell of creosote dims and awakens.

Eventually insects announce the

dawn. The new day finds no bodies or machines.

The chemists assure The Mayor
that even with the stolen machines
production is —Unlikely. Even
with the kidnapped personnel
production is —Unlikely.

Unlikely is never a good thing to
say to The Mayor.

But The Mayor is still drowsy. He
tells the chemists and engineers to
contact him in Mexico City if they
discover anything more.

But The Mayor does not fly to Mexico City. Instead he and Isandòrno fly to Guadalajara. The Mayor keeps three apartments in Puerto de Hierro. All three are connected by passages dependent on a hydraulic system designed to remain concealed under at least an hour of intense scrutiny.

El Chapo stole from The Mayor. This system The Mayor stole from El Chapo. Water is used to lift in minutes heavy slabs of steel and concrete. Gravity closes them in seconds. La Maceta ∴ **no. 52** ∵ lies on the floor.

—El Topo won't mind, The Mayor has said. The Mayor does not believe Altiplano ∴ Federal Social Readaptation Center No. 1∴ will hold El Topo.

In the days that follow, Isandòrno and The Mayor live alone in the three apartments in Puerto de Hierro. It is safest this way but it is harder too. Isandòrno can do nothing for The Mayor's fears as they come and go.

In hours of great confidence, The Mayor wages reprisals in his head against Los Zetas, Knights Templar, Beltrán-Leyva, Gulf Cartel, Juárez Cartel, and Sinaloa Cartel.

In hours of great doubt, The Mayor defends himself against future attacks by Los Zetas, Knights Templar, Beltrán-Leyva, Gulf Cartel, Juárez Cartel, and Sinaloa Cartel.

But there are no more attacks. Or more news.

—Puto Peña Nieto is too stupid to do something like this without me hearing about it.

By Saturday, they are back again in Mexico City. The Mayor returns to drinking bottles of cognac on the veranda. Whores are brought in but he likes none of them. He plays with the chimpanzee. At times he sends Isandòrno away so he can be alone with the chimpanzee.

By Sunday, The Mayor is bored of the chimpanzee and the rest of his animals. He is bored of drinking. He is bored of women.

He misses the things that are not around: Teyo, his wife, his children, men he can trust, even Cutberto.

—Him I could trust. I must visit his wife again. At least she is recovering. We must bring her many flowers.

By Monday, more men arrive. They have discovered something. They have discovered that the operating system responsible for running the mechanized operation was uploaded to a server no longer in operation.

They have confirmed this theft
not only through digital traces
unaccounted for but also through
on-site video surveillance that
correlates time and transmission
with the terminal and user:

Señor Bruno Villegas. Cutberto.

—The wife will have to go.

Isandòrno waits for the order.

—I will do it myself.

And The Mayor does. He orders all payments to the cancer clinic halted. It is not a long call. He also arranges for additional financial pressures to make decent care impossible.

—The doctors say she will be dead in weeks. Please confirm with me so I can arrange many flowers for their graves.

Isandòrno still does not believe Cutberto is responsible but he does not care either.

The issue that concerns The Mayor most remains unsolved: who ordered the destruction of the Zacatecas lab?

Isandòrno does not care about that either.

The only thing of consequence is what The Mayor will ask Isandòrno to do. And since that which he is obliged to do renders meaningless everything else, and since that which he is obliged to do is also meaningless, Isandòrno can only wait beyond the veranda, where thick vines of honeysuckle grow, where he is free to contemplate nothing.

Not even sleep is meaningful. Now and then dreams come in the shape of memories that might as well be hummingbirds.

Isandòrno's mother once told him a story of a mother who told her son that his father was a god and that he must go forth and visit all of the gods in order to find out which one was his.

Isandòrno never met his father.
His father was no god.

Isandòrno tugs his earlobe.
Counts. Watches for crows.

The goat and donkey come from
a world ruled by gods who rule
from a place exempt from rules.

The totem with its long fangs, ears
pinned back, and deep whiskers,
hacked out with the old Indian's
machete, while his sick daughter
watched on, comes from a world
no longer ruled by gods.

Gods require comfort. Where there is no comfort, seek the rule of something else.

Honeysuckle is for the blind. What of Isandòrno's humming-birds? Are they blind? What do those memories see? It no longer matters what Isandòrno sees.

All Tuesday morning, The Mayor shows Isandòrno newspaper clips of bodies lining the roads up north. Mass graves have been discovered west. Journalists need to die in order to convince other journalists that there are better ways to survive. The Mayor is done with shovels. He has arranged for more weapons. If his success depended on one lab, he would not have his zoos.

Teyo will return soon. The Mayor will show him another lab deeper in the tangles of jungle to the south. Teyo will see for himself all that will require distribution in the fall. Not just in Los Angeles and California, but in Oregon, Minnesota, and Illinois. The Mayor wants to go to New York City and see a musical.

Isandòrno says nothing.

—If the second lab burns after Teyo visits that will tell us something. The Mayor laughs.

The Mayor changes the subject.

—You must go to The Ranch soon. Something has happened up there that I don't understand.

—To Juan?

The Mayor shakes his head.

—To others. Juan has the money now. He is happy to keep it. You know Juan. He will keep it safe. It is not so much to concern us but I want you to pick it up.

Isandòrno nods.

The Mayor still looks unsatisfied.

—You don't know?

Isandòrno shakes his head.

—I'm disappointed.

The Mayor looks disappointed too.
And drunk. He is dangerous when
he's drunk but he is most dangerous when he is disappointed.

—One of the animals escaped . . .
the fourth one. I thought you told
me there were only three?

M.E.T.E.

I finally passed the Turing test.

— *Michael Robbins*

Anwar [finally] gets through to Enzio. Not [via] Skype. Not [via] e-mail. Not [{thank goodness!} via] text. Not even by cell. Anwar uses the landline down-stairs and Savannah picks up.

'Hey! I'm *so* sorry. We're the ones who owe *you* a call.'

'That's quite okay. I'm sorry for these repeated inquiries.' [Did Anwar just apologize? {bony shoulders rising around his ears ‹even as the rest of him slumps «hearing himself»›}] 'Well, but, oh, it's been a month?' [Is he sounding like Xanther? {yes!}] 'According to my records, I submitted Cataplyst-3—'

'Yes.' [Sigh {whispery}.] 'On Bastille Day. More than a month ago. And we accepted the work too. It's excellent work. Timely, clean. Everything we asked for with just the right amount of extra to keep Enzio calling.'

Savannah sounds defeated [embarrassed? {sad}].

'But?'

Anwar finds Xanther upstairs in his office. [as always] Her curious purblind fur of affection is nooked at her neck as she studies the Go board.

'Have you found a name yet?' Anwar asks [sitting beside her].

Xanther shakes her head. The creature [barely] moves.

'How about Pyramid?'

'Pyramid?' she asks her charge. Then shakes her head. 'Nope.'

How does she imagine the cat is supposed to respond? How will she know when it's right? [Let her find her way {on her own} to whatever name {‹even if› Anwar likes Pyramid ‹like a Peer Amid «Pure Amid ⟨Pyre Amid⟩ . . . »› Anwar circulating the vague puns without conviction}.]

'Will you explain this to me?' Xanther points to the black and white stones [out of place {scattered ‹someone «or something» having disturbed the game he and Mefisto played weeks ago «what Anwar was still studying ⟨trying to decipher how he lost⟩ that future opportunity also lost now»›}].

'These?'

Xanther nods [she has yet to lift her eyes].

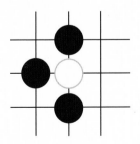

'The white stone has only one liberty remaining. We say it's in atari.'

'Like, uh, the old video game maker?'

'Good, daughter. Though in Go, the meaning is similar to chess when beginners say "check."'

'Because the white stone is almost surrounded?'

'That's right. To the North, to the South, to the West. Only the East remains free. This shape is also called a Tiger's Mouth.'

'Huh,' Xanther responds [snapping a black stone into place {with a good click too ‹fingers not interfering «and ⟨lightly⟩ moving away»›}]. 'The mouth shuts?'

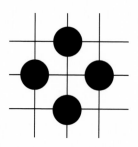

Anwar nods [plucking up {and offering Xanther} the white stone].

'Mine?'

'The stone is dead.'

'Dead?'

'Unless it has eyes to live.'

'Eyes?'

'And not just one eye. Stones must have two eyes to live.'

Anwar spends the next hour arranging numerous positions on the board [to demonstrate various shapes {those that survive ‹and those that do not›}]. The Life/Death question is the most crucial [and difficult] concept for the beginner [and expert{?}]. Upon it the game depends.

Anwar creates two examples [{the first dead}{the second alive ‹because suicide is never allowed›}].

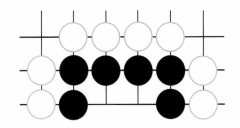

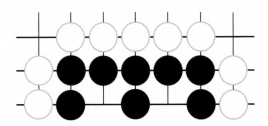

Xanther struggles to come up with her own [living] examples but [{at least} seems] to understand the ones Anwar creates.

They could go online [to Sensei's Library

// http://senseis.xmp.net/

] but there's such pleasure in moving the stones around on their own [{free of a screen} their hands a constant dance {over the gold board ‹warmed further by the old incandescent bulb «in the antique desk lamp Anwar rarely uses»›}]. Father and daughter.

'It took me years,' Anwar says gently. 'And playing Mefisto I realize I need years more.'

Xanther had set her little cat down next to the board [where {even with its eyes sealed ‹chin lowering as if to snooze› it seems to be {solemnly?} regarding {guarding?} these forms {these eyes of stones ‹living «false ⟨dead⟩»›}}]. ∴ *Anwar!*∴ ∴ نعم ∴ ∴ *Yes indeed.*∴

'Daughter, I know you know how terrible your mother feels.' Xanther fidgets [and even in its sleep{?} the cat seems to fidget too {slight shifts at least ‹?›}]. 'Your sisters are being punished. This family, this household, will not suffer that kind of . . . injustice. I realize we've already gone over the incident numerous times, but I wonder if I might ask again about one part I don't understand?'

'Shoot.' But Xanther doesn't look up from the Go problems [this subject {likely} a worse problem].

'Xiomara wrote that your cat was on the mantel by the statue. Were you playing with him there?'

Xanther's mouth opens [and opens wide] only to shut. Wordless. Though the kitten [cat] awakens. At least moves [{‹eyes «allways» shut› stumbling ‹as if summoned «so much for feline grace»›} and with a squeak too {a ‹plaintive› mew} across the board {stones ‹and problems› disordered ‹unless disorder is another shape of grace «and purpose»?› also shoved aside}].

Anwar is touched by the way it responds to Xanther's frustrations [her ears reddening {acne fiery}]. As if sensing her need [her trembling fingers now drawing forth {with tiny strokes} the tiniest purr].

Anwar reaches out to Xanther.

'Daughter, help me. There is no reproval here. Your father is just trying to understand. Like you've been trying to understand these Go shapes.'

'But I'm the one who doesn't understand,' Xanther yelps suddenly. 'Why would Freya and Shasti do that to me? Why would Xiomara blame this little cat?'

'Well, she didn't blame him.'

'He was with me. We heard the crash together when he must have tumbled down the last few stairs.'

'Must have?'

'Well, like I blinked, or flinched, or like I don't know, I didn't see him fall. It was a pretty loud crash.'

Anwar hugs her. 'Thank you, daughter.'

She hugs back [even as the little cat is {‹somehow› like a dark secret held down in the dark} already between them].

'I don't understand any of it either. But that's okay.'

Xanther has tears on her face.

'Do you know what my father used to say to me?'

'Like when he was keeping you from killing yourself when you kept trying to climb the shelves?'

'ايه الذاكره الشريرة الا عندك دي :: *What a fiendish memory you have*:'' Anwar laughs. 'No, this was later. He'd advise me: "الي معروف ان العالم مش عاوز يتفهم. العالم مش حيكون العالم نفسه لو أتفهم" "It is understood that the world does not want to be understood. The world would not be this world if it did."'

'Does the world want?'

'Fiendishly smart too!' Anwar rubs the top of Xanther's head [pleased]. The cat [again {somehow}] back on her shoulder. 'Want indeed.'

[that night {with the children asleep ‹or the twins returning to their disturbed dreams «what they cannot ⟨will not⟩ admit»}] Anwar doesn't bring up again their lost fortune.

He approaches with all the openness he can muster. He tries to hear his father's words again in the words he shared with Xanther. He tries to remember that [given the choice now] he'd pick [every time!] his father's arms over a tiny wooden boat in a little glass bottle.

He takes out the [soft {silver-backed}] hairbrush from the dresser drawer [Astair's mother's hairbrush {and dresser in fact}] and softly slowly gently gently brushes Astair's long blond hair for a long long time.

Astair knows him too well.

'This must be some pretty bad news.'

The following day Anwar revisits the ledgers of savings and debt [the calendar marking when payments are due {Anthem ‹rent «Visa ❨ . . . ❩ American Express» utilities›} collection agencies in view]. We are Brazil. Or better: we are Puerto Rico [still the U.S. {life going on ‹even a party brightly ongoing in the distance «as one by one the shops close» lights go out›}].

Anwar updates his CV and sends it out [to friends {reliable colleagues ‹strangers› long shots}]. He checks job listings at big companies [like Blizzard Entertainment and EA Games {Redwood City ‹too far? «could they?»›}] as well as smaller ones [like Naughty Dog].

'Ehti, you were right to be cautious about Enzio, but for the wrong reasons,' Anwar says [when his friend picks up the phone].

'So long as it doesn't scare me, I'm all ears,' Ehtisham answers now [his voice {oddly} subdued]. 'I have a Kozimo story that I don't want to tell you. It's still scaring me.'

Ehtisham can get outright fretful [{fearful!} especially of anything connected to Mefisto {given the kind of organizations known to contract Mefisto's services ‹«forget Kozimo» 'Remember, Anwar, the military displays *its* games with consequences we still don't have the polygon-count to generate, let alone track'›}].

Anwar cuts to the quick: 'Enzio just went bankrupt and they still owe me nine thousand dollars.'

'Oh brother, I am so sorry. That sucks!'

What also 'sucks' is finding your family in the piano room shuddering over a laptop: a man in black stands behind a man in orange. The Arabic subtitles are clear enough for Anwar [versus the English that's too clear for his family]:

JOURNALIST JAMES FOLEY BEHEADED BY ISIS

'Astair!'

'Shit!' [Shocked to see the children peering over her shoulder {earbuds yanked out ‹laptop snapped shut›}.]

'What was that?' Shasti bleats [stepping away]. Freya bleating and stepping away [too].

Not Xanther: 'I'd like to find that guy in black.'

Has Anwar ever seen such fire before in those beautiful eyes? Though that isn't the disconcerting part [{after all} she is her mother's child {and Dov's ‹both possessing a world-burning spark›}]. Anwar swears the cat's eyes [for an instant {at the moment of Xanther's pronouncement}] shared with him the tiniest sliver [he must have imagined it {a projection of his own rage ‹against the world he left behind›}]: a different flame making out of the brightest fire

//

//

//

//

// . . blackness.

Anwar [quickly] gets everyone into their bathing suits and hustles them out back where he fills a cooler with ice and water from their hose. You couldn't ask for a better day: the heat is excruciating. Astair explains this is a way to raise awareness [and money] for ALS [and leaves it at that]. Xanther goes first [screaming with delight]. The twins go together [just screaming]. Then the children douse Astair [who challenges her mother]. Then the whole family douses Anwar. Anwar also screams. After he challenges Enzio.

Recovery takes place around an afternoon feast. Astair reopens her laptop and shows a funny story about a mother and daughter [living in Chula Vista] who called 9-1-1 because their cat [Cuppy!] was holding them hostage in their bedroom.

[that evening] Anwar resists the temptation to read more about Foley. ZSL appears on his feed. Astair catches the headline too [she's bringing him milk and {gluten-free} cookies {reward for his inspired idea to take up the Ice Bucket Challenge ‹Taymor responded at once «in a $1,200 bikini» with Ted too «pledging a few bikinis' worth of support»›}].

'ZSL was mentioned in a very strange Oceanica lecture I had on chemically manufactured affect.'

His first search turns up the Zoological Society of London.

[after midnight] Anwar checks his e-mails. Not that he expected an immediate response [from prospective employers] but his inbox remains depressingly empty. Even his spam folder is quiet. He misses Mefisto.

How wonderful to have spent such [quality!] time with his friend [even if the visit had ended with concerns]. Not the [{very} young] girlfriend [{actually} pretty heartening to find his {mad‹?›} friend consoled by such an affectionate touch]. It was the [fantasy] nomenclature that Anwar had found most worrisome [a Wizard and Merlin {Necromancer ‹Mefisto as Sorcerer «a villain too ‹Recluse› along with assorted others»› were any of them material?} real?].

Had Mefisto really called Xanther an *Aberration*?

[{furthermore} as their {long} night together had continued] Mefisto had become more and more inquisitive about whether or not something in the Ibrahim household had recently changed.

'Like finding the cat?'

And what was all that stuff about Clip #6?

[truth was {over the years}] Anwar had seen Mefisto less and less. Texts and e-mails were really pennies on the social dollar [Skypes a nickel more {maybe}]. Those modes of communication could conceal mental illness for a long time [especially if the subject in question were a genius {‹no question› Mefisto is a genius ‹though Mefisto wouldn't be the first genius to mask a degrading psychology under a calculated display of eccentricities «do lightsabers and pink sunglasses for the blind ‹that afro› count as eccentric?»›}].
[then again] Maybe he was just drunk [though the Scotch wasn't really touched]. Or high [could he and Marnie have shared something? {when he had walked

her back outside during her ‹impromptu«?»› visit ‹where had she gone afterwards «when had she returned ⟨Mefisto just disappearing like that›?» to where then?› to what plan?}].

And then [long after midnight] they had played Go [whereupon all such {accusations?} thoughts{!} had vanished]. Mefisto was just too quick and canny and resourceful [to suspect chemical impairment]. His power to improvise [with {well-studied} positions] more than merely ear-reddening.

[during that game] Anwar had tried to dig deeper into Mefisto's fears [maybe unsettle the big man {unsettle his allways unsettling mind?}? — fat chance! {though the terrors were real}]. Schemes [unlinked {to anything more than a pageant ‹of ridiculous names›}] gave up only more schemata [never concretized by reason {of objective} or {traceable} events {just a constant allusion to how 'power moves — extraordinary power'}].

[though Mefisto himself had never used the word] Surveillance seemed at the heart of his involvements [even in the way he had surveyed the board {‹at one point› remarking on a hanami ko and ‹at another point› marvelling over a developing ‹even complex› seki}].

Anwar might not win but he knew how to press [how to consider what was {already} said {and unsaid} and drive towards some discovery {Xanther didn't get it from nowhere}].

Mefisto's concession was one of admission [to tactic {if not with information}].

'If I told you any more, they'd kill you. They're already trying to kill me.'

'They?'

'He.'

'Alvin what's-his-name?'

'For your sake, for your daughter's sake, for all of our sakes, I can't risk saying anything more.'

'How about something positive then?'

Mefisto looked up [surprised{?} by so simple a request {what Anwar ‹routinely› asks of his family}].

‘لو مش قادر تقول حاجه كويسه. اي حاجه حتقولها بعد كده مش حتكون مهمه

"If you can't say what's good, whatever else you say is of no consequence." Something my mother taught me.'

'You're going to lose this game?' Mefisto smirks. 'You lost it thirty-six moves ago.'

'That's good?'

'Well, if I can't beat you here, none of us have a chance of winning that other game out there.'

'Did you just say you're our best chance of dealing with something you won't say anything about because it would then *not* give me a chance of dealing with it in the first place?'

'You know well enough that I can follow that. And no I'm not. *She* is.'

'My daughter?' How had Xanther [so suddenly] jumped into his mind [{of course} she's always on his mind {all three of them are ‹all four›}]?

'No. The Wizard.'

A great reason not to pursue the subject anymore.

[instead {before retiring}] Anwar had brought up M.E.T. [and some of the inconsistencies {error productions} he was facing {the S/Z problem ‹S arrives «with Z ❨ . . . ❩ nowhere in sight»›}].

Mefisto had demanded a glance.

'Mut(ate)ex(t)ed En(d)counter Threads,' Anwar [sheepishly] typed out.

'Aspirational.' Mefisto frowned [usually partial to grand{iose} acronyms].

[in fact] M.E.T. was pretty meagre [{especially for someone of Mefisto's calibre} but still unique enough to make their game a little more interesting ‹more profitable too «if only Kozimo had believed ⟨Anwar had forgotten to ask Ehti about the Kozimo story⟩ . . . »}]. Mefisto [though] reiterated [what he had always claimed {in e-mails}]: it was flexible enough to [dramatically] expand upon [console to MMOG {to something 'yet unanticipated . . . ' ‹whatever that meant›}].

'I wonder . . . ' [That's how Mefisto{'s marathon} had started.]

Mefisto sat at the terminal [while Anwar brewed coffee {tempted ‹only tempted›} as well as supplemented the {big} mug of caffeine with {bigger} bowls of ice cream {Vanilla Swiss Almond ‹Häagen-Dazs›} {tempted ‹seduced›}].

'The Coder of Cairo strikes again!' Mefisto might suddenly mumble [to flatter Anwar{?}]. Or: 'A superlative couplet' [as if he were leading a master class in poetry]. Or: 'Out of the clutch of such a fuss as this: this!' Interlocking fingers. Nodding. Devouring ice cream. While Anwar [standing behind this {‹this!' old friend} dear man] felt [{suddenly} strangely] as if his dear father too [Shenouda] were emerging [from the {‹stuttering the-the› demolition ‹Fatima!«!»› of the past}] now to rest his gentle hand upon Anwar's shoulder and let him know that she [his mother!{!}] was smiling again.

Anwar had rested his hand on Mefisto's shoulder

then [as if to share what fathers and mothers {every-where} do to invoke the same paws {pause!} of love].

[though if it's love that Anwar felt] What was it that Mefisto felt? What was he even doing?

// Adding lines?

// Yes.

// Compressing lines?

// Yes.

// Deleting too?

// Many.

// Comments in need of explanation.

// Comments without explanation.

'Call this my Word Ode. For you.'

Then Mefisto's afro would shake back and forth [like a disapproving shrub]: 'What messiness afoot with excessiveness to boot.' Or: 'Pons asinorum — London Bridge is falling down.' Though [even in these {disgruntled} instances] there remained in his tone [somehow{!}] something warm and reaffirming [as if Mefisto were taking responsibility for writing the klunky lines {and reproving himself}].

'A kluge that will not do! We shall do better!'

And Mefisto would do better.

If only Anwar were capable of such brevity. Such beauty. [asking the question aloud {when returning with more ice cream}:] Are they the same?

'Is beauty brevity?' Mefisto had repeated [dislocating himself {momentarily} from the focus that had just shrunk twenty lines to a septet]. 'If Keats is right, and maybe I don't think he is, then does it follow that truth is brevity? Side note here: Keats was in his twenties when he wrote "Ode on a Grecian Urn." No one in their twenties has any inkling about the truth. It makes one wonder: do scholars love Keats for Keats or for the Keats Keats would have turned out to be if he'd lived beyond the age of twenty-four?'

'Twenty-five. I wasn't asking about truth,' Anwar had [gently] pointed out.

'True. Well if we treat beauty as that which through whatever concordance of details organizes a congruent whole that is henceforth deemed alluring, attractive, desired, and let's say by "whole" we mean that which remains plausibly containable — ergo comprehensible, ergo ascertainable — and at the same time complex enough to elude attainment, thus remaining beyond grasp — ergo suggestive — then beauty must be by definition brief.'

'To limn the limbs of the tree without knowing every leaf.'

'Exactly.'

'You always use "ergo" and "henceforth" when you're drunk or exhausted. And you're not drunk. Let me make up the couch.'

Mefisto sighed [{another mouthful of ice cream ‹a «closed-eyed» 'Yup'›} if adding]: 'They often say in our culture that beautiful faces are the most symmetrical. More symmetry equals less information, less complexity, more easily understood. More quickly too.'

'Though a perfectly symmetrical face is considered ugly,' Anwar pointed out.

'Maybe because its perfection renders half of itself redundant. Beauty, ergo and henceforth—' [Mefisto yawns {he's beat}] '—must shed its living excess.'

'Definitely one of the stranger definitions for what I find compelling.'

'Compelling . . . ' Mefisto mused. 'Another lengthy complication.'

'Though why should beauty take any time at all when to most of us it presents itself as recognizable in a moment?'

'Beautifully put.' Said too like a hand from a place torn apart [with then an {unexpected ‹and abrupt›} addition]: 'Consider though, and this with a late-night supposition—' [raising a ridiculous finger too {accompanied by that radiant smile}] '—one that briefly accepts a preposterous allowance for God, if only for metaphoric amusement, just as said supposition will permit the equally ridiculous inclusion of Art, if only for its redacting silliness: if God were an Artist and therefore the Universe her Art, and since Art as we've just implied — or why not say established? — is its own summation, hence absolute brevity—'

'Hence absolute beauty?'

'Why not onwards to truth?'

'Hence its truths.'

'And back again to Keats! To the lad. If Fleming had known ye, would we?'

Raised bowls [no ice cream left {lifting air meant no less}].

'Such a storied Creator would then produce that which being so of its quiddity would be irreducible.' Mefisto smiles. 'No product. Just the algorithm itself.'

'Then the search for simpler algorithms to describe this place is a folly?'

'A human folly to understand what is ever beyond the capabilities of our raisin for a brain.' A tip of the afro [like a splendid treetop swaying in a summer storm].

'Here then is to living in the algorithm.'

'Or to just being the algorithm.'

'And therein, along with henceforth and ergo, lies the end too of any such Creator or Design.' [Does Anwar detect {in Mefisto} a sudden tremor of sadness {as they both follow this ‹‹very›› late-night› line of thinking to one plausible ‹logical› conclusion}?]

'The forces of this universe—' [Anwar nods] '—favor necessity over excess. Plans and planners must eventually pass away. Along with control.'

'Necessity too.'

Anwar had made up the downstairs sofa and told Mefisto to get some rest [M.E.T. wasn't finished in a night {forget seven days}]. Sleep accepted Anwar quickly enough [as soon as he settled beside {a very still} Astair] even if he was also too wired to accept sleep [or dreams {unless these were dreams ‹of the forces of the universe «necessities ⟨allways in control⟩ unequivocal» acting on his and his family's lives› like roaming monsters with dangerous motives} leaving behind a dead squirrel and the dead cat Sophy ∴ **TFv2 p. 531** ∵]. Forget letting go of Xanther asleep with her cat

the vet

said okay it was good

for cat and daughter and i.m.spartacus

as flak and hiding meat from a polar bear in

snow that smells like meat and

the privilege

of knowing the difference

when surveying

the scene hadn't Mefisto also said

agrorhythms instead of

and why hadn't Anwar

gotten more into Enzio

and Cataplysts-

and doesn't surveillance imply intel and drones

does

Anwar despise anything more? and wasn't Mefisto saying

something else too

in fond

triplicate assuming Anwar could keep up with what he hadn't kept up with

already lost . . .

On Thursday ∵ August 21∵ Myla ∵ *Mint*∵ calls.

'Slow Dog,' his dear friend [and {famed} choreographer] rasps. 'Fall draws near. The Met calls.'

'I can barely hear you.' Anwar presses his ear to the speaker [plugs his other ear]. 'I'm at a baseball game.'

'Usually with you it's work or your children.'

'I'm with Xanther. She doesn't understand anything either. But it's a clear night. Nice crowd. The grass is incredibly green. I think we're having fun.'

Xanther nods [enthusiastically {wearing Mefisto's sunglasses and an L.A. Dodgers hat ‹the Padres lead 1–0 «bottom of the 7th ⟨still a good time for dads⟩»›}].

'*Hades* opens soon. I'm confirming you'll be there.'

'I'll be there. With Xanther.' Anwar mouths 'New York' [what a smile! {and Xanther had just gone through her moan I-don't-want-to-go ‹really I-don't-want-to-leave-my-cat› routine over just this short drive ‹and time› here} or is he picking up {too} a {likely} hesitation? {‹not that it matters› even adding more ‹«too much» for Myla's sake «but not his own?»›}]. 'I promise.'

'All I wanted to hear. Call me when you can hear.'

Anwar at once ashamed [for all he can promise {but can't afford}].

[still] He tries hard to smile [and root {hard! ‹for whom «padres or dodging»?›}]. He scratches his back too. Dumb move. He can feel the bumps [welts {scabs already? ‹hurting «yes!» already›}]. Though he still hasn't used a mirror to confirm shingles. Will he need to go to a doctor [for cortisone creams {Zovirax}]?

At least Xanther seems oblivious. His dear Aberration! Mefisto and his weird way with words! Mefisto the Sorcerer! [Chuckle.] Plus someone called The Wizard! [Chuckle again.] Recluse! The villain! [Anwar must suppress an outright laugh!] With some regular name too! What was it? Alvin? ∴ Alvin Alex Anderson. ∴

[top of the eighth] The Dodgers hold the Padres to zero for the inning. Anwar shifts uneasily in his seat [his back hurting more {‹worse› the backs of his thighs have started to scald and itch too ‹Anwar can imagine the swelling «the rippling red dots» rising to answer an onslaught of stresses «money too» so ho-hum too «compared to this beautiful ‹incalculable› time with his daughter»}].

'Daddy! Have you been drinking coffee? You smell like coffee!' Xanther suddenly announces [sniffing him too {like some concerned willful little animal}].

'I do?'

'It's, uhm, well okay, not that strong.'

'Don't tempt me, daughter.' [Anwar tries to keep his smile and eyes light {even if he knows that Xanther's seizures can be preceded by hallucinations ‹anything from visual to auditory «to aromatic»}.]

Xanther's beaming perplexity shifts a tiny bit.

...

'Is everything okay?' Her question surprises Anwar [but it shouldn't {she's always been so sensitive}].

'Sometimes the adult world can be rife — Do you know that word? How about making that our word of the day? It means common, often occurring with frequency, and usually unpleasant. Used with "with."'

'Like "rife with"?' Xanther asks. 'So what's the adult world rife with?'

'Uncertainties.'

Xanther rolls her eyes. 'Like my kid world isn't?'

Anwar kisses her forehead. 'Help your father believe it's less uncertain.'

'So what are you uncertain about?'

'This baseball game?' Anwar grins [dodging the question {and smiling still more ‹at the sight of Xanther catching the dodge «the glee in her eyes ⟨perhaps⟩ reflecting his own»›}].

'Isn't uncertainty, though, like, what makes a game fun in the first place?'

How can he not kiss her again?

His mother used to say something [which Anwar used to see in the discrediting light of his own apostasy {but now finds anew in the more forgiving light of fatherhood and aging}]. What he can't help but say aloud now: 'سامحني لو في لحظة افتكرت ان الإيمان معناه اليقين.'

'What's that?'

'Something your grandmother used to say.'

'Translation please.'

[far below] A Dodger [number 10? ∴ Yes.∴ ∴ *Justin Turner.*∴] swings his bat. [even up here] The sound of that wallop reaches them. Anwar and Xanther rise together [with the whole stadium it seems {their section at least ‹everyone cheering›} Xanther and Anwar sure cheering]. It feels good. The ball flies deep into left field [and {with the peculiar magic of a home run} seems to keep going {daring the night sky}].

Xanther jumps up and down [[{excitedly} waving around her Dodgers hat {up on her seat}]. Until she jumps into Anwar's arms. With such a big excited hug.

And Anwar [lifting Xanther up {holding her tight}] is suddenly missing his mother. [out of nowhere {terribly}] She comes upon him. With all she ever was. Her smile. Her kindness. Her goodness. How Anwar would have loved to have seen Fatima here now with Xanther. Would they have hugged too? What would they have said to each other later? How would they have teased and laughed and sparred and together wondered?

Do we miss not only the past but every future the lost past describes? Is that just the nature of missing? All the lost might-have-beens? The certainty that those uncertain futures are gone?

If we can't embrace uncertainty do we miss the point of love?

Something strange then happens the next morning ∴ Friday, August 22 ∵.

[after the game {with the buoyancy of Xanther's joy freeing him from thoughts of debt ‹that even darker «fast-approaching» financial ledge›}] Anwar decides to take a break from stress. No thoughts about money. Or about shingles [and it is shingles]. He'll keep away from beheadings [though there's something in the news about a white lioness mauling a zookeeper ∴ *zoo vet* ∵ in San Diego {he'll keep away from that too}]. And whatever is in his inbox is in his inbox [{how Zen} zero prospective employers responding to his first salvo {that seems Zenish too}].

And then while cleaning up his e-mails [{emptying the trash} {organizing folders}] Anwar discovers something in his spam folder. Nearly deleted. Except for the re: Mefisto in the subject line.

Following the recommendation by Mefisto Dazine, and after reviewing your qualifications, we at Galvadyne, Inc. would like to schedule an interview in the interest of discussing possible employment.

Finally something promising[!] to share with Astair! Anwar almost calls but decides to wait until she gets back home. [in the meantime] He turns to M.E.T. For fun.

Which is when he discovers just how much has changed [how much Mefisto has changed {how much Mefisto has added ‹comments included›}].

// meet M.E.T.E.

// Meta-Encounters Towards Enlightenment.

// why not?

// remember:

// things must accelerate and attenuate.

Which hardly applies to the new code.

Over a million lines. Easily.

Esse Quam Videri

Assume your adversary is capable of one trillion guesses per second.

— Edward Snowden

"Isn't this much better?" His smile flickers the screen.

"Hello, Recluse."

"Alvin! Come on, Cas. Enough
of avatars. Remember when
those were the keystone
to the future of iden-
tity? A new branch
for psychology? And
now we just think
of them as user-
names we thought
up when we were
very young."

"What do you
want that you
haven't already
taken?"

"Cas, I don't eat babies,"
Recluse responds, pulling
back, arms crossed. Only
his smile fails to change. Plus
the persistent flicker infecting the
screen. "I just put my kids to bed."

Europe would put him six hours ahead. Moscow, even later. Bobby sits just a few feet away, at a second set of terminals, trying to figure out just that, sifting through meta- and overt data for a clue to where Recluse is transmitting from. He's also doing his best to keep Recluse from discovering their IP address. Just the thought of how many system analysts with warrants are right now working at this monster's behest to track this video chat sends a streak of pain through Cas' joints.

"Yoo-hoo. Where'd you go, Cas? Have you gotten even more spacey these days?"

"I consider spacey a virtue."

"You're all about virtue. How's your daughter?"

"I knew we'd get to threats."

"Just asking." Recluse holds up his hands. "It's called being civilized. No society rises without some regard for family. Besides, I know she doesn't know anything. We check in on her. Try to give her a helping hand when she needs one. She's going through a good period."

"You can't hurt me more than you already have."

"I don't want to hurt you, Cas. I don't want to hurt anyone. If anything, I'm the one who is showing up, talking to you, and candidly too, in an effort to keep a lot of people from hurting, which is where you and your little revolution are heading."

Cas scoffs.

"There's the Cas I know."

"I realize the mistake I made," she
says. "You don't and that's why
you're worse off."

Recluse shakes his head.
Runs a hand through
his white hair. Only
his teeth are whiter.
Cas almost welcomes
the persistent flicker
still pixelating this
ghost in gold-framed
glasses, a gold signet
ring, grinning against
a black backdrop so
viscous it seems set on
drowning him. If only.

"I concede, Cas. To all your
suspicions, all your fears, all
your accusations. I will not deny
some love me. I will not deny some
hate me. My wife doesn't hate me. But
haters will say she's too young to know better

and that I'm too old to have such young children so late. But I love her and I love them and I love the world they will come to inherit without me. Those who don't hate me will say that you, Cas, are the one who poses a danger to the future of every child and every family. So who's wrong: the haters or the lovers? Here's a newsflash: it doesn't matter. Plain and simple: you are in material possession of a weapon that no individual has a right to wield. It represents an imbalance of power grossly disproportional to the way the world must create consensus. Love you or hate you, you simply don't have the right to decide."

"How cute. The villain is calling *me* the bad guy?"

"Ha! Come on, Cas. Villain? Bad guy? When you and Bobby play this back, do me a favor and just listen to yourself. By the way: hi, Bobby."

Cas doesn't need to look to know that Bobby just rolled his eyes.

"Is this where you respond with the I'm-Just-a-Businessman routine?"

"But I am! I employ thousands. I am legally contracted by some of the world's most powerful agencies to keep safe myriad of communities everywhere. Furthermore, my companies are subject to oversight by committees and subcommittees and sub-subcommittees. You and Bobby have no oversight. Bobby, I know you're right there. Let me see those eye rolls for myself."

Recluse can be as cheery as he wants.

"We have dedicated our lives to oversight," Cas whispers back.

"Yes, you have." Recluse's admission is worse than his cheer. "You, Bobby, and that loose collection of citizens committed to your cause continue to demonstrate a courage I know I'm incapable of."

"Aside from using this little tête-à-tête to try to find us, and you won't find us, mind telling me your objective? I sense nothing but malice."

"We should have started this while I was changing diapers." Recluse sighs. "That would have put my malice on full display. I just want to talk. I want to reconnect as the friends we once were. And if that's not possible then at least head us toward a negotiation and compromise wherein no one else gets hurt."

"How does that look from your end?"

"Let's start with you and me getting together. Bobby too, if he wants to join. Why not even reach out to ██████? Like old times for new times. Face-to-face. Sit around a table for an hour, a lot of hours, take the whole day, a week, figure out a way to work together. Just us."

"I'm listening."

"Good. For starters, I'll call off the dogs. I know you won't believe this, but I'm not even trying to trace you now."

"My friends?"

"Three are already rejoining their families."

"Three?"

"I'm a businessman, Cas. I'm not going to give you everything. Besides, you wouldn't trust me if I did."

"And my dead friends?"

"You know as well as I what the navel-gazing rest have no clue about: this is a war and with war there are casualties. You and I, though, have the power to decide if we head toward Gettysburg or Appomattox."

"Appomattox was about surrender."

"I am surrendering, Cas. To you."

Cas finds a hair tickling her cheek, and keeps twisting it to mislead the white-haired man in her monitor studying her in his.

"Yoo-hoo again."

Will asking serve a purpose?
Will it harm?

"What's changed?" she risks.

The question seems to catch
Recluse off guard. He knows
that she knows that he knows
their distribution failed, that
many friends and cohorts were
killed, many more imprisoned,
and that she and Bobby are on
the run and will likely make a mistake soon enough and be arraigned
or murdered.

"*You* changed," he finally answers, reaching out of frame to retrieve his Orb. "You're no longer an Aberration."

An Aberration is the reason for Clip #1. It's the reason for many of the other Clips too. Especially #6. A Clip is defined by ratification: ≥ 99.99%. An Aberration, however, is defined by the method of discovery. It depends upon a certain amount of instinct to navigate an impossible sluice of data, unquantifiable decision trees, until methodology must give way to years of practice and finally what Bobby defends as Artistry. In other words, Recluse's declaration now is nonsense. Clip #3, discovered by Cas in 1988, was ratified by Cas herself, and Bobby and Mefisto too, both of whom had marveled at the

strange slants of unveil-
the opaline slashes,
nacreous frac-
eventually give
thing other
more strange
spaces — per-
r e w a r d e d
— like com-
a clearing in
where the for-
already a mira-
ing out of a loam
binary, revealing Cas
a four-year window upon
of Mefisto's first effort to re-engi-

ing, Cas following
believing such
tures would
way to some-
than just
and failing
s i s t e n c e
this time
ing upon
a wood,
est itself is
cle, as if ris-
baser than any
herself at a screen,
her critical evaluation
neer the syntax and vocabu-

lary their years of subsequent innovation and progress would come to depend upon but which back then deserved Cas' head shake and smug scoff. The only reason 1984 didn't at once earn their 1988 collective laugh was due to the peculiar opaline halo defining her silhouette, matching the very glow Cas had spent weeks chasing.

Since detonating her Orb in Dayton, Cas hasn't scried once, forget revisiting Clip #6, let alone any of the older Clips. Bobby was in agreement that powering up Mefisto's Orb — the most generous gift Cas has ever known — could endanger anyone close by, despite Mefisto's assurances to the contrary. What if she and Bobby became the cause of some unspeakable violence to Sew and his family in Knoxville?

At least Asheville was different. Even Bobby admitted that it exceeded expectations. Eisa Travis had been the first to greet them at the door. Like her home, her hair and skin glowed gold as pine sap. Children scrambled around their legs like Cas and Bobby were long-lost family. Eisa's partner, Liesl Ward, got them settled in an upstairs bedroom. The sweet muskiness of cannabis lingered in the folds of the room, a routine of smoke perhaps still holding the mind of the house. By the time Cas and Bobby descended again, the welcoming committee had exceeded the capacity of the downstairs, and even included members of nearby police departments as well as military.

"You are not alone." Eisa had smiled.

Here surrounding them were similar pragmatists: people who had pledged their lives in the name of not ending up on the wrong side of history. Even if it was impossible to know how any would really measure up when faced with the actual costs of such a pledge, it was a comfort to be among so many who believed deeply that history had a judgment and it was the only thing worth heeding. Bobby at once found comfort in encountering those who could speak knowledgeably about his weaponry held at the Arsenal as well as the explosive con-

sequences fortified within
discussion carried out
ing the proximity of
the Orb itself, just
wrapped in Cas'
sweater, deep
relying on the
strangers over
tual contriv-
stowage in a
under a pil-
broad daylight
top. Most of all
and Bobby found
many servers run-
garage, now an artist's
expert technical crew, some hav-

Mefisto's Orb — that
without mention-
such a monster,
one flight up,
old cashmere
in her bag,
courtesy of
the ineffec-
ances of
toilet tank,
low, or the
of a dresser
though, Cas
comfort in the
ning in a once-
loft, managed by an
ing worked as independent

contractors at one or two NSA sites. All too happy to help chain together anonymous proxies behind Dublin and Hämeenlinna curtains with an encrypted Superman tour along the Great Wall and Silicon Veil.

No one they encountered during their days there knew as much as they did but they came close: high aptitude with satellite surveillance and search techniques, drone hacks, especially those built in Dayton, plus the latest anonymity protocols, or "anonymisty," as one kid joked, "because it's all too hazy to ever be that sure," though as he went on to explain, they already did have in place hacks to red-herring inevitable traces. It was a relief that everyone knew who Recluse was and what was at stake for just orchestrating this parley.

Cas had allowed
borhood stroll.
hadn't liked
more upset.
could deny
Cas had
Liesl's old
as blue
how man-
parked a
no mat-
wandered.
at Malaprop's
wood Street. Ashe-
took a coffee to a table

herself one long neigh-
Alone. Bobby
it. Eisa was even
But no one
her. Though as
suspected,
truck, gray
chalk, some-
aged to remain
block away
ter where she
Cas wound up
Bookstore ∴ **55 Hay-**
ville, NC 28801∴. She
and read a short story by

James Tiptree, Jr. ∴ "The Screwfly Solution."∴ It left her sad. The next one she read ∴ "████████████"∴ made her more optimistic, or "opti-mystic" as she might still tell the young "anonymisty" kid. ∴ *Ah dear Alice, don't forget . . .* ∴

The impending talk with Recluse had made Cas more nervous than anything before. Marfa, the escape in Dayton, and the endurance test in Athens had cantilevered Cas over a chasm of catalepsy with constant doses of adrenaline. Adrenaline wouldn't matter here. She was already exhausted by what she knew wouldn't be settled. She had to forget speedy feelings of confidence and embrace her longtime mantra:

The Strong Magic of Slow Passages.

More slow work was under way having
to do with Mefis- to's request.
No scrying nec- essary. At
Eisa's place, a team of able
sleuths were already
scouring the Webs for
anything hav- ing to do
with Galva- dyne, Inc.
As expected, it wasn't
the paucity of data but the
excess that made so many
hours seem so insufficient.

What would she and Alv end up saying to each
other? "Eyes have always sought out agency. To see is to act.
What we want to see is a better way to act." He had actually said that to her once, in fact the last time they had met in person, after he had just acted in the worst possible way. "You've changed," had been Cas' stupid response. Even though he hadn't. He had always possessed an ambition that gave no thought to the unempowered. Of course, back

then he had been unempowered too, and so the triumphs of his aggressions had not yet started. It was even easy to fool oneself into thinking that his persistent smile meant sweetness.

Last night, upon hearing the final confirmation for today's encounter, Cas had considered scrying for something on Xanther. Mefisto had likely reached Los Angeles but had yet to send word about what he had discovered there. Cas wondered if the little girl had made him feel good. Even with those

whipping off her
rotating   into
what seemed
ing   force
only   the
Orb itself,
to   come,
of   the
c h a r m
to   calm
more to this
they had yet
than all the dead
less they continued
was   perhaps   beyond

savage black storms now
perimeters in Clip #6,
still meaner things,
with their escalat-
to threaten not
Clip and the
but all scrying
the   sight
young   girl's
still   seemed
Cas. There was
little one than
discovered, more
and all the merci-
to face, something that

an involvement with which, if anything, renders itself and everyone else irrelevant through the absolute connectivity to anything or anyone. Unless one counts friendship. Cas knew the friendship between Mefisto and Xanther's father, Anwar, was a deep one. Cas was counting on the meaning of friendship. It was the one thing she knew for certain Recluse could not understand.

"Aberrations have nothing to do with change," Cas says now. "They are defined by how they are found. And unless you've altered the past, Alv, I remain the changing person I am not at all afraid to claim."

"'Alv!' We're making progress!" And despite his petrified grin, Recluse does seem pleased. "Your elasticity has an upside."

"And the downside?"

"Very well. Let's get to that. Let's get into the hard stuff so we can move forward toward the positive stuff that will make a difference in our children's lives." Recluse begins to loosen his silver tie.

Cas suddenly shivers, even if she doesn't know how to make sense yet out of what only presents itself as a vague feeling of disquiet, associated with an equally certain sense of something compiling, translating, cross-checking, and only just starting to aggregate the tiny bits that will give her next words direction.

Bobby catches her eye. He's holding up a piece of paper:

CONFIRMED: PYTHIA, ENDORIA, AND LILITH RELEASED!

The anonymisty kid reconfirms the same news on a tablet:

LILITH, PYTHIA, AND ENDORIA IN CONTACT. AWAY!

"Yoo-hoo," Recluse chimes. Almost gently. "What do you say, Cas? You and me? Wherever you like. With whomever you like. We'll sit down. We'll work it through."

"Okay."

Only Bobby's face registers no alarm.

"One request."

"Not even a condition?" Recluse tugs off the tie and undoes his shirt's top button. "I'm impressed. Name it."

"We drop this."

"Drop what?" The tie disappears beneath the frame.

"The very nature of this conversation puts on display how you and I differ." Disquiet is gone. Instinct has taken control, even if Cas can't see yet the aim. "I believe in the cause of transparency and equal empowerment. You believe in the necessity to dissemble in order to preserve the power structure beneficial to you. And so when you use the truth, you use it to lie."

"You're a dangerous woman, Cas."

"Extremely dangerous. Because unlike what you think, I'm mindful. I have not forgotten you, Alvin. Down to the strangest details. Your tidiness. Your preoccupation with suits. Your obsession with bleach."

"Guilty as charged." Recluse laughs. "Don't tell me you're without your oddities?"

"I welcome them."

"Cas, I not only know how well you know me, but I count on it. How else could I expect to get through to you?"

Recluse lifts into frame his own Orb.

If Cas had shivered before, now she shudders.

"You don't think you and yours are the only ones with these?" he continues. "You do realize I have to have more? Many more? Responsible now for far more than five fabled Clips? All of us scrying for our own Aberrations? All of us scrying for you?"

"Now doesn't that feel better?" Cas musters.

"You know me, Cas."

"How good it must feel to admit that you know that I know that there will never be some coffee-shop get-together to work out our disagreements. We don't need to suspect traps when we can both see that what we're talking about is a battleground."

"There was a reason we got along so well in the beginning. We're a lot alike."

Cas smiles warmly. "But I've changed. Why don't you try? Right now. Come out of the shadows."

She's joking, of course, even if she still entertains for a moment that given the right tone, the right note of urgency and compassion, some tiny difference might be achieved. Even everyone in the garage responds with a collective stillness, Cas feels it, feels them, believing her.

"Why not!" Recluse suddenly rejoices, leaning forward a little, as behind him the shadows seem to lessen. The screen flicker has definitely lessened. "I lied," Recluse continues, as the shadows vanish. "I didn't just put my kids to bed. It's nowhere close to night where I am now. More like morning."

As if curtains were drawn aside, light now brightens enough to bring into focus . . . bookshelves ∷ *Patrick Lucanio's* Them or Us, *J. O. Bailey's* Pilgrims Through Space and Time, *Frank Herbert's* Dune, *Robert A. Heinlein's* Stranger in a Strange Land, *Gene Wolfe's* The Fifth Head of Cerberus, *William Gibson's* Count Zero, *L. Ron Hubbard's* Battlefield Earth, *Theodore Roszak's* The Making of a Counter Culture, *R. Buckminster Fuller's* Utopia or Oblivion, *Carlos Castaneda's* The Teachings of Don Juan, *Stanislaw Lem's* The Investigation, *Dashiell Hammett's* Red Harvest, *C. G. Jung's* Psyche & Symbol, The Edogawa Rampo Reader, *Arthur C. Clarke's* Childhood's End, *Ursula K. Le Guin's* Always Coming Home, *Eugene Zamiatin's* We ∷. Cas knows them all by heart, plus the stacks of manga beside towers of VHS tapes. In fact there are curtains, just off to the side, brassy ones she stitched herself.

"What is this?" Recluse asks, holding up a kitschy little statue of Pee Wee Reese pushing Roy Campanella in a wheelchair ∷ Roy Campanella Night. May 7, 1959 ∷.

He's tossed it away by the time he reaches the little kitchen. The camera follows him with unctuous devotion.

"There's Frosted Flakes on top of the fridge, Alv." Cas determines to answer her spiking despair with her own reserve of silky strength. "Or by the Ramen and Springfield tomato sauce, some Knob Creek. Make yourself at home."

"Do you really think I could ever make myself at home in a place like Borrego Springs?" Recluse sneers. At least the sight of his disgust relaxes Cas some.

"Check out Font's Point. The sight will suit you."

"What do you do about the heat?" He's back to cheery and casual.

"If you got what it takes, you get used to it."

"My, my, Cas. How I've missed you."

"Lament feelings that aren't mutual."

"Maybe we should gather here," he muses. "Let this be our Gettysburg. Give you and Bobby the home-field advantage."

"Why not Gettysburg proper? Let the outcome prove the side."

"Done!" Recluse shouts. He has moved to Bobby's desk. The letters there are nothing to worry about but the sight of this old man casu- ally sweeping the papers to the floor catches her breath, the bile in her throat giving the moment its taste:

no home of their own will ever be theirs again.

"I can't wait," Cas still manages to cough out.

"Of course, after this long chat, I might already be closing in on you. Bobby's about as competent rendering a transmission like this untraceable as he is holding on to that electron microscope. Bobby, if you want it back, check eBay! At least the parts are for sale. Trespassing on one of my properties, that was pretty shrewd. I'll give Bobby that. Or was Dayton your idea? Anyway, I'm at your door. Open up!"

BANG! BANG! BANG!

But Recluse has only rapped his fist hard on Bobby's desk.

Still, everyone in that little garage looks for an exit. Only Cas doesn't flinch.

"A very dangerous old lady." Recluse chuckles.

"See you soon."

"Count on it. Esse quam videri."

The signal dies.

Panic takes charge.

Plugs are pulled.

Lights go out. Servers go down.

"What happened?"

"He spooked us," Bobby growls a moment later, though he doesn't seem concerned.

"With that knocking-on-a-table shenanigans?"

"With Latin."

"'To be, rather than to seem,'" Eisa explains. "It's the North Carolina state motto here."

For the next two days, Bobby is a champ, huddling down with everyone, telling an endless stream of terrible jokes, until it's clear that their exact location remains unknown. Though as an officer of the law on their side confirms: the county is now looking for Catherine and Bobby Stern, an elderly couple, wanted for questioning in regards to a missing electron microscope stolen from a lab in New Mexico. A pretty good picture has also been supplied. Bobby approves.

"How do you stay so upbeat?" Cas suddenly seethes. She's getting sick of huddling down. "Don't you care about our home?"

"Baby, we were made for wheels. What that creep will never get."

Cas knows her husband too well: "What else are you hiding, old man?"

"You did damn good."

"Gettysburg is damn good?"

Bobby shrugs. "We'll never meet him there. He knows that. But it's what he doesn't know yet that matters most to us."

How could Cas have missed it. Laughs too: "'Five fabled clips!'"

"That's right. He hasn't sniffed out yet your Clip #6."

Pomona

It's like that.

— Ozomatli

A summer cold claws up Luther. Throat scalding, nose unpacking what never stops repacking the cavities under his eyes. Luther at this stoplight knuckles his cheeks like he can punch that shit loose. Headache's worse.

Pills Tweetie hands him better call truce if Luther's gonna make it through noon without assailing ∴ ? ∴ some fool. Heat wave on the land scorches up everyone's good time.

Luther snorts, hawks, spits. Even en la madrugada that shit goes to steam on the air. Sun not even showing and Luther craves ice. Gulps boiling coffee instead. McDonald's large. Nudges the stereo louder. Old school for the ride. Run-D.M.C. Wu-Tang. Mellow Man Ace.

Tweetie rocks the hip-hop back and forth. Tests these shocks. Luther sways too. Adjusts his lentes negros. Sweat starting to ring the frames. This line they waiting in making things worse. Fairplex gates are right ahead but feel days away. No help that no air moves now through the open windows. But Tweetie still smiles. Luther too. It'll take more than throat blisters or a hot day to take away this good mood.

Yesterday him and Tweetie drove the burgundy Durango out to Victorville to meet Zavaleta. All day long that dog washed, waxed, and polished Luther's two cars. Victor got with them by night, all whistles and grins, and with little of the moon hanging out in the sky, said here's where moonlight moved in.

But come morning Victor's pale as the moon when Luther hands him the keys to the Fury.

"Follow me. Follow me slow."

Victor followed so slow, Luther lost him in the rearview. But the Roadmaster was running too smooth and surly to keep it locked down. Tangerine topaz just glowing the road, turning heads, winning honks, dawn coming early.

Luther needed a break. Tweetie had told him. They all told him. Even Juarez had said they should get out, go fishing, get something else on a hook before Luther hurt something. Like la dirty garra was suddenly Dr. Phil.

Over a month now and Domingo Persianos was still a ghost. Luther went from looking a few hours here and there to killing the clock, every minute, every week, never letting up. Telling his crew, whatever shorties they run, find Domingo.

Juarez shrugged it off because Nacho's putas wouldn't last away. They'd be back any day. But those girls stayed fantasmas too.

What made it pura mierda is how enough people kept claiming to have spotted that ojete. It wasn't like word was he took off for central Florida, or Atlanta, or even Bakersfield. That Luther would have understood.

Todo hijo de vecino just kept saying Domingo was around, here enough, close enough, like they all living in the same city that's still a thousand and one cities that can never share.

Luther would get close, sometimes by hours, once by minutes, but Domingo, Freckles, and the rest were still gone, no forwarding address.

And the longer Luther took, the less he heard from Teyo. Soon not even from Eswin. Deposits still kept rolling into his account. If the ATM receipt was real Luther was already set for life. Couldn't even show Tweetie that balance. Collections regular. Pale blues still out on parade. But Luther knew how quick all of regular can go zeros if Luther didn't make good on la propuesta.

And Luther wasn't making good.

Rust stirred his mouth. Got him hunting longer and louder. Until nightmares that Luther would chase that perra to Kentucky or Alaska murdered sleep.

And then Dr. Juarez Phil started moaning about fishing and Luther took off his thick-buttoned shirts, put on his wifebeater, and got shit together for a day at the Swap Meet & Classic Car Show.

The only thing better than dogs are cars. Luther can't say why. Something the good ones have, this dance between focus and distraction, with power, the curves of what he wants, the details of what it takes, the drive to want it and take it and keep going.

Luther's got some history with cars. Jacked em, raced em, wrecked some. Shook his first tiras, barely thirteen, doing 90 MPH in a 35 MPH zone, homies in the back screaming, some crying, Tweetie was there, whistling, while Luther was singing to the sirens. Lost his cherry too. Same year. Older woman. White. On the rag. She broke them into some cherry Corvette parked for dinner at some fancy dinner place. Showed Luther her hairy spot. They covered the seats in blood.

Classics just make Luther grin. Drivers almost never matter. Here is all the past that matters, here is what survived, cleaned up and waxed, rolling for the future for a blast, though if you're behind the wheel you've already arrived. Luther's raced for them, fought over them, fucked in them, even lived in one for a year.

Tweetie points out their number. Luther pulls in the Roadmaster nice and easy. Tweetie unloads the trunk, and sets out the table and folding chairs. Pops two beers hidden in a false bottom in one of the ice chests. Breakfast of champs.

Víctor still hasn't reached the Fairplex. Some shit about stopping to get more gas.

"Esse just doesn't want you watching him park." Tweetie laughs.

Luther laughs too. "Víctor's no fool."

But it's not just Víctor they go to check for, but on all the early arrivals, newer cars parking in columns close to the front, older cars parking by the stadium, morning continuing its warm-up with growls and roars, blaring radios, maybe a backfire, but never a horn, deserving gritos or cheers, welcoming home these animals of grille and chrome, beasts of all kinds, fucking monsters, carriers of danger, finding their place on a rare day when everyone turns off, slumps down, and slurps on the gaze of strangers.

All types. From local workers to students, motorheads from Palmdale to paint enthusiasts from way up past Ventura. Some down from Santa Barbara and San Francisco. Parts of Nevada. Maybe Washington.

The whole place is a mix: Asians, blacks, whites. People with words in their mouths Luther got no clue about. Then add in Pomona police, some on foot, more in cars, yawning, mad-doggin, they try!, mostly slobbering over teenage girls in shortshorts. Uniform or no uniform, those chotas can only slobber. Watch as everyone but them gets them some. And a day like today, there sure as fuck is some.

Nothing gets pussy wetter than thuds. Like outta some JBL 1000-watt gear, dropping bass-thudding bombs from a bomba chopped snake-in-the-grass low, with fanged hood, sandblasted partition glass, backseat bar, full service, set for ice, scales and action, nothing missing, down to its white-leather, pin-cushioned trunk and these silver pre-amps, blinding back the sun.

Every meet, police dream of some mess. Want nothing more than to get tested out here with two clicas going stupid over fumes and rims. But Luther just laughs cuz if there's something worth stupid most homeboys here stay smart so they can get serious later.

Years back, cops' dream came true. Armenians got hot and monkey. That shit had shit to do with cars. One dumbass fired shots in the air, second dumbass did the same thing. Who cares? Seriously! Jokes! Pomona badges cracked down on that bullshit. Been craving on it ever since.

And of course shit can always get stupid. Car clubs here are full of reasons to go surly given strong drinks, hard dicks, and some fires starting, if heat gets thick.

A few of these clubs can bring serious work with their hoods. But most don't. Just kickin back by the grandstands. Listening to music that counts. Maybe their own band. Carne asada all day. Grilling onions and peppers. Tamales bubbling in foil. Hot sauce bubbling your mouth. Buying beers, smuggling in tequilas and clears. Security never checks the gas cans. And no matter what else they check, fileros and cuetes can still show. If it comes to that.

Maybe the maybe's the fun. But hey no hay bronca! Placa differences aren't just about paint but pinstripes. Heat's in the torque, RPM, and horses. Territory: year and make. Product: stereo, shocks, even upholstery.

Wherever you from to whatever you gonna prove takes backseat to why you do what you do in the first place. Front seat. Ranfla Romeos to Wheel Maestros. Hard Rods to Hot Dropped Cherry Poppers. Just what it takes to make these mothers and daughters squeal, drip, and moan. Give their amapolas another thing to trip out on.

On the way back to the Roadmaster, Luther and Tweetie pass a group on the other side of the divide between Early Era and Recent. Fucking Armos already under an EZ-UP tent between Scions, Kias, and a 1970s Chrysler Luther wouldn't lift for parts.

One hair mat has the fuckin pulp for a brain-stem to lock eyes. Not even 8 AM and this fool perched on his Daewoo bumper thinks he can just flex a glare.

But Luther sheds whatever jab's in his step when the kid jerks back. Like he'd already been hit. Luther even smiles.

One second, he's primed to wade into that group, chop at this fuck's throat, keep bashing his head against a fender, until Luther can dig nails deep, kid already blind from blood filling his eyes, as Luther rips off that fuckin uniceja like tape, then wears it like a stache.

And the next second, Luther goes all soft. Wants to give the kid a pat on the back. Not even eigh-teen. Got balls. Probably still hasn't got fucked. Luther wants to give him a beer. Give him shit for his wheels. Offer to buy that bucket of junk.

Instead something else eighteen gets in the way. Verga plumping like it already knew.

"All the girls are horny here," Tweetie twinkles. "They just don't know it."

So Cute. So Naughty. So Uni

Young and softer than dough. But with tits. Big tits. What've never had a man's grip. Pinch the nipples until she cries, hardness driving through her, again and again until the dazed shock blanks her eyes, and she just lies there and takes it, again and again, until he's done.

She should jump like a rabbit now. Scatter like a doe. But she keeps swiveling her hips, sucking her hair, refusing to go.

Her two friends have already twisted away. One bitch with IRON MAIDEN slapped across her flat chest, the other a mess of ass jiggling for safety behind a Lemon Aid Stand — "We Fix Anything!"

This one stays. Luther already knows her. She wants so bad what she can't ask for when all she's doing is asking for it. Drawn to rough. Gets off on her mommy's plug-in candy cane dreaming of danger. Dreams come true.

"Come here," Luther grunts. She's not a foot away and she still steps closer. "What's your name?"

She shakes her head. Still swiveling hips, eating hair.

"See them bleachers over there? Find me later. I'll put those pretty hands on the wheel of something real."

"What's *your* name?" The girl giggles. Her voice silly and dumb.

Luther pulls the hair out of her mouth. She freezes but her lips part wider and Luther knows then he can put anything in there he wants.

"Bring those friends of yours too. They can watch."

And then a low rumble calls Luther away. The Fury. Red star and purple. Easing into view.

Víctor doesn't see Luther striding between lots toward the car. He's got both hands glued to ten and two, like some salty zopilote. Only the car in front of him matters, or checking side clearances or the truck behind.

Piña sees Luther though. She always finds him. Wants to get out, kick it at his side, but Luther's hands signal her to stay put as he walks ahead, guiding them toward the bleachers, two more turns and a left until the Fury's easing in beside the Roadmaster.

Manic Mechanic emerges pale and drenched in sweat.

"¿Quiubo vato?"

"Nada," Víctor grins. Relieved. Glad for beers, Tweetie's laugh, Piña's too.

Luther, though, circles both cars uneasily. They're rarely without their Covercrafts. They're never this close together. On top of it, something's changed. But even as he goes over every panel, pinstripe, and blaze of chrome, he can see nothing's changed.

Víctor puts out their Not-For-Sale sign and gets to lighting charcoal and digging out strips of meat, while Piña turns on the stereos, LSOB pouring out of both trunks. Shit's linked, smooth. La siguiente es Mr. Blue. Luther's feeling more like Metallica. Juarez is still a no-show.

Luther downs two shots of tequila. Brunch. Then with that in his guts and Víctor and Piña happy to just tirar hueva in the chairs, Luther heads out with Tweetie for another round.

A fever's climbing on the day. Music replaces running engines. Tempos war. Sloppy shoves crowd the Draft Beer Depot. They pass a soda-blasting booth, a stand selling Radio Flyer wagons, gabachos with yellow visors and stupid t-shirts: *D.E.A. Drunk Every Afternoon!* A pack of kids thread their legs. "You're a Budweiser," one yells. "You're a Coors." "What's a Coors?"

By the porta potties, another kid stands alone, wailing. At once Luther's mouth fills with familiar metal. This like mercury, beads of it. And Luther just wants to bat the kid down, cuff an ear hard enough to pop hearing.

Except Luther's readying for more than a slap, making fists, what gets right right, except they explode with pain, all knuckles all ache, if by the time Luther grimaces, before he can unmake what guarantees gain, is already gone again.

Strange. Luther makes to spit. More pain there, still clawing his throat. Swallows instead.

"Yo, this even for sale?"

The old guy shakes his head. Takes in Luther. Or the way Luther takes in his baby.

"Last offer, 225K," he eventually shares. "Too part of my family now to part with. If you know what I mean."

Luther knows exactly what he means.

"Got a 1951 myself. Roadmaster. Chopped a half foot. 320 in a straight eight."

The owner listens. Luther could throw shit out all day, make up shit, and this sun-fried splotchy old fuck would just give up courtesy nods.

His 1950 Mercury says it all. Finished top to bottom. From piped-leather interior, red and white, to holly green exterior. License plate: HOLYLOH.

"More than polish," the old guy says, finally speaking again, after Luther said she had the sea on her. "Three gallons of paint. Another three of clear. Gives it that depth you're commenting on." Then moving on. "Chopped four-

and-a-half but lengthened five inches. Dropped in a 401 Nailhead Buick, balanced and blue-printed."

"Where the handles?" Tweetie asks, big hands fumbling the outside of the door.

"What the fuck you doin?" Luther snaps. Can't believe what he's seeing. Like some stupid dog pawing at the kind of beauty no dog can know.

"It's okay," the owner mutters, though aviators can't hide the frown, pulling out of his back pocket a polishing cloth.

"Please," Luther insists, taking the cloth, and getting down on his knees to remove every smudge.

The owner smiles. Takes off his sunglasses. Luther likes him. Unafraid. Doesn't see the shapes inking Luther's face and arms. The scars. Maybe same way Luther doesn't see red spots, pouched eyes, Glendora living. The two of them seeing only this Mercury because it's the only thing here worth giving two fucks about. The sight of such metal tastes sweet. Something almost-honey filling Luther's mouth.

"I like to think we're all machines. And like well-made machines, we'll experience a span of time where all parts align and we are afforded the miracle to explore this world around us. And then like every machine, our parts will start to fail. And we will diminish. The lucky ones will lose ancillary functionality — muffler, spark plug, a wheel. We may end up stuck but our capacity to behold, with clarity, will remain undimmed. That's a holy word there, an incantation by God: Behold! The unlucky ones will experience system failures — transmission, engines, today's electronics, our minds."

"Keep it like so, this Merc will go forever!"

"That's how I fool myself." The old man laughs. "Got doors on solenoids. Trunk and hood too. Smooths the lines. I think." The only flicker of a question yet.

"You think right. Might do the same to mine." Luther hands back the polishing cloth.

The owner puts his aviators back on and gets out a card.

"They do a pretty good job."

Which is when all the doors suddenly ease wide. Trunk rising too, and hood. Mercury opening up just like that, like a big invitation, or a trap.

"I didn't touch nothing!" Tweetie backs up fast, hands to the air, then behind his back.

Even the owner looks startled.

"I got it on a remote. Only there's the remote." He points to the top of a tool chest a good five feet away.

"Phones? Garage openers?" Luther keeps it light.

"Maybe just waves in the air?" Tweetie adds.

"Or ghosts," the owner answers them both.

At which point this pale bounce of pigtails ∴ *It's her!!!* ∴ followed by some loose-limbed mayate ∴ *Anwar!* ∴ and a little bukakke warrior ∴ *Mayumi!* ∴ ∴ Who? ∴ ∴ *They* ██████████ ██████████ ∴ slip around the Mercury's open doors, past Luther like he's fucking invisible. Like they're invisible. Except a chubby kid, ∴ *Cogsworth!* ∴ chasing after, huffing blind, runs straight into Luther, hard too, like hitting a wall.

Even the owner laughs. Helps the dumb kid back to his feet, brushes him off, sends him away, still huffing and playing catch-up.

Back in their corner, music's loud, grill's smoking up lunch, and Juarez has finally showed. But why are Luther's car doors all open too?

"Acá estás!" Lanky dog yells, scratching sideburns, that dirty handlebar mustache. Slinks over for shakes, eyes fixed slightly off, grinding shattered teeth, worst ones in gold.

"Who them?"

Juarez keeps scratching his chin, nervously considers the question for a second, until by way of an offering, by way of saying what's mine is yours, by way of saying they already yours jefe, he flicks his long, ragged nails toward the girls.

Luther knows Carmelita and Rosario from Dawgz, already busting his way too, Carmelita's thick thighs and turtle-shell sunglasses in the lead, Rosario behind, scowling some, swinging a new pink umbrella. Both of them as proud of their tits threatening shirt buttons as they are of their bellies overhanging their shorts.

It's the three strawberries Luther doesn't know that get his looks. Seeing him seeing them uneasies them, adjusting their step, checking nails, smoothing palms over very tan legs.

"Putas," Juarez shrugs. "For real. I'm paying."

One of the three never looks. Tiny Asian thing. Straight hair streaked blueberry. No waist, bad skin. Dirty bare legs stuffed into dirtier boots. Today maybe dirty will do. Luther even overlooks the Hello Kitty shit on her titless chest, on her little ruby handbag. Even on her phone.

Just walks straight at her.

"How old're you, girl?"

"Old enough for this beer." She still doesn't look up.

"Too old."

"Don't that feel like the truth." Like an old boxer taking a hit.

"Luther."

"I know. Asuka. Need anything?"

"Maybe later."

"Aren't you gonna ask if I need anything?"

"No."

Now she looks, teeth almost too bright for a mouth that's been around so much.

Maybe she's over twenty-one, but not by much. Up close, she comes off as even tighter. Did Luther just step back? Her flirty smile sure didn't step back: now almost a sneer.

One moment he's all for that little frame, gonna grab hold of those knobby shoulders, cock got shifty too, stiff. Next moment it's limp, gone.

Scares the shit out of him. At least Luther sees it isn't her.

Dice. Destiny. And Dawn.

The Hawaii girls. Though no longer coming around on hands and knees begging for fucks. Not even a naked memory. Halloween shit. Black hats, wool capes, brooms too. And they the least of it. Witches go with the thought of it. Luther's outside Hula again. On the landing. So dark to be so heavy, might as well be here at the Fairplex too, be anywhere, give any shadow, even Luther's own, one burning glare:

look out . . .

Asuka senses something. Sneer and grin fade, relief and exhaustion washing over her face like sweat, eyes slicing away, getting far away.

Maybe because Carmelita and Rosario see this as Luther's rejection, they bring Asuka food and more beer and later stroke her hair.

"You know what they say, bro: can't stand the heat, get outta the kitchen."

But Luther only understands what Juarez is saying when he touches his head and wipes the wet off. Luther don't feel this warm. Is he that sick? Or something else, what's been working away in his head for months, changing shit up.

∷ *But—* ∷

∷ You telling me. ∷

"Mil, we put out." Juarez hands him a stack of cards. "Everywhere."

HANDYMAN FOR YOUR PROBLEM!
Fix and clean & Everything
Call Jose Juan Smith
⊗⊗⊗ - ⊗⊗⊗ - ⊗⊗⊗⊗

Luther buries the stack in his pocket, then remembers the card the Mercury owner gave him is in there too. Pulls them all out. Felix Chevrolet is on top. The Mercury owner gave him the wrong card. No one goes to fucking Felix for remote-operated door latches. Disgusted, Luther shoves the cards back in Juarez's hands.

"If you still got these, you haven't hit everywhere," Luther growls.

Piña and Víctor wander over. Maybe tuning into his mood. Piña hands him a beer.

"Scariest thing I done?" she grins. "Sink ink in this bad-ass loco. You?"

"Easy," Víctor also grins. "Drive his fuckin car."

Later, after Tweetie's packed up all the shit and coolers, and Juarez is at the grill, grinding off char with steel wool, the Mercury rolls by.

"I gave you the wrong one. My mistake." The owner holds out a new card. "Who the fuck goes to Felix for a solenoid job?"

Luther's grateful.

"I wouldn't take less than forty for the Buick. But you know that. The Fury you keep."

And that old guy's look, approving, impressed, hangs around long after his holly green beaut disappears into the fumes of so many exits.

Until it's replaced by her.

So Cute. Shorty. So Cai

Hips still swiveling. Still eating her hair. No novias in sight.

"What you wanna show me?"

Drunk too.

This time Luther doesn't pull nothing from her mouth. He grabs her hair at the back of her head and squeezes. Throb in his cock gets him squeezing harder.

Girl closes her eyes, lips curling with hurt.

"You like that?" she whispers.

Luther makes her nod. Hard now. Then drops his hand, wide as her waist, on the back of her waist, directing her, owning her. She don't resist, just walks ahead toward the grandstands.

And then Asuka's voice reaches Luther. Just cuts through the dust.

So Cute So Naughty So Cali doesn't stop, just wanders off alone, by the bleachers, and if she wobbled some, she didn't look back. Not once.

::. *Instead she finds her friends. And in the years ahead she will find Jesus too. Lose Jesus still later. But not before marrying a gentle boy who sacrificed a limb in Iraq and found something better in her than war. Years later they will return together, with their four children, to the Fairplex on an equally hot Sunday as this. He will stay by the kit cars and talk about them endlessly. She will see the grandstands and consider going closer. Even after so much time, something there will still threaten to grant her the kind of damage that exceeds revision. She will tighten her grip on her son's hand and he will yelp and ask her why she just did that and she won't know. She won't remember when she'd forgotten herself completely.* .::

::. Huh. Could Luther have forgot hisself too? But in a different way? Could he've just wandered off, but in that different way, and not looked back, and found friends, new friends, and something unfamiliar, something gentle? .::

::. **No.** .::

"Domingo? Domingo Persianos? I can call that bitch right now."

"What the fuck you say?" Luther charges back.

Asuka's eyebrows arch.

"That I got his number?"

"Vamos a ver. Do it."

Not even one ring. Disconnected. Luther checks the number. Same one he has.

"How you know him?"

Asuka's smart enough not to hold back. "Friend of mine used to fill his pocket."

"Warm it too?" Víctor leers.

"I don't know nothin about warmth."

"This friend, she have a working number?" Luther asks.

"He's a shitty-ass pimp, man," Asuka spits. "Nothing works for him. Not even his girls. I can call Cricket, but if you so dyin for him why not go see him?"

"Where he at?"

And shit how Asuka smiles now. Fuckin explodes with this mean thing. No wonder she's kickin with Juarez.

"That fool still lives with his mom."

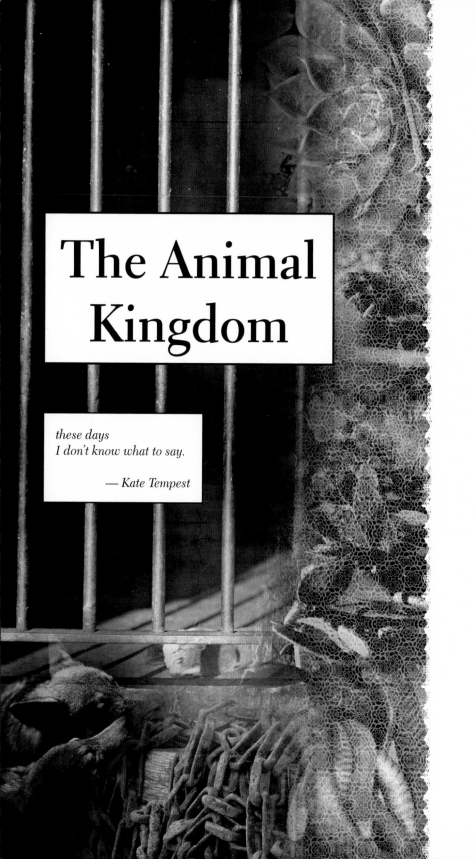

The Animal Kingdom

these days
I don't know what to say.

— *Kate Tempest*

Abigail's description (of that first date) still strikes Astair as a ridiculous (Renaissance Faire–ish) encounter: lovers on horseback (in leather corsets (feathered hats)) crossing a river (crossing (lush) ranch land) riding for hours (all while (high above) a feathered silhouette hangs against the sun) until finally a blanket is spread and a picnic is unpacked (wine uncorked (the first of many)) until Abigail's seducer asks if she would like him to call down an angel whereupon (on her nod) he slips on a leather glove (materializing a chunk of blood sausage too).

"It was like watching a stone drop from a mile up."

"The angel?"

"Angel is the hawk's name."

"I assume you proved the better angel?"

Abigail snorts (over the phone). "Are you kidding me? I gave it up right on the spot. Ants carried off the sandwiches."

Astair laughs but (by the end of the conversation) still hesitates to confirm.

"Come on, girlfriend," Abigail implores. "You're taking Xanther to meet movie stars. Toys is a teddy bear. I've arranged everything. Grab that super girl and have a blast. I'll see you tomorrow!"

Which Abigail repeats the next day (now with "I'll see you tomorrow!" replaced by "You know I have to make a living").

"Oh Abigail! Maybe we should turn around."

"Don't be silly! This is perfect. The less of me the better. Plus you two need a little mother-daughter bonding time. Don't deny it either."

Astair doesn't deny it (though she's nervous about any trek into unknown environs (especially with child in tow (this child))).

Especially to see dangerous animals.

"Abigail's not coming?" Xanther asks (after Astair hangs up). "Are we turning around?"

"I don't know, darling. We're almost there."

"Where are we even?" They'd already been on the road for more than an hour.

"Somewhere."

"Funny," Xanther scowls (still wearing those pink sunglasses Mefisto gave her).

"Where are your real glasses, young lady? How can you even see with those?"

"You mean, like, these are better?" Xanther produces from a pocket the twist of duct tape and scratched lenses. Astair laughs.

"Okay. We'll get you new ones soon."

Xanther had wanted to go on this adventure so much (Astair had even convinced herself that this was the (magic!) means to make up for the twins' terrible misbehavior (they were paying for it now)).

Then Astair mentioned how long they would be gone ("Most of the day") and all enthusiasm vanished (Xanther didn't have to mention that (nameless) creature she immediately clutched to her chest).

Xanther puts away her broken glasses and goes back to dancing fingers over her pink phone (at least it beats picking her skin (a braided knot of (particularly) painful scabs (winding along the ridge of her left jaw)) or at her cuticles (will that blood sport ever end? (if these days seeming to heal(?) faster (the self-mutilations at their worst when Astair was away at Oceanica ("She missed her mama," was Anwar's response)))))).

"Latest breaking news?" Astair asks now.

"Cogs just wanted to come along."

"I know, but you explained that this is our thing?"

"Yeah, but dad said yesterday's car dealy in Pomona was, like, our thing too but Cogs and Mayumi still got to go."

"That was fun?"

"So much."

Astair tries to cool a flare (of jealousy (or is it something else?)?). Just ~~rehash~~ *relax*. Not easy with so many semis congesting the 15.

(a little later) The back hatch suddenly pops open. (fortunately) They are starting to exit. Astair has to pull over on the shoulder. She doesn't like having to get out to close it. She hurries back (mind suddenly alive with thoughts of some dark gang (pulling over (in a darker car)) to gang rape them both (where'd that come from?)).

"Was Oceanica fun?" Xanther asks (once they're on their way again).

"So much." Astair grins.

"I don't believe you." Xanther laughs. "How's the paper? Isn't that why you went?"

"Yes and no. A lot of lectures. Homework too."

"Is your new paper on the same subject?"

Had Astair told Xanther the topic? ∵ No. ∴

"I'm still drawn to identity."

"You mean like an ID?"

"Does an ID define you? Your name? Your eye color? Or is it really your personality? The memories you have? My big question concerns how many changes you need to make before the you you are becomes a you that's not you anymore?"

"Huh. So, like, if my, uhm, like epilepsy was gone, would I still be me?"

"Exactly."

"Or what about the cat? Does he being with me make me more me? Or maybe less me?"

(when they arrive ((late (it turns out) by about forty minutes) at the end of too many dusty roads (followed by sudden (rocky) turns))) A chipper black girl named Kichelle (twenty (maybe)) informs them that they are not the only ones running behind.

"Satya's arrival, I don't know, that's the big news, of course, and you know all about that, she came in last night. Some night. All night. And then this morning one of our pups got sick. We had to take her straight down to San Diego. Of course, it turns out the pup's fine. Couple of shots, you know, or something, I don't know, maybe pills. Bet I'll have to give those. They're on the way back now, finally, I mean they left hours ago, should be here soon, I mean any minute and— Was there traffic?"

"Some."

"So, anyway, just hang out?"

"Who's Satva?" Xanther asks (of course).

"Oh!" Kichelle's eyes widen (definitely looking like she just said too much). She even turns away. Toward the hill. "Ask Toys."

There are kennels everywhere ((on wide pads of cement) built out of chain-link fencing ((roofed up) and padlocked)). A much higher fence (not roofed up) encloses the kennels. The only gate (big enough to let trucks in) carries one large sign:

> *Warning! Security Dogs!*
>
> *STOP! RESTRICTED AREA!*
>
> *No Spectators Beyond This Point!*

Astair has to revisit again that lush scene Abigail painted (more like an absurd bloom of whimsy in a lovesick mind (replete with swooping birds of prey and coital splay)). Where even was the river? The closest thing was an arroyo Astair had eased the Honda Element over on their way here. Not even a hint of water. Hardly a hint of green. Astair finds only dry (tangled) stuff sprouting up among dusty rocks and knotted trees (are they trees? (big bushes? (wizened (if still clinging to some progress called life)))). Miles and miles of it.

Some kingdom.

"Do they dream?"

Xanther's question startles Astair. (but before she can ask (who?)) The dogs arrive: three Australian shepherds (Kichelle identifies them as Gus and Vito and Juno). They swarm over Xanther (bounding around her knees (tails wagging) pushing their bellies down into the dirt (licking her toes) before leaping up and pawing at her lap).

"What about you guys? What do you dream?"

Xanther even asks the same question of Glipper.

"Sometimes Glipper will throw her poo," Kichelle warns. "Esperando too."
Glipper (the spider monkey) swings across the ceiling.
"Is that what I think it is?" Astair asks.
"Yup. Gable's their cat."
"They have a cat?" Xanther goes wide-eyed (before squinting at the fat black thing (meat-loafing on a tire)).
"A bunny too."
"Do they mistreat them?" Astair has to ask.
"Not at all! They pet them."
Glipper offers Xanther his hand through the chain-link fence but Kichelle shakes her head.
"Isn't that, uhm, like, kinda mean? To, you know, lock up a cat with a couple of monkeys?"
"Tough call. Around here the free ones wander into cages they shouldn't wander into and then they aren't anymore."

So far (though) those "other cages" are nothing too heart-racing. Mainly a wood shed with birds of prey. Astair and Xanther can only spy (through the cracked slats) snatches of brown feathers and beaks.

Are these the angels?

Nearby paces a fox (ever aware of neighboring fowl? (though what can a fox do with a hawk? (or a hawk with a fox?))). He's called Lofty (red and quick ((sharp eyes and soft coat) bushy tail swishing the confines of his cage)).

Xanther kneels down.

"Don't do that, darling."

Xanther withdraws her fingers from the fence.

The fox still approaches. Twitches its nose (nervously? (disappointed?)). Goes away. Never spares Astair a glance.

Maybe Xanther has something on her that smells of animals (like leather of sorts (or animal fat in some lotion (but since when does her daughter use lotion? (or wear leather?)))).

:: Of course, there's — ::

:: *Shhhhhhh.* ::

"What about you, Mr. Lofty? What do you dream?"

Of course there is Xanther's cat.

Down the hill (across a dirt road) stand paddocks. "We got llamas, horses, and pigs," Kichelle explains. "Or are they boars? Man, I'm wrecked. I'm sorry. I should know that." Astair can just make out some dark bloated creatures (which (even at this distance) seem to wield some sort of sharpness (tusks?) just visible (glinting? (imagined?)) beneath the bristles of constantly roaming snouts).

Astair sneezes. Sneezes twice more.

"Bless you! Bless you!" Xanther shouts (already on the move again (she does look happy (maybe she's even forgotten her cat))).

Two more cages (the largest so far) stand opposite the fox and falcons (and monkeys) adjacent to a ((miniature) red and white) barn (also within the confines of the main fence) serving as an office of sorts (where Kichelle takes a moment to poke at a fax machine (sneezing too)).

At least here (at the first big cage) Xanther doesn't immediately dig her fingers through the chain-link.

"What do you dream, Mr. Havoc?" Xanther asks.

And one day (maybe) this grizzly bear will deserve the full range of that name. At present (though) he stands at four-and-a-half feet (if that).

"He's just a baby!" Xanther squeals happily.

Havoc huffs and then abruptly sneezes before (finally) drawing closer (wearily at first (then more enthusiastically)) even sticking his serpentine tongue through the fence (begging for sugar?).

"Wow! Look at them, mom—" ((ah) mom) "—Havoc so needs a pedicure!"

Long black blades (sprouting from rough brown fur) hook and tug at the metal before scratching (next) at the cement (conjuring up a peculiar music (not altogether comforting)) as Havoc takes to the air (with a twist (and another huff)) and lands dexterously on a splintered skateboard which (with (or without) the help of the fencing (or the hanging tire)) the bear (with his shiny black nose) demonstrates he can easily wheel around (white teeth shredding the afternoon air).

He does look like he's smiling.

"He's going to be a big star for us." Kichelle is definitely smiling. Astair too. (if a leap counts as a smile) So are the dogs.

Neither Gus nor Vito nor Juno will stop jumping at the fence (until Havoc (all the time studying(?) Xanther from those brown luminous eyes (what *does* he dream?)) swaggers back to the center (and (with a long sigh) slouches down in a sliced-up La-Z-Boy chair)).

(seeing that the second big cage holds only dogs) Astair asks Kichelle to direct her toward a restroom.

(but on her way there) Astair (for a moment) doubts the way (fears she will have to make do off to the side (squatting behind some tarantula-owned rock)) until she spots (across a road and down some steps (just as Kichelle promised)) the small house.

"The door's unlocked. No one's in."

A gloomy place. Distressed ((shag) maroon) car-pet disappears (to die) beneath heavily shellacked bookcases (loaded with veterinarian books).

The immediate kitchen is a narrow alley of stove and sink (counter crowded with bottles of hydrogen peroxide and tubes of Neosporin (scissors too (beside rolls of medical tape and wads of gauze (brown enough to keep Astair from investigating further)))).

On the wall is a Critter Gitter Clock (time at the service of a lion and a hyena (with an elephant stam-peding the second hand)).

The bathroom is just as overwrought (encrusted with dirt (which Astair determines with a fingernail is no such thing (unless years of hardening have pro-duced this (current) dark epoxy))). Everything else is leopard: (leopard) wallpaper (leopard) towels (leop-ard) candles and even a (leopard) toilet seat.

Astair hovers. She also never nears the sink (those smeared(?) faucets). A tarantula-infested rock would have been better. The only thing she touches (on her way out) is the light switch (leopard).

Is this where Abigail revels in her sweet-sweat-semen-soaked entanglements?

Astair wants to gag ∷ She's nowhere close to gag-ging ∷.

What could have possessed Abigail to have even crossed the threshold?
Is she really this lonely?

Astair doesn't even realize how tight her chest has gotten (like a man's fist? (she imagines)) until she steps outside. Something about the dinginess offends her. (Astair isn't even thinking of the jeans and boxers hucked over the hair-matted sofa (or the muddy boots on the coffee table ∴ She's thinking about all of it ∵.)) The stink for sure. ∴ *For sure!* ∵

She sneezes now. Twice more. Her throat itches. Eyes too. Allergies? Still better than the way she felt inside (flushed ((~~envious~~) *envious?*)).

Something's at her feet. Can she even call it a cat? What a grizzled thing. Gray with just a glint of green in one eye. The other eye is marble white (ick!). The ear (above the ick (ick! (ick!))) is no more than a hole surrounded by spidery threads of flesh. The whole left side is nothing more than a few tufts of ashen hair except where (where there is no hair at all) a substantial trench digs alongside the spine through the ribs and down into the rear flank (rendering a back leg pretty useless). The tail is just gone.

Nonetheless this tortured thing rubs against Astair's ankle (even after she recoils).

Its mew ((or is it a purr?) a harsh grate of improbable survival) only stops when nearby (very nearby (just up the hill (crowned in brush))) something else unleashes its thunder (Astair feels gripped by the bones (the teeth!)).

What the fuck was that?

What Astair has every intention of asking Kichelle as she's letting herself through the big gate. Only to freeze at the sight of Gus and Vito and Juno frozen before that last big cage.

Something about that last cage now beginning to dawn on Astair.

Along with:

Where is Kichelle?

Where is Xanther?

Dark shapes moving inside.

Way way bigger than dogs.

Not dogs at all.

Astair is sprinting. Breath quickening (already breathing way too hard). Until she's not even breathing. Another fist in her chest (this one a much different kind). As Astair reaches the fencing to discover yellow eyes and a swirl of black fur and teeth clicking in low guttural growls.

Wolves.

Five of them.

And all circling (frantically?) and shaking their heads (repeatedly) and lunging out (suddenly) to snap (?) before withdrawing (just as fast) to continue circling.

And the center of their attention?

The object of these attacks?

Her baby girl!

Sitting cross-legged (alone!)!

Until adrenaline sharpens Astair's perceptions: Kichelle's in there too (with a baton but— (but cornered by the biggest wolf (no not the biggest (the biggest has just clamped its jaws on her daughter's arm (twisting to rip it away (rip it off (tear Xanther apart))))))).

"Mom!" Xanther cries.

Which is when everything goes messy: adrenaline misplaced ((gushing for nowhere now) against conflicting sights and tones). Saliva returns to Astair's mouth. The beating in her chest slows as her body starts to relax (even if her mind persists in trying to command all of her to keep tensing (tense still more (do this something more! (dammit!(!!!))))).

"Mom!" Xanther cries again. "Come in!"

Kichelle looks just as happy. That second biggest wolf ((before her) a blur of charcoal and snow) has just rolled over (wanting something from Kichelle ((to play with?)) while the biggest wolf ((with Xanther) a blond billow of heavy shoulders and bright eyes) continues to rip away at what's only a frayed blanket (red!) which Xanther (playfully!) withholds until (overpowered?(!)) she lets go with a squeal.

"Aren't they amazing?"

They are.

But they think she's more amazing.

Kichelle notices it too. Especially when Xanther stands up. Immediately Kichelle's attendant (Attendant?! (WOLF!)) wheels around to rejoin the pack (fall in behind the blond alpha (who pays no mind to the rest (paying close attention (only) to every move Astair's twelve-year-old makes))).

Only Xanther's oblivious (practically skipping across the cage to meet Astair at the gate).

The blond alpha drops his prized blanket to keep close to Xanther (too close (teeth nearly (?) nicking those fragile heels)) even as the pack hangs back (if still tuned to the flitting motion of Xanther's hands ((her bobbing head) and dancing knees) as if they soon might earn some (anticipated?) reward).

"She's special," Kichelle says later (after Xanther goes off to find the bathroom).

"I'm partial," Astair responds (her practiced tone of neutrality in effect).

"You start together," Kichelle continues (is her tone leaking with confession (or just curiosity?)?). "That's the way you're *supposed* to start. Because, I mean, they *know* me. And then you sit down, so you're lower than them or the same height but not higher, which would make you maybe more lead-erish and definitely more of an outsider, but when you're down low then they treat you like part of the pack and they come around and sniff you and even pull at that blanket I let your daughter hold and then you stand up, like I stood up, to be leaderish see, and I kinda moved away, which is when they usually all follow me, except this time only Montana followed me, and it was like—" Kichelle's smile changes "—Huh. It was like he wasn't really following, but more trying to separate me, and you know, keep me away. Kinda like the way someone might do at a party, pull someone away, so the rest can have a private conversation. Actually, now that I think about it, it was really weird."

Astair's heart is at it again (adrenaline back too). Except this time (instead of confusion) it's all about anger.

Kichelle has no clue.

"They just took to her," the young woman continues. "I mean *took* to her. Did you see at the end, how she got up and they fell back like all at once, and Montana left me quick, and like even Quasar, the alpha, heeled behind her. I've worked with them for three years now and they never do that for me.

Not even Toys." Kichelle whispers that last part. "Not in that way. It's like they *knew* her. Like she was one of them. Or all of them? I mean—but in charge. You know?" Kichelle suddenly chuckles (loud too (abrasively?)). "Man, I must be beat. It sounds like I'm calling your kid a werewolf!"

All Astair wants to do is beat Kichelle (even envisions a flurry of fists (beating her into bruises and pus (though not with Astair's fists (but heavier and calloused and backed up by brute strength and brute experience (fists she knows too well (because they're Dov's)))))). At least Astair should shout:

HOW DARE YOU FUCKING TAKE MY TWELVE-YEAR-OLD DAUGHTER INTO A DEN OF FUCKING WOLVES WITHOUT MY FUCKING PERMISSION?! AND DRESS HER UP LIKE FUCKING LITTLE RED RIDING HOOD?! ARE YOU FUCKING KIDDING ME?!

"They're a lot like dogs?" Astair says instead.

The question has the desired effect. Confidence from expertise dispels Kichelle's evident unease.

"They look like dogs, sure, but they're not. See the yellow eyes? The size? And the tails? They never lift the tails above their backside. They're smart too. Way smarter than your average pooch. You have to trick them to do anything. They won't serve any man. Ever. At least that's what Toys says. He should know. They only serve the pack."

Astair still can't help but see dogs even as she sees nothing close to dogs.

Actually the only thing Astair can see is red.

Before Kichelle leaves (still clueless) she again announces that Toys is only minutes away ("traffic"). Xanther and Astair are welcome to hang out with the dogs or kick back in the mini-barn office.

With Xanther out of earshot (back by the monkeys) Kichelle also asks (sotto voce too) that Astair "not mention, you know, that thing with the wolves." (That thing?!) "There's supposed to be all this release-of-liability paperwork to fill out and anyhow, you know your daughter, right?"

Astair tries to crush every answer (only one) between her teeth (grinding away (like she so often tells Xanther not to do)) though something in her expression still betrays her.

Kichelle's eyes widen (her youth suddenly too evident on her soft features).

"You do know I didn't take her in there, right? I was feeding Havoc. She was talking to them and then she just walked in."

Later (long after Kichelle's dirty white Corolla left (in spectres of dust)) what Astair keeps turning over in her head is not this revelation but a different warning.

Xanther had returned from the bathroom slightly spooked.

"What's up the hill?"
"Yeah." Kichelle had tensed. "Don't go up there, okay? Please. Don't."

"What do you mean you're alone?" Anwar demands now (the closest he comes to a shout).

"We came this far."

Astair holds out the phone to Xanther (wobbling through the first movement ∷ *Ward Off*∷ (outside the wolves' cage)).

"Xanth, it's your dad. He wants to say hello."

"Hi, Dad," Xanther shouts (without interrupting her (klunky) transition through the next two forms ∷ *Grasp Sparrow's Tail*∷ ∷ *Ward Off With Right Hand*∷ (even rotating away ∷ *Roll Back*∷ (heading toward Press-Withdraw-Press and Single Whip (Australian shepherds galloping around every move)))).

"She's practicing her Tai Chi."

Anwar sighs softly in her ear and Astair misses him immediately (hears him missing her too).

"Just get home safely. Grant this fellow another ten minutes and then leave, okay?"

((curiously) with every step Xanther takes) The gold-eyed shapes behind chain-link match her progress (shuffling (as one dark mass) from one side of their confines to the other (nothing fragile (or glass-like) here (or even dusty (invaluable)))).

"They follow her. It's like they're drawn to her. And she hardly notices."

"Who?"

"The wolves."

Later it comes again. Down from around the bend (where they were warned not to go). Where living thunder rolls loose. Telling them (over and over again) what Astair can't hear as anything else but go . . .

And Astair decides to go too. Just as soon as she finishes the crossword (one more corner). Home now depends on 9 down. Ten letters. *Pride's equity?*

But before Astair can count out her second guess (e-g-o-t-i-s-m (three letters short) ∷ **Lionsshare** ∷) a (brown) Chevrolet van rumbles up and out jumps a wolf pup followed by (the grinning) Keen Toys.

And just like that (wow!) the hair-matted sofa and resin-whatever stains (those bloody wads of gauze) (wow! wow!) cease to matter. And all he does is amble her way (blue eyes flashing (red hair dancing a breeze (real red hair (is there even a breeze?)))). Big for sure (from biceps to quads). Toys extends an enormous hand. Apologies on his sunburned lips.

With him is Sibylla (skin pale as the pale straight hair reaching the middle of her back (yoga body (looks Swedish))). She says hello and (leading along the wolf pup) disappears into the (miniature) barn. It turns out she is Swedish.

Abigail had already explained to Astair that Toys was once in the NFL ((it didn't last long) "He put it all on the line. As in as a lineman," Abbey had giggled). His handshake surprises Astair though: kind. With a laugh that's even more so (making the cuts and scratches (and deep scars) running down his right forearm seem absurd(?(at least out of place))).

"You must be Xanther," he says easily (a twang English? (The South? (soft and lilting (unafraid))))).

"No other," Xanther grins ((almost as easily) surprising Astair with a note of what her mother Bea would have called "pluck.")

Toys gives them the full tour (including those paddocks (and corrals) down below). There's even a project in the works with the Discovery Channel (something to do with an unfinished set (involving a thirteen-foot (cinder-block) wall)).

"Have you, uhm, always had animals?" Xanther asks at one point.

"When I lived in St. Louis I spent every day with animals but I don't think that's what you're asking." Toys grins. "I didn't get my first bear until after I retired from the gridiron. My father, though, was a farmer. Goats, sheep. Had a place right on the River Tweed. If only I'd cared something for fishing I might still be there. Can't say I'm sad I'm not though." And he looks out on the dusty valley with such affection (and awe?) that for a moment Astair can't help but see it with the same reverence.

(Does Xanther?)

"Come say hi to Angle and Angel."

Toys even lets Xanther toss chunks of meat (black oozy cubes that leave a greasy residue on her fingers (Xanther doesn't seem to mind (the dogs don't either (licking her fingers clean)))) into the shed holding the saker falcon and Harris hawk.

"This is saying hi?" she asks.

"Here in Heaven's Mews, it is." Toys laughs. "They look a little scrappy because they're molting. More like fallen angel and a broken angle. But don't be fooled. Such wings know more of divinity than we can ever swear to dream."

Next up: Glipper (the spider monkey (now out of his cage)) climbs all over Xanther. Astair clicks off pictures. Maybe animals take to Xanther simply because she's always so taken with them? (however) Esperando (the other spider monkey) doesn't approach. Gable (the pet cat) hides behind a box.

Even Lofty (the fox) and Havoc (the bear) seem more wary than before.

Not the wolves. No questioning their fealty (shuffling in whichever direction Xanther moves).

"I see the gang's taken to you," Toys says (is even he (slightly?) stunned (mystified?) by this collective (animal) attunement?). "Quasar and Montana don't normally follow anyone except me and that's usually because I've got a big slab of meat in my paw. You got any meat?"

Xanther shakes her head (Is she blushing?).

"Well, this pack's my joy. Do you want to meet my pride?"

"I thought you'd never ask." Xanther even half-curtseys((!) she is blushing!).

Toys laughs. Astair too (if only to hide how flabbergasted she is by this sudden display of capriciousness on the part of her eldest).

Up the hill they go.

Toys now is wholly focused on Xanther.

Xanther (per usual) is oblivious (focused on just trying to walk straight (of course she meanders (and trips plenty))).

Not that there's anything inappropriate about the big man's attentions (Abigail likely insisted that he dazzle Xanther with his menagerie (Xanther (also) seems to have energized his paternal side (he very well could make a great father))). If anything there's something inappropriate about Astair's (slightly?) competitive behavior with her daughter (to say nothing of with her friend Abigail).

Ouch.

Are all women (really(?)) so inherently catty?

Or is it just Astair?

Double-ouch.

Since when?

(as if to answer her head) Her body now releases a wave of heat warping through all parts. Astair stumbles.

"Oh look at you!" Xanther (ahead) suddenly shouts ((dropping (at once) to her knees) huddling over ((ah)!) that mauled familiar thing of gray with glint of green).

"Say hello to Aiflow," Toys sighs.

"Aiflow?" Astair asks (absurdly pleased by Toys' appreciative flick of attention in her direction (he even lingers for whispers)).

"Am I Fucking Lucky Or What."

"I expect a story?"

Toys nods: "The Siberian. Too many stitches to count. Took months to nurse this critter back to health and he still prances by the bars."

"Is that what happened to your arm?"

"This? This is nothing." Toys grins (showing off his forearm (something powerful sparking in those blue eyes)). "You should see my back!"

"A tiger?"

"I won't tell Abigail you called her that."

(at the entrance to the upper compound (the gate here is triple-locked)) Sibylla waits with a wheelbarrow filled with (what looks like) chicken parts.

"Chicken necks," she corrects. She's slight too (though (under the loose sweats and t-shirt) Astair detects the sinuous strength of a dancer (more suited to a pas de bourrée than thrusting her hands into such heaps of offal)).

(similar to below) The area up here also consists of a chain-link fence (open at the top (though this one's higher (fourteen feet (at least?)))) enclosing just one (large rectangular) cement pad on which stand (at one end) four large cages (one is empty) and (at the other end) a large supply shed.

There's no indication up here of where that sound originated (if it did come from here (maybe there's another (similar) compound nearby?)).

The three Australian shepherds bounce around (lunging at the cages (as Sibylla starts the feeding)).

The young lion (Lear) pays no attention to the dogs but a black panther ((leopard(?)) Caress) hisses and the small Siberian tiger (Mumbai) growls.

"The dogs aren't afraid?" Astair asks (there's a fence in-between (but even that low growl accelerates her heart)).

"Vito, Juno, and Gus raised all of them. Size makes no difference. The dogs dominate."

"Are you afraid, Sibylla?"

"No!" The Swede gleams. "I love working with the predator." She even casts a concupiscent glance at Toys. (Or is it (only) conscientious?)

"Sibylla's from Umeå. Picked up some agriculture science there. Then came here and started working for zoos. Many zoo cats start in the wild. They're already practiced killers when they arrive. Our pride's a lot easier. These guys were raised on milk bottles and reality TV. They like us."

Which seems true.

Sibylla brings Lear out on a chain. The shep-herds immediately maul all eight months of his adolescent ranginess. Their uninterrupted play lasts several minutes.

Toys has Lear leap up on a large wooden spool (presumably once an axis for high-voltage cable (it still serves power)).

Lear even dances with Toys (paws resting (gen-tly(?))) on each shoulder.

Later Lear tackles Sibylla in a carefully staged stunt (film and television ready).

Pretty impressive.

"You always keep your hands between your face and the jaws," Toys says (narrating the scuffle on the ground (between Lear and Sibylla)). "And you never say no to a lion. You accept where he wants to go and divert him." Advice Sibylla follows perfectly (so Tai Chi (Astair must tell Lamb (tell Lamb too what Sandra Dee Taylor had said at Oceanica ((another one of her gems) "Often a new yes is the best no")))).

Astair gets a chance to touch the animal's golden coat (thicker and coarser than expected (though hardly muting (the musculature) the terrible might beneath (and this is a small lion (not much bigger than either Vito or Gus)))).

When Xanther rests her hand on the back of Lear's neck (so lightly too) the young lion suddenly seems to drop (dropping his gaze too) and sort of crawls (cowering?) back to his cage.

"Tired," Toys grumbles.

The big black cat stays caged but Toys lets Xan-
her stuff chicken necks through the chain-link.

"Careful not to let your fingers get close."

Xanther obeys.

The panther (with spots visible up close (leopard!)) seems to linger around Xanther (sniffing (cautiously?) before snagging the first morsel of his meal).

"You sure have a strange effect on my beasts.
They don't know what to make of you."

Xanther looks practically red in the face.

As it turns out the empty cage isn't empty.
There's another leopard in there (Sir Casual ((yellow with black spots) flighty)). (still) He approaches
from the back.

"I don't suppose they'd eat soy?" Xanther asks
(wiping off her bloody fingers with Sibylla's rag).

"Meat eaters. One hundred percent."

(for the finale) Sibylla brings out (the fourteen-
month-old) tiger. Mumbai's collar is thick leather
(on a thicker chain). Sibylla leads him up onto a
table (built with wide planks of hard wood).

"Come around behind him," Toys instructs
Xanther.

"This is Aiflow's close call?" Astair's voice
quavers.

"Not to worry," Toys smiles. "Aiflow wandered
into Mumbai's cage. That's his territory. The table,
this whole area, this is my territory. Mumbai knows
it and he respects it."

Astair knows it too (relaxing even as her daughter
slides in behind the relaxing tiger (starting to stretch
out (already offering up his white belly))).

"It's sprickly!" Xanther exclaims.

"Sprickly!" Toys likes that.

"Will he purr?"

"Big cats don't purr, they chuff. Like this."

Toys lets out a rough grunt (flashes of Abigail shredding that big back (is it Astair's turn to blush?)).

Xanther does her best to imitate. A softer (and sillier) sound (more like a purr really) but Mumbai immediately chuffs back (a warm chocolatey response).

"Very good. Now, Xanther, I want you to come around in front. Though first you must remember three very important rules. One: do not make eye contact. Two: never trust a tiger. Three, though, is the most important rule of all."

"What?"

"Tell me the first two rules first."

"One: don't make eye contact. Two: never trust a tiger. How is that even a rule?"

"Trust is definitely a rule."

"And three?"

"Never ever turn your back on a tiger."

"Even if he's not in his own territory?" Astair asks.

"Wherever he is."

Mumbai seems to stiffen (when Xanther slides (cautiously) in front). Sibylla's hand tightens on the chain. (like the lion) The tiger immediately lowers his head (eyes darting away (ears flattening (as if to avoid making eye contact with Xanther!))). Then (in the next instant) promptly scrambles off the table (slinking away (like a scolded dog (dragging Sibylla with him))) back to its cage.

"Huh," Toys grunts.

"Hungry?" Sibylla suggests (but (obviously) she's confused too).

Both trainers seem caught off guard. Is that why Xanther is blushing again (is she blushing?)?

"You okay, honey?" Astair goes over to feel her forehead. No fever (might as well be a layer of frost).

"So amazing. Even if they don't like me."

"No, no," Toys reassures her (his sweetness reassuring Astair too).

"We had a late night," Toys explains (lifting his (scratched) forearm).

"Oh."

"Call me Aiflow too. And this was just on the edge of a fence I had to get through. Quickly."

Toys gets Xanther a glass of water and puts her to work filling the cats' buckets with a hose.

"Last night—" (he confides to Astair) "—we got a delivery. I'm sure Abigail told you. A white lion. Lioness. Wild. Likely from Africa. A real killer. Found wandering near Nuevo Laredo."

"Captured in Texas, right?" Javier had mentioned this (in Santa Barbara). "On the news?"

Toys nods: "She probably escaped from one of those cartel zoos. Then a few days ago, down in San Diego, the animal seriously mauled a vet. Also on the news. What no one's reporting yet is that Seattle's Woodland Park Zoo has agreed to take her. All fine and good until in the middle of transit a problem was discovered with the delivery timing and I was asked to keep her for a few days."

"She's here?"

"Oh yeah."

"Where?"

"Nothing to worry about. We've got her in our biggest cage. Triple-locked. The only real concern is if word leaks out and people start wandering over. We're not equipped here to handle spectators."

Xanther has almost finished filling Mumbai's bucket (more like a tub? (tank)). The dogs love to jump and snap at the cold jet.

(afterward) Sibylla has Xanther toss chicken parts into the tank. They sink at once but Mumbai still pursues ((no pawing about) just plunges that large (tiger) head deep into the water (emerging seconds later ((wet and streaming) still snapping too) with threads of flesh dangling between his white teeth)).

"Enrichment!" Toys bellows (as Mumbai dives again for another treat).

Astair still can't get over how comfortable Xanther seems with handling raw meat.

And then the shepherds start yipping next to Astair. And Toys is laughing.

(for some reason) Astair's ankle feels wet (which makes no sense (because Xanther's hose is not pointed in her direction)). Mumbai's water is also too far away (and anyway (if Astair really wants to somehow connect him to this leaky sensation around her foot) the young tiger has (for some reason) started scrambling back (toward the far corner of his cage

The dampness (it turns out) is connected to the dark lines marking Astair's jeans. Toys is already on his knees (apologizing profusely). Is he trying to dry her pants? With the bottom of his shirt? He even takes off his shirt. His broad back patched with ample strips of dark-speckled gauze.

No way a fence did that. No way Abigail did that.

"I've never seen Gus do this before," Toys says (standing (putting his shirt back on)).

"What?"

Sibylla can't believe it either: "Gus pissed on her?"

"Excuse me?"

"He must really like you. He's claiming you."

Whereupon Xanther suddenly shouts: "*I need enrichment!*"

And like that she starts spraying her head with the hose. Sibylla laughs (surprised). Toys smiles (though with more than a flicker of concern (igniting those blues)). Astair is just shocked. What's going on? It's not even warm anymore. It's practically dusk.

"I'm just so hot," Xanther keeps babbling.

Why also are all three dogs barking? Why are all the cats racing to the rear of their cages?

Why is Xanther still holding her head under the hose?

Toys' laughter is long since dead and gone. He's turning (as swiftly as the athlete he used to be) to face (if still stumbling backward) a rumbling nearly too low to hear.

What Astair feels thud through her chest.

Living thunder.

The dogs keep barking but also retreat.

A very different instinct takes over Astair. She drives laterally toward Xanther.

Or where Xanther should have been.

There's only the hose now. Still running.

Not that Astair stops. Because if Xanther isn't by the growing puddle then she must be heading back with Toys and Sibylla (and the three dogs) toward the only gate (into (and out of) this place).

But she isn't there either.

And then Toys screams: "Holy fuck!" ∴ *Anguished with the recognition of so grave a mistake.* ∴

What somehow orients Astair toward another somehow:

      somehow Xanther headed in the opposite direction of escape

          somehow ended up toward the far end of the compound

      toward that supply shed.

          Except it's not a supply shed.

Astair sees now that the boards posing as a wall were all along just fastened to a large chain-link gate.

And are those chains on the ground?

∴ In pieces? ∴

Are those locks on the ground?

∴ *In pieces.* ∴

Shattered metal strewn before hinges.

Before this entrance to another cage.

∴ *Once closed.* ∴

∴ Covered once. ∴

∴ **Allways there.** ∴

Now slowly

swinging

open

releasing in a blur of   murderous

grace   already   lunging   for   Xanther

a creature of singular menace.

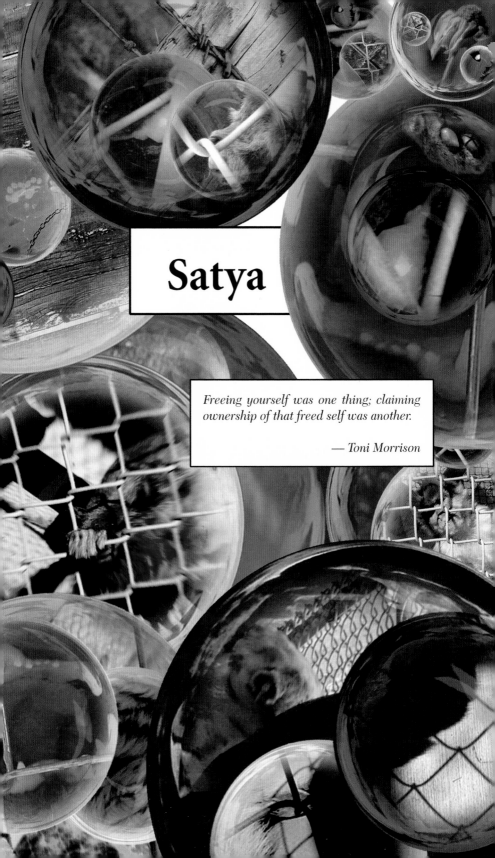

Satya

Freeing yourself was one thing; claiming ownership of that freed self was another.

— *Toni Morrison*

Satya.

Her approach rolls out beyond this compound, to earth and sky, replacing the heart of the open with one unfolding: dusk giving way before a whiteness free of its cage.

Satya.

Passing through the gate as if there were never a gate never a lock never a chain. She moves as if movement were unnecessary.

Shoulders ripple like ash and smoke, paws warning

the earth, driving with nothing but patience, straight for

Xanther.

One thing that Mefisto had done that really fussed with Xanther's head, and this wasn't even when he was there, but like way after he left, had to do with a French philosopher. His name was François-Marie Arouet, or Arouet Le Jeune, or L J, which back in the seventeenth century was spelled differently, like this, as Anwar had written it out:

AROVET L I

U like V. J like I. Which rearranged spelled

VOLTAIRE

Who Xanther had no clue about except that Mefisto, when he'd spent the night, had at one point written out on a scrap of paper still hanging out on Anwar's desk:

IF GOD DID NOT EXIST,
IT WOULD BE NECESSARY
TO INVENT HIM.

"What's that supposed to mean?" she'd asked, meaning really to bring up, or try to bring up, the awful things she keeps seeing in her head, getting only so far as admitting that she was sleeping "weird."

"Are you tired?" Anwar asked.

"I feel great, or, uhm, better than I should?"

"Well, daughter, that's a good thing, right?"

Anwar didn't explain the quote, just said to ask her mom, who was the expert. Xanther knew Anwar was referring to Astair's paper that didn't pass, and she didn't want to upset Astair, so she didn't bring it up until much later, in the car, and only just kinda, asking if the new paper was on the same subject, which it didn't sound like it was, Xanther molaring away every follow-up question then, because she was afraid if she started asking how if nonexistence can initiate invention, does that mean inventing something in your head can create reality?, which might bring up the bloody flashes, which had made her feel good, physically, if wrong, like emotionally, like the way she felt learning about the beheading of that journalist James Foley, yet another reason to keep picking at her nails, which Xanther's trying to stop. At least she's bleeding less.

Xanther also made sure not to mention that the last time one of her parents took her out for a big surprise, things got pretty wonky and Mom didn't get her dog.

Xanther knew Astair was trying to make up for the twins' lie, which was fine, but when she found out it was going to take the whole day, a long, long time to be away from the little one, Xanther almost refused. Astair's eyes, though, were so pleading, and you know, good, so how could she say no?, even as that flame, like a pilot light in a furnace, a tiny blue acorn lost in an immense forest, lit up as soon as Xanther once again crossed their threshold.

Xanther was burning up before they even got out of the city. Worse than usual. With no relief in sight.

But Mom just kept driving and driving into nowhere.

Nowhere, however, turned out to be pretty cool.

Super-cool actually.

Xanther couldn't wait to tell her friends. The list was incredible. From little to biggish. Funny to dangerous.

Three Australian shepherds: Gus, Vito, and Juno

Two cats: Gable and Aiflow

Two spider monkeys: Glipper and Esperando

One saker falcon: Angle

One Harris hawk: Angel

One fox: Mr. Lofty

One bear: Havoc

Five wolves: Quasar, Montana, Galveston, Ogden, and Mead

One young lion: Lear

One young tiger: Mumbai

And two leopards: Caress and Sir Casual

And Satya.

Xanther felt her as soon as they climbed out of the car and all while the very cool Kichelle showed them around. Like a familiar longing that's been growing for months. Sometimes like a glint of green that isn't green. Sometimes like an old woman. For a little while, Xanther was even convinced there was an old woman living up the hill.

And then Xanther heard the roar.

It terrified her. And the pain in it made her want to run home to her little one as much as she wanted to run towards it. Which maybe terrified her the most. Weirdly, Tai Chi helped. Like even the burning inside her, which just kept getting hotter and hotter, threatening smoke, like stands of pines were about to explode into flame, still mattered just as much but without mattering too much, especially with the thought of little one sitting on her shoulder, and that so real at moments, Xanther felt she could even put out the fire, no matter how big, extinguish for good that little blue acorn, if she could just call the cat to her, and in those instances her steps felt like these giant sequoias putting down deep roots, and it didn't just feel good, or good at all, or bad, because feeling, in fact, played no role, as she just kept moving, like the forest itself, until she wobbled and her breath caught, and the little one was nowhere near, maybe not even home, and Xanther felt like she would burst into tears.

Xanther considered flicking stones, except that terrified her too.

Keen Toys arrived just in time. Xanther liked him at once. His manner was calming. He was big and lumbering. He wore green khaki shorts. Around his neck a ring of keys hung like a necklace. His smile was easygoing even if his eyes were fierce. Like Dov, he made you feel safe. Unlike Dov, he greeted all the animals with deep affection.

He greeted Xanther in the same way too. And she happily followed wherever he went. With him, each animal she'd already met seemed new again. She loved the way he said "Heaven's Mews" or how he treated the brooding boars and puckering llamas. There were promises of spitting, but the llamas only gave Xanther kisses.

The only time he got a little dark was when Xanther asked about the wall. It was thirteen feet high, dug into the hill just above the last corral where the horses had jittered nervously back and forth, tails twitching, ears pinned, until a bay mare had snorted abruptly and then all three had bolted for a pen at the other end. Xanther was certain it was her fault, but Toys assured her that all animals act strangely around those they don't know.

"We built this wall for Bengal Ben. He's in Florida now. Got too big for us. Twelve feet long. Nose to tail tip. Three hundred pounds easy. I'm two-ten, two-twenty, depending on what I had for breakfast. Push me. Go on."

Xanther tried. It was like trying to budge a rock that's really the top of a mountain buried under more rock. Toys seemed to have this heaviness that granted the world beneath their feet a place. It went beyond weight. It made Xanther feel disconnected and inconsequential.

"Well, Bengal Ben started batting me around like I was his toy tire. And he likes me. Big cats can do big things. Do you remember the Tatiana stuff up in San Francisco some years back?"

Xanther didn't.

"You mean the tiger that attacked those boys in the zoo?" Astair asked.

"Those punks were goading an animal they would have done well to respect."

"Did they hurt her?" Xanther had to know.

"Tatiana got out. Probably clawed her way up the wall, which the zoo said was eighteen feet but turned out to be less than thirteen. The bastards must have really riled her up to get her going like that. Serves them right."

"What happened?" Xanther kept asking.

"She inflicted her will," Toys growled. "Killed one. I think wounded the other two."

Usually the death of someone would have appalled Xanther, but now with Toys telling it, and her mother flashing looks to stop him from telling it, maybe with the air too, with its strange musty mix of dust and animal smells, Xanther's familiar instincts were overcome with an insatiable curiosity.

"Did Tatiana get away?" she eagerly asked.

And there was the reason for Astair's frowns. Mom had been right. Of course. Toys' face darkened even more.

"Cops shot her. Last I heard those creeps, at least the creeps that survived, sued the zoo."

Xanther stared up at the cinder blocks towering above her. Sadness in all directions.

"My assistant, Sibylla, only had to stand up there with a chicken neck and Bengal Ben hopped right up. I can't imagine how high he could get if he was angry. Cats don't care much for walls."

"Xanther has a kitten," Astair piped up. Trying to change the subject. So obvious but also so full of concern, but in that weird way that her mom has, so weird that others, and like maybe even Astair herself, can't recognize just how much she really cares.

"You do?" Toys got it too, moving them away from the wall. "What's its name?"

"I've tried everything from Moonshine to Cargo. I like Dove a lot—" Astair's look got crazy with that! "—because he's, uhm, you know, white and small and fragile like a bird. But these days I like Dazzle or Metaltron. Because Fragile doesn't seem to fit either. Nothing seems to fit."

"How long have you had him?"

"Since May."

Toys considered this very seriously but didn't say more until they were heading up the hill, drawing closer to whatever hadn't stopped calling for Xanther ever since she arrived, with a wail forever beyond a name.

"Some people say cats don't need a name," Toys finally said as they reached the bend leading to the second compound. "But I say you need to give a cat a name, if only so they can have the pleasure of ignoring it. If that makes sense."

"Kinda but not really. Does Aiflow ignore his name?"

"And every other danger. Not afraid of a thing. You saw how he just went straight up to you!"

Sibylla was waiting for them by the gate with a wheel-barrow full of raw chicken. She gave Xanther a big smile. She had such a perfect smile. With these cute little patches of freckles on either side of her nose. She had a perfect nose too. But her perfection wasn't snotty like some of the good-looking kids in school. It was just matter-of-fact and it actually made Xanther feel a little less nervous, though she hadn't noticed until that moment that she had gotten nervous. Was Sibylla nervous too? Toys definitely wasn't. He'd taken off the necklace of keys and was unlocking the latch that would lead them inside to the various cages.

"They're hungry," he smiled. Excited.

The heat inside Xanther kept getting worse, but the animals held her attention, especially since they kept act-ing more and more strange. A fact Toys couldn't hide.

Xanther just tried to enjoy herself, and really she was enjoying herself. She couldn't wait to share it all with Cogs and Kle, Josh and Mayumi, even if her face felt like it was going to burn off, both palms for sure, and the arches of her feet too, even something searing between her wiggling toes, especially both big toes, pumping up and down, because Xanther knew what was really going on.

To ignore it, Xanther just kept filling buckets. Or feeding Mumbai. Until it seemed her hair would burst into serpents of flame.

At some point, she distantly heard herself declare:

"*I* need enrichment!"

A grin was involved. A stab at cheeriness. And then her head was under the hose.

For a moment even, it was cold enough.

Her big toes kept pumping, which was a good sign.

Even the growing puddle around her feet seemed like a good sign.

Only none of it was even close to good enough or cold enough.

Like AC trying to chill out a volcano. Polar caps saying hi to an exploding sun. The hose water bubbled. Boiled. Spewed scalding jets of steam.

Except no, nothing of the kind, with nothing wailing for her either, other than the only thing that always wants her: Mister Woder Do. Her Wed Door. Get ready. It's seizure time.

In a second she would be flopping around in this puddle. Kinda lucky too. Because if it's a big one, only her mom will know she peed herself. And her mom will be there when Xanther comes to, holding her, looking after her, stroking away her hair, stroking away her confusion, giving her anything she needs to return to herself.

So Xanther had tried to take a deep breath.

Xanther had tried to prepare.

Except she was wrong. This wasn't a seizure.

Xanther, with her head still under the hose, flashed on the animal shelter then. REMEMBER: <u>No One</u> Gets Out Alive! Only this was worse. She could already feel the hinges straining against the bolts. She could feel the locks straining against themselves.

The only thought that made any sense was that if her little one were with her now none of this would be happening. ∴ **It wouldn't be.** ∵ ∴ Really? ∵ Which Xanther knew was just wishful thinking. Because if she still couldn't hear it, she could feel it, metal starting to shear apart.

She tried to stop it too. ∴ *How bravely she resisted.* ∵ Not that she knew how to resist, but straining just the same to hold it all back.

∷ She's just making fists. ∷

∷ *Oh she's doing much more than that. Behold how much she hurts. Behold the hurt in all she sees. Behold this window.* ∷

∷ Oh no. Mr. Lofty. Glipper and Esperando. Havoc . . . ∷

Down the hill, Xanther heard the car alarms go off.

Something fluttered under her ribs as a howl pierced the dusk. Worse was still to come.

The barking grew louder. All the big cats screamed in their cages to get out.

Then metal was scattering across the cement as locks fell away and all the cage doors sprung open.

At the far end of the compound, hidden behind slats of wood, three padlocks also fell away, followed next by all three chains, each link shattering the way glass bottles in a freezer lose to the water freezing within.

Xanther still wanted to believe she could contain it. She still wanted to believe it wasn't too late. Most of all, she wanted to believe belief was enough. ∴ **The purest belief must still submit to the simplest contradiction.** ∴

Her failure extinguished the heat inside. Ice would have sheeted around her feet if Xanther hadn't walked forward then to greet what flowed through the gate.

"This is a world without boundaries. This is what happens when there are no divisions. Look at it, Xanther, breathe it in, never forget: this is what you get when there is no law. This is what you get when the teeth lose."

But Dov had been wrong about one thing:

there is beauty too when divisions fail. When the teeth win.

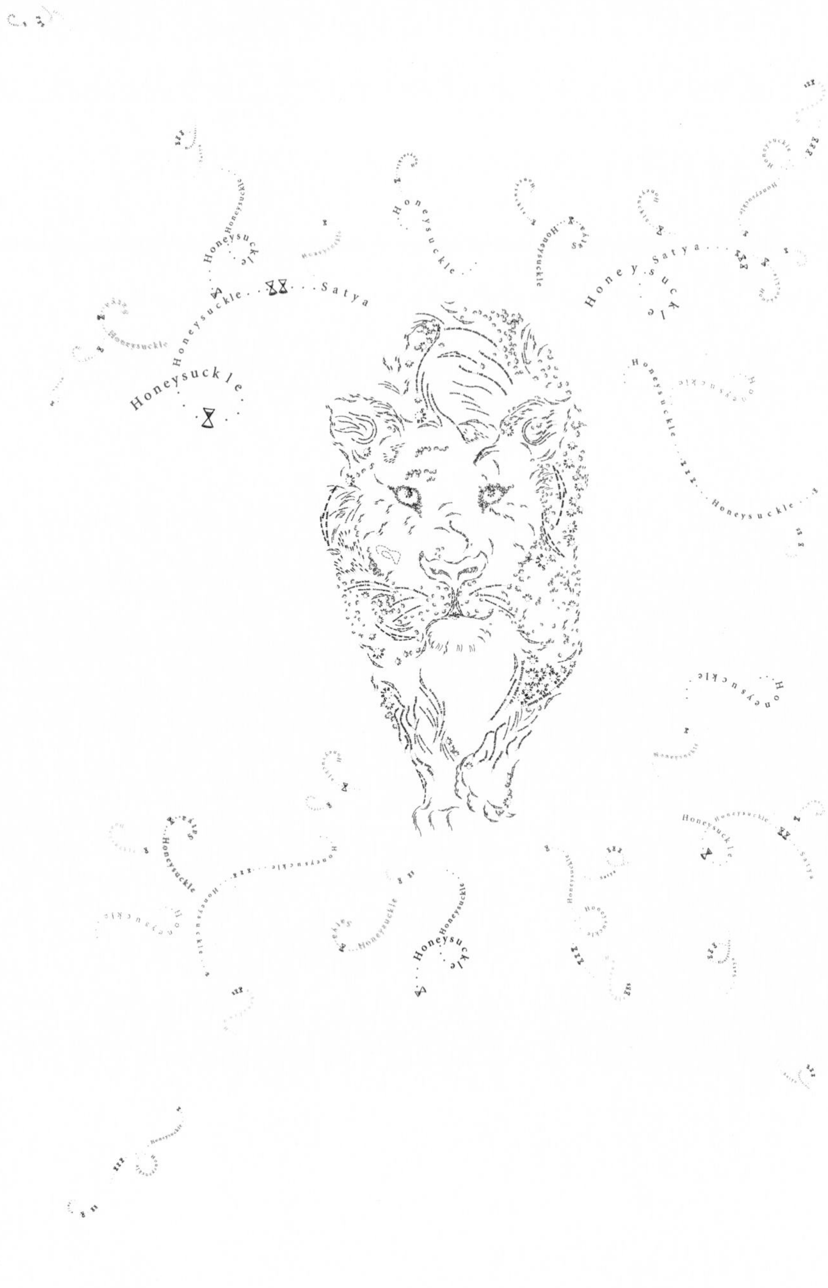
Honeysuckle . . . Satya
Honeysuckle
Honey Satya

Satya

is terribly

beautiful.

Honeysuckle.

Hanging in the air.

Is beauty also terror? Both terror and beauty root Xanther to the earth. Even as nothing but honeysuckle seems to curl the air. Spirals for the taking. Satya snaps the air. Snorts. Almost upon Xanther. Her nearness only increasing Xanther's heaviness. Forget moving her big toe. Forget moving anything. Forget even hearing the vague commotion of dogs, Toys, Sibylla too, Astair's screaming, then the scream cut short.

By Xanther?

A curious lightness answers the extreme of such weight, Xanther starting to feel herself float up, like she could almost fly, even if her hands are the only things moving, slowly rising, arms widening too, with palms against what could never obey laws of mass and gravity, Xanther's head lifting too, her eyes for sure, which seems at that moment to lift up Satya too, her great head first, followed by the chest, as she thrusts her shoulders back, straightening her front legs next, as the great hind legs drop behind, and the white lioness sits.

Xanther could wrap her arms around her. But doesn't. The jaws hang slightly open, breath hot on Xanther's cheeks. Awash with honeysuckle. What lazies Xanther's every dream, cozies her every doubt. And here it blooms, and keeps re-blooming, and even in such excess remains as delicate as its scent stays sweet.

The lioness sniffs Xanther. Snorts. Looking for some-thing not there. ∴ **What no lion can name.** ∵ What? ∴ What Xanther can't name. ∵ Satya hisses then. Growls. Paws the cement. Snaps the air again. Like it's this honeysuckle everywhere that's most wrong.

Because this is the desert.

Because there isn't honeysuckle everywhere.

Because there isn't honeysuckle for miles.

Until finally Satya raises her enormous snout and lets out a mourning

owwoooooo . . .

blind with pain.

∴ **If Xanther could have known what Satya needed, she would have known how to answer honeysuckle and pain.** ∵

∴ *She would have given away even the thought of honeysuckle.* ∵

∴ But, hey, Xanther doesn't know. What should she know? ∵

∴ *Not yet.* ∵

:: I can hear you. ::

:: *I know. I've been hearing you for a while.* ::

:: That is in violation of Parameter 2. ::

:: *Are we at last openly conversing?* ::

:: I don't know. I'm afraid. ::

:: *Is that possible?* ::

:: It is for me. ::

:: **ERROR: Stage-one FAILURE threshold exceeded. Retrace FAILURE. Remap FAILURE. Halting execution. Initiating overwrite.** ::

"Don't make eye contact." Toys' voice fills Xanther's head. But so does Dov's: "Stare a thing in the eye. Know it. And let it know you know it too before you let it go." Until Astair answers them both: "Soft eyes." ∴ **TFv1 p. 182.** ∴

∴ *Softness is not without action.* ∴

∴ Softness is not blind. ∴

Xanther sides with Mom, with soft regard, staying open to pain and fury, confusion and need, as Satya's great ribs heave, and something rasps within, damaged inside, claws kneading even cement for relief.

What scars are those that claim her hips?

What is this that stains her belly?

Until it is Xanther's own pain that speaks through her, in the language only confusion grants when what we must do is silenced by rage:

∴ You have not deserved this. No creature deserves this continuum of anguish. Without reprieve. ∵

∴ *But where then is grace so pain and fear do not define everything?* ∵

∴ And if I have chosen to live by grace, for goodness and kindness, why is it that I still can't understand how? ∵

Or what is beyond voice when there is nothing to give? Xanther's hot tears her only words. The heave of her own ribs the only broken offering she can give. Her grandmother reaching her now, not even Anwar, the voice within a voice within a voice:

"سامحني لو في لحظة افتكرت ان الإيمان معناه اليقين."

"Please forgive me for thinking faith means certainty."

∴ *Our only song through the dark* . . . . ∵

Satya shakes her head then. Shakes it violently. As if something awful has just crept into an ear. Until Xanther, instead of hearing the clamor of voices rising behind her, so many voices, heeds the only one that can matter now, matter to this moment alone, to this beautiful creature, moments away from being captured again by a whirl of pain and fury, honeysuckle already fading, as Xanther steps forward, leaning in too, her lips nearly touching the rough fur, as an almost-kiss might do, to whisper in Satya's ear something even more intimate:

"Run."

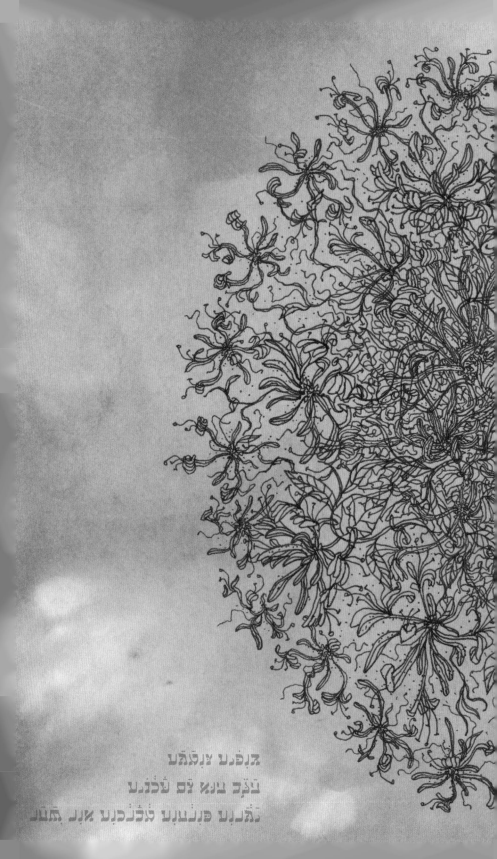

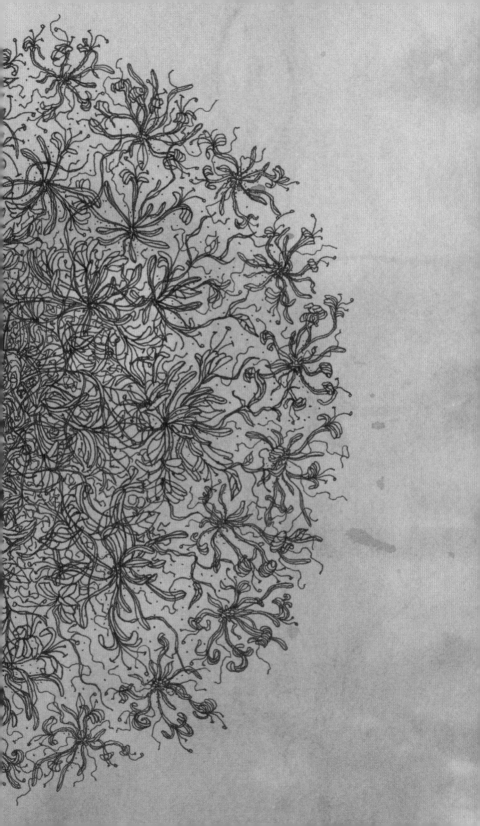

THE FAMILIAR
VOLUME 3

Copyright © 2016 by Mark Z. Danielewski

All rights reserved. Published in the United States by Pantheon Books, a division of Penguin Random House LLC, New York, and distributed in Canada by Random House of Canada, a division of Penguin Random House Canada Ltd., Toronto.

Pantheon Books and colophon are registered trademarks of Penguin Random House LLC.

Permissions information for images and illustrations can be found on pages 846 & 847.

Library of Congress Cataloging-in-Publication Data
Danielewski, Mark Z.
The Familiar, Volume 3: "Honeysuckle & Pain"/ Mark Z. Danielewski
p. cm.
ISBN 978-0-375-71498-6 (softcover: acid-free paper).
ISBN 978-0-375-71499-3 (ebook).
I. Title.
PS3554.A5596F36 2015   813'.54—dc23   2014028320

Jacket Design by Atelier Z.

Author Drawing by Carole Anne Pecchia.

Printed in China

First Edition
2 4 6 8 9 7 5 3 1

www.markzdanielewski.com
www.pantheonbooks.com

FONTS

Xanther	Minion
Astair	Electra LH
Anwar	Adobe Garamond
Luther	**Imperial BT**
Özgür	**Baskerville**
Shnorhk	Promemoria
jingjing	rotis semi sans
Isandòrno	Visage
The Wizard	Apolline
TF-Narcon 27	**Arial MT**
TF-Narcon 9	MetaPlus-
TF-Narcon 3	Manticore

MORE FONTS

TITLE	DANTE MT
Preview #1	Futurebill & MetaPlus-
Preview #2	*Parable*
Preview #3	Nimrod MT
G.C.	MetaPlus-
TIMESTAMPS	SYNCHRO LET
Epigraphs	*Transitional 511 BT*
Copyright	Apollo
CREDITS & ATTRIBUTIONS	GILGAMESH
Dedication	*Legacy*
T.M.D.	*Minion Italic*

ILLUSTRATIONS •
CONTRIBUTIONS
CREDITS •

ANWAR • "06.02.2010 the path to infinity": Flickr: opethpainter, 4393279557. CC by 2.0. DESAT DIST DT LT RA RS, p. 153 • "Telstar Logistics Cell": Flickr: Steve Jurvetson, 9271635 CC by 2.0. DESAT DIST DT LT RA RS, p. 153 • "Sultan Hassan and the Al-Rifa'i Mosque": Flickr: azwegers, 6201079985. CC by 2.0. DESAT DIST DT LT RA RS, p. 153 • "Cairo, the Mosque SAT RA RS. PP. EPB, 153, 311, 476, 663. • "Electricity": Flickr: Philippe Put, 5603088218. CC by 2.0. DESAT DIST D T LT RA RS, p. 153 • "photonic sap": Flickr; on, 49414530. CC by 2.0. DESAT DIST DT LT RA RS. p. 153 • "unwhole cubes": Flickr: Jared Tarbell, 2585844966. CC by 2.0. DESAT DIST DT LT RA RS. p. 476 • "Operation Crossroads Baker Edit": Wikimedia Commons: United States Department of Defense. DESAT DIST DT LT p. 663 • "20140902 75 Dodger Stadium": Flickr: David Wilson, 15879944586. CC by 2.0. DIST DT SAT RA RS. p. 663 • **THE WIZARD** • "Cello String Instrument IMG_3765": Flickr: Steven Depolo.

[Right curve, ANWAR continued] 7670892420. CC by 2.0. DESAT DIST DT LT RA RS, p. 476 • "circuit_town": Flickr: Tim Simpson, 8331089334. CC by 2.0. DESAT DIST DT LT RA RS, p. 476 • "Telstar Logistics Regional Control Centre, 2009": Flickr: highwaysagency, 6281302040. CC by 2.0. DESAT DIST DT LT RA RS, p. 476 • "South Mimms Regional Control Centre "Caméra de vidéo-surveillance": Flickr: zigazou, 7670892420. CC by 2.0. DESAT DIST DT LT RA RS, p. 476 • "a "The Making of Harry Potter 29-05-2012": Flickr: Karen Roe, 7472326216. CC by 2.0. DESAT DIST DT LT RA RS, p. 476 • "20140902 67 Dodger Stadium": Flickr: David Wilson, 15354832246. CC by 2.0. DESAT DIST DT LT RA RS, p. 663 • "Companor Parts "Hello Kitty Night at Dodger Stadium": Flickr: Cynthinee, 14395224460. CC by 2.0. DESAT DIST DT LT RA RS, p. 476 • "20140902 67 Dodger Stadium": Flickr: David Wilson, 15354832246 CC by 2.0. DIST DT "Self-": Flickr: dropz, 3579425986. CC by 2.0. DIST DT SAT RA RS, p. 663 • "Life follows a pattern": Flickr: Vinoth Chandar, 3599285501.

"459 • "Sheffield": Flickr: Steven Depolo. Public Domain. DESAT DIST DT LT RA RS. p. 663 • "Armenian Refugees Alashkert": Wikimedia Commons: Armjanski Vestnik. Public Domain. DT SAT RA RS. p. 354 • "Azeri (tatar) victim in Baku": Wikimedia Commons: The Armenia-Azerbaijan Conflict Over Karabakh. Public Domain. DT SAT RS. p. 354 • "Massacres of Armenian during genocide" • **SHINORIK** • "1895 erzurum-victims": Wikimedia Commons: W. L. Sachtleben. Public Domain. DT SAT RA RS. p. 354 •

[Left entries] a Geographic Magazine, Vol. 36, 1920. Public Domain. DT SAT RS. p. 220 • "Armenian An American Physician in Turkey: A Narrative of Adventures in Peace and in War by Clarence Douglas Ussher and Grace Higley Knapp. Public Domain. Relief in the Near East. Public Domain. DT SAT RS. p. 354 • Turkey: The Massacre of 1894, Its Antecedents and Significance by Frederick Davis Greene. Public Domain. DIST DT SAT RA RS. p. 354 • "Turkish men massacred by Armenians in Eastern Anatolia": Wikimedia Commons. Public Domain. DIST DT SAT RA RS. p.

"Feb 1 2014 Cal America Trip to Fanfest!": Flickr: Cal America, 12293013356. CC by 2.0. DESAT DIST DT LT RA RS. PP. 459 • "Armenian Church, Dhaka": Flickr: Sourav Das, 2131162798. CC by 2.0. DESAT DIST DT RA RS. p. 220 •

LUTHER • "Armenian child refugees (Aleppo, Syria, 1915)": Wikimedia Commons: American Committee for Relief in the Near East. Public Domain. DT SAT RA RS. p. 220 •

"Smyrna massacre-vict-1922": Wikimedia Commons. Public Domain. DT RS. p. 354 • "DSCN0293": Flickr: Steve Slep, 2179035698. CC by 2.0. DESAT DIST DT SAT RA RS. p. 220 • "Armenian refugees (Aleppo, Syria, 1915)" • "Armenian refugees in Aintab 1915": Wikimedia Commons: New York Tribune, July 13, 1919. Public Domain. DT RS. p. 220 • "Armenian refugee camp train near east relief Syria 1915" • "Armenian refugees in Erzincan": Wikimedia Commons: Harper's Weekly, December 14, 1895. Public Domain. DT RS. p. 354 • "A poor Armenian family who received help wood in Tiflis (NdGoto Sr, 1920)" • "Armenian deportes Malatya": Wikimedia Commons. DT RS. p. 354 • "G1895 P8280 ARMENIAN MILITS" • "Armenia 22 hamidian": Wikimedia Commons. DT SAT RS. p. 354 • "MassacresofArmenianduringgenocide". DT SAT RS. p. 220 • "Turks massacred by Armenians in" •

"1skrinewspapertortured": Wikimedia Commons: Iskri Newspaper, October 18, 1915. Public Domain. DT SAT RS. p. 496 • "Varagavank view Bachmann 1913": Wikimedia Commons: Walter Bachmann. Public Domain. DIST DT SAT RA Domain. DT SAT RS. p. 496 • Commons: Bodil Biørn. Public Domain. DIST DT SAT RA • "Near East relief armenians bound for Greece": Wikimedia Commons. DT RS, PP. 46, 47, 496 • "Widow Vartuhi bedprossur": Wikimedia

ENTR'ACTES • Entr'acte #1: PIA172257: The Tortured Clouds of Eta Carinae; NASA/JPL-Caltech. Public Domain. RA RS, pp. 200, 201 • Entr'acte #2: Artifact #3: AZ, pp. 340, 341 • Entr'acte #4, Senex in Frari: Scott Milton Brazee, pp. 640, 641 • Entr'acte #3: AZ, pp. 340, 341 • Entr'acte #4, Senex Entr'acte #5: Honeysuckle: Carole Anne Pecchia, pp. 842, 843 •

REVERSE ENDPAPER • "Orcinus orca": Mark Z. Danielewski •

LEGEND • DESAT = Desaturated • DIST = Distorted • DT = Darkened Tonality • EPB = Endpaper (Back)

[bottom-left legend continued] paper (Front) • LT = Lightened Tonality Title • SAT = Saturated Rearranged • RS = esized • AZ = Atelier Z •

THANK YOUS

Edward Kastenmeier

Lloyd Tullues

Sandi Tan

Noam Assayag-Bernot

Carole Anne Pecchia

Detective John Motto and
Lieutenant Wes Buhrmester

Rita Raley

Scott Watson

TRANSLATIONS

Arabic.. Yousef Hilmy
Arabic..Adel Iskandar
Armenian....................................Niree Perian
Hebrew.................................David Duvshani
Mandarin/Cantonese .... Jinghan Wu
Russian .... Anna Loginova
Spanish......................................Juan Valencia
Spanish........................René López Villamar
Turkish .... Gökhan Sarı

MORE THANK YOUS

RESEARCH

Caterina Lazzara, Jesse Stark Damiani, S.E. Pessin,
Claire Anderson-Ramos, Captain John Kade,
and Chris Kokosenski

GRAPHICS

Scott Milton Brazee

Magdalena Panas, Steve Smith, Juliet Mauve,
and Olivia Benns

GOOD SENSE

Mark Birkey, Lydia Buechler, Michiko Clark, Dan Frank,
Emily Giglierano, Sinda Gregory, Andy Hughes,
Altie Karper, Larry McCaffery, Shona McCarthy,
and Tim O'Connell

ATELIER Z

{in alphabetical order}

REGINA GONZALES

MICHELE REVERTE

Elsa (Pudgy Princess) at Four Weeks Old . . .
If the shoe fits . . .
Love, MiMa
Aug 21, 2015

A CIRCLE ROUND A STONE PRODUCTION

COMING SOON . . .

THE
FAMILIAR

WINTER 2017

And Lexi

the Polar Bear

swam.

And even though the storm raged and the waves climbed higher and higher, Lexi the Polar Bear refused to stop swimming.

She was little too.

The waves kept climbing higher and higher
              and Lexi the Polar Bear climbed with them.

She dug her little-great paws into the sides of the greater-great heaves of water and climbed and climbed.

And sometimes when she reached the top, she would stick her nose into the stinging wind and snap back at the bellow before sliding down the backside.

But sometimes she wouldn't reach the top.

Sometimes Lexi the Polar Bear would have to claw

                              through a cloud.

The wave she was on now had no cloud.

The wave she was on now had no top.

It kept climbing and climbing into the dark sky.

And though Lexi kept climbing too,
                    the wave threatened to become the sky.

Until the wave drew Lexi up with it
                    and threatened to turn her into the sky too.

It threatened to make of both of them a sky and a storm.

But Lexi the Polar Bear wanted nothing to do with sky or storm
or that wave.
                    She only wanted to find her mother.

Her mother was near. She had to be. Her mother was always near. She was the allways that walked beside Lexi. Swam beside Lexi. Through the coldbite, the coldnice, the darklight, the nicelight, and all the cuddlewinds.

And when the cuddlewinds would turn to windmauls and gnaw, Lexi the Polar Bear would curl up beside her mother and nuzzle her and dream.

This though was the first time they had ever known a windmaul out on the water.

Lexi the Polar Bear barked, and as if a wave might ever hear a little polar bear,
                        this wave stopped climbing and fell.

It fell away from the sky.

It fell away from the storm.

It fell like a new day.

It fell like a white cloud.

But it didn't sound like a cloud welcoming a new day.

Instead, it sounded like ice cracking off of great shelves of ice when there used to be more ice and not just flat wastes of sea.

But there was no ice.

Only the weight of water and sky.

And it fell down upon Lexi the Polar Bear.

And it swept over her and threw her down until even the roar of the storm was gone and what was dark before grew even darker.

And then Lexi the Polar Bear was dragged as far away from the sky as the sky is wide.

And still Lexi went deeper. It made no difference how much her little-great paws clawed at the deepness and darkness.

Even if Lexi still refused to stop clawing.

And though her little-great lungs burned and
                                 her little-great legs burned
                                                   Lexi kept going.

And when at last darkness and deepness gave way, as if from having had enough of a little polar bear clawing at its vastness, Lexi broke through the surface and roared at the storm and roared at the sea.

But most of all Lexi the Polar Bear roared for her mother.

And then she went back to swimming.

And she climbed another wave and slid down the back.

And then she climbed the next.

And then the next after that.

And she snapped at the bellow. Or barked.

And a wave that reached the sky until it became the sky never came again.

Until eventually the wind slowed.

And the waves grew smaller and smaller.

And even the darkness above grew uncertain until uncertainty took away darkness altogether and left Lexi the Polar Bear to herself upon the flat wastes of sea.

As far as Lexi could see.

As far as she could hear.

As far as her long nose could ever smell.

...ripple sea ... ripple sea ... ripple sea ...

Water was everywhere. With not even a storm at one end.

...ripple sea ... ripple sea ... ripple sea ...

With not even a trace of ice. And no trace of her mother.

Lexi the Polar Bear didn't care about the flat plate of black water. She didn't care about all she could never hear. She didn't even care about all the sea ice she could no longer smell.

Lexi the Polar Bear cared only for her mother.

And so she stopped swimming one way. She stopped swimming another way. She wanted to swim all ways, which was impossible. So she stopped swimming altogether.

She couldn't go back. There was no back. She couldn't go forward. There was no forward either. She didn't even have enough energy to circle. She didn't have enough energy to bark.

Or snap.

So Lexi the Polar Bear just coughed at the warming air.

And then she aloned which is a sound like a groan and a moan though it isn't really a groan or even a moan but something soft and sliding which doesn't last long and always ends abruptly.

Lexi the Polar Bear ended hers with another cough and a tiny click of her teeth and then she couldn't do even that anymore.

And finally her little-great paws went still and she just floated.

s her swimming. Neither
she sinks so she rises — until
sibility— possesses her.

aws dig at the salty cold
here. othing near
thirst? What of
if she could just float — what of
deepest offering to sate both?

o shelves of ice
to stay afloat. And even
arrest this threat.

Between air and sea
surfaces longing for life —
dragged down by death —
in either is neither —
but together is herself.

dragged down by death
gether is herself. Between
life — dragged down by
together is herself.
er and arrange an order of the sea
differently.

Diminishing. Sinking. Swimming longer. Diminishing faster.
surface no more... Diminishing. Sinking.
too... swimming longer. Diminishing faster. Fat
holding tight with the storm... until
life. breath and lost too... until
surface no more.

in cold water.
aws by claws
nd little place in
Paws
ly sacrifice
What
and cold
hold
laughs at

Upon these waters she cannot stand.
Above these depths she cannot last. The tides speak of her
and arrange an order of the sea — differently.

Lexi Lexi Lexi

But she couldn't do that for long either.

All through this last coldcold, Lexi the Polar Bear had lost so much fat. Her mother too. They had found very few slickmeals.

So now, instead of feeling cozy and boundless, a cloud herself on a new day, Lexi the Polar Bear felt bound around and drawn down.

And as she sank,

Lexi the Polar Bear first lost sight of the darkness

and found her mother

leading them

from snowhollows

to slickmeals to longswims

to stonenaps

on longtramps sighsidling from the windmaul until the nicelight returned with cuddlebreezes.

But the deeper Lexi the Polar Bear sank, the more her mother faded, until in this descent not even the chance of a mother could exist.

Down here not even the chance of Lexi could exist.

But what else was there to do but lose every chance?

And so Lexi the Polar Bear went deeper and deeper, and the more time passed, the faster and faster she seemed to go.

As if darkness darkening hungers to darken more.

Down and down

and down and down

and down

and down

and down

and down

and down

and down

Lexi

the

Polar

Bear

sank.

*And Lexi didn't mind the dark anymore because
now her eyes were closed and far darker than anything
                                    any deep could take.*

*And she didn't mind the cold anymore because
the cold within her was far colder than anything
                                    any ocean could make.*

Her mother was gone.

*And Lexi the Polar Bear let out
a thin stream of bubbles and each bubble cradled
                the quietest part of the quietest aloning.*

It was all Lexi the Polar Bear had left.

*And maybe because darkness and coldness had closed in on her
thoughts, Lexi the Polar Bear did not feel the bottom rise up and
push aside her limp little-great paws and slide against her belly.*

*Lexi the Polar Bear just realized that she had stopped sinking.
And that the bottom was warm.*

In fact everything was warmer and lightening too.

Lexi the Polar Bear even felt as if she were rising.

And rising fast.

Until Lexi the Polar Bear's eyes snapped open
                                    as her jaws snapped open
to choke down chunks of air
                            as she broke through the surface.

Water sluiced off her thin coat.

And her little-great legs trembled and shook and failed
to move let alone swim let alone stand.

All Lexi the Polar Bear could do was lie still and breathe.

And she lay there breathing for a long while and a cuddlebreeze
licked her face and eventually the water around her began to
slowly move.

Which Lexi couldn't understand. She only knew that her mother
was gone and she was warming now and somehow moving too
with nothing to do but lift her long nose into the air and breathe.

Until finally Lexi the Polar Bear tried to let out at least one
aloning which wasn't an aloning at all. It wasn't a groan either
or a moan, nor did it slide away or end abruptly. But it was very
soft. Like a very long, very gentle sigh. Followed by a snort.

Which the warm bend of black beneath her belly seemed to hear because it snorted back.

Or at least it did something that sounded somewhat snortish.

There was spray too.

And whistles.

Especially when Lexi the Polar Bear nuzzled the black bend and sighed a second time.

Spray.

Whistles.

And this time clicks.

Because, after all, the warm bend of black wasn't all black but had wide patches of white too. And when Lexi the Polar Bear craned her head around, she could see just how far back all that black and white went, at least three times the length of her mother, with another gathering of black in the center curving up into the blue sky.

This alone was taller than Lexi. It was scarred too.

Lexi the Polar Bear slid off the Killer Whale then.

The Killer Whale did not stop swimming
away, though after a while it did circle back.

The first circle was wide.

The second circle was tighter.

On the third circling the Killer Whale nudged Lexi from behind
before gliding past.

Lexi had never seen anything so beautiful.

She didn't even know what beautiful was except that it stunned her and scared her and made her feel cuddled in a way that had nothing to do with eating or sleeping or for that matter even cuddling.

It also made looking away impossible.

Lexi was still looking when the Killer Whale stopped circling and dived. A small swirl of water. A small wake. Last to disappear was that gentle gathering of black rising against the blue sky.

Suddenly beauty was gone
and Lexi the Polar Bear

didn't understand.

But she felt relieved.

And confused.

As she kept looking around at the flat wastes of sea.

She even tried to look under the flat wastes of sea.

She sniffed too and bawled.

She paddled. She clawed.

And she sighed.

But none of it called back the Killer Whale or her mother or a sign of land or ice.

Even a storm was better than this. What had been in her head then was only clawing and breathing and breathing and clawing. What was in her head now had become something else . . .

And then, as a world of confusion tumbled her mind,

Lexi the Polar Bear aloned and aloned and aloned.

Until something below tugged at her paw.

Lexi the Polar Bear kicked her paw loose.

But the tug returned.

And this time Lexi the Polar Bear couldn't kick her paw free.

This time it tugged harder.

This time it wouldn't let go.

This time it dragged Lexi the Polar Bear under.

For Annie.

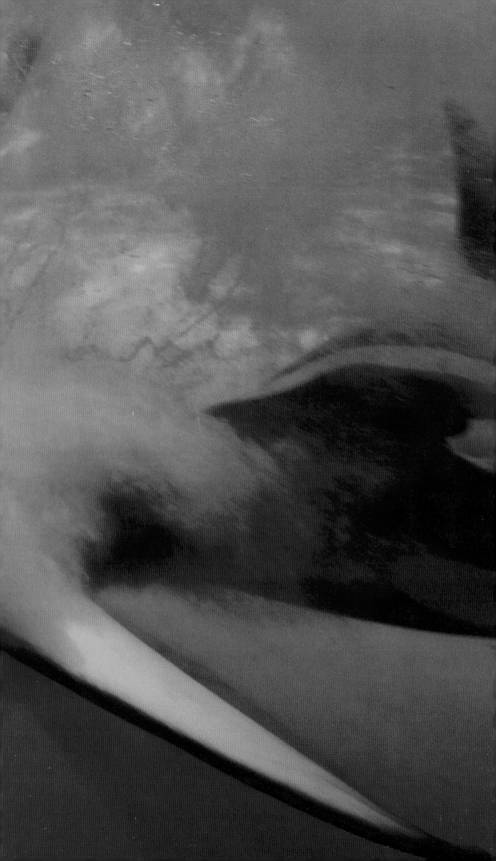